The Heir AND THE ENCHANTRESS

THE ENCHANTRESSES BOOK FIVE

PAULLETT GOLDEN

Also by Paullett Golden

This book is dedicated to all my loyal readers who inspired the writing of Hazel's story.

Praise for Golden's Books

"An amazing book by an author that has honed her craft to perfection, this story had me gasping with laughter and moping my eyes as the tears rolled down my face."

— Goodreads Reader

"Paullett Golden isn't afraid to weave complex family matters into her historical romance… The author's strong points are her ability to reveal the vulnerability of her characters while showing you how they work through their differences."

— Readers' Favorites Reviewer

"Character development is wonderful, and it is interesting to follow two young people as they defy the odds to be together. Paullett Golden's novel is compelling and a stellar work that is skillfully crafted."

—Sheri Hoyte of Reader Views

"It's thoughtfulness about issues of social class, birthrights, gender disparities, and city versus country concerns add provocative emotional layers. Strong, complex characterizations, nuanced family dynamics, insightful social commentary, and a vibrant sense of time and place both geographically and emotionally make this a poignant read."

—Cardyn Brooks of *InD'tale Magazine*

"The author adds a few extra ingredients to the romantic formula, with pleasing results. An engaging and unconventional love story."

—*Kirkus Reviews*

"The well-written prose is a delight, the author's voice compelling readers and drawing them into the story with an endearing, captivating plot and genuine, authentic settings. From the uncompromising social conventions of the era to the permissible attitudes and behaviors within each class, it's a first-class journey back in time."

—*Reader Views*

"[The Enchantresses] by Paullett Golden easily ranks as one of the best historical romances I have read in some time and I highly recommend it to fans of romance, history, and the regency era. Fabulous reading!"

—*Sheri Hoyte*

"The author Paullett Golden has a gift for creating memorable characters that have depth."

— Paige Lovitt of *Reader Views*

"Golden is a good writer. She knows how to structure plot, how to make flawed characters sympathetic and lovable, and has a very firm grasp on theme."

— *No Apology Book Reviews*

"What I loved about the author was her knowledge of the era! Her descriptions are fresh and rich. Her writing is strong and emotionally driven. An author to follow."

— *The Forfeit* author Shannon Gallagher

"I enjoy the way Golden smartly sprinkles wit and satire throughout her story to highlight the absurdity of the British comedy of manners."

— *Goodreads Reader*

"Paullett Golden's writing is so good that I was completely entranced, and could barely put the story down."

— *Goodreads Reader*

"With complex characters and a backstory with amazing depth, the story … is fantastic from start to finish."

— *Rebirth* author Ravin Tija Maurice

"Paullett Golden specializes in creating charmingly flawed characters and she did not disappoint in this latest enchantress novel."

— *Dream Come Review*

"…a modern sensibility about the theme of self-realization, and a fresh take on romance make the foundation of Golden's latest Georgian-era romance."

— *The Prairies Book Review*

"What a wonderful story! I have read a number of historical fiction romance stories and this is the best one so far! Paullett does a masterful job of weaving so many historical details into her story…."

— *Word Refiner Reviews*

"The novel is everything you could ever want from a story in this genre while also providing surprising and gratifying thematic depth."

— *Author Esquire*

"I thoroughly enjoyed meeting and getting to know all of the characters. Each character was fully developed, robust and very relatable."

— Flippin' Pages Book Reviews

"It is a story that just keeps giving and giving to the reader and I, for one, found it enchanting!"

— The Genre Minx Book Reviews

"This is one of the best books I've read EVER! It made me smile, it made me laugh, it made me angry and then it made me very happy."

— FH Denny Reviews

"One of the best historical romances I have ever read. Everything about this book is empowering and heart touching."

— Goodreads Reviewer

THE ENCHANTRESS FAMILY TREE

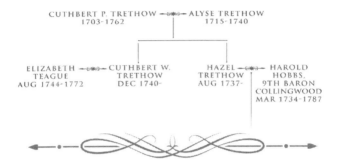

CUTHBERT P. TRETHOW ⚭ ALYSE TRETHOW
1703-1762   1715-1740

ELIZABETH ⚭ CUTHBERT W.   HAZEL ⚭ HAROLD
TEAGUE   TRETHOW   TRETHOW   HOBBS,
AUG 1744-1772   DEC 1740-   AUG 1737-   9TH BARON
                                          COLLINGWOOD
                                          MAR 1734-1787

Visit www.paullettgolden.com/the-enchantresses
to view the complete Enchantress Family Tree

Prologue

September 1754

The anteroom to the Trelowen study smelled of cigars, leather, and beeswax polish. Animal horns and skins adorned the dark wood of the walls. Hazel dabbed the corners of her eyes with a wadded handkerchief.

Beyond the adjoining door, she heard the voices of her father and Lord Collingwood, muffled one minute then raised the next. She flinched each time her father blasphemed.

One voice shouted, "Ruined!" The remainder of the sentence was lost through the door.

"Scandal!" shouted another voice, or maybe it was the same voice.

She did not strain to hear or listen at the door. How could she? She could not bear to listen to the accusations, however true. She was ruined. Nothing could save her reputation. Her father would not secure the marriage he had planned for her; her brother would never become a Member of Parliament; her father's investment plans would not come to fruition. All because of her.

Her only hope, her family's only hope, was Lord Collingwood.

"Whore!" a voice screeched.

Hazel's tears flowed anew. Without bothering to stifle her sobs, she pressed the damp kerchief to her face and wailed.

Chapter 1

One Month Earlier

The squeeze of the year was to be the party at Longfirth Hall. Miss Hazel Trethow pinched her cheeks in the vestibule mirror. This would be a coup if she had her way. It was, after all, her birthday. Not every day did a young lady turn seventeen.

Her curls assessed, her bosom primped, and her rouge heightened, she opened the drawing room door. A babble of voices cut the hallway's silence. The hostess, Miss Agnes Plumb, sat with her friends near the double doors to the garden, all tittering and fanning themselves. But where were the gentlemen? Hazel's heart sank to think they might have declined.

"Hazel!" Agnes rose from her chair.

"Oh, Hazel, they've *all* agreed to come," said one of her friends, relieving her unspoken worries.

Agnes kissed Hazel's cheek. "Even *him*."

With deft hands, Hazel fluffed the skirt of her *robe à l'anglaise* to ensure the outline of her panniers showed to advantage before taking a seat.

This party was no ordinary house party. Agnes's overbearing parents were visiting friends in Hampshire, leaving her in the capable hands of her governess. As luck would have it, this particular governess was in love with the gardener and willing to make a deal with her charge: Agnes could host a party in her parents' absence on the condition that the governess could spend the week's end undisturbed in the gardener's cottage.

Agnes looked to her friends. "While none of our esteemed guests have yet arrived, I'm positive they will. When they do, the butler will escort the gentlemen here, and we will greet each with all the delight our fair bosoms have in store."

The ladies exchanged glances, giggling with accelerated fanning.

"Once we've each claimed our gentleman for the party," Agnes continued, "we may spend the remainder of the next two days in his company, uninhibited by guardians or parents. At last, we can all *live*. Whoever thought up this ridiculousness of chaperones should perish in a duel. No one can find love from observed conversation and arranged matches."

"But what of the butler and staff?" voiced one of the girls.

Agnes sniggered. "Don't worry about them. I caught the butler with a scullery maid this summer. He won't breathe a word of our transgressions and will ensure the silence of the staff."

The honored guests of the occasion happened to be the most eligible bachelors in the West Country. One such gentleman was the love of Hazel's life: Anthony Faldo, Viscount Brooks. Granted, she had not been formally introduced to him, but she knew enough *of* him to know he was the one — fashionable, handsome, desirable. What more could a woman want? She was determined to have him.

Her lips ached to know the pleasure of Lord Brooks. Should all proceed as planned, Hazel would, at long last, have her first kiss.

It was difficult to ignore the peeling wallpaper, the worn cushions, or the frayed upholstery. Nothing escaped Mr. Harold Hobbs's notice as he stood in his father's study, still wearing his travel clothes, dusty and exhausted. His father Eugene Hobbs, Baron Collingwood, kept his son waiting. Harold did not fidget, nor did he become impatient. With infinite discipline he waited.

His father's voice boomed behind him. "Welcome home, my boy!"

Before Harold could turn, Lord Collingwood slapped his son square between the shoulder blades.

"Nearly three years it's been." His father clasped Harold's shoulder to angle him. "Let me have a look at you."

Harold took in the sight of his father. In the time he had been in India, his father had aged, new worry lines creasing the man's forehead, a rounding of the shoulders apparent, and a sloppiness present in the styling of his periwig. The sight tugged at Harold's heart.

"Bit darker in complexion, eh?" Collingwood eyed his son, hands still grasping the shoulders. "A touch more powder will remedy that. Can't have you looking like a savage, now can we?"

Lips pursing at the insult to an olive complexion — the skin tone of the friends he held most dear — Harold cut straight to business. That was, after all, why he had been summoned without delay, without time to rest, bathe, or change.

"You received my letter?" Harold asked.

Collingwood moved to the other side of his desk and sat, inviting his son to do likewise.

When his father affirmed, Harold said, "Then you know we made a tidy profit. I was prepared to reinvest a portion of the earnings for additional ship charters until I received your letter. I returned as soon as I could. You understand why I declined the alternative investment opportunity you proposed?"

Index finger to temple, the baron propped up his head. "Not in the slightest." He waved a hand when Harold made to speak. "Yes, yes, you scribbled several nonsense reasons, but that's all they were—nonsense. Why didn't you await my reply? If you had, you would know I instructed you to carry out the deal." He grunted his displeasure. "It'll take far too long for you to return to India. I suppose my solicitor must make the necessary arrangements now. I'm quite put out."

Lacing his fingers in his lap, Harold waited for his father to finish before saying, "The deal is too risky."

Another wave of a hand. "You're too young to understand. There are debts to pay. Our priority is to make money. We *need* more money."

"I disagree. Our priority is for the estate to sustain itself. Fallow fields and empty tenant farms will not support Trelowen. I intend to take the profits to the steward so he may purchase new equipment and begin repairs to the cottages. With more tenants and working farms, we'll be back in the land's good graces."

"I've let the steward go."

Harold sucked in a breath. "Then rehire him."

Collingwood slapped an open palm to the table and leaned forward. "Here's what we're going to do. We're going to invest our earnings in the new deal, double that amount, invest again, and double again. My ear has been to the ground. I *know* this is sound. We'll be wealthy and back in business, my boy!"

Shaking his head, Harold said, "I've spent nearly three years in Calcutta, Father. *I* know what's sound, and this deal is not. The Nawab of Bengal is discontent to the point of raising an army. The French East India Company is at odds with the British East India Company. There's already a war in southern India. Trouble is brewing, as I said in my letter. More importantly, I refuse to be involved in opium trading. Chartering ships of coffee, tea, and textiles is one thing, opium quite another. Either from greed or risk, the capital required to invest has tripled since the first offer, far and above what we earned from the recent charter. We don't have the money. Even if we did, I wouldn't do it. It's too risky, not to mention unethical."

"Poppycock," Collingwood said. "Nothing about money is unethical. We need more, and this is our way in. Tripled, you say?" He tugged at the edge of his periwig, the part slipping askew to one side. "You won't earn the capital here. You should have stayed in India." Stroking his chin, he added under his breath, "Unless…"

Harold squeezed his eyes shut for a moment, straining against exhaustion and frustration.

His father's palm slapped the desk again. "You'll marry an heiress, someone with a dowry large enough to provide the capital."

"And what will you tell Mr. Trethow when he dis-covers you've broken your word?"

Harold thought of the pink-faced young Hazel Trethow to whom he was intended to marry, the daughter of his father's childhood friend. She had only been ten years of age when Harold had seen her last, he having just turned fourteen and not at all interested in the arrangement. He would not be disappointed to walk away from the match, but there had always been a certain security in knowing whom he would wed—security and resignation.

Collingwood leaned back in his chair, a gleam in his eye. "Don't you worry about Trethow. I'll handle him." Talking more to himself than to his son, he added, "Your mother will know an heiress or five. We'll invite them for an evening of supper and enter-tainment. Let them compete for your hand. We'll secure the capital before you can say 'hoodwink.'"

A knot tightened in Harold's chest. He had no intention of marrying a woman for money, nor did he intend to invest in a deal that would surely ruin them. For now, he could only placate his father until he devised a sounder plan.

Chapter 2

On the bright side, Miss Agnes Plumb was enjoying herself. Hazel watched her from the other side of the room, laughing with Lord Driffield, Lady Melissa Williamson, and Melissa's husband Sir Chauncey.

Lord Driffield's eyes rarely left Agnes's face as she talked with animation. There was no denying he was enamored with her. Agnes needed more fun in her life, more glimpses of love, more time with her beau. Unlike Hazel's father, who doted on her, Mr. Plumb was a tyrant, refusing Agnes a come-out, refusing the suit of Lord Driffield based on an old and ridiculous rumor of his being a rake and gamester, and refusing her just about anything. This party was as much for Agnes as it was for Hazel, if not more so in Hazel's opinion.

A good thing since Agnes was having more luck in love than Hazel. Lord Brooks had yet to approach the birthday girl. Not even after they had been introduced had he seemed interested in continuing the acquaintance. While she had no experience with flirtation, she did not think her strategies too terrible, or so her mirror showed when she had practiced batting her eyelashes and striking conversation.

He stood across the room from her, talking with a group of his friends.

Hazel huffed.

She was not the only lady disappointed by the affair. A multi-day party yet the gentlemen had not bothered to show until the second day, arriving late afternoon at that. What did they expect? To be compromised into a leg shackle? That was not at all the intention. After all, there were no chaperones to catch them.

The party was not completely improper, as it would not do for the ladies to be ruined when they each had high hopes to marry. Although the party was devoid of proper chaperones, it did host several married couples who would keep the occasion decorous should word of the party spread — couples who would also turn a blind eye to kisses in dark corners. And besides, no harm came from a little fun.

Hazel's attention returned to Viscount Brooks. The rumors had not exaggerated. The man defined fashion. His heels were tall, his frock coat frilled, his blonde hair curled with a teasing dash of powder, his figure the slimmest in the room, and the corner of one eye adorned by a delectable heart-shaped patch. A perfect specimen of manhood!

Pinching her cheeks, she plucked her courage. If he would not come to her, she would go to him.

One of her mirror's favorite flirts was her smile. Hazel flashed it now as she walked across the room to the tune of a Bach prelude and the accompaniment of conversation and laughter. Her approach would be subtle. *You're my guest of honor*. More subtle. *Good evening*. Less subtle. *Would you care to kiss me?* Fiddlesticks. All her well-planned words flew out the drawing room doors, a lump lodging in place of witticism.

As she drew near, her path was intercepted by Lady Melissa Williamson. An ebony beauty from the West Indies, she had married for love a week after her seventeenth birthday, an act that inspired all her friends to want to marry for love, shaking their quiet submission of marrying whomever their parents desired. With a knowing smile, Melissa tucked her hand under Hazel's elbow and walked with her to join the group of gentlemen rapt in conversation.

Lord Brooks's first reaction was a creased brow at being interrupted. His second reaction was to school his features into placidity and offer a bow promptly mirrored by his peers.

"Ladies," he greeted, drawling the word with a sensual promise that forgave the creased brow.

With an encouraging nod from Melissa, Hazel curtsied and said, "I hope you're finding the party to your liking, especially the company." However unpracticed her flirting, she slipped into the role with the ease and comfort of donning a favorite pair of shoes. She sidled next to him, touching a hand to his forearm. "You may think me bold, but it *is* my birthday. That grants me special privileges. Will you dance with me?"

Brooks partook in a thirsty perusal of Hazel from head to toe and waved a ringed hand to the young lady at the pianoforte.

Conversation around the room buzzed as guests realized the onset of dancing. Couples paired off to join the set as others moved to the perimeter to continue their tête-à-tête, hope for a future partner, or observe the fun. Not that Hazel noticed. Her gaze was riveted on Brooks. They took their positions, facing each other for the first dance of the evening, and waited for the music to begin. The wait proved long and awkward as the miss at the pianoforte did not know what to play and begged for a friend to take her place.

Hazel stared at Brooks.

Brooks stared back.

"Are you fond of dancing?" she asked when the silence stretched.

"Yes."

Her smile broadened as she gifted him with the full force of her wiles. He replied with a tight-lipped expression that might pass for a smile in any other company, but Hazel's heart beat an erratic rhythm to realize he was not as taken with her as she was with him. She needed to try harder. How else was she to get her first kiss? How else was she to make this man fall in love with her?

Once the dance began, their witty banter of question and one-word response halted. They moved away from each other and back together throughout the set, a heavy silence weighing their steps.

In many ways, the evening was far too short for Hazel's liking. In other ways, it dragged forever and could not end soon enough. Agnes had already approached Hazel with the news that Lord Driffield planned to escort all single gentlemen out of the house before he took his leave for the evening, his way of protecting his ladylove and her friends from scandal.

Not all ladies present wanted his protection, but he meant well. His intentions were among the many reasons he was a perfect match for Agnes, making her parents' disapproval all the more heinous. That he was not any aristocrat, but an earl made no difference to them. Rather than get to know the gentleman, they trusted rumor alone, ridiculous rumors of gaming and rakish behavior. This unfounded belief in gossip went to show how little parents knew or cared about the happiness of their daughters and how wrong society was about love and matrimony.

Hazel's opportunity to isolate Brooks was diminishing with every tick of the clock. He had returned to his friends after the dance and had stayed with that same group, using them as a protective shield, or so it seemed to her. Did he not find her attractive? Had she not given him obvious enough overtures? If he gave her the slightest of chances, she was certain she could sway his opinion. For the course of the evening, she danced with others, circulated for conversation, envied Agnes and Driffield their love, as well as Melissa and Chauncey their marriage, and pined for Brooks to notice her.

Her chance arrived when Agnes sneaked next to Hazel during a conversation with a group of guests.

Agnes leaned in and whispered for Hazel's ears only, "You *must* visit the terrace to admire the stars."

With a playful pinch to Hazel's arm, Agnes drifted to another group. Hazel made short work of excusing herself for fresh air. In truth, she would not mind the cool August air, for the room had become stifling. She could not be certain why Agnes wanted her to visit the terrace, but she could hope.

Aside from the candlelight spilling onto a portion of the terrace, outside was shrouded in darkness. No moon shone tonight, brightening the twinkle of the stars. A soft breeze tickled Hazel's skin. The room had been overly warm, but she did not realize how hot until the autumn night air prickled the perspiration at the back of her neck. After a few deep breaths to give her eyes time to adjust, she searched the terrace for Agnes's birthday surprise.

She spotted him a short distance away, leaning a shoulder against a Grecian column. Rustling to Viscount Brooks, her hands pressed to her embroidered stomacher to still the butterflies, she readied herself for the most pivotal moment of her life — when the man of her choice would fall in love with her.

"Lord Brooks," she said, lowering her voice to a husky imitation of how she had once heard Melissa speak to Chauncey.

He turned, surprise etching his features. Despite the shadows, his face spoke the truth: he had not been expecting her.

"Miss Trethow," he replied with a frown. "What brings you outside?"

Her attempt at allure was lost to the night, for he would not be able to catch the sultry way she looked at him from beneath her lashes, not with the light of the room at her back. Words would have to win her love rather than seductive glances.

"Desire," she answered. "I desire to live a life of my choosing. Without the interference of well-meaning relations, I aim to live and love. This party is the beginning of my forever."

Brooks coughed.

"Have I shocked you?"

"Not for the reasons you might think. As it is, your *desires* are none of my concern."

Hazel wringed her hands. Her nerves were failing her with each passing second. "What is it *you* desire, my lord?"

"A new pair of riding boots, but the best cord-wainer is in London. If you'll excuse me, Miss Trethow."

With a hasty bow, he left her alone in the darkness.

Chapter 3

Harold met his friend's knowing glance across the dining table, the two sharing a silent understanding regarding their supper companions.

The sweet voice of his mother, high pitched and melodious, rang out in continuation of her story. "And I said to the gentleman, 'What do you mean you *practice* medicine? Shouldn't you know by now what you're doing without needing more practice?' I wouldn't want him *practicing* on me!"

The guests shared in the laughter as Helena Hobbs, Baroness Collingwood, tittered.

From the head of the table, Lord Collingwood said, "You needn't understand such matters, Lady Collingwood. You need only be beautiful."

His mother simpered at what she must have thought a compliment.

One of the guests, a young lady who made her eligibility known by way of flirty poses, offered her own pearls of wisdom. "I believe a woman's greatest accomplishment is to decorate the arm of her husband. Don't you agree, Mr. Hobbs?"

His friend Patrick suppressed a cough.

"On the contrary, Miss Evans," Harold said. "A woman should possess a myriad of skills, least of which is serving as an ornament. A keen mind, ingenuity, compassion, companionship — I could list a dozen I would value over superficiality."

Nonplussed, Miss Evans looked to the other guests. "What a gentleman says he rarely means." She laughed, the others joining in. "By a keen mind, do you mean a woman who *reads*? Such marked intelligence is the ruination of beauty!"

The young woman sitting next to him concurred. "It's a known fact education leads to madness in women. We simply haven't the sensibilities for it."

Harold spared a glance for Patrick who raised his wine glass in mock salute.

The last course before the women would return to the drawing room dragged. This was the second supper party — in what he suspected would be a long line of supper parties — hosted by his mother in the hopes of arranging a marriage with a woman of means. Dowry, holdings, inheritance, anything would do. The previous supper party had entertained two wealthy widows and one spinster. Tonight's guest list included three misses of reputable lines.

The parents of each attended, giving Harold unsolicited insight into what marriage might be like with such in-laws, for good and ill. One young miss had such sensible parents, he would be tempted to pursue the match to further *their* acquaintance, but not even their company could entice him to consider the suit with so shallow of a girl.

His only pleasure of the evening was the company of his closest friend Patrick March, Viscount Kissinger, heir to the Winthorp earldom. In Patrick, Harold knew his own thoughts of the evening reflected. There was a multitude of reasons Harold was pleased to return to England, the reunion with Patrick being one of the most significant. The two had enjoyed a friendship since childhood, thrown together on many occasions since Lord Collingwood set stock in wooing the Earl of Winthorp as a potential investment partner, a success he never could realize.

"Come, ladies," his mother said at last. "Join me in the drawing room where we can make ourselves pretty before the gentlemen join us."

Chairs scraped. Dresses swished. Panniers swayed.

Thanks to his father, he was released from the obligation of conversing with the fathers, for Lord Collingwood launched into talk of his investment plan, something each of the men were enthralled to hear. Not only did Harold not wish to hear the lunacy, he also did not wish to give any of the men false hope that he would court one of their daughters.

"Whichever one will you choose?" Patrick asked, his words hushed as he slipped into the vacated chair next to Harold. "The one who values beauty above brains? The one who wants to raise swans…inside the house? Or the one who needs confirmation from her mother after every voiced thought? A shame you can't have them all."

Harold snorted. "Somewhere there's a gent for each of them. I'm not that man."

"Pity. The one with the pink hair powder—who told her that looked good?—was so set on having you, she twice dribbled bits of food on her bosom in hopes you would notice her assets."

"Did she?" Not that he would want to see such silliness, but the absurdity made him laugh. "Observant of *you* to notice."

"How could I not? Only twice was she successful. The other three times, the food deflected and landed in my lap instead."

Once the gentlemen joined the ladies in the drawing room for tea, Harold's mind wandered to an unlikely person — Miss Hazel Trethow. He had not spoken to his father about the matter since the first day of his arrival, but he wondered if the baron had written to Mr. Trethow yet about the understanding, releasing their children from the arrangement and freeing Miss Trethow to marry whomever she wished. He could not imagine her being disappointed. In all likelihood, she did not remember meeting him those many years ago and may have already set her cap at someone else.

And yet he could not help mourning the loss of a match with a woman he did not know. His plan had been to return from his father's business ventures and pay her call, an easy distance from Trelowen in Devonshire to her home in Cornwall. If the initial conversation went to plan, he would have used the winter months to court her, and they could have married before spring or waited to marry in London.

They probably would not have suited, he told himself, turning his attention to the ladies bickering over who would play the pianoforte first.

"London?" Harold stared at his father in disbelief. "I've only been home for a week."

Lord Collingwood drummed his fingers on the desk. "You'll be back in time to greet our guests. I need this done before the hunting party begins."

"I realize you don't agree with how I managed the earnings, but there was ample time for you to send a message to our solicitor in London with instructions before I docked. As it was, there was no message, and it was left to me to sort."

His father's drumming slowed, each finger falling with a disapproving *thud*. "A quick trip will *un*sort it and *re*sort it to my liking. I need that money at the ready for the new deal. Key players will be attending the hunting party, and I aim to gather additional backing from them. If I can think of a way to better represent the deal, I could potentially gather enough capital to cover my portion as well, and they'd be none the wiser. Unless you've taken to one of the girls your mother has introduced this past week?"

Harold scowled.

"Thought not. Yes, this is the way of it." Although Collingwood continued, he spoke more to the desk than to his son, as though working out his own plan rather than collaborating with Harold. "Driffield is invited, you know. A wealthy earl is just who I need to convince. That man has too much wealth for his own good, but the tables have done him no favors; already gambled away a sizable portion of his inheritance I heard. This investment is far more sound for his pocketbook. Butterbest is attending, also. He could be influential in convincing others."

While his father continued to mutter about the guest list, Harold eyed the table clock, wondering if it was too late to make headway for London. No sense in wasting time at home.

His ears perked at his father's next words.

"I have the highest hopes for Trethow. Wealthy, sensible, loyal. I've already written to him about the potential lucrativeness of this deal, so if I can persuade him to join with my refigured numbers, his capital could cover what I'm lacking. He'll want what's best for his son, and with the money we could make on this deal, his son could purchase a far grander estate than Trethow's modest Teghyiy Hall. Or at least that's how I aim to convince him."

With a tilt of his head and furrow of his brows, Harold asked, "You would cheat your friend? More to the point, you would cheat him with a deal I've warned you could fail?"

"Have faith. It will not fail. I'd be cheating him if I stole his money. As it is, I'd be borrowing it to help make him a great deal more. If anything, I'm thinking in his best interest. He'll double, even triple, his wealth with my guidance."

"By using a portion of his money to pay your capital." Harold flexed his fingers then clenched his fists behind his back. Not in a lifetime could he imagine lying to Patrick or having the man lie to him on such a scale. Loyalty in a friendship was reciprocal.

"You aren't seeing the full scale of the plan. That's what's wrong with you. You've never seen the bigger picture. Details, semantics, they're nothing to the larger stratagem. In time, you'll understand. With age, you'll understand. You're far too young to know the decisions a man must make, a peer of the realm. Follow my lead, my boy!"

When Harold returned to his room, he shut the door quietly behind him, a contrast to the rush of blood in his veins.

His father planned not only to ruin them with this deal but to bring down others in the process, including Miss Hazel Trethow's family. Had his own future not seemed bleak, he would pity her the fate she did not yet see coming, a fate she may not fully comprehend even when it came crashing down; that is, should her father agree to invest. Perhaps Mr. Trethow was wise enough to decline. There was the slimmest of chances his father was correct and that this deal would make them all wealthy beyond measure, but Harold did not believe it for a moment, not with the trouble brewing in Bengal, not with the opium trade, and not with Lord Collingwood's risky choices.

He looked about his bedchamber, a last look knowing he would not see it for another two weeks or so.

Not even after a week of being home had he accustomed himself to life in England. One would think he would have slipped into his four poster on that first night home and slept like a babe, or nestled into the well-cushioned chair by the fire for an evening read, even relished in the bedside coffee that appeared as though by magic every morning. Instead, he spent his nights restless, could not find comfort in the chair, and considered it unnerving that someone brought the coffee so soundlessly he did not notice.

Life in India had been different. A cot for a bed. The room sparsely furnished. Staff nonexistent. After a time, he had accustomed himself to the sweltering heat, even in the evenings, so much so that England seemed in perpetual winter in comparison.

He left the bedchamber with a sigh, entered his dressing room, and rang for his valet.

However short the wait, he was impatient to be on the road. Grabbing one of the bags tucked in the corner, he began clearing the table of his shaving equipment and sundry items.

"You rang, sahib," Abhijeet said.

Harold spared the valet a look before returning to his packing. "We're to London again. Only long enough to meet Father's solicitor."

Swatting Harold's hands from the bag, Abhijeet emptied it and began packing anew with meticulous care. With a refined British accent, only edged by a faint Bengali cadence, he commanded, "Sit. Leave this to me. Tell me of your father's plan while I pack."

Harold knew a battle he could not win and shrugged himself into a chair. "While we're there, you should open your own shop. You've enough money and skill to be the most sought-after tailor in London. I'd much rather us share a drink as equals than have you dress me."

"How many times do I have to tell you? A passion for fashion I may have, but I care not to do business with any Englishman but you. This is what I enjoy."

"Dressing me?" Harold ribbed.

"Come, think what life I would live as a tailor. Not the life in a grand estate, living in luxury as a king, my belly full of the finest albeit blandest of England's foods."

"If we're to be on the road to and from London every few weeks, you may change your mind about living in luxury."

Abhijeet shook his head as he packed at least two weeks' worth of clothes in a trunk. "You're stuck with me, I'm afraid. I've had the taste of life in a grand estate and won't give it up."

Only after returning to England did Harold hire Abhijeet as a valet. It was the fellow's own suggestion as they stood on the dock, Harold bidding farewell to a man he had come to consider a trusted friend. The Indian had spent too many years as a munshi for the East India Company to want to return to a life of business, but he had an inheritance significant enough to live the life of a gentleman, become a textile merchant, or do what he loved as a tailor. He preferred instead to live an easy life with purpose, pride, and ample time to himself.

Harold chuckled as he watched his valet work. "You simply don't want the bother of owning your own home."

"You see through me." Abhijeet waved Harold out of the chair to change him into traveling clothes.

"I fear this trip is only the beginning, my friend," Harold said. "He's determined to follow through with the opium deal. My hope is the hunting party solicitations will be denied, and he'll be left empty handed of capital. If he can convince his guests to invest, he'll go through with it, and back to London we'll go to make the arrangements."

The valet stripped Harold down to his shirt before replacing the silk breeches with buckskin, the waistcoat with a utilitarian sleeved vest, and an unadorned frock coat pleated at the hips. "His lordship knows the Company is taking control of the opium farms in and around Calcutta?"

"He does." Harold stood still for Abhijeet to bag his hair at the nape and tie it with a black bow. He favored this style when traveling, a more practical alternative to curling and powdering.

Abhijeet tutted. "Should the Company discover the ship, his investment will be at the bottom of the bay."

"More like in the Company's possession — ship, cargo, and capital."

"You'll pardon my saying but your father is a fool."

Harold could not agree more, but saying so was disloyal, even said to a friend. "He's in a tight spot and trying to save us all in the only way he knows how. If only I could make him see there are other ways out of this bind."

Packed and ready, Harold nodded to his valet and headed to wish his mother well before departing.

Chapter 4

Hazel admired the passing scenery from the Trethow carriage window. The rocky and sheep-dotted landscape of their seaside home gave way to hills and hedgerows as they traveled farther from Trevena in Cornwall and closer to Exeter in Devonshire for Baron Collingwood's hunting party. They were but a mile from Agnes's home at Longfirth where they would stop briefly to collect Agnes before continuing the journey. How her father had managed to convince Mr. Plumb to allow Agnes to join, Hazel would never know, but she was eternally grateful; a hunting party of lords and landowners sounded the dullest of droll drabbers.

Her father, Mr. Cuthbert Phineas Trethow, was not the dull sort but rather a man of vitality and spirit. He had spoken nonstop since leaving Teghyiy Hall. Much of the monologue centered on hunting. But some he reserved for his disappointment at not bringing his son, Hazel's brother Cuthbert Walter Trethow, a young man mere months from his fourteenth birthday. Almost a grown man, Mr. Trethow argued. Should be introduced to the right sort at an early age, all in preparation for his career as a Member of Parliament. Cuthbert had other ideas for his future, but neither he nor Hazel had mentioned that to Mr.

Trethow. Their father had a plan for the boy's future and would stop at nothing to see it through to fruition, just as he had a plan for Hazel's marriage, a sentiment she felt as strongly against as her brother felt on the political front.

"Promise me," her father was saying as she realized he had been talking about her, not just to her, "you'll make a favorable impression."

"Of course, Papa," she said, uncertain to what she committed herself but confident she could make a favorable impression on just about anyone.

"This is something we've hoped for since our youth. To see it happen at last — what proud papas we shall be!"

Hazel eyed her father with narrowed gaze.

Papa rubbed his hands together, a greedy grin glinting.

"The investment you mean?" Hazel hedged.

"Have you not been listening? The betrothal!"

Her gaze narrowed further; her lips pursed. "What betrothal?"

"Between you and Collingwood's heir, of course. If my suspicions are correct, it's the reason he's hosting the hunting party. He hopes to announce the betrothal in front of his important guests."

"Oh, that." Hazel made an unladylike snort. "Not likely, Papa. That's *your* dream, not mine. I will marry for love, not match myself to some stranger."

To her mind the conversation was concluded. Score one for Hazel, Papa zero.

"Don't say that, my bird. I *need* this. It is my dream and Collingwood's too. Think, you'd be a baroness one day! Rather than for a come-out, you could attend the London Season and be introduced to the Queen as a future peer's wife."

"Hmm. And this has nothing to do with the investment?"

Her father cast his eyes to the floor of the carriage, a sheepish pink to his cheeks. "Understand, Collingwood's letter made promises of wealth beyond measure. We could move into a grander estate, one to rival the baron's own! He's hesitant to do business with a friend, not wanting to combine friendship and business, he said, so he aims to interview potential partners at the party. Hazel, love, I can't be overlooked. I know I'm a simple man. I know his guests are more apt to laugh than consider me a partner. But should you be his future daughter-in-law, well, he can't possibly exclude me, now can he? This will be the making of us!"

As her father's animation increased, so did her foreboding for this party.

So close to finding love, she had been. So close to that elusive first kiss of love's lips. And now she was being auctioned at the town fair to some dullard. Why was he still a bachelor if he was such a catch? Likely as ugly as a sheep's bottom with the manners of a toad. She could see him now, the heir of the Collingwood barony, teeth rotted and the breath of a fermented chamber pot, his ideas of wooing a woman being to douse her with his perfume to hide his stench, and spray her with spittle as he professed an undying affection for his snuff box.

In memoriam, she recalled Anthony Faldo, Viscount Brooks. Blonde locks waved in the night's breeze, teasing her to run parted fingers through the tresses. She pouted to remember there had been no breeze, his hair had been tightly curled at the sides, and he would not have welcomed her roaming fingers. As embarrassing as the memory, the idea of him held fast in her heart. He represented a man of her choice. No arranged betrothal between interfering parents. No toad with foul breath. No unhappy marriage. He represented freedom.

When the carriage turned along the Longfirth Hall drive, Hazel realized her father was still talking, doing his best to convince her to make a good impression before the conversation would need to change for Agnes's sake.

Setting her teacup in its saucer, Hazel leaned towards a giggling Agnes. "I wager he's a connoisseur of monocles. Always looking about the room with one eye magnified."

"His idea of courting a lady is," Agnes said with a pause, "showing her his periwig collection."

The two dissolved into laughter.

The object of their fun was Mr. Harold Hobbs, the notably absent Mr. Harold Hobbs. Hazel might have felt a twinge of guilt at poking fun at the man if she could remember him or, more to the point, if her father had not pressed his marriage ploy. As it was, Mr. Hobbs was not in residence to rebut their silliness. He would return from a London trip by the end of the week, the Collingwoods had promised their guests, hopefully in time for the soiree.

Not that he was missed. The only guests who had thus far arrived were the Trethows with Miss Plumb and a Mr. Butterbest with his wife and two sons. All other guests were set to arrive on the morrow.

The drawing room was no less lively this evening, despite the drizzle of rain tapping at the windows. Lady Collingwood enjoyed the company of Mrs. Butterbest. Lord Collingwood entertained Mr. Butterbest and Mr. Trethow. And the Messrs. Butterbest made eyes at Hazel and Agnes from across the room. All through supper, the two gentlemen had flirted with them. Agnes had a heart only for Lord Driffield and so gave them a polite albeit frosty reception, while Hazel considered them for all of two minutes before dismissing them as suitors.

Wealthy as Croesus, she was to understand, but milksops. The twins were in their early twenties with hair so powdered she could not say with confidence its natural color. They deferred to their parents on every score. *Is it not a fine day?* Hazel might ask. *Our father says we'll pay for this fine weather with three days of rain.* One of the twins might answer. *Will you be riding to hounds?* Agnes might ask. *Our mother feels it prudent we look after our safety, we mean to say the ladies' safety, by staying behind with the women on hunting days.* No, these young men would not do. They could never hold a candle to someone like Lord Brooks.

Agnes touched a hand to Hazel's arm to draw her attention from the twins. "You don't think your father is serious, do you?"

"Of course not. He would never force me to marry. His words were meant to encourage me, nothing more. Papa believes he can curry favor on this business deal if I'm engaged to Lord Collingwood's son."

"But hasn't this been arranged for years?"

"Informally, nothing serious." Hazel reassured her friend as much as herself. "Papa would never force me. You know how he is."

Agnes grimaced. "He was fibbing, then, when he told my father this was to be your betrothal party?"

"He what?" The teacup rattled against the saucer.

"That's the only reason Father allowed me to come. Was your father playing mine to ensure I could attend or…."

Or indeed. Hazel was not overly concerned, but it was a troubling turn of events. When they returned and she was *not* betrothed, there would be a price to pay with Mr. Plumb, not only for his being misled by Mr. Trethow, but also to her own reputation in the man's estimation, not to mention to whomever he then spoke about it.

She would not think ill of her father. He must have a plan in mind, for he would never force her hand nor fall out of the good graces of Mr. Plumb.

Before she could respond to Agnes, she caught sight of Messrs. Butterbest making their way across the room to them, intent on flirtation if she could judge by their overly eager expressions. With a bow, the gentlemen eyed Hazel's and Agnes's bosom.

A stir at the drawing room door caught Hazel's attention, caught everyone's attention. All heads turned at the sound of a shriek and a grunt.

"Unhand me, you cretin!" cried a woman as the double doors flew open. "Where's Eugene? I must see Eugene to bed."

The twins snorted laughter as a shivering woman shuffled into the room, her nightdress soaked through, clinging indecently to her frail figure, her mobcap flattened against frizzed grey curls. She looked all about the room in confusion.

"Nana!" Lady Collingwood was at the woman's side in an instant, her husband following suit.

"Mother," said the baron, shielding the figure from view, "did you walk here from the dower house in the rain? You're not even wearing shoes!"

Two footmen shadowed her, faces crestfallen and apologetic.

Hazel and Agnes exchanged glances of both sorrow and curiosity as their hosts ushered the woman from the room.

"It's Eugene's bedtime," she repeated as they led her away.

When the doors closed behind them, the twins' guffaws trumpeted.

Hazel set her saucer on the table and rose from her seat. She squared her shoulders, lifted her chin, and glowered at Messrs. Butterbest. Their expressions sobered.

With a withering glare, she hissed, "Stop your shameful silliness this instance."

They had the decency to look abashed.

Hazel was not finished. "You both ought to be ashamed of yourselves. That is no less a personage than the Dowager Baroness Collingwood, who deserves the utmost respect. If you've no more manners than this, I'll see to it you eat in the stables for the remainder of the week."

That Hazel was younger, two heads shorter, and a guest on equal footing with no power to have anyone eating in the stables did not seem to occur to either of the young men. They stared at their feet and mumbled apologies, red splotches coloring their cheeks. Giving a satisfied harrumph, Hazel offered a bright smile to her father and Mr. and Mrs. Butterbest across the room then sat down, turning her attention back to Agnes.

Agnes's lips curved into a grin.

"Don't look so smug," Hazel said. "We're no less guilty with our gossip about Mr. Hobbs."

"That's different, and you know it."

"Is it?" Hazel asked under her breath, her eyes on the closed door.

The next morning, Hazel enjoyed a cup of chocolate in Agnes's dressing room, the latter clad in her shift while her lady's maid curled her hair.

It did not escape Hazel's notice that Agnes's suite was not as nice as her own. Although the suite was the same size with the same view of the gardens, Agnes's bedchamber and adjoining dressing room appeared tired. The wood had dulled, the rugs faded, and the curtains frayed. The most attractive aspect of the room was the strapwork of the ceiling, but even it needed new plastering and painting.

Perhaps Baron Collingwood could not be bothered with a guest such as Miss Plumb. He was, after all, exceedingly wealthy, a man who favored the finer things and hosted lavish parties, or so her father had explained in his impassioned speech in the carriage.

Agnes sighed at her reflection, admiring the first set of completed curls in her *tête de mouton* hairstyle. "If I could drink chocolate every morning, I would be the happiest of persons. Father would never approve. He thinks chocolate sinful." She turned to wink at Hazel. "That makes it all the more divine!"

In response, Hazel savored her chocolate with a dramatic moan. "When you're the Countess of Driffield, you may have a cup of chocolate at every meal."

She eyed the lady's maid but knew their conversation was confidential. All who attended Agnes, be they governess or lady's maid, were loyal to their mistress, if not outright protective.

"But when will that be?" Agnes's smile slipped at the corners. "Nathan promises he'll find a way, but until then I'm trapped."

"An elopement would be romantic. He loves you, so what's stopping him? Once under his protection, your father will have no control over your life."

"He's afraid of the scandal an elopement would cause."

The lady's maid finished Agnes's hair and shifted position to help slip on stockings and shoes.

"If he's against that," Hazel reasoned, "then I don't see why he can't procure a license with or without your father's permission—he's an *earl*! He must have some sway."

"He's trying to find another way," Agnes said, lifting one leg then the other for the maid. "His grandmother is determined to marry him to someone of her choosing and would make life difficult if she didn't approve of me. A little more time, he says. With a little more time, he can convince his grandmother to accept me."

"And then what? It still comes down to elopement or license. Your father would lock you away if he heard the banns read."

Agnes's shoulders slumped as her maid slipped the underpetticoat over the shift. "Nathan doesn't like to talk about it."

"Well, Lord Driffield needs to—*what are those?*"

Hazel gasped when the lady's maid tightened the stays, the movement tugging the short sleeves of the shift further up Agnes's bare arms. Only the arms were not as bare as they should be. Old, yellowing bruises encircled each upper arm.

Agnes waved away Hazel when her friend rose from her chair. She nodded for her lady's maid to continue dressing her.

Not meeting Hazel's eyes, Agnes said, "You know how Father can be."

"He's never been like *that*." She pointed at the bruises even as Agnes tugged at the sleeves to cover the evidence.

"They don't hurt if that's your worry. He held my arms a little tighter than he anticipated is all."

"But why?" Hazel could think of no rationale for anyone holding someone so tightly they left marks.

The lady's maid secured the panniers before turning to the petticoat.

"He was concerned. He saw me having a word with the gardener, you see, and was fraught we might have spoken about more than the flowers." With a laugh and smile that did not meet her eyes, Agnes said, "Imagine his reaction if he found out about our party. How diverting!"

Hazel scowled. "There's nothing diverting about it. Have you told Lord Driffield? Tell me you tried sneaking a letter to him. He must do something! I don't care what his grandmother says; if he loves you, he needs to bring you under his protection."

With the stomacher pinned in place, the lady's maid retrieved the *robe à la française* from its hanger, slipping Agnes's arms into elbow-length lace and satin sleeves before pinning the gown to both stomacher and petticoat. Agnes watched her lady's maid in the mirror, ignoring Hazel for a time.

Hazel fidgeted, her cup of chocolate forgotten on the tray. If only there were something she could *do*! Lord Driffield needed to make good on his promises. The life of an earl was not uncomplicated, she knew, but love should not be *this* complicated. She could not see why the two could not marry now and sort out the details later, the grandmother being an easy conquest once she got to know Agnes. Who would not adore Agnes once they got to know her?

Her friend twirled and tittered. "Do I look good enough to marry?"

"One look and any man would be besotted."

"Perfect. Because Nathan is coming to the hunting party." Agnes laughed at Hazel's widening eyes.

The afternoon sun reflected off the diamond windows of the Elizabethan manor. It was a perfect day for a garden party. Nothing could keep the partygoers indoors, not even the dampness of the lawn from yesterday's rain or the chilly September air. Guests arrived at their leisure throughout the morning and afternoon. Dotting the landscape an array of colorful dresses and frock coats pranced, posed, and lounged, worn by more aristocrats than Hazel had ever seen in a single gathering at one time. Mr. Trethow was known to host a gathering from time to time but never like this. Never so posh. Never so well attended.

Agnes sat across from Hazel on a decorative picnic sheet, twirling her parasol. They were a contrasting pair, Hazel observed, Agnes in her ivory and Hazel in her periwinkle, Agnes with blue eyes, Hazel with green. Even their features opposed. Agnes bore a lean, slender face with an aquiline nose, and showed to advantage a figure to match, long limbs, sultry bosom, and hips to envy. Hazel was all hearts. Her face was heart shaped, her nose pert, her lips cherubic, and her physique an inverted triangle with shoulders wider than hips, an ample enough midline to take the stays to task, and a cherry bosom, that was to say, more the size of cherries than the shape, although they were that too. No one seeing Agnes and Hazel side by side would confuse them for sisters, but they did share one similarity: their hair. Although both ladies sported brown hair, Agnes's being hickory and Hazel's auburn, the powder dusting their curls transformed the shade to a matching snowy white.

Hazel never envied Agnes her beauty, for there was nothing in the mirror Hazel did not like. Never vain, but confident. The gentlemen waggling their eyebrows at her from across the lawn felt likewise.

Ah, the gentlemen. A veritable cornucopia of available bachelors! If a young lady could not find love here, there was little hope for her. The competition would be stiff. Unmarried ladies, each with their own beauty, moved from one intimate group to another, sheep herded by the scent of eligibility.

"No more talk of Nathan," Agnes was saying.

Hazel turned her attention from the frocked fops under the yew tree to her friend.

"Let's talk about *you*," Agnes continued. "You never told me what happened with Lord Brooks."

Leaning back, palms to the lumpy sheet, Hazel said, "Because there's nothing to tell. He took his leave the moment we were alone."

"That's unexpected. From the rumors I've heard, he's on the lookout for a wife." Dropping to a whisper, Agnes added, "Not to mention the *other* rumors."

"About his being Casanova in hiding from the law?" Hazel snorted a laugh.

"No, about his being…*you know*." Agnes mouthed her next words. "A grand lover."

Hazel barked a laugh loud enough to turn a few nearby heads and send Agnes diving for her fan to cool her reddening cheeks.

"I shall never know."

Wafting the fan until her cheeks lightened to pink, Agnes said, "Don't be discouraged. He might only need a stronger nudge. But if not him, you'll find someone else, someone who makes your soul sigh, your heart pound, and your resolve melt. We'll both marry our true loves in the end.

Wait and see." She set her fan aside to squeeze Hazel's hand.

Movement from the terrace caught their attention before Hazel could reply. More guests had arrived. Agnes craned to see around the group blocking the view of the double doors. Hazel spotted them first.

"Melissa!" She squeaked.

Clamoring to her feet, she waved her arms to catch her friend's attention. A few other heads turned in the process, accompanied by snickering. Hazel did not care a whit. They could call her an uncultured West Country bumpkin if it suited them.

Hazel did what she did best. She flashed a smile.

Chagrined, the heads turned away. Meanwhile, Lady Melissa Williamson caught sight of them, gave a little wave in return, and excused herself from Sir Chauncy and the group that had stopped them upon entering the terrace.

She was pretty in pink, Hazel admired. Green eschelles laddered her stomacher with matching green bows where the satin met the lace at her elbows. The hem of her dress-robe, framing the petticoat, flounced and bounced more green bows. Not to be out fashioned by her friends, Melissa's ebony hair was curled in rows above her ears and powdered white, a pleasing contrast with her dark complexion.

"Hazel. Agnes." Melissa approached with out-stretched hands, kissing Hazel's cheeks first, then taking Agnes's hands in hers as she knelt to join the ladies. "I'm relieved not to be the youngest here. Is it me or is this hunting party intended for the dotage?"

Giggling, Agnes said, "Look under the yew tree. They've gathered en masse, Miss Evans leading the unmarried ladies on rounds to tempt the eligible gents."

"Yes, I see." Melissa wrinkled her nose. "When did you both arrive? I've not yet had the opportunity to rest. I hope we'll have time to do so before supper."

Hazel's attention turned once more to the terrace as another set of visitors arrived. "Yesterday. A tedious supper with the Butterbests." Before she could elaborate, she gasped a breathy, "*Oh my*."

Agnes and Melissa followed her gaze.

Viscount Brooks stood next to the Earl of Driffield, the pair exchanging pleasantries with Lord and Lady Collingwood. Hazel's heart caught in her throat to see the rogue who had rejected her. Across from her, Agnes made to rise until Melissa's hand caught her arm to stop her.

The trio watched the gentlemen in silence.

However impossible, Lord Brooks was more handsome than he had been at the Longfirth party. Ringed fingers waved in a bed of lace as he spoke. A beauty patch adorned the corner of his mouth, drawing attention to his rouged, supple, kissable lips. Hazel sighed. Her father would be disappointed to know the train of her thoughts, but it was not her fault Lord Brooks was here rather than Mr. Toad Hobbs. She could not very well sigh over the baron's heir if she had not yet met him. Although she doubted he could contend with Brooks's foppish fabulousness, without doubt the most desirable man present.

Or so she thought for a full minute. Hot on his buckled heels, another pair appeared at the terrace doors, causing a stir from the guests near enough to greet them.

"*Who* is *that*?" Hazel hoped she was not gawking.

"Poor Lord Brooks. Forgotten already," Agnes chided.

Melissa, who had moved in fashionable circles ever since her marriage to Sir Chauncy, knew everyone worth knowing. "Ah. That's Viscount Kissinger and his father the Earl of Winthorp."

Hazel's "Oh my" this time held a far different meaning than before. How could she possibly be in the presence of so many finely figured men? Love must be in the air!

Melissa laughed. "Yes, he's available."

"Did I ask that aloud?" Hazel fluttered her eyelashes.

"Your expression asked on your behalf."

Agnes poked Hazel in the arm then said to Melissa, "Our Hazel is under strict orders from Mr. Trethow to make a favorable impression on our host's son. We'll have to rein her in."

"Best of luck," Melissa said. "Rumor has it Lady Collingwood has been inviting the wealthiest women west of London to dine. The wealthiest and most available, that is. No difficulty guessing why. And from the look of some of the guests, I suspect those same women will be vying for his attention the whole of the hunting party."

"Better to wish *them* luck than me. He's not even here to be wooed. How disappointed they must be." Hazel brushed off the talk of Mr. Hobbs, her eyes riveted on the terrace.

She may have luck in love yet.

Chapter 5

Giving his frock coat a firm tug, Harold descended the main stairs at Trelowen. Although his letter to his father had promised he would arrive in time, supper had started half an hour ago. He was late. Inexcusably late. It could not have been helped. During the trip home from London, he had made good time, but as he reached the outskirts of Exeter, a toppled farm cart had blocked the road. The only reason he had made it in time for a late supper rather than arriving well past dusk was his insistence on helping the man restore order to the felled cartwheel and fallen goods before sending him and his donkey on their merry way.

And so he was late. His mother would be suffering from silent fits of hysteria to see an empty seat at her perfectly planned table, and his father would be piqued. They would experience a greater shock when he walked through the double doors: his hair was unpowdered and bagged. With time against him, he had the choice of either bathing or recruiting Abhijeet to style his hair. He opted for the bath.

Two footmen opened the dining room doors upon his approach. With a grand entrance sure to catch everyone's attention, whether or not he wanted it, he marched into the room to face a tide of turning faces and stilled cutlery.

"Ah. My son," Eugene Hobbs, Baron Colling-wood, announced, rising from the head of the table and sweeping a hand. "Allow me to introduce my son Mr. Harold Hobbs."

Harold bowed.

Not until he took his seat and a footman filled his wine glass did the din of voices resume. In a single survey of the room, he assessed the guests.

His first reaction was shock. How much further debt had his father accrued with this extravagance? They could not afford this. A hunting party alone was beyond affordability, but this was going well beyond their financial reach. While the wear of Tre-lowen remained evident under Harold's scrutiny, care had been taken to buff, wax, and cover. The dining room shimmered with not just any candles but beeswax candles, the same he had seen in the hallway, stairwell, and vestibule, all burning with-out the benefit of observation or use, irreplaceable money torched in each sconce and chandelier. The wood paneling, banisters, and floors gleamed with polish. The table fare was one of the finest Harold had ever seen with the choicest meats and a selection of dishes so varied the guests could not possibly try them all in a single meal.

Given this was the third day of the hunting party with several days remaining, Harold could have wept to think of the expense. His father must be confident he could convince the guests to invest at a higher price point so he could recoup the money spent and cover his capital. Harold was not so certain. In his single survey, he had taken the measure of those in attendance.

Prior to leaving for London, he had seen the guest list; some of the names he knew, some he did not, but it was not difficult to distinguish who was who at the table. Only the West Country's wealthiest were present. The wealthiest and the most likely to take risks. The presence of the wives and children was a red herring from his father's goal, for his intended guests were the gentlemen, all invited for their pocketbook.

The first eyes to meet his were Patrick's, his friend seated at the opposite end of the table near the Earl of Winthorp, father and son separated by a stunning young woman who engaged in turn both Patrick and Lord Winthorp. Harold arched an eyebrow at Patrick. He hoped his eyebrow conveyed the question, *Lord Kissinger, the eligible bachelor?*

A few of the guests surprised him. The Earl of Driffield, for instance, for the Driffield he knew had been an older man. At some point during Harold's time in India, Driffield must have passed, and this man inherited. The new Lord Driffield looked a decade older than Harold, but he was a popinjay if ever Harold saw one, frilled and laced to the point of foppishness. His demeanor spoke of a man of leisure, one who spent money faster than his estate could earn and one who thought himself God's gift to ladies. The man eyed his supper companion — Mr. Worthington's daughter, if Harold was not mistaken — from beneath hooded eyes. Harold's jaw ticked.

Viscount Brooks sat across from Driffield, a gentleman who Harold had known by reputation at Oxford. The viscount would not have been a guest Harold would have thought to invite. Wealthy, yes. Risk taker, yes. Sensible, no. Perhaps Lord Collingwood banked on that lack of sense.

Butterbest's hearty laugh dominated the table, never mind that he sat at the far end near Harold's mother Helena. Gauging from his conversation, Butterbest would be unlikely to favor the investment plan, for he was in the process of detailing the new horses he had purchased, the new carriage, and the new lake at the east end of his property. If the man had any money remaining, Harold would be surprised.

The chinless Mr. Worthington might also reject the investment opportunity, for he was telling the lady at his side of his extensive travel plans, expensive travel plans to be precise.

Harold's gaze fell on each guest, gentlemen and relations, and assessed their likelihood of agreeing to the baron's scheme. As much as Harold regretted the money spent on the hunting party, he held out hope fewer guests would be persuaded to invest, thus deterring his father from finding the capital and proceeding with the deal.

The perusal was not yet completed when Miss Evans, seated to his right, engaged him in conversation. Or tried to. Not to appear rude, he asked her about her modiste, which saved him the trouble of conversing as she launched into a monologue of next Season's wardrobe and how complementary she would be to the gentleman at her side — wink, wink, her expression said.

Many of the sons and daughters of the guests he did not recognize. None were under seventeen, but they certainly would have been when Harold saw them last, before his departure to India.

The Butterbest twins were among the easily recognized. They sat on either side of a young lady Harold did not know, both singling her out for conversation. The poor girl blushed in demure silence, the pink of her cheeks accentuating the blemishes that no amount of face paste or powder could cover. She seemed just the sort for the twins. If they had not changed in the time Harold spent in India, and he doubted they had, they would prefer a simpering and shy gel, for both men were intimidated by any woman who spoke her mind.

So engaged in his assessment of the guests, his gaze nearly moved past her. *Her* being his once upon a time intended.

Miss Hazel Trethow sat across the table from him, three chairs removed. Her head was bowed in conversation with the gentleman to her left, Sir Chauncey if memory served. Had not the gentleman married recently? Harold could not recall. He gave little thought for the baronet and focused his full attention on Miss Trethow. It was absurd that his heart skipped a beat at the sight of her. After all, his memory was of a wide eyed and pink faced ten-year-old girl, as silly and giggly as most ten-year-old girls. But she was no longer a young girl.

To think, he had planned at this point to be in Cornwall, calling on her with the intention of marriage.

Her eyes were bright, full of aspirations and dreams, full of the search for eternal love. With a subtle flick of his gaze, he took in her physique, what he could see of it above the table, and just as quickly shifted his attention to his plate. She was perfect.

Interjecting monosyllabic responses to Miss Evans, who was still chattering, Harold glanced back to Miss Trethow.

In that moment, her head turned.

Their eyes met.

Harold's heart thumped.

With no more than a pout of her lips to acknowledge him, she turned back to her supper companion and laughed. In the space of the next course, Miss Trethow laughed more than anyone else at the table and, in fact, laughed so much that Harold found himself scowling both at his plate and Miss Evans. Only his mother laughed that much.

So a beauty Miss Trethow may have become, but a woman she had not. Immature, vapid, and silly, the antithesis of his desired wife, an antidote to sensibility. He may be only a few years older than she, but he felt like a fossil.

Not for the first time since his father announced he would write to Mr. Trethow to discourage the childhood match did Harold wonder how the family had taken the news. No doubt with enthusiasm. Miss Trethow was the type of girl foolish enough to think marriages ought to be love matches. How fortunate, then, that he had not traveled to Cornwall to court her.

He refocused on the guests, his ears perked to learn more about them. Only his eyes, those traitorous eyes, found their way back to Miss Trethow, insistent on admiring her even while his mind disengaged from her.

Lady Melissa Williamson's suite rivaled Hazel's, confirming for Hazel that the Collingwoods had, indeed, set Agnes in their shabbiest of guestrooms. It was a slight, to be sure. Hazel hoped Agnes did not notice.

Although, now that she made the observation, she would swear the corner of the wallpaper behind the dressing table peeled, a mustard yellow peeking from the edge. Perhaps the Collingwoods did not use these rooms often.

"With our help," Melissa said to Agnes, "you'll be engaged before the end of the week."

Hazel beamed at her friends, excited to set their matchmaking into motion. "We must convince him to marry you *before* he speaks to his grandmother rather than after. With us at the ribbons, we'll steer you straight for love."

All titters and blushes, Agnes looked from one to the other of her friends. "We exchanged poetic declarations of love today in the library, enough to make you both green with envy. Even you, Melissa. He *wants* to marry me. I know he does." She fingered the edge of the blanket wrapped about her legs. "Do you truly believe he'll make a formal announcement at the party?"

"Yes!" Melissa and Hazel said in unison.

"With the right persuasion, he could marry you *during* the party. Wouldn't that be grand?" Hazel tucked her feet beneath her bottom, snuggling deeper into the chair in front of the fireplace. "The timing is perfect. A last day elopement. Or if he can find a way to get the license without your father's permission, which I'm positive he could, then the two of you could marry before the end of the party, all the guests here to celebrate the nuptials."

"Do you think it possible?" Agnes asked wistfully. "I would never have to return home. It *would* be perfect timing. And together, he and I could convince his grandmother that we're well suited and that I would make the best Lady Driffield."

Melissa cast them a rueful smile. "And then our goal will be to matchmake Hazel."

Agnes giggled anew, her giggles increasing when Hazel harrumphed. "The delectable Lord Kissinger could be a contender—what a delightful conversationalist he was at supper this evening, and how lucky was I to sit between him and the Earl of Winthorp—but we needn't bother matchmaking. Hazel's already met her match. Mr. Horrid Hobbs."

Melissa frowned. "Now that you've seen him, do you hold to your conviction that the two of you wouldn't suit? Personally, I thought him handsome and well mannered."

Agnes answered for Hazel with a fictionalized telling of Mr. Hobbs's hobbies of cataloguing mushrooms and collecting wigs. Had it been earlier that day or any day before, Hazel would have joined in the fun. In truth, now that she had seen him, she was not so sure.

Mr. Harold Hobbs was a curious contradiction. In one part, he was wholly unfashionable. His attire was plain, although well-tailored. He wore neither wig nor powder, his russet hair bagged and bowed in dishevelment, strands frizzing their escape in unruly curls at the nape of his neck. His complexion was as sun bronzed as a sailor's, his shoulders broad, and his chest expansive. He overshadowed the other men at the table.

Yes, he was wholly unfashionable.

And yet arresting.

Hazel's stomach had fluttered at the first sight of him. She was simultaneously intrigued and appalled.

The contradiction was that despite his unfashionable physique and presentation, he was the poshest man at the table. Hazel both hated him for it and fell a little in love with him. He wore no smile, revealed no emotion, and acted a proper toff. But there was a poise to him, a natural polish and grace no one else at the table embodied. No artifice, no pomp, no flair. He was the most aristocratic man present, despite his being at a table of earls, viscounts, and barons.

She had not wanted to encourage him and so had avoided meeting his eyes. Her gaze, however, had a willpower of its own, for it found its way back to him time and again throughout the meal, roaming his direction even when she aimed for Lord Brooks or Lord Kissinger.

Had Papa not pressed her to make a favorable impression or reminded her of the childhood dreams he shared with Lord Collingwood, would she have given Mr. Hobbs an encouraging nod? She suspected she would have. Since supper, she reminded herself he was everything she did not want. She wanted passion. That man, that strait-laced bore who showed no flirtation, no emotion, no reaction, not even an assessment of her figure, could not offer passion. Not that a maiden of seventeen knew anything about passion. She had never even been kissed. But she knew *of* it and knew there was a deeper mystery to it than even she could dream, for the looks she spied passing between Melissa and Chauncy spoke of the passion she wanted. Looks that spoke of a love so deep and eternal that nothing could break the bond, not even death.

That was what she wanted.

Passion.

Agnes's rising from her chair and folding of the blanket interrupted Hazel's musings. "Go on, then," Agnes said, shooing Hazel to the door. "You heard Melissa."

Hazel had not. She glanced to Melissa with a nod to pretend she had been listening.

Melissa's mischievous smile revealed what Hazel had missed even before her words said it. "Don't be so shocked that I'm going to his room rather than him coming to mine. This is, after all, an advantage of a love match."

The next morning was the first day of the hunt. The gentlemen had gathered early for the much-anticipated ride to hounds on the north side of the estate. The ladies, after sleeping late, now milled about both inside and outside, entertaining themselves with lawn bowls, archery, poetry, and whatever else it was women did to find pleasure amongst their numbers. Lady Collingwood played the dutiful hostess, initiating games and circulating between guests outside and inside.

It proved the perfect opportunity for Harold to visit Nana.

He cut across the lawn with a nod here and wave there, his destination the wilderness walk through the woods. The path would fork at approximately a quarter of a mile, splitting one way to circle the lake with its boathouse and lakefront vistas, and splitting another way to the dower house. His grandmother had always preferred to reside in the dower house, demanding her independence. Before Harold left for India, she had grown increasingly forgetful but without cause for concern, a far cry from the condition in which he found her on his return home. Her state had shocked him, to say the least. Nana may live with a full staff and companion, but she was in no state to live independently, certainly not with only a companion whose responsibility it was to keep her company, not serve as a nursemaid.

If Harold had anything to say about it, she would move into the main house before the month ended. His father would object. His mother would object. Nana would object. Harold would not take no for an answer.

The lawn gave way to trees, English Oak and Common Beech towering in splendor with their autumn foliage, golds, coppers, purples, and reds painting the canopy. The park woodland consisted of a combination of native and non-native trees cultivated or hybridized, gathered from the world travels of the sixth Baron Collingwood, Harold's great grandfather, and gifted by gardeners of neighboring parks, such as the newest acquisition, the Holm Oak, courtesy of the head gardener at Mamhead Park, Mr. William Lucombe.

Hours he could spend studying the texture of the bark, admiring the veil of leaves, contrasting the uniqueness of the various genera. Countless pages in his sketchbook captured the tapestry of light dancing in the shadows of the forest floor. Long years he had spent away, too long. As much as he already missed India, nothing could replace the parkland at Trelowen.

The underbrush would crunch and crackle beneath his buckled shoes should he veer from the path, but the groundskeeper kept the walk clear, only hardpacked soil underfoot. Had the gardener not done his job so efficiently, Miss Trethow would have heard Harold approach before he saw her. He had the pleasure of first sight. Leaning against a tree trunk, she stared at the handkerchief in her hand. From this distance, she looked to be tugging at the threads of the embroidery, unraveling the work one string at a time.

He cleared his throat to announce his approach. Not before taking her in with a sweep from head to toe—as beautiful as she had been at supper, and no doubt as silly. She was shorter than he expected, or would it be more polite to call her petite? Her pleasingly plump torso tapered to slender corseting inches above wide panniers that flared in teal satin to meet shapely ankles, luckily for him visible because of her stance. There was nothing silly about her at present. No laughter or flirtation. With her head bowed, her bottom lip pouted, and her shoulders slouched, she was a woman in repose, a woman awaiting skilled, deft fingers to master charcoal against paper. As had happened at supper, his heartbeat accelerated.

When she gave no notice of his initial throat clearing, he tried again, louder.

Like a rabbit spying a fox, her head jerked up, eyes wide. Skittish, she stepped away from the tree and looked about her, as though scanning for a means of escape.

With a bow, he said, "Good morning, Miss Trethow."

"Quite."

She gave a nervous laugh, or rather it sounded nervous to Harold's ears. Her eyes flitted between him and the surrounding woods. Were they not alone? Was she expecting someone?

"What brings you to the wilderness walk alone?" he asked.

"Your hair."

His lips creased at the corners in a confused half-smile, half-frown. "My hair brings you here alone?"

She waved the kerchief, as if his response was illogical, not hers. "Your hair, it's different." A pucker formed between the thin arches of her brows.

"Ah, yes. I apologize if my appearance offended you yesterday evening. I had not intended to be late."

His hair, as with his attire, was impeccable today. Nana would expect it, as would the guests. Powdered and curled in tidy rows above his ears and bowed at the nape of his neck, his hair made him look like a different man, although he refused to lighten his tan with cosmetics, making him not a completely different man from whom Miss Trethow saw at supper.

Hazel returned his half-smile with one of her own, the sight doing strange things to his pulse. "Do people often take offense when your hair is unpowdered?"

He made to answer then caught the twinkle in her eyes. She was teasing him! While racking his brain for a witty reply, he lost himself in her eyes. Never had he seen their likeness. They reflected the forest, an earthy green, darker around the outer ring. What was a man to say when caught unawares by such beauty?

Her laugh intervened. It was not the affectation from supper, but a deeper laugh of genuine amusement. An onlooker might assume he had made a witty retort after all. Rather than reply, he chuckled along with her, sharing the moment, feeling a thread of something between them, though he could not put a name to it. There was a chance she was laughing at him, but he thought not; rather she was laughing at a shared joke.

Then an idea struck him. Impulsive but desirable.

"I'm for the dower house," he began.

Seconds before his invitation for her to join him reached his lips, he saw a movement in the woods beyond. A flash of white.

He squinted.

Lord Driffield, free of coat and waistcoat, sat upright from the underbrush, propping himself against the trunk of a tree.

Ah.

A lover's tryst. Between Driffield and Miss Trethow. Harold's jaw tightened and his fingers curled into fists.

This was none of his concern. He should bow and leave her to make her own mistakes. Alas, he could not in good conscience do that.

"Allow me to escort you back to the house before I continue for the dower house," he said instead.

Miss Trethow's laughter died. She hesitated, made to say something, stared at the handkerchief still clutched between her fingers, and then nodded.

To his relief, she did not turn to look back into the forest. It was awkward enough for Harold. He did not wish for her to know he had seen her lover or caught them in the act of a clandestine meeting.

To his relief, Lady Melissa Williamson entered the wilderness walk before he felt obligated to make conversation. She smiled in greeting and reached out to take Miss Trethow's hands, the passing of the charge from Harold to the baronet's wife.

He did not see the Earl of Driffield on his return walk to the dower house. Another relief. Had he seen the man, he would have been hard pressed not to confront him. To say what, he was not certain, but to say *something*, for who else would champion a maiden?

It was not his concern, and he would do well to remember that.

Chapter 6

According to Harold's valet, the household was short-staffed. Lord Collingwood had admitted to dismissing the steward, but the dismissals ran deeper, all in an effort to avoid unnecessary expenses. *Yet the man used beeswax candles.* Harold scoffed. This was one of several points of contention he aimed to discuss with his father before the partygoers took to the lake for an afternoon of boating and lakeside strolls.

The most pressing matter was Nana.

She had greeted him in good spirits yesterday morning. All would have appeared well, nothing unusual, had she not mistaken him twice for his father, mid conversation no less, and thrice made whispered accusations that her companion was a man in disguise who plotted to steal her jewels. In the lightest of manners, he had indicated how welcome she would be at the main house. She saw straight through his machinations. For a quarter of an hour, she had lectured him on the need for a woman to maintain independence. She refused to be fussed over. She was not *old*. She did not need a nursemaid. How dared her green grandson think he knew what was best for a mature woman who knew her own mind.

Chastised, he had kissed her cheek, wished her well, and returned home to mull over a plan that would not insult her or undermine her wishes.

Yes, there was much to discuss with his father. Lord Collingwood's study, accessible from the entrance hall by way of a reception room, faced the Elizabethan knot garden through a semi-circular bow window with diamond-shaped, latticed windowpanes. While the reception room was a manly monstrosity of dark woods and animal skins, the study was a garish rococo with pastel blues, gilded scrollwork, and ornamental plaster. A fortune had gone into renovating the room to the baron's liking, albeit a decade ago. A fortune that should have been spent on the home farm.

Harold visualized the study and how the discussion might take place as his purposeful strides took him across the upper gallery, down the main stairs, and into the entrance hall. Before he reached the reception room, he heard muffled voices coming from the study. Nudging the anteroom's door open, he peered in. Empty. The door to the study ahead was closed. He shut the reception door behind him and perched on the edge of a chair. Within the walls of the reception area, the voices were no longer muffled, not loud, merely hearty.

Father and Mr. Trethow.

It was not eavesdropping if he was waiting in good faith to speak to his father and if the present company happened to be speaking at an audible volume. Or so he assured himself.

"After all our years of friendship?" Mr. Trethow was saying. "What if I increased my contribution? I could pull from the estate. I could pull from the estate if the deal is guaranteed."

"I won't have it, Cuthbert. Never mix friendship and business. I couldn't forgive myself if aught went wrong. No, no, not even if you doubled the offer."

"If I tripled it?"

Harold ground his teeth. It took all his willpower not to burst into the study and point a finger at his father. The man was fleecing his childhood friend. Although he had known his father's intentions even before the guests arrived, hearing it happen infuriated him. But what could he do? His hands were tied. Aside from the initial supper when he first set eyes on the guests, he had avoided observing the interactions between his father and the gentlemen, especially the private conversations. Even during last night's port, he had excused himself to join his mother in the drawing room to entertain the ladies. In the end, it did not matter who or how many men invested, for his father would do what he wanted as long as he found a way to cover his portion of the capital. Harold's hands were tied.

Saving his conversation for later was best. He need not discuss anything with his father in this state of outrage. When he stepped into the entrance hall, Mr. Quainoo, the butler, was waiting, coat in hand, anticipating Harold's next move.

"You're a mind reader," Harold said.

It was a good thing Harold had brought the butler with him—along with Abhijeet—when he returned from India, for that was another staff member, an essential staff member, who had been missing from the roster, dismissed along with who knew how many others. Mr. Quainoo had been a postillion in India. Taken from his home in Africa as a young boy, he had made a life for himself in India until news came he would be sent to the West Indies as a laborer. But the man was shrewd. When Harold offered him a position as coachman, Quainoo said he would take butler or nothing. Harold would not deny he had been nervous on the return home, expecting mass confusion when the new butler met the residing butler. Luck had been on their side.

Coat snug about his frame, Harold faced the crisp air of the outdoors. Grey skies shrouded the estate. Guests milled about the lawn, anticipating the walk to the lake.

At the far end of the knot garden, he spied a small group of ladies, namely those his mother had invited for him to consider for a potential bride. They collectively twirled their parasols at the sight of him. Luck would not be on his side today for he knew he would have to row each out onto the lake. If he did not volunteer for the task, his mother would find the means to arrange it. For now, he could delay the inevitable. Patrick stood at the center of the garden, sharing a word with his father the Earl of Winthorp.

Hastening his steps before one or all of the ladies intercepted him, Harold approached the gentlemen duo.

After the earl excused himself, Harold jested, "May I use you as a shield?" He indicated the ladies with a discreet angle of his head.

"I have more need for a shield than you do. A pity you aren't still intended for Miss Trethow — who

I notice is conspicuously absent from festivities again. As is her friend Miss Plumb. Quite the pair, those two."

Harold's thoughts flashed to yesterday. "I believe her attention is engaged elsewhere."

Patrick eyed him in question, but Harold refrained from sharing what he witnessed.

Instead, he turned the conversation. "Did your mother decline to come because her schedule overflowed with invitations or because she's still angry you didn't take to her nudges of marriage with Miss Snow?"

"Hardly nudges." Patrick snorted a laugh. "She invited the poor girl to dine with us *every night* for a week and spoke of nothing but how much she wanted to arrange a wedding breakfast. Some of the more indelicate remarks included her description of how delicious we'd look side by side at said breakfast. Yes, she's furious at me and sees this party as a wasted effort for her matchmaking." With an expression that was partly sheepish and partly smug, he added, "I might have refused to attend the final supper with Miss Snow."

Harold chuckled. He could readily imagine the Countess of Winthorp's reaction.

"Don't laugh. Her antics were mortifying! One of these days she'll land me in real trouble."

"Or," Harold suggested, "you could pick one, marry, and be done with it. The heir must ensure the line and all that."

"Do you think Mother would have an apoplexy if I brought home Lord Brooks?"

"Brooks? I thought you had better taste."

Patrick cast a sly smile. "Then you've not heard his reputation."

"About being Casanova in disguise?"

Patrick threw his head back and laughed but said no more on the subject. His attention turned to something or someone beyond Harold's shoulder.

"Joy. Your admirer Miss Evans has brought a friend."

Harold turned to find the ladies descending on them like vultures. With a practiced skill, Miss Evans directed her friend to take Patrick's arm, then took the arm Harold had not yet offered, and nudged him to walk about the garden.

For whom he should feel more pity, he could not say. They would both need to find a bride at some point in life, but neither faced an easy task. Harold had expectations for his future wife that not many women of his acquaintance could meet. Meanwhile, Patrick would never find a woman who met his expectations since his desired partner could only be found among the sterner sex. And yet here they were, persuaded none-too-gently to walk Miss Evans and Miss Whateverhernamewas around the garden.

How much simpler life had been when he had known his bride would one day be Miss Trethow. As wealthy as her father, it would seem the man had not set aside a tempting enough dowry for Lord Collingwood, perhaps because he never thought he would need to with an alliance arranged between friends. Alas, it was for the best they were no longer paired by their parents. As attractive as Harold found her, they would never suit, and he would not soon forget her dalliance with Driffield.

Hazel peered out of the narrow casement window at the end of the upstairs hall. Unlatching it, she nudged the window open, hoping to catch a word or two from below. Mr. Hobbs was walking the garden with Miss Evans. A short distance from the pair Lord Kissinger and Miss Lytle strolled together.

With a wistful sigh, Hazel imagined she was walking the knot garden. Missing the boating would be the worst part. Ever since discovering there was a lake, she had longed to ride in one of the boats. Instead she was stuck indoors on a perfectly remarkable day.

Hazel sulked and slumped a shoulder against the wall.

Now, now, Hazel. Pouting does not become you. She scolded herself, pouting nevertheless. This was not about her; she tried to remember. There would be ample opportunities for her to find love. Agnes, however, was not so fortunate. Agnes was the priority.

Hazel's only concern now was seeing to Agnes's happiness, marital bliss, and security. Luckily, she had not had to do much work in securing clandestine meetings between Lord Driffield and Agnes, for the earl sent Agnes discreet invitations every so often to meet him somewhere private. Each time, Hazel escorted Agnes and stood sentry. Just as she had done yesterday in the woods. Just as she was doing now while the two conversed in an upstairs parlor. It would not be long before he made their betrothal known. It would not be long before he whisked her away to elope. Once married, Agnes would be free of her father. When seen from that perspective, wanting a boat ride on the lake seemed trivial. How childish of Hazel to pout in the hall when her friend's future hung in the balance. How selfish.

And yet...

Hazel's gaze flicked back and forth between Lord Kissinger and Mr. Hobbs, each time resting on Mr. Hobbs for longer stretches of time. Kissinger was undeniably handsome, arguably the handsomest guest. His look was not as fashionable as Driffield's or Brooks's, but he bore a confidence that surpassed their arrogant ennui, a genuine sort of confidence, as though he were the kind of man a lady would want by her side should a highwayman accost the carriage. As handsome as he was, Hazel's eyes betrayed her. They found their way back to Mr. Hobbs every time.

Was it the fairy tale romance of the forest with the slants of light filtering through leaves in a diamond mosaic that had enchanted Hazel for the briefest of moments yesterday, or had she felt an inexplicable connection to Mr. Hobbs?

He was as contradictory as he had been at supper, if not more so. Prim and proper of dress, no frills but fine tailoring, all with a conflicting element of savagery about him. It was not the tan of his skin or the dishevelment of his hair this time — his hair, after all, had been styled and powdered — rather a certain something in his tawny brown eyes. He seemed, for all the world, like a man in his element, at home in the woods and outdoors, a man full of natural *passion*.

Hazel had tingled from head to toe. What if she heeded her father's desire for an alliance with the family? What if she made herself agreeable to Mr.

Hobbs? Was it possible that he could incite the sort of passion that—but no, how silly.

Thinking of passion and Mr. Hobbs in the same sentence was wholly ridiculous. He was stiff and polite, nothing more. Not even his appealing aroma of spices, coffee, and starched linen could convince her there was passion, not even the impishness in his eyes. If she set out to turn his head, she could be stuck forever with a lifeless, loveless marriage to a dried stick.

She watched him lean closer to Miss Evans to hear whatever the shameless flirt was saying. As Hazel admired his profile, she could not recall what it was she disliked about him.

"Allow me to show you…" said a trailing voice from the main stairwell in the hallway beyond.

There was a chattering of voices, a group in conversation, all audible above the creak of floorboards as they moved from the stairwell to the hall. Hazel cast a longing glance at the knot garden then readied her smile to greet the guests.

Guests.

People coming down the hallway.

Good Lord!

It struck Hazel like a chamber pot to the head. She was supposed to be standing guard, the ever-mindful sentry, championing Agnes who met privately with her true love to arrange their wedding or elopement or whatever it was they would plan. So enraptured in her own selfishness Hazel had forgotten her purpose. Why were guests coming upstairs? They were all supposed to be heading to the lake!

This was a disaster.

But it need not be so. It had all been well planned. *Follow the plan, Hazel. Follow the plan.*

Hazel darted to the parlor door. Her heart galloped. Her hands shook. Her ears buzzed.

For the split second she had before the guests would round the corner into this hallway, she inhaled a lungful of air to calm herself. Cool, calm, collected. There was nothing improper about two young ladies sharing conversation with a gentleman in a parlor, each other acting as chaperone. She would make for the chair by the window, take a seat, and strike up the most mundane conversation. All as planned.

Lump lodged in throat, Hazel rapped smartly on the door, then stepped inside as casually as her trembling limbs allowed. She clicked the door shut behind her and surveyed the room.

She gasped.

Her hand covered her mouth to muffle the sound. So loud and so startling had been the gasp, it would be any wonder that the guests down the hall did not hear it.

On the couch was a tangle of limbs. A tangle of everything. A tangle of impropriety and sin and... *passion.* Driffield, coatless, leaned over a partially clothed Agnes. Her lips were swollen, her neck puckered in red, her dress unlaced and lowered about her shoulders. Before Hazel could determine if that was a bare shoulder, a bare knee, or a bare breast, a flutter of fabric flew about Agnes as she shrieked, leapt off the couch, and bolted for the adjoining door at the back of the parlor into what Hazel hoped was an anteroom and not another hallway full of guests.

What must have been mere seconds felt like hours. For at least two of those hours, Hazel could not move. She stood stunned. Appalled. Intrigued.

Then she panicked, although she aimed to affect calm. It would not do for anyone to see her panicking. This situation was still under her control. However, she could not very well follow through with the plan of taking a seat and starting conversation, neither could she leave by the door she had come since she would be seen leaving the parlor which now only Driffield occupied. Her only option was to follow Agnes.

From Driffield's expression, he had not been made aware of what Hazel's presence signified. He looked, briefly, sheepish, as though Hazel was the intruder who had caught them in a sordid embrace rather than the chaperone meant to save them from impropriety. But then, his expression changed. She did not fully understand the change. His eyes roamed over Hazel head to toe. Assessing her level of threat? Assessing her level of secrecy? Assessing...*what*?

Not caring if she ever found out, she gave a little curtsy then walked across the room, intent on dashing to the adjoining door as soon as she passed the couch.

Driffield met her halfway. "Am I to take it it's your turn?"

Hazel blinked her confusion as she made to step around him.

He caught her waist in a severe grip. "Had my little colt not been so skittish, we could have enjoyed a *ménage à trois*."

Before she could grasp his meaning, he pulled her against him and captured her mouth with his in a suffocating force of hard lips, abrasive teeth, and saliva.

Her first kiss, the one she had dreamt about for so long, happened in a startling moment of horror and disgust. Bile rose to her throat. Her lips clamped close against his probing tongue. Her body turned cold.

Recoiling, she pressed her hands against his chest and tried to angle her face away from him.

He released her more swiftly than she expected, his expression reflecting her own confusion and anger. She stumbled away from him just as the parlor door opened to a cacophony of voices.

Chapter 7

The silence was more accusing than words. Hazel stared wide eyed at the astonished faces of no less personages than her father, Lord and Lady Collingwood, and Mr. and Mrs. Butterbest.

Mortification flushed her face crimson as she realized how damaging the situation must look, her lips likely as red as Agnes's had been, her skin as pink, never mind for far different reasons. Driffield reaching to don his coat did not improve the circumstance.

In all ways, Hazel's life had been one of ease, her future bright with promise. Her father doted on her. Her brother admired her. Her mother, who she had no memory of since Mrs. Trethow died in childbed with Hazel's brother Cuthbert Walter, was said to have adored her. Teghyiy Hall was as lucrative as a modestly sized estate could be. Never once had Hazel wanted for something. Although her father had made that childhood promise with Lord Collingwood to marry their children, it had not been much spoken about, Hazel understanding herself free to choose love if she wanted rather than an arrangement. Yes, her future had always been bright, full of possibilities, promises, and freedoms.

How curious that in a single second, life could shift irreversibly. Like a branch snapping. A cup shattering. She watched her life splinter as though she were removed from the situation, as though she were a spider perched in a far corner of the room, observing the scene from its web. *Poor girl*, said the spider. *From champion to harlot.*

Mr. Trethow spoke first, his cheery voice contrasting the gravity of his daughter's having been compromised. "Are we to be the first to share in congratulations?"

Lady Collingwood spoke next, her words trilling with excitement. "How diverting! Tonight's supper will feature a betrothal announcement!"

Plans escalated faster than Hazel could comprehend. One moment she was staring at a doorway full of shocked faces, and the next she was listening to plans for her wedding to Lord Driffield as she remained dazed and silent.

No! she shouted above the commotion, not realizing her mouth did not move and her voice did not sound. *No! He's Agnes's love, not mine. And for all his charm, he fooled us. He's a rogue; don't you see?*

"In the chapel, of course, the morning of the soiree," Lord Collingwood was saying.

"No, I want to organize a wedding breakfast; we couldn't possibly hold it the same day as the soiree," Lady Collingwood was responding.

They all carried on saying and responding, Hazel hearing naught but a quarter of it.

"Ahem." A throat cleared. Loudly. Pointedly.

A few voices died down.

"Ahem." The throat cleared again. Louder. More pointedly.

Silence filled the room again.

Hazel's eyes met Lord Driffield's.

"I'm afraid," Driffield began, "your plans are not to be."

A pregnant pause.

"You see, I'm already betrothed."

Hazel closed her eyes and exhaled. And so, it was all settled between him and Agnes. Hazel was one part relieved and one part distressed. How was she to tell Agnes the truth of his character? To do so would break her heart, and should Agnes cry off because of it, she would return to her father, a worse fate in Hazel's estimation. She dared not ask the more pressing question — what would happen to herself?

After a collective gasp, Driffield said, "To Lady Felicia. We'll be making the announcement at her mother's opening ball this Season, followed by a wedding at St. George's. I trust you all to keep my confidence until then."

With that, his lordship gave a curt nod and took his leave of them.

For half an hour Hazel awaited her fate in the anteroom to the Trelowen study, staring sightlessly at animal décor and inhaling the stench of cigars. Her handkerchief dangled limp and sodden from her fingertips. She had cried until there were no more tears to shed.

It was not for herself she cried, although there was a great deal about her situation to mourn — her planned come-out in the spring, her trip to London, her chances at love, her relationship with her father; the list was long. Despite all, she cried for the repercussions her loved ones would face for her poor decision. Nothing would change the disappointment her father must feel. All the countless freedoms he entrusted to her had been slapped in his face with this situation, with what he thought she had been doing in the parlor. Her fault or not, she must face the consequences, the censure, the damage to her relationship with her father and how he viewed her. His own reputation would be damaged. Her brother's reputation would be damaged. Lord and Lady Collingwood would face censure, as well, since this had happened under their roof.

Even if she explained the situation, it would make everything worse, for she would be confessing to aiding two unmarried people in a tryst. Not only would Agnes be dragged into this and ruined, but Hazel's reputation would not be salvaged, for she was an accomplice to impropriety and caught in a compromising position with the very man she had supposedly set up to meet with Agnes. No, explaining the situation would make everything far worse.

Hazel could laugh. Of all the upset, what made her cry the hardest was her first kiss. It was beyond absurd to mourn *that*, but there it was, her handkerchief as evidence. The kiss she had longed to receive had been stolen. How could she ever rid herself of the memory? Of the taste? The cut on the inside of her bottom lip where tender flesh had met teeth would heal, but the memory would remain. May she never be kissed again. She washed her hands of the whole business of kissing.

So childish, she thought, wadding the soggy kerchief in her fist. So childish to be upset over a kiss. Hazel sniffled.

Her nose burned. Her eyelids ached when she blinked. She must look a fright.

Voices carried stray words through the study door, none Hazel cared to hear.

"Ruined!" someone shouted.

"Scandal!" someone else shouted.

"Whore!" Mrs. Butterbest screeched.

Mrs. Butterbest demanded the Trethows be cast out; she would not have her boys under the same roof as a harlot. Either the Trethows go, or her family goes, she threatened.

Had it only been Lord and Lady Collingwood with Mr. Trethow this situation might be brushed under the rug. Hazel would have had to live with the shame of it, but in all likelihood, the baron and his wife would not have said a word more about it, leaving the reprimands to Mr. Trethow. As it happened, the Butterbests had seen all. Nothing could be swept under the rug. Before nuncheon, the guests would know everything, certainly if Mrs. Butterbest had her say.

Hazel could see no way to resolve this aside from her and her father, along with Agnes, leaving for home, heads bowed, never to darken the Trelowen doorstep or those of any good society again. If there remained any hope, Lord Collingwood controlled it. He had the power to save her from scandal. *How,* she did not know, but he was wealthy enough, well connected enough, and respected enough to resolve even this problem. With Mr. Trethow being his childhood friend, surely he would do something to help.

The door to the study cracked open wide enough to admit Cuthbert Phineas Trethow.

Hazel drew her shoulders back and lifted her chin, ready to face the gallows with strength and determination. From the room beyond, she could hear murmurs but not distinct words.

Mr. Trethow gripped the front edges of his coat, his gaze meeting Hazel's shoes. Without making eye contact, as though ashamed to look at her, he said, "Best return to your room. I'll sort this; don't you fret. I'll see this to right. Stay in your suite until you're called. Understood?"

Hazel nodded, her eyes warm with fresh tears, though there could not possibly be more to shed.

With a tentative pat to Hazel's shoulder, Mr. Trethow returned to the study, pulling the door closed behind him.

Chapter 8

Harold took the servants' stairs two at a time to his bedchamber, his clothes soaked, his mood grey. The boating on the lake had been tedious at the best of times, but Miss Evans's behavior frayed Harold's nerves. When she first stepped into the boat, the sun shone overhead. From one side of the lake to the other, she had twirled her parasol and regaled him with a never-ending tale of her new bonnet — he assumed in an effort to offer her conversation skills as an admirable quality of a potential bride. At worst she was tiring. Until the surprise rain shower.

The unassuming cloud that drifted overhead was initially a godsend, truth be told, signaling the end of the boating and his hopeful return to sanity. Then her shrieks echoed those of the other ladies on the lake as she rocked the boat in some inane attempt to gain a better look at shore or prompt him to row faster or whatever her logic. Water sloshed onto their feet, sending her into further shrieks and panic until they came dangerously close to tipping into the lake.

Her primary concern? That the rain would ruin her parasol. Yes, her parasol. Harold would have laughed had he not been trying his hardest to steady the boat and calm her. The rain, after all, was only a drizzle. More than once on the way back to shore he had considered intentionally tipping her into the lake. Ungentlemanly perhaps, but any man in his position would have thought the same. He resisted. Only just.

After seeing her to safety, Harold had lingered at the shore, watching the groundskeeper's crew pull the boats into the boathouse, ensuring all guests had returned to the wilderness walk for the path to the house, and avoiding the gaggle of ladies accompanying Miss Evans.

When Harold reached his dressing room at last, Abhijeet stood waiting.

"Bless," the valet said under his breath.

"I see it as my duty to keep you busy." Harold smirked as Abhijeet began removing the offending clothes.

"After seeing the guests racing the rain, I expected dampness, but you've outdone yourself."

Undressed, Harold donned a banyan and took the chair next to the fireplace. A chill seeped into his bones with the wet clothes removed. He shuddered.

Abhijeet cast him a sideways glance as he hung the sodden garments. "A warm bath then? Or are you remembering the company you were entertaining?"

Pulling the collar of the banyan higher about his neck, Harold barked a laugh. "Both." He felt foolish for shivering, but there it was. A grown man shivering by the fire. As long as he did not catch a chill.

"I know one lady's company you weren't keeping today."

Hands tucked under his armpits and legs crossed, Harold dipped his chin for Abhijeet to continue.

"Miss Trethow."

His valet held his full attention.

Abhijeet carried on with the garments before fetching a blanket for Harold to wrap around himself. He carried on some more with bath preparations, ringing for water to be boiled and brought up, setting out the soap, and Harold knew not what else. The daft man was dragging out the suspense. From time to time, the valet glanced his way with a coy grin as if to say he had a secret Harold wanted. And he did want it.

"Out with it!" Harold insisted with a laugh.

The sadist hummed to himself for a few more moments before saying, "Miss Trethow spent her lake time in the parlor."

"And?"

"With the Earl of Driffield."

Harold's blood turned cold.

"Let me be the first to tell you they were not whinging over the bland English food." The valet gave him a knowing look.

Whatever humored curiosity Harold had felt drained, leaving him angry, frowning, and chilled. "Tell me."

The valet nodded, his expression sobering. "Everyone has a different tale of what transpired in the parlor, but enough of the staff saw the comings and goings and overheard the conversation in Lord Collingwood's study to satisfy their curiosity. Miss Trethow was caught alone with the earl. Some say she was in a state of undress. Some say they were embracing." He shrugged. "No one will ever know the truth. The baron and baroness, her father, and two other guests caught them in the room alone, and that's enough truth for the masses."

Leaning forward to rest his elbows on his thighs, Harold released the edges of the blanket to rest his head in his hands. "I never took her for a title hunter. It would seem she caught her man."

"No, indeed. He's refused to marry her. According to his valet, he's already engaged to the eldest daughter of the Duke of Milford."

Harold looked up, shaken. Had Driffield tricked her with false promises or…was she the man's lover? He was torn between being appalled that this happened under the Trelowen roof and pitying her naivety.

Abhijeet continued, "Nothing's been decided, but one of the lady guests who witnessed the scene is demanding the Trethows leave."

"I can't see my father allowing that. He wants Trethow's investment capital too much. My guess is he'll hush it up."

Whistling, the valet shook his head. "To think, not too long ago she was to be your bride."

Of one truth Harold was certain. A woman like that would never be mistress of Trelowen.

"Life is ruined!" she wailed. "How can I ever face him again? How can I face *you* again?"

Hazel patted Agnes's back, the former dry eyed, the latter burying her face into a pillow that muffled whatever she said next.

Seated at the edge of Agnes's bed, both Hazel and Melissa offered equal portions handkerchiefs and reassurance. Hazel was stoic. She had little choice. To console Agnes meant to disguise her own concerns.

Melissa crooned. "He fooled us all. Don't take it to heart."

Hazel nodded to the back of Agnes's head. "You'll find love again, and next time, he'll not be a scoundrel but will love you back on equal terms."

Fresh sobs shook her shoulders as Agnes cried louder against the pillow. "I've ruined *your* life too. You must hate me. You're a fool if you don't."

"Then call me Miss Fool." Hazel leaned down and rested her cheek to Agnes's tangled hair.

She meant what she said for she could never blame Agnes for what happened. It had been her idea for Agnes and Driffield to meet unchaperoned and her idea to stand sentry. Even beyond that, Agnes did not make the rules of propriety or spread malicious gossip and was as much a victim as Hazel, never mind that Agnes was not directly tied to the scandal and could continue forward with life to find a new love. Agnes was touched by this in far different ways. A broken heart. Guilt. Trepidation to return to her father. That was a different kind of hopelessness. Hazel would much rather face her problems head on than be in Agnes's shoes.

A half hour of soothing softened the tears but did not ease Agnes's pain. Melissa and Hazel retired from the room after calling for the lady's maid.

With Melissa's hand tucked in the crook of Hazel's arm, she guided them both away from Agnes's room and down the hall towards Hazel's door. With a glance down the hall, she lowered her head to say, "Rumor has already spread."

Hazel had known it would. One afternoon was all it took with Mrs. Butterbest at the helm.

"If your father doesn't insist on removing tomorrow morning, you ought to suggest leaving. You can't remain among the guests now. Agnes is in no shape to stay either and is likely to make the situation worse if left to her own devices. Chauncey and I will do what we can to staunch rumor, but if you stay, the guests will cut you. Or worse."

Drawing back her shoulders, Hazel said, "Unless Papa forces it, I will not leave. Even if it means sitting at the same table as Driffield for all to see. By leaving, I admit guilt. By staying, I draw doubt to Butterbest's accusations."

Melissa shook her head. "Leaving is about self-preservation, not an admittance of anything. You're already guilty in the eyes of the guests whether you stay or leave."

"I'll not be cowed."

Chapter 9

Harold was still dressing for the early morning hunt when a footman brought a summons from Lord Collingwood.

Was it too much to hope he would be granted a reprieve from the hunt? Not that he disliked riding to hounds. Quite the contrary. But there was far too much to do. The past several days had been devoted to entertaining his father's guests. Time wasted in his estimation. Aside from calling on Nana, he had accomplished little in the way of estate management, which now fell on his shoulders with the absence of the steward and the distractions of his father. He needed to visit the tenants, see to repairs, walk the farms, and a long list of tasks. Instead, he was planning a social morning with a foxhunt.

There was little doubt the nature of the summons: the Trethow debacle. While no one said a word aloud about it during supper, it was all anyone could focus on, everyone exchanging knowing glances, eyeing the empty chairs, chatting louder than normal about marriage and morals and *polite* society.

If Harold wagered a guess, he was being summoned so his father could tell him what happened — assuming his son was none-the-wiser — and inform him the Trethows, along with Miss Plumb, had departed well before dawn that morning.

Even while censuring her behavior, his heart went out to Miss Trethow. There was no coming back from this incident. Be it by her naivety or failed manipulation, this would ruin her family irrevocably. How could his heart not go out to her? There was a double standard between the behavior of men and women. Despite her reasons, she took the brunt of the blame while Lord Driffield enjoyed his supper, port, and drawing room tea, unaffected by the incident.

Yes, his heart went out to her. Loose morals or not, she was a young girl to be pitied.

Once Abhijeet fitted him with riding boots, Harold made haste to his father's study.

"Come in, my boy!" Eugene greeted him with a broad smile and waved him to take a seat before the desk. A footman followed with two cups of black coffee.

Harold tensed.

His father was never this cheery or thoughtful unless something monumental had gone his way, or he was about to have something monumental go his way. Perhaps both.

To prepare, Harold fortified with the coffee.

Eugene leaned back in his chair, lacing his fingers over his chest and grinning. "We've done it! We've enough to see our plans through, all set into motion."

The hairs on the back of Harold's neck stood on end.

"I've found a way to resolve all our problems," his father said when Harold did not respond. "We've enough to cover the capital and line our pockets for the years to come without being inconvenienced with stewards and all that. Oh, my boy! We. Are. Set."

Nursing his cup, he eyed his father over the rim.

"My secretary has personally dispatched the contracts to the London solicitors to seal the deal. After all is settled, I'll have you return to London to see to the accounts, the investment, and so forth." Eugene waved his hand as if to brush off the unpleasantness of details and London trips. "For now, the necessary paperwork is drawn, signed, and soon to be delivered."

The empty cup met its saucer with a muted *clink*.

Eugene's grin slipped at the corners when Harold did not follow with a request for more information or a cheer of celebration. For Harold's part, he saw little reason to celebrate. By the sound of it, his father had convinced the gentlemen to invest at an inflated enough amount to cover his own portion. A pity.

"If we set the wedding for Monday," the baron continued, "that will encourage the guests to stay a few days longer, allow travel time for family to arrive, and permit time to secure the common license from the bishop—a quick trip to the Diocese of Exeter to meet with Lavington will do the trick. I had hoped to set it for Friday, the morning of the soiree, but your mother helped me see reason."

Ah. Harold understood. The mention of a wedding startled him at first, so jarring from the original conversation of contracts and investments, but on further thought, it made sense. Driffield had agreed to marry Miss Trethow after all. Sensible to host the wedding at Trelowen, see it all through, have the guests present as witnesses, and turn gossip into excitement—and how much more exciting to share tales of witnessing the union of a love match than to claim to have spent a week under the same roof as a rake and his mistress.

Clearly, his father had been hard at work the day prior. Investment gathering *and* wedding planning. All completed while Harold rowed the ladies across the lake, recovered from an afternoon chill, and supped with the guests.

"I assume you have something appropriate to wear?" Eugene asked.

"To the wedding?" were Harold's first words in the conversation. "I hope I won't be expected to attend the ceremony, only whatever breakfast or tea Mother has planned for afterwards."

The baron stared at his son with mouth agape. "But of course, you'll be attending the ceremony. You're the bridegroom."

Had Harold been holding the coffee cup, it would have slipped from his fingers onto the rug. Thankfully, he held only his composure, which slipped instead. "I beg your pardon."

Eugene's smile returned. "The dowry couldn't be refused. We'll not easily find its equal. It took some convincing, but in the end, he saw reason, saw the noose tightening, as it were. When a man sees the end of the rope, sees his opportunity for investing closing, the ruination of his daughter, the ruined future of his son, scandal…Well, it makes a man realize that the aid of a dear friend is the only solution. Now, the scandal will be silenced, and the son will look forward to a future of far more wealth."

Harold heard the words but could not understand them. Perhaps his father intended it to be that way, or perhaps Harold was so stunned he could not make sense of any words spoken.

Gripping the arms of his chair, Harold asked, "Whom am I marrying, pray tell?"

With a clap of his hands, Eugene said, "Miss Hazel Trethow, of course!"

He heard the words, and this time he understood them, but they made no more sense than the rest of his father's announcements thus far.

Before he could respond, his father launched into an impassioned speech. "We. Are. Set! If you had seen me working over Trethow, you would have been proud of your old Papa. I convinced him to convince himself this was the only way to save his family. In the end, it'll work out for all of us, rest assured, so I've done him a favor he could have never done for himself. When this investment sees the earnings I expect it will, his son can marry any woman he wants, someone to bear his sons and negate the entailment. All the while, we'll be living as kings!"

Harold interrupted. "What entailment?"

"It's brilliant what we agreed to, my boy. Brilliant. First, I had to convince him I wouldn't allow him to invest in my deal with a scandal overhead. And then I had to convince him I might consider *you* as a husband if the dowry were enough to compete with the other ladies' dowries. If the two of you wed, the scandal would be hushed, and then he could invest. You see the brilliance? There was a touch of difficulty, though. Nothing I couldn't handle. You see, he didn't have as much ready money as I had anticipated, not for both dowry *and* investment."

Harold interrupted again. "This has nothing to do with saving her reputation, I take it. Or even me marrying. This is all to do with your opium deal. She's a pawn." His disgust tasted acrid. "You've made the girl a pawn. You've made us both pawns." He looked away, his mind working and reworking through scenarios, all unlikely but none beyond his father's cunning. "Was Driffield part of it too? Did you set them up to be compromised so you could hold the scandal over Trethow's head?"

"Don't talk nonsense." The baron waved his hand to dismiss the accusation. "Now, where was I? To meet the capital, since he didn't have ready money, I promised to front him the funds — using her dowry, of course, but he needn't know that. To reimburse me for what I've covered, plus interest, he agreed to allot a percentage of his annual estate income to our accounts until the loan is repaid. We'll earn money from his estate, you see. Brilliant. What sealed the deal was the entailment — I wouldn't accept the dowry without it. He agreed to a fee tail special, entailing his property to Miss Trethow's first-born son, unless Trethow's son has a son of his own, of course. You needn't be concerned, my boy, for in all likelihood his son will have a boy of his own, but if not, Trethow will make so much money from the investment, it'll pay for the dowries of a dozen granddaughters. Meanwhile, we'll earn the annual percentage and know that any son you sire from Miss Trethow might look forward to one day possessing that estate, and a lucrative estate it is."

"No." With the single word, Harold removed from his chair, turning his back to his father. He paced once. Twice. Then gripped the edge of a bookshelf and frowned at the leather spines. "I refuse to be part of this."

"Don't pout, son. It's unappealing for a man of your age. Had you an eye for Miss Evans?"

Harold scoffed, digging crescent nails into the woodgrain and letting silence stretch before speaking. "This is despicable. Unforgivable. Manipulation of the worst sort." He ground his teeth. "You're extorting your childhood friend."

"You're not seeing the bigger picture, son. *He'll* benefit as much as we will. I know you have doubts on the opium deal, but I assure you it's sound. He'll be rich as Croesus after this, all because of my generosity, or as you call it, manipulation."

Harold heard the creak of the desk chair as his father shifted position.

"Perhaps you've misunderstood the situation in which Trethow finds himself," Eugene said, his tone lowering, the cheer gone. "His daughter's actions have ruined the family. The man has two choices. He can disown her to try to salvage his family's reputation, or he can do what's necessary to save her reputation and thus the family's. If not for me, what options would he have? Bribe someone else? What will that someone else require for his daughter to marry their son, I ask you? I'm seeing to the security of the family."

Resting his forehead against the shelf, Harold said, "In case you've forgotten, this is *marriage* we're talking about. *My* marriage. I will be tied to my wife for life. She'll bear my children. She'll one day be Baroness Collingwood. *My wife.* I don't take this situation lightly."

"And you think I do?" His father's voice dropped an octave, his words gruff, choked.

Harold turned to watch his father's shoulders round as the baron leaned over the desk and clasped his head in his hands.

"You don't understand the straits we're in," Eugene breathed, the words little more than a groan. "The amount of debt is...exorbitant. We need money *now*."

His anger defused as he watched his father diminish into an older, frailer man. "There are other ways," Harold said, his voice softening. "If we use the money we earned from this charter to rehire the steward and take his advice to purchase new farming equipment, we would have an income to pay off whatever smaller debts have accrued. With each season's profit, we can build new homes that will draw more tenants, more farmers, more laborers, increasing the income and paying more debts. Steady, reliable income."

Eugene shook his head. "It would take too long and too great an expense. How long until the fields yield crops? How long until tenants pay their rent? Years? We need money *now*. Yes, yes, we can rehire and purchase and build, but we can do all of that with the annual income from Trethow's estate. For now, we need ready money to pay the debts. We *need* the opium deal."

Exhaling from his cheeks, Harold said, "Let's suppose I agree to marry Miss Trethow. We would have the dowry. We would also have the profits from the charter on top of those figures. Why not use the dowry to pay debt—however much that might cover—and then use the charter profits to rebuild the estate? Or vice versa. I would need to see the estate ledgers, the vowels, and the marriage settlement to better assess the situation, but you understand me. If we can't do it with the charter profits alone, surely we can with the dowry. There's no need for the investment and no need to siphon from Trethow's income."

His father's hands slapped the desk with such ferocity, Harold jerked backwards.

"You're a boy of twenty. You know nothing of life. I need money that flows, not the kind that trickles." He smacked the desk again. "It is my moral obligation to invest Trethow's money. That's what he entrusted me to do. That's the whole point of the deal — this investment. The contracts are already signed."

Harold's fists clenched at his father's "moral obligation." As quickly as his father's strength had drained to frailty, it now swelled with authority — angry, exasperated authority.

"You *will* marry the girl," the baron commanded. "Until you reach your majority, you will do as you're told."

"Not to be the eternal optimist, but you did fancy her when you first saw her," Patrick said to Harold. "A physical attraction could become more. Given time."

Harold grunted.

Morning sun filtered through the diamond-latticed windows. The two gentlemen sat in the parlor, both dressed for the hunt, neither attending the hunt. Harold slumped in his chair. One hand drummed a rhythm on his thigh, the other rubbed his bottom lip as if to stimulate thought, his booted ankle propped on his knee. Patrick, conversely, sat upright, one leg crossed over the other, his teacup and saucer poised for enjoyment.

"You'll marry her?"

Harold gave a curt nod.

"Because your father commands it."

His gaze snapped from the window to the curiosity of his friend. "No. There's a host of reasons, none of which owe to Father's mandate. At least not explicitly. The house is full of guests, expectant guests, guests who demand satisfaction. I may not be responsible for her, but I can't now stand by and watch her fall, not knowing what my father's done, not considering I was intended to marry her before my father's greed."

"Guilt?" Patrick questioned.

"No. Yes. I don't know. I *feel* responsible for her. Had I not listened to my father in the first place, I would have been courting her, and Driffield never would have worked his charm on her." His fingers worried his lip, a thought occurring to him. "Do you think she'll resent me?"

Patrick quizzed him with a look as he refilled his tea.

Pushing himself upright, Harold dug an elbow into the chair arm and leaned forward. "Rather than see that I'm helping her, what if she resents me for trapping her in an arranged marriage? There will be no further opportunity to continue her dalliance or vie for Driffield's hand, no return home, no say in marriage to me."

"It's possible. Women are funny creatures. Honestly, I don't know what you see in them." Patrick took a single sip from his cup and set the saucer on the table. Looking at Harold directly, he said, "Know this. Whatever her sentiments, you can prove to her you're a good man and win her affection. With a bit of motivation, I think you can do more than turn the tide with her."

"In what way?" Harold asked.

"Try to take control of the financial situation in so much as your hands are tied. Think. You've a mind for numbers. There must be a way to follow through with your father's deal but protect the family when the investment goes belly up, as you know it will."

He listened but did not know what to make of the possibilities. Dealing with his father was like watching a captain punching holes in his own ship. He needed time to think, yet there was no time.

"What if she loves him?" Harold asked. "I can't compete with that."

"Then don't. She'll fall for you on your own merits."

Harold snorted.

Voicing the deeper worry was not as easy. His words hitched when he asked, "And if she's already carrying his child?"

Patrick exhaled sharply. "Ask her. Before the wedding."

"I can't ask her something so improper. She wouldn't tell me even if I did. And what if she is? I can't halt the wedding. But what if our first child is his, not mine?"

"You'll be the best father you know how to be."

Surprising them both, Harold laughed. "You *are* an eternal optimist. When they force you to marry, I'll remember this and torture you with happy outlooks on life."

The heart to heart with Patrick did ease his mind somewhat. He felt more confident about the decision. That did not stop him from fretting that he was about to make one young lady unforgivably unhappy by proposing an unwanted marriage. His one hope at present was that all parties involved would allow him to propose to her in private of his own volition rather than corralling her in Collingwood's study and forcing the news in the harshest of ways. If he could present himself as an ardent suitor, no matter how ill-timed — or should that be absurdly well-timed — they might have a chance together.

Hazel gawked at her father. "What do you mean I'm to marry Mr. Hobbs on Monday?"

The words she wanted to say in protest caught in her throat — she did not love him; she had barely spoken to him; she wanted to return home.

Her father turned to Lord and Lady Collingwood. "What she means is will there be enough time between now and Monday to arrange the wedding?"

Hazel pressed her lips together at her father's warning glance. It would not do to appear ungrateful. To save the family, the baron and baroness were offering their only son, the heir. Despite the situation, they had not withdrawn the childhood promises between

Lord Collingwood and her father that she and Mr. Hobbs were to marry one day, rather they had agreed to rush the wedding, thus saving her and her family's reputations. Truer friendship had never been known. More compassion had never been shown.

But this was marriage. *Her marriage.* Her forever! Had her father found no alternative?

Blast and double blast. She hated to sound ungrateful. She owed her future to the baron's kindness and machinations, but... *marriage.*

Hazel's heart beat more rapidly than it had when she first heard the baying hounds return from the hunt. All morning she had waited at the edge of her bed, dressed and braced for the summons that would determine the rest of her days. At the sound of the hounds, she had strangled the bedpost, her resolve fraying.

Now a different kind of fear quivered her limbs and sharpened her breath. Not the fear of the unknown. This time was the fear of life without love. How could a man forced into marriage feel anything but resentment for her?

The drawing room door opened behind her.

Before she turned to look, Lord Collingwood rose from his chair. "There you are, son. We were discussing the wedding."

"You've already told her?" At Mr. Hobbs's disapproving tone, Hazel faced her husband-to-be.

His expression spoke volumes. His brows furrowed. His lips curved into a frown. He looked, if not angry, stormy. His expression, from the tense tick of his jaw to the narrowing of his eyes, said to her that he did not approve of the match. She remembered seeing him walking with Miss Evans, the two paired on more than that occasion—had he a *tendré* for her?

He came to stand at Hazel's side, his profile to her.

Lady Collingwood, all smiles, as she always was, clapped her hands. "How lovely you'll look on my son's arm at the soiree. Oh, but how silly of me. Your most pressing concern must be the breakfast. Set your mind at ease, Miss Trethow, I've already begun the arrangements. As a bride once myself, I know the importance of these matters."

Rather than respond, Hazel glanced to Mr. Hobbs again. His expression was now chiseled of stone.

"At the risk of appearing rude," Mr. Hobbs said, "may I request a moment alone with my intended?"

Hazel's surprise was echoed by the others in the room. Lady Collingwood squeaked. Lord Collingwood harrumphed. Mr. Trethow coughed. No one spoke for long minutes.

At length, Lord Collingwood returned to his feet and said, "Shall we see what Mr. Quainoo has in mind for the soiree now that it's to be a betrothal party?"

The only fortification Hazel received was an encouraging nod from her father as the group departed.

Once alone with Mr. Hobbs, Hazel clasped her hands at her waist and raised her chin. What must he think of her? Her betrothed walked across the room to the fireplace, resting a hand on the mantel.

When he finally looked at her, her breath caught in her throat. Brown eyes studied her, searching for answers to unspoken questions, the brown eyes she had seen at the first supper of his attendance rather than the brown eyes she had met on the wilderness

walk. The eyes of a man here on business, not pleasure. He disapproved of her.

"I had hoped to propose to you alone rather than
have it mandated," he said, the words contrasting
his expression.

"Would that have made a difference?" She
squeezed her fingers.

"You tell me. Would you have preferred I come to
you as a suitor with an honest proposal or be forced
by our parents into matrimony?"

"But you're not a suitor with an honest proposal.
Are you?"

He stared at her in silence, those piercing eyes
trying to read her. When he spoke again, he turned
away, his attention on the fireplace. "I apologize for
the manner in which you were told. It was badly done.
I take it, however, you're not opposed? The match is
acceptable?"

Hazel almost laughed. He asked as though she
had a choice in the matter.

"You're to be my savior, Mr. Hobbs. How could
I object?"

He nodded once, a curt inclination. "I leave
tomorrow morning for Exeter to obtain the license.
The guests will be invited to stay through Monday
to attend the breakfast. Some may leave the morning
after the soiree as originally planned, but I suspect,
given the circumstances — " He shifted from one foot
to the other, propping a leg on the marble surround.
"They'll stay."

Hazel took her time studying him in turn. This…
this…*stranger* was to be her husband in four days.
Would she ever become accustomed to him? Could

she make him love her? Did she want him to fall in love with her? He was nothing but a stranger.

"I ask this not to be indelicate," he continued, "but I must know. I will not judge you ill. But you owe it to me to be honest." He hooked a finger behind his cravat and cleared his throat. "Is there a chance you could be with child?"

Hazel gasped and reeled backwards. "How…how dare you." The audacity! "That is the most indelicate and inappropriate question I've been asked in my life. Have you no shame? Have you no sense of honor?" What a base man!

"I'm marrying you, Miss Trethow. I would say that makes me the most honorable man of your acquaintance."

Hazel looked around the room at anything but him. "I—I don't wish to be alone with you anymore. Please, leave."

Her cheeks flamed. So *this* was what he thought of her. Given the circumstances, it should not surprise her, but she was out of her element. To know he thought of her as a…a whore. To know they all thought of her in those terms. It was too much. Her throat burned. *Oh, please leave before I further humiliate myself by weeping.*

She heard the creak of the floor as he walked to the door. "All will be settled soon, Miss Trethow. Together, we will turn a scandal into a celebration."

Chapter 10

Had Hazel known how swiftly time would pass, she would have made a concentrated effort to memorize every moment. How could she later remember her wedding day when it rushed by in a blur?

The evening prior, it had rained so heavily, she had lain awake all night, fretting about carriage wheels stuck in the mud, overturned vehicles, and sinking horses. Even without the rain, she would not have slept a wink. Sleep was an impossibility, just as it eluded all brides. This was her last night as Miss Trethow. Her last night alone. The darkest of rooms could not hide the blush that stole across her cheeks. However much she wanted her marriage to be to someone she loved, she was *to be married*. Worry crossed her mind but outweighing that was undeniable exhilaration.

She was not opposed to marrying Mr. Hobbs, not even after his probing and indecorous question. She did wish she knew him better, knew him at all, really. They had never shared a conversation outside of polite exchanges. At the soiree, they had spoken only briefly, the whole of the evening focused on receiving congratulations from the guests—the same guests who whispered behind their hands when she was not looking, and a few who whispered even when she was looking. In a funny sort of way, she wondered how many of the unmarried ladies envied her. Their congratulations had been offered on sharp tongues and with narrowed eyes. With Mr. Hobbs's family being wealthy and well connected, he could marry anyone of his choosing, and yet they had arranged for him to marry *her*. Yes, the unmarried ladies must be envious. She had seen the way they looked at Mr. Hobbs, especially Miss Evans.

Whatever misgivings Hazel had were nothing compared to her realization that in the morning she was marrying one of the most eligible bachelors in the West Country. More than once through the thunderstorm, no, make that more than a dozen times, she had thought of how handsome he had looked when their paths crossed on the wilderness walk.

The trouble was his impression of her. She could spend eternity convincing herself how swoon worthy he was, but if he spent their married life thinking her a whore, that would not get them very far. Wounded pride encouraged her to tell him the truth. Common sense warned he would not believe her. And so spun her mind through thunder, lightning, and the relentless rain.

The morning of the wedding dawned with sunshine.

Escorted in carriages, the family proceeded to the chapel. Hazel traveled with her father and brother, while Mr. Hobbs rode with Lord and Lady Collingwood. The chapel was on estate grounds, a small family chapel not far from the dower house. They had planned to walk there. The mud had other ideas.

"Stop grinning at me." Hazel glowered at her brother.

"When you stop blushing."

"I'm not blushing. It's simply the exertion of the journey," she defended.

"In a carriage?" Young Cuthbert Walter howled with laughter. He ribbed his father and said, "I knew she'd marry the first gent to turn her head."

"I did *not*." Hazel huffed. "It's not a love match, if you must know. It's...it's convenient."

"Hence the blush?"

"I should have known you'd be bullheaded. If I had given it any thought, I wouldn't have invited you."

Cuthbert continued grinning, more so after Hazel stuck out her tongue. Her final action as an unmarried woman, she thought with amusement.

Having her brother present was a godsend, although she would only confess it under duress. He had made haste upon receiving the missive, accompanied by his tutor. No one seeing Cuthbert would guess him a young boy shy of fourteen, not with his long legs and remarkable eyes, the sort of eyes that shone green in the sunlight but brown in the shadows. He did not look a day under seventeen. The only aspect that gave him away was his unforgivable use of youthful slang, not that many guests would hear past his nearly unintelligible Cornish accent, all the stronger to antagonize his family.

Once the carriage pulled to a stop at the entrance of the red sandstone chapel, Hazel experienced each moment as a succession of flashes. One moment she was staring at the door. The next she was midway down the aisle. In a blink, she was at Mr. Hobbs's side, repeating after the curate.

The only moment she could recall with perfect clarity was the pronouncement of man and wife.

Hazel turned to Mr. Hobbs, arching her neck to look up at him. *My husband*, she thought with a peculiar tingle in her toes. He lowered his head to kiss her, and she mistook the moment, thinking he meant to kiss her on the mouth. With a pucker of her lips and a tilt of her head, she angled to meet him, only to realize a second too late that he had been aiming for her cheek. His lips collided with the corner of her mouth. Her stomach fluttered — from embarrassment, of course, nothing more. When he leaned back, frowning, she gurgled a laugh, feeling a right ninny.

In another blink, she faced both sets of parents, dazedly made her way to the carriage on her husband's arm, and headed back to Trelowen, a married woman.

His wife's leg bumped against his each time the carriage wheels slid in the mud. Either she did not mind, or she was too nervous to adjust her seating. He could not explain why, but he found the contact reassuring. Without turning his head, he eyed her profile.

His wife.

Mrs. Hobbs.

Hazel Hobbs.

Would they ever be familiar enough for given names?

She must think him rude, for as a gentleman, he should be sitting across from her with his back to the horses, and yet he had ignored the bench and sat next to her. It seemed the natural thing to do. They had, after all, exchanged vows.

Clearing his throat, he said, "We've not discussed a honeymoon. Would you care to visit London? Travel the continent?"

It had been a pressing thought during his sleepless night. Despite her situation and poor choices, she was a young woman who had undoubtedly never traveled outside of the West Country, not had a chance to plan the wedding of her dreams, nor had an opportunity to share plans, wishes, or desires with her betrothed. Rather than spend a lifetime resenting the match and judging her decisions, he would prefer they build a life together, starting with his attempt to see to her happiness. Assuming she did not choose, instead, to pine for lost love.

Mrs. Hobbs took her time in considering his question. Her leg bumped against his four times before she answered.

"I hardly see the point," she said.

Ah.

Harold turned to face the opposite window, not wanting her to see how deeply her words stung. This was not a love match with two lovesick youths desperate for alone time, desirous to see the world together. The words stung, nonetheless.

"I didn't mean that how it sounded." Her words rushed together, her voice breathy. "What I meant was I don't see the point of gaining a new home and family only to travel away from it all. I would like to learn what life is like as Mrs... Mrs. Hobbs."

Harold angled away from her for a better view of her expression. She stared at her knees, a tell-tale pink bridging across her nose and cheeks.

As he studied her, he searched for a reply but found none that would do justice to his thoughts, for where would he begin to say he had not the foggiest what life would be like for the bearer of the name of Mrs. Hobbs? In many ways, he had his own multi-faceted role with which to acquaint himself. Life in England, his return to Trelowen, his struggle with his father and the finances, his concerns for Nana, his new position as a husband. He was one part flattered — his heart drumming a syncopated beat — that she was most interested in her new role as his wife and one part disappointed that she did not want to escape all of this with him — two strangers forsaking responsibility to run away for a few weeks, perhaps falling in love in the process.

If Patrick could hear his thoughts, he would snort with laughter. Never had anyone accused Harold of being a romantic.

Trelowen visible from the window, the carriage turned down the drive.

"My mother is nothing if not a party planner," he said. "The breakfast should not disappoint." After a short pause, he added, "I hope you were not too disappointed by the ceremony. It's my understanding brides dream of London weddings."

What a ridiculous thing to say. Of course, she was disappointed. If he could unsay the words, he would.

A quick glance to him then back to her knees, she said, "Not all women. I liked it as it was. If I had planned our wedding—" She stopped with a sharp intake of breath as though to recall her words just as he had wished to recall his. "Well, if I had planned it, it would have been as it was."

He doubted she had ever envisioned *him* as the bridegroom. She did not say ought to the contrary, however. Instead, she laced tensed fingers, her blush deepening, causing him to question his doubts. Who *had* she envisioned? The carriage rocked to a halt, but Harold's gaze remained on Mrs. Hobbs's profile. The door opened, but his eyes held steady. In the span of a five-minute carriage ride, this stunning stranger had managed to shock him to his powdered roots, infusing him with hope.

What should have been the most awkward wedding breakfast of the year was a raving success.

When Harold stepped over the threshold with Mrs. Hobbs, the two were greeted with a party already underway. One of the guests was playing the pianoforte while a sizable group danced in the drawing room, never mind that it was well before noon, and in fact earlier than any of the guests had risen in a week save for hunting days. Perfumed flowers, most fake except the predominant ones from a hothouse, adorned both the dining and drawing rooms. A feast stretched across two sideboards. A cake large enough to feed the family for a week centered the table.

Everyone attended. *Everyone.* Never in Harold's wildest dreams would he have anticipated the turn-out. Every guest, even the Earl of Driffield, stayed for the wedding breakfast.

No sooner had the newlyweds entered the drawing room than Mrs. Hobbs was whisked away by

Lady Williamson and Miss Plumb, the three disappearing into the dining room. The absence of his wife did not stop the guests from congratulating him on the nuptials. He would have preferred her to be at his side. Only minutes after feeling the stir of hope for their marriage did he feel robbed. One hand after another he shook. One smile after another he exchanged. Propriety worked its magic, for the scandal that instigated the event transformed into gossip of how handsome a couple they made and how everyone swore they witnessed the budding romance the whole of the hunting party.

Just as he turned towards the dining room to find his bride, Mrs. Butterbest approached. Smugness did not become her. Wrinkles creased her over-powdered upper lip as she awarded Harold a complacent smile.

"I'll be telling everyone I had a hand in the matchmaking," she said in way of congratulations.

His second attempt to head for the dining room was intercepted by Messrs. Trethow, his father- and brother-in-law. The elder Mr. Trethow embraced him and called him son. The younger Mr. Trethow shook his hand heartily, the youth's other hand holding a plate piled with food. The boy looked more man than youth but had not quite grown into himself, a lanky fellow, all legs, and bearing the brightest smile in the room. Harold would hazard to guess the youth knew nothing of the circumstances that had united his sister in matrimony to the man before him other than impulsive infatuation or the desires of both parents to wed their offspring together. Were that either could have been true.

Harold's third attempt to head for the dining room to extricate his bride was foiled but this time not by someone in his path, rather Mrs. Hobbs herself, Nana on her arm. Nana patted Mrs. Hobbs's hand while chattering until her companion laughed. His grandmother was in good form today, as spirited as he had seen her since his arrival home from India. The two ladies approached him, Nana with glistening eyes, his wife with a shy smile. He kissed his grandmother on the cheek before she drifted in the direction of a group of guests.

Mrs. Hobbs stood before him, eyes trained on his cravat. "Lady Collingwood is under the impression my name is Helena rather than Hazel. For all my corrections, she can't be dissuaded."

Harold's lips twitched into an almost smile. "Don't take it as an insult. She's confused you for my mother. Lucky for you, she adores my mother."

She made to reply but nodded instead.

Offering his arm, he escorted her about the room. They made as much conversation as they had at the soiree—hardly any. With each attempt to strike up a discussion or ask a question, they were interrupted by well-wishers of one type or another. Harold gave up his efforts after a time.

Not long into the breakfast did he find himself stepping back altogether, positioning himself in a corner to observe the festivities. He was not forgotten. On the contrary. His blushing bride looked more to Harold than to anyone else in the room, even while she spoke with guests, and each time their eyes met, the pink across her cheeks darkened. Not a bride blushing with love but more likely the embarrassment of having married a stranger; nevertheless, he found flattery in each blush.

Although she had little more than a couple of days to prepare for the occasion, she was stunning, easily the most beautiful woman in the room by his estimation. There was more in this world than beauty. He wanted more than beauty, far more, but that did not keep him from admiring her. Her dress, the same she wore at the soiree, was adorned with a new embellishment of embroidery along the hem and bodice. If he were not mistaken, a few extra bows had been added, as well. The dress showed her figure to advantage, so much so that he had to turn away to keep from thinking of the wedding night. The thought brought as much pleasurable anticipation as it did pain.

His eyes flicked to the Earl of Driffield.

His thoughts turned stormy. How intimate had they been? Harold had little reason to believe his bride a virgin, not if she were under Driffield's spell. The fear of pregnancy still pressed its way into his conscience. The last thing he needed to do on his wedding day was observe the two lovers, but he found himself doing just that.

He watched his bride. He watched Driffield. He searched for signs of something, anything, stolen glances, wistful exchanges.

The two masked their affection well, for as far as he could tell, neither paid the other any mind. Had it not been for the scandal, he would not assume they were acquainted. Hazel acted so much the part of a bride that no one outside present company would dare suspect her of being forced to marry a stranger to save herself from ruin. More curious, her gaze continued to find *his* rather than the earl's, the ever-present rosy cheeks teasing him into a half-smile in spite of the direction of his thoughts.

By the close of the wedding breakfast, he spared little thought for the earl, scandal, or guests, his attention riveted on Mrs. Hazel Hobbs.

Shadows danced across the wall, furniture becoming ghostly outlines in the flicker of the hearth fire. Harold's hand rested on the door handle of his bedchamber. He ran a finger across the cold metal.

Ought he?

So long had he stood at the door, his left hand tingled, the arm weary from being held at an angle, weighted by the candlestick holder.

Ought he?

One sitting room away awaited his wife. Or he assumed she waited. She could have refused to move from the guest wing to the family wing. She could have refused to take the room adjacent to his, only a small sitting room between, so small in fact it could nary be called a sitting room. A reading closet was more apt. Space for a narrow window, corner fireplace, and chaise longue. Nothing as extraordinary as the lord and lady's suite.

Had she accepted the new room but locked the adjoining door? Had she barricaded herself with pillows and furniture, or perhaps hid behind a door with a fire poker?

Images of how the evening might proceed flashed through his mind. He could take her in a passionate frenzy, prove to her he was a superior lover to Driffield, vanquishing the earl from her mind. He could propose they talk instead, get to know each other before consummating the marriage. He could not attend her at all, give them more time, give her more time. She could not possibly want him to go to her.

Yet how could he not? Regardless of circumstances, he wanted this to be a real marriage. Had his father not gotten in the way, had Driffield not gotten in the way, they could be enjoying tonight as two newlyweds in love.

Another factor remained ever present: the possibility of a child. Going to her tonight meant protecting her.

Resting his forehead to the door, he decided if he stood there any longer, his toes cold and numb, he would lose all courage. He pressed the handle and stepped into the sitting room.

The fire, however quaint, lit the space with vibrant light and heat. He took another moment to breathe, smooth a hand over his banyan, switch the candlestick to the opposite hand to shake the pins and needles from his left, and still his beating heart. So fast and so loud did it beat, Harold could hear little else. Not the crackle of the fire. Not the hoot of the owls. A hand to his chest, he made the ten steps across the room to his wife's bedchamber door.

Ought he?

Butterflies fluttered in his stomach.

Deep breath.

He rapped on the bedchamber door thrice, waited, then pressed the handle.

Unlocked, the door yawned before him. Harold surveyed the room, half expecting to find it empty. The hearth fire cast shadows just as it had in his room, the longer shadows of a tired fire. In the middle of the room, cozied against a canopied alcove, stood the four-poster bed, the curtains drawn to tease at the figure beneath the bedding. He swallowed, his heart pounding more furiously, if possible.

Mrs. Hobbs was most certainly in the room. The bedding was pulled up to her chin, the only visible part of her being her head. He would have laughed had he not been so arrested by the scene. Unpowdered auburn hair fanned across the pillow, curling a halo about her face. Her eyes widened at the sight of him.

Wordless, he walked to the bedside table and set down the candlestick holder. She watched him. He watched her watching him. Parting the banyan to reveal his nightshirt beneath, he slipped the robe off his shoulders, folded it, and set it next to the candle.

When he lifted the edge of the bedding, she squeaked. "The candle."

Sheet half raised, he stared blankly.

She burrowed further under cover. "Could you douse the candle?" In a near whisper, she added, "Please?"

Flame extinguished, he climbed into the bed next to her. Although their bodies did not touch, he could feel her heat along his side. Could she hear his heart? Feel the wings of the butterflies?

A sliver of moonlight peeked through a narrow parting in the window curtains. He stared at the beam, shadows licking at its edges. The side of his body closest to her beaded with sweat, the other side still chilled.

"Are you ready?" he asked, his voice cracking, much to his dismay.

Silence.

He rubbed his feet together and watched the imperceptible movement of the moonlight.

"We can wait," he said at length.

In the quietest of voices, his bed companion said, "I want to…tonight."

His body needed no more invitation than her lips forming the word *want*. Anticipation alone had hardened him before he stepped into the room, but now he felt the stoke of the fire in his loins, his body yearning to know the pleasure of his wife.

However experienced she might be, he dared not take her swiftly. He wanted to savor their first coupling and show her tenderness. Turning to face her, he took a moment to admire her cherubic face before leaning to kiss her cheek. His lips lingered, gauging her response. She remained still, her breath jagged. He kissed her cheek again, brushing a finger over her lips. She made no movement, her breath sharper. Kissing the corner of her mouth, he moved his hand beneath the cover to lace his fingers with hers. She squeezed his hand with painful tightness.

Harold propped himself on his elbow to gaze down at her. The tip of her tongue flicked her bottom lip before tugging it between her teeth.

Untangling their fingers, he swept his hand over her leg to find the edge of the nightdress. She quivered at the touch, her lips parting in a gasp. He tugged the fabric up and over her hips. His body throbbed with longing. Cheek inches from her lips, he felt her hot breath.

Rolling his leg over hers, he parted her thighs with his knee. He slid his torso across her, wanting her to feel all of him and he all of her as he nestled between her legs. He slipped a hand between them. When his fingers caressed the wet curls of her mound, it was the final enticement he needed. Harold positioned himself, rubbed against the sweet nectar for but a moment, then entered her with a steady albeit lustful thrust.

His moan of pleasure as groin met groin was answered with a startled cry. Mrs. Hobbs went rigid, her body tightening around him, her fingers grasping his upper arms, nails digging into skin.

He went still.

They remained locked in an embrace of confusion and shock. Harold tried to think, tried to rationalize her response, but his body's needs overpowered his mind's ability to form coherent thought. All he could concentrate on was the titillating sensation of being buried in the heaven that was Hazel Hobbs and the sudden pulse of awareness that he was her first and only.

His eyes met hers, but he could not read anything beyond the shadow of his own form blocking the firelight from her features. Holding himself still, he waited for a sign. Withdrawal? Continue?

She relaxed beneath him. The next thrust was slow, tender, tentative. Her moan was soft but permissive, encouraging him to continue.

If he could have started the night over, he would have. If he could have lasted all night, he would have.

Alas. She intoxicated his senses. The velvet of her skin, the sound of wet suckling, the scent of musk and roses—it was his undoing. His thrusts quickened until the wonder of release surged through him, blinding and paralyzing.

Hazel stared at the underside of the bed's canopy. At least an hour had passed since Mr. Hobbs returned to his room. So shocked was she when he asked if he could remain the night that she had shaken her head an emphatic *no*. Had she hurt his feelings? She hoped not. No one had mentioned that two people could share a bed the entirety of an evening. The thought excited her as well as flustered her. Would he have taken her again had he stayed? Would they have conversed? Would they have held hands again?

It was too late now to ask those questions.

The canopy was coffered. Or maybe that was considered paneled. Sixteen squares. Rectangles? No, they were squares. Each with a centered, carved diamond, or perhaps that should be with an angled square. Yes, if she tilted her head just so, it was another square. Thirty-two squares if she counted the smaller ones. Oak? Mahogany? Cherry?

At the end of the room, a log shifted in the hearth with a crackle, the fire nothing more than glowing embers.

Her nightdress stayed bunched around her hips. She could not bring herself to lower it as though the evening had not happened. Not that her body would let her forget. Between her legs throbbed and ached in pleasant memory. Was it pleasant? Yes, she believed it was. A pleasant intimacy. And yet…

Was that all there was to it?

Earlier that evening, she had waited for so long that she had lost track of time, worried he would not come to her. The worry stemmed from fear he was displeased with the forced marriage, distress he would not want what he believed to be used goods, concern that he would wait to ensure she was not with child. Bottom line: had he not come to her, she would have known he believed her a whore.

But he came.

From the moment he stepped into the room, her heart knew hope.

Although she had no experience on which to base her assumption, she believed he enjoyed the encounter. She was not disappointed herself, not really. It had not been enjoyable, but neither had it been unpleasant. The trouble was, she knew there was more. Was there not? Outside of this evening, she had no knowledge of what occurred between a husband and wife, for her married friends never divulged details, but they *had* shared enough that Hazel was positive there was more to this intimacy.

Passion. Would she not know if it had been passionate?

Silly thoughts for a wedding night. What she should be feeling was contentment. If this was all there ever was, it was enough. The family had come to her rescue. *He* had come to her rescue. Even knowing she had been involved in a scandal with another gentleman, he had been gentle — of that much she was certain.

Was he thinking the same as she, that had it not been for their parents pressing the match since childhood, had it not been for the circumstances of the scandal, they might have courted of their own volition? She would never know if they would have, but she thought they might. Those brown eyes she had spied on the wilderness walk had promised passion, even love, those irresistible eyes of Mr. Hobbs.

She wished she had not told him to douse the candle.

Chapter 11

Wiping the sweat from his brow, Harold tucked the handkerchief in his waistcoat pocket before stripping off the garment and rolling his shirt-sleeves above his elbows. Abhijeet would curse him out of the dressing room, he mused.

With a grunt, he hoisted the sledgehammer, arced it overhead, and drove the fence post into the ground.

A short distance away, Patrick and Mr. Jones, one of the tenant farmers, worked together to fit a rail into the corresponding mortise. It was not every day the heir of a barony and a viscount mended fences, but on this day, that was precisely what they found themselves doing. When Mrs. Jones directed them to the paddock, she had failed to mention Mr. Jones was tackling a fallen fence. They could not very well tip their hat to the man and canter back to Trelowen without offering assistance. At least the morning air was chilly. Not that it prevented the evidence of hard work: perspiration.

His post set, he lent a hand with the next rail.

Mr. Jones wasted no time in asking, "When do we have the pleasure of meeting Mrs. Hobbs? My Effie is champing at the bit to see who's stolen the heart of our own Mr. Hobbs."

Harold chuckled while lifting the next rail in place for Patrick to secure. "Give her time. The wedding is only three days past."

"With a new bride, you'll be staying on home soil, I expect."

Mr. Jones hedged at the very question Harold had been asked by three different families that morning: would he be returning to India? While he could be mistaken, and he did not believe he was, there was a restlessness among the tenants, each witness to, recipient of, or rumored about the recent decisions of Lord Collingwood and his financial straits. When staff were dismissed, lands left barren, and repairs ignored, tenants noticed. Their own livelihoods depended on the estate as much as the estate depended on them.

"You have my word," Harold said, turning to Mr. Jones. "I won't be returning to India or leaving England anytime soon."

It would not be long before his father sent him to London to sort the investment, but London was a far cry from Calcutta. He had no intentions of leaving England, not now that he had a wife to care for and an estate to rebuild, even if he had to do the latter with his bare hands and no money.

Half an hour later, they steered their horses towards Trelowen. Patrick would part ways for his own home, not but ten miles away, once they reached the lake.

"Well?" Patrick prodded.

"Well, what?"

"You know perfectly well what I'm welling about."

Harold considered his reply. As much as he wanted to share the finer details of his marriage with his friend, if for no other reason than to help him work through his own thoughts of the situation, such topics were best not aired outside of the bedchamber. He wondered at how much to say and how to phrase his words.

"I'm resolved to help her feel comfortable here," he finally said. "While I can't control her sentiments on the marriage and can't turn this into a love match, not if her heart belongs to another, I can and will do my part to see to her comfort."

"I see." Patrick was silent for a stretch, as though considering his own words. "She's given you reason, then, to believe her heart remains with Driffield?"

"No, actually." He cast a sidelong glance at his friend. "To be honest, she's more akin to a scared rabbit than a lovesick mourner."

"She came for a party only to end up trapped. Dreams dashed with a flash of a scandal."

Forcing his company on her seemed a disservice, so he had, admittedly, been avoiding her outside of the obligatory meals, not that she had made herself available outside of those meals. Even the evenings were quiet. He vowed not to return to her bed until they knew each other better and until she invited him. Granted, it was only the third day. Three days, however, felt like a lifetime. Harold's struggle was *how* to help her accept Trelowen as her home.

Patrick snapped his fingers. "Better said than thought. You're wasting a good ride by brooding."

"I'm not brooding."

"Yes, you are. Best say it before I launch an interrogation."

Harold tossed a smirk at Patrick. "Right. You brought this on yourself." He took a deep breath then said, "I need to know how to turn a stranger into a lover. The trouble is that each time I attempt conversation, she becomes more of a stranger. There's a chasm between us I don't know how to bridge."

"I see," Patrick said again. "Let us revisit the lovesick mourner. If there's no indication she's longing for lost love, that should give you hope, yes? No secret letters? No murmuring of the wrong name in, *ahem*, intimate moments? No wistful stares out rainy windows?"

"Take this information with you to the grave, for if you don't, I'll put you there myself. Understood?" He narrowed his eyes until Patrick nodded. "She and Driffield were not intimate. At least not intimate enough to beget a child."

"Oh. Oh, that *is* interesting." One hand guiding the reins, Patrick rubbed his chin. "What do you suppose that means? If anything. While you've been away too long to know Driffield's character, allow me to educate you. He is *not* known for affairs of the heart. A first-rate rogue. Think it was her first meeting with him rather than a lovers' tryst?"

The memory of catching her in the wilderness walk haunted him — Driffield waiting for her in the underbrush, stripped of his coat.

Unwilling to part with the memory, Harold said, "Perhaps he had not yet had the opportunity to inflict more damage."

"Perhaps."

"Be honest. Do you think there's a chance there was a misunderstanding? He targeted her, but she had not yet fallen in love?"

"It's possible." Patrick slowed his horse as they approached the lake. "I say that for your sake because I want you to have hope you can win her. You *will* win her. My sage advice? Stop worrying about the rogue. Focus instead on winning your wife."

Idle was not a word in Hazel's vocabulary.

So busy had she been that she had not seen Mr. Hobbs except at mealtimes, an unintentional avoidance that nevertheless guilted her conscience. The first day after her wedding was filled with letter writing. The guests had departed that morning, and although she had only wished farewell hours before to her family, Agnes, and Melissa, she set out to write each a letter to thank them for their love and encourage them to visit again soon. Only for the eyes of her two friends, she added a brief mention of what a kind and gentle soul was Mr. Hobbs—not that she knew this for certain, but she wished to reassure them this would all work out for the best.

The second day after her wedding, she had toured the house in its entirety, met the staff, and spent a great deal of time with her new mother-in-law Lady Collingwood. Bless, the baroness was the height of fashionable prettiness but had not a thought in her head outside of being decorative. If Hazel's new husband wanted a wife such as that and expected Hazel to be *decorative*, he had quite the surprise in store.

Mr. Hobbs remained a mystery to her, but she had gleaned information from her lady's maid who subtly plied answers from downstairs. According to her lady's maid, his days had been equally as busy, all estate business, paying calls to tenants, taking tea with his grandmother, and any number of other tasks. Industrious fellow, to be sure. His busyness helped ease her guilt.

On this sun-shiny day, Hazel decided to call on the Dowager Lady Collingwood, affectionately referred to as Nana by all in the household. Not since the wedding breakfast had Hazel seen Nana, the same woman she recalled bursting into the drawing room in her nightdress the first evening of the hunting party, and the same woman who insisted Hazel was Helena. From Hazel's estimation, the woman needed a friend, possibly more than Hazel herself did.

A friend would be lovely. Better than lovely. Keeping busy was in Hazel's nature, but it also held the shock at bay, the shock that she would never return home. This was her home now. She had come for a party but would never leave. With both her father and brother she had a strong bond, but rather than leave with them to Cornwall, home to Teghyiy Hall — no, no longer home — it was Agnes who traveled in the family carriage. Hazel had with her the belongings she brought for the week's party, nothing more. Her things would be sent by her papa to arrive within a week or two. Fretting over her circumstances did no one any good. She owed it to this family to be the best Hazel she could be, to prove they made the right decision in saving her and her family.

With a smile on her lips and a tune hummed under her breath, she stepped out of the house and across the lawn for the wilderness walk. The dower house, the butler had directed her, was on the left path.

Hazel made it all the way to the split in the path before stopping in her tracks.

Walking straight for her from the lake path was Mr. Hobbs.

A feeling she had never before experienced swept through her. Raw desire. The fluttering in her stomach, the throb at her apex, and the warm, desperate need gave it away in an instant. Desire.

He halted as abruptly when he saw her. They stared at each other. With a sweep of hungry eyes, she took in his dishabille. His shirt, with open vee, clung to his torso, soaked through. His coat and waistcoat were slung over his forearm. His breeches were dusty and splotched with damp. His boots were caked in dirt. When he took the first steps forward, she inhaled a whiff of his cologne — sweat and lake water.

However disgusted she ought to be with a man who had heretofore been the poshest toff she had ever laid eyes on, she instead was struck by another rush of desire.

"Good afternoon," he said with a bow. "Pardon my state. I must look a fright. My only excuse is I hadn't expected to see anyone." He ran a hand through his hair, the curls tangled, unbound, and clumped with wet but determined powder. "I mended a fence at the Jones' farm, then after seeing my horse to the stable thought I would visit the lake before being reprimanded by my valet. You don't want to know any of this, do you?"

Swallowing, she nodded. "On the contrary."

Keeping her eyes from roaming was becoming a challenge. She pressed the palms of her cold hands to her cheeks to hide the blush.

Mr. Hobbs gave a curious half-smile, his brows puckering as though he were sorting out a puzzle. "Are you available?"

Her mind flashed to their wedding night. Could he mean... "Now?"

He swept a hand over his wet attire and chuckled. "I need to change. But I thought you might walk with me to the dower house. In an hour?"

"Oh." How silly that she thought he meant — well, never mind. "I was on my way there now. I can wait."

"Meet me in the entrance hall?"

Only after he proceeded to the house did she realize she had never removed her palms from her cheeks.

Hazel's heart skipped a beat when Mr. Hobbs made his way down the stairs. The posh toff had replaced the irresistible rogue by the lake. Starched linen, crisp and well-tailored satin, hair combed and bagged, eau de rose, and a serious expression. All that was missing was the hair powder, but given he had only taken an hour, there would not have been time for his hair to dry. The russet color offered a glimpse of sensual rusticism. Her lips curved up at the corners.

He stopped at the bottom step, his hand on the newel post. "You're exquisite, Mrs. Hobbs."

His words stole her breath. His first compliment to her. And as unexpected as if he had announced they would be riding an elephant to the dower house.

Exquisite.

No one had ever called her exquisite. Never pretty. Never beautiful. Never anything save slightly plump and petite.

Exquisite.

"As are you," her lips formed in reply.

His expression was as startled as she imagined hers must look. With a curious frown, he approached the silently waiting Mr. Quainoo, accepted the coat and gloves, then offered Hazel his arm. She slipped a hand in the crook of his elbow.

The day had warmed since that morning, so much so that one would never guess it was September. Earlier in the morning, a cold, grey haze had shrouded the lawn surrounding the house, the fog so dense Hazel had not been able to see past the garden. Each hour brought a brighter, hotter sun. So warm it had become, Hazel wished she had not worn her *pet-en-l'air*. The additional layer was overwarm. Or maybe it was the company.

They made it all the way to the tree line without speaking. Every passing minute after the auspicious start chipped away her hope that they would say more.

Her disappointment was short-lived.

Once under the cover of naked tree branches, he slowed their pace. "How are you settling into your new home?" he asked.

"Far better than I expected if I'm honest. Your mother has been welcoming, as have the staff."

"I'm pleased to hear it." He turned to her with a shy smile. "And duly chastised. I've neglected you."

"Oh, but you've been busy! Calling on tenants, mending fences—" She clamped her mouth shut before he realized she had been gathering information on his whereabouts. At least he had admitted as much when they met earlier.

"Trifle excuses. We're newlyweds, and I should be lavishing you with attention. Even my failure to bring you to call on neighbors has been remarked on. Much to my chagrin, Patrick heard every word of my dereliction of duties."

He guided them to one of the larger trees and leaned against the trunk to look at her more directly.

Hazel clasped her hands at her waist. "You're forgiven, but only if you tell me who Patrick is."

"So derelict I've spent more time with him than you." Mr. Hobbs chuckled. "I promise to remedy that. Soon. As to Patrick, I refer to Lord Kissinger. You remember him?"

She did. The handsome viscount, heir to the Winthorp earldom. Yes, she, Agnes, and Melissa had exchanged many whispered giggles about him. She nodded to her husband.

"He's been my closest friend for as long as I can remember. Although not his father's county seat, they've resided in their country home here in Devonshire since his father's inheritance. About ten miles north. We grew up together." Mr. Hobbs stared at his feet in thought. "I've not yet mentioned it because I thought you might not be ready—presumptuous, I know—but he's invited us to dine this week."

Her breath caught. To dine with an earl's family?

"I'd love to. Yes. I accept." She gave a little bounce then checked herself. Dignity. Ladylike dignity.

He gave a half-smile. "Well, well, Mrs. Hobbs. Our first supper engagement."

"About that," she interrupted.

His half-smile slipped.

"As thrilling as it is to be called Mrs. Hobbs, it's rather silly for you to call me that, don't you think?"

The smile turned to a frown. "I'm not to address you by name? Wife, then?"

Hazel giggled, although she could not be sure that he had made a joke. "If you don't call me Hazel, I shall cease to answer to you. I will turn my head and pretend I cannot hear you."

One corner of his lips lifted. "As you wish, Wife."

She crossed her arms and turned up her nose.

Pushing against the tree to give her a bow, he said, "It's lovely to meet you, Hazel. You may call me Harold — if it would please you."

Eyeing him down the length of her nose, never mind that he was at least a full head taller than her, she presented her hand for him to kiss.

"Harold," she declared. "Yes, that's pleasing to me."

What she had meant to say as a tease sounded so naughty to her ears that she laughed and blushed furiously, hoping he could not guess the direction of her thoughts. He studied her over her knuckles until her laughter dissolved, his expression as serious as always but his eyes twinkling with what she thought might be mischief.

They continued their walk along the wilderness path, but at snail speed, her hand once more tucked in the crook of his arm.

Seeing this as her opportunity to better know her husband, she opened a new line of inquiry. "You've been in India?"

"I have. For the past three years. I returned a nudge over a month ago."

"Is it strange being home, or were you happy to leave India?"

His hand slipped over hers, capturing it between palm and arm.

However thoughtless or instinctual the movement on his part, she found it intimate, a touch between lovers rather than strangers or spouses of convenience. It made her giddy, lightheaded. How different would it all have been had she listened to her father from the outset and set her cap at this man intended for her since birth? Was this how he would have courted her? A walk in the park. A hand over hers. A bashful smile. Would their first kiss have been tender and sensual?

"For a time," he said, "India was home rather than here. Even after a month, I've not fully adjusted; yet there's a rhythm to England one never forgets."

"Why were you there?"

Harold clucked his tongue, hesitating before speaking. "Business. On my father's behalf."

She waited for him to elaborate. When he did not, she asked, "What was India like?" A glance his direction awarded her a change in his expression from cloudy to wistful.

"The sun, however relentless, has a way of reflecting off the Hooghly River so that light glints and shimmers on the surrounding buildings. An asymmetrical landscape. A straw hut next to a manor, a fort next to a warehouse, park greenery next to industry. The people themselves are as varied as the land, a mixture of cultures and languages, formal attire contrasting with undress, an array of color where the livery shade distinguishes the house, all walking the same dusty street, smelling the same aroma of garam masala spices, smoke, and sweat."

Hazel tried to envision it, then tried to envision *him* walking those streets. Her first vision was of the posh heir with his powdered hair and starched linen, but then she transposed that image with one of him as he had looked coming from the lake — shirt vee open, clothes drenched and molded to his frame.

She turned her head to stare down the lake path as it veered away from them, Harold guiding them down the left path towards the dower house. "What did you do there? Not the business but day to day?"

"There was no limit to entertainments. Dinner parties, balls, whist. I toured the countryside for a time, made friends. There were several families living in Calcutta with whom I befriended. Abhijeet, my valet, being one of them. He's more friend than employee and is only my valet by his own insistence. Stubborn man."

"What of Lord Kissinger? Did he travel with you?"

Harold shook his head. "I'd not seen him since I left for India. One happy reason to return was to reunite. We'd missed three years of friendship, not that we didn't write, but letters abroad take a great deal longer than they should and oft lose their way. I noticed you have close friends, as well. Lady Williamson and Miss Plumb, yes?"

Hazel grinned. He had noticed her. Not that it was difficult to know with whom she spent her time during the hunting party, but she would wager Lord Brooks would not have been able to name her friends. Harold had noticed her.

"They are my dearest. I've known Agnes, Miss Plumb that is, ever so long. As with Lord Kissinger and you, she lives not far from my ho—I mean to say Teghyiy Hall, my childhood home. Melissa's father and mine did business together for a time, although I couldn't tell you what business. It was something to do with the West Indies, but he never shared the details with me. Sir Chauncey was involved, as well, Melissa's husband, and they met in the West Indies. There was a great to do when he and Melissa's father returned to England. We hosted a supper party, and there Sir Chauncey introduced his bride. The three of us—Agnes, Melissa, and I—became fast friends after that. She's supportive of all our endeavors and has the heart of a saint. She and Chauncey are a love match, you know, and to hear her father tell it, he put up quite the fight to have her."

Realizing she was rambling, and carrying on about love matches, no less, Hazel pressed her lips together. Here she was, determined to get to know her husband, yet at the first opportunity, she rambled. He must think her a silly nit.

And to talk of a love match! *Oh, Hazel!*

To her surprise, he said in response, "I wish I had become better acquainted with them. In a month or two, shall we invite them to stay for a few days?"

Hazel clasped her hand over his and squeezed. Despite her best efforts to maintain her dignity, she squealed with delight.

Watching their approach and witnessing Hazel's departure from decorum was Nana. The Dowager Baroness Collingwood waved from the front door of the dower house, calling out a greeting to Helena and Eugene.

Chapter 12

The Countess of Winthorp peered at Hazel over her wine glass. Her expression indiscernible, she gave the glass a gentle swirl, set it down, then said to Lord Kissinger without moving her lips or removing her gaze from Hazel, "You see how easy it is? Find a woman and marry her. Never would I have thought Mr. Hobbs wiser than you, but the proof sits before me."

Lord Kissinger mumbled inaudible words into his own wine glass. Harold cleared his throat. The Earl of Winthorp cut a piece of venison. Miss Hale stared at her plate.

The supper was not a disaster, although it appeared that way with each poke and prod from Lady Winthorp. Quite the contrary. It aided Hazel in feeling *married*, a strange concept, perhaps, since she was irrefutably married, but being so legally did not always translate to emotionally. This was not the first time, rather the second time that week Hazel felt married, a woman part of an exclusive two-member club.

The first time had been during tea with Nana and Harold two days prior. Although Nana confused them for Lord and Lady Collingwood on several occasions during the visit, she remained lucid for the majority, regaling Hazel with stories of Harold's youth and his seriousness as a boy. What was so monumental about tea was Nana's ability to paint them as a pair, a unit, a whole. She saw them not as two individuals sitting awkwardly across from her on the Rococo canapé but as a duo, a love-struck duo at that. So often she referenced the twinkle in their eyes that Hazel began to blush and believe just such a twinkle must show, even while she knew the truth. By the time they left the dower house, she could not meet Harold's gaze without wondering if he could see this mysterious twinkle of infatuation. Despite circumstances, she felt *married*.

The second time was during this supper party at the Winthorp's country home. Hazel was seated at the dining table with her husband to one side, Lord and Lady Winthorp at each end of the table, and Lord Kissinger across from her, a pretty young lady by the name of Miss Hale sitting next to him.

Lady Winthorp's comments were not complimentary; yet she spoke of the marriage so often and referenced so frequently Hazel and Harold as though they were the same pair, unit, and whole that Nana had recognized, no one could doubt that they were *married*. Given the only person at the table Hazel knew was Harold helped the sensation of being one part of a pair. The fact he watched her through most of the meal contributed, as well. She was ever aware of him. Her *husband*.

How many arranged marriages, and especially under the circumstances, had turned bitter and resentful? How many husbands punished their wives for being forced into an unwanted marriage? Hers could have ended this way, and perhaps it still would, but if he continued to stare at her as he was, and if she continued to feel such inexplicable elation each time she caught him staring, then surely this would be written in the annuals as one of the successful marriages of their time. She could only hope.

Hazel looked up with a start to realize Lady Winthorp was talking to her.

"You must talk sense into my son. His father won't live forever and needs to be assured the line is secure. This title is our family's legacy. Our lineage must be preserved. Is that not right, Lord Winthorp?"

The earl grunted as he cut another piece of venison. The man did not look a day over forty, hardly on his deathbed.

Hazel glanced at Lord Kissinger before saying to her hostess, "Wouldn't you prefer him to marry for love?"

The countess sniffed. "Do you mistake us for commoners?"

Hazel's eyes widened, fearing she had insulted Lady Winthorp.

Before she could respond, her ladyship continued, "Miss Hale is sensible. Do you not think they would make a stunning couple?"

The sensible Miss Hale was as red as a poppy and had not eaten a single bite of supper, her attention riveted on the plate. Next to Miss Hale, Lord Kissinger raised an eyebrow at Hazel. Rather than be annoyed or angry, he bore the smirk of amusement, as though this were the greatest of entertainments for the week. Her heart went out to Miss Hale.

A quick peek at Harold revealed he was staring at her again. There *was* a twinkle in his eyes. Undeniably.

Not the twinkle of Nana's imagination but that twinkle of mischief she had seen before. One corner of his lips rose in a teasing smile. Right there at the dining table, in front of complete strangers, she blushed.

"Mrs. Hobbs? Are you listening?"

In a moment of confusion, Hazel realized yet again that Lady Winthorp addressed her, and from the woman's expression of sour lemons, had been addressing her for some time. Had Hazel been so caught up in Harold's smile, or had she not registered the name as her own? Hearing herself addressed as this new persona was akin to dressing in an unaltered gown. It fit, but it did not hug her curves, the sleeves ever so loose, the petticoat too short, the neckline too low. She was *not* Miss Trethow anymore, she reminded herself. She was, indubitably, Mrs. Hobbs.

"Mrs. Hobbs. I'll not be ignored."

Hazel smiled at her hostess. "It's not for me to say if they would make a stunning couple, my lady, although I'm honored you value my opinion."

Her ladyship narrowed her eyes then turned her attention to Harold. "As I understand the situation, you and Mrs. Hobbs were intended since birth. Being party to an arranged marriage, you can speak to its success."

Although more of a statement than a question, it sounded like a command.

Harold took it as such, for he replied with, "I attribute the success to destiny."

The only lighting in the carriage came from the first quarter moon, hanging low in the sky, and the coachman's carriage lamps, swaying with the drive. Harold could make out Hazel's profile against the carriage upholstery but not her expression. She chattered with animation. Her tone alluded to a smile. Not yet a full week of marriage, and he already craved that smile. He did not know how to win a woman's affection nor how to transfer a woman's love from another man to himself, but he fancied from all her blushes that he was not doing a half bad job of the task. The next time he spoke with Patrick, he would badger the man about her every expression — had Patrick noticed her looking at him overlong? Had he seen her flush when Harold spoke to her? Had he sensed any attraction between them?

"Poor Miss Hale," Hazel was saying while Harold tried not to think about when it would be appropriate to revisit her bedchamber — too soon; far too soon; they had only just begun to talk to each other. "I would pity Lord Kissinger, but it was Miss Hale who received the brunt of her ladyship's not so subtle innuendos."

"Patrick's plight in life. He calls on me as an escape from his parents. If Trelowen weren't nearby, I suspect he would move to one of their other residences."

"Do they hound him so often?"

Harold nodded but realized she could not see him clearly in the darkness. "To my knowledge, yes. It's why Lady Winthorp didn't attend the hunting party. She was disappointed he had refused the newest of sacrificial lambs."

"Bless. Is he waiting for love, or does the countess have abominable taste?"

"A combination, you could say." Harold shifted on the bench.

"Has he not thought of marrying to appease them?"

He tugged at his waistcoat. "From time to time."

"Well, I hope he does wait for love."

Harold hoped that would be the end of the conversation. It was going in an uncomfortable direction, one he was ill equipped to handle.

Across from him, Hazel gave a little squeal. "I know! Yes, that's it. I have it."

Waiting for her to elaborate proved futile. She *hmm*ed and *ooh*ed under her breath, deep in thought, with no indication of sharing with him.

The more time he spent with her, the more curious of a young lady she became. His first impressions of her being anything like his mother were unfounded, although there was a sort of simple pleasure about her. Simple was not the correct word, but he could not think of a better one. She garnered pleasure from the least significant of things, be it delight in an autumn bloom along the wilderness path or glee from Nana having the very biscuit she favored most.

"Care to share your thoughts?" he asked with a chuckle.

"I'm determined to find him a bride! I have in mind a young lady from home, one of my neighbors, who would suit him perfectly. She's—"

"No matchmaking," Harold interrupted.

"I promise to be discreet. I won't be as gauche as Lady Winthorp. Neither will ever know I'm—"

"No matchmaking, Hazel," he snapped. He had not meant a harsh tone, but the last thing he needed was his wife meddling with Patrick's love life.

"There's no need to worry that I'll—"

"He prefers the company of men."

The words slipped before he could stop them. Better said than thought, as Patrick oft told him. At least now she would understand.

To his surprise, she laughed. "Well, of course, he does. Just as I prefer the company of ladies. But I'm not speaking of a *friend*, Harold, but of a *spouse*."

"He. Prefers. Men." Harold enunciated each word. "Unless you have a gentleman in mind, you needn't bother."

Although he could not see it, he could sense the pucker forming between her brows.

"Oh." Was all she said before lapsing into silence.

They both stared out the carriage window into the darkness. As refreshing the silence and as relieving the revelation, Harold's annoyance mounted. Only moments prior, his wife had supported love matches, but now she disapproved. He had given her reason to judge his closest friend, someone who would call on them frequently, dine with them often, and be a permanent fixture in their lives. This was a conversation he had never expected to have and certainly not with a woman he had known for two weeks, less than two weeks if he counted the days. The longevity of their parents' intention for them be dashed, and brief prior meetings during their childhood be damned; he had *known* her for thirteen days.

Harold scowled at the passing silhouettes of trees.

Hazel clapped her hands, shattering the silent night. So startling was the sound, Harold braced against the bench.

"I know the perfect gentleman! Sir Chauncey's cousin dined wi—"

Whatever Hazel was about to say was disrupted by a howl of laughter. Of all the things he anticipated her saying, that had not been one of them. Harold threw his head back and bellowed the heartiest laugh he had shared in years, so hearty he had to retrieve his handkerchief to dab at the corners of his eyes.

Not yet the master of his humor, he said between chuckles, "No matchmaking, please, not even with Sir Chauncey's cousin or whatever gentleman you had in mind."

Hazel harrumphed. "I think they would make a stunning couple, to steal his mother's words. You underestimate my matchmaking skills."

"I promise that is one thing I will never do— underestimate you. But let's leave Patrick to sort out his own love life."

On Sunday, their sixth day of marriage and their fourteenth day of acquaintance, Harold searched the house for his wife, eager to devote the afternoon to winning her affection. The morning had been spent at church, but the afternoon would not be wasted with idleness. He had a woman to woo.

After visiting their shared sitting room, the parlor, the drawing room, the dining room, and every other room he could think she might be, he finally found her in the morning room, hunched over the table with quill and paper. Since his presence had not been detected, he took a moment to admire her heart-shaped face, the pout of her cherubic lips, the pertness of the low and corseted décolletage. Every day since their wedding night, she wore her hair powdered and curled. The contrast struck him each time he saw her. Etched in his memory was the vision of her nestled in the bedding, naked auburn hair fanning against the pillow as a halo. So help him, he would see that sight again. The next time, he hoped to see far more of her than undressed hair.

Shaking his head of the enticing and distracting vision, he stepped into the room to catch her attention. His heart thundered when she smiled at the sight of him.

"I wondered," he said as she returned her quill to its stand, "if you might like to take a boat on the lake with me?"

Her smile broadened, her emerald eyes brightening. "Row on the lake? With you?"

Was it his imagination, or did she sound breathless with anticipation? Perhaps that was himself as he waited with bated breath for her answer.

Task forgotten, she pushed back her chair to stand. "That would be the loveliest of lovelies."

He took that as a yes. "I didn't mean to interrupt. We could go after you finish writing your letter. Say in an hour?"

Hazel waved her hand at the letter. "I'm ready now. The letter can wait."

A ray of sunshine, she approached, all smiles, and tucked her hand under his arm. With plots of how he might strike up conversation once in the boat and a hopeless desire to win a kiss, he saw her to the entrance hall.

They were intercepted by Mr. Quainoo.

The butler offered an apologetic bow and said, "Your father wishes to see you in the study, sir."

"Not now, surely. We're for the lake."

"I'm afraid now, sir."

Hazel's disappointment was palpable. She squeezed his arm.

"Wait here?" Harold implored. "I won't be but a moment."

The magic of the excursion dimmed.

When Harold stepped into the study, his father signaled to close the door and waved him over to the desk. Lord Collingwood poured two glasses of brandy, the one in his hand twice as full.

"Sit, my boy. We've plans to make."

Harold remained standing. "If we could postpone for an hour, I would be grateful."

"Nonsense. Sit."

He clasped his hands behind his back. "Mrs. Hobbs is waiting for me in the entrance hall. We're for the lake. I'll return in an hour for whatever it is you have in mind to discuss."

"Sit. You have all the time in the world for distractions. This, however, cannot wait."

Clenching his fingers into fists, Harold pursed his lips. He needed to choose his battles. She would wait, and once his father had his say, they could continue with their plans, only a few minutes delayed. What he wanted to do was command his own time by telling his father he would not be bullied into sacrificing even a second with his wife. But it was senseless to defy his father. Choose his battles. She would wait for him.

He accepted the seat but ignored the brandy.

"I've prepared everything for you." Eugene pushed a stack of papers across the desk. "You need only follow the instructions I've provided. My solicitor is expecting you."

Harold frowned at the stack. "What's this?"

"An itemization of the investment amounts. I've adjusted the numbers from the capital provided by our guests and figured our own contribution. The solicitor should have received the marriage settlement by now, but I'll need you to explain to him the adjustments I've detailed in these papers, namely the percentage of Trethow's annual income to be allocated to the investment and the portioning of the dowry."

Squeezing his fingers until his knuckles cracked, Harold glowered, burning a hole into the stack with his glare, or so he hoped would happen if he stared at it long enough. "How much of any of these figures has been allocated to the debts? How much to the estate for new supplies? How much to rehire the steward?"

Eugene leaned back in his chair, resting his glass on his chest and propping his feet on the edge of the desk. "I'll not waste a ha'penny. All is to be used for this investment. If we go in short, we could lose the deal. The more we're in, the wealthier we'll be. This is the making of us, son! Don't be short-sighted. You'll leave before dawn tomorrow. The solicitor is expecting you."

"You won't listen to reason, will you?"

His father snarled. "It's *you* who's unreasonable. Just a pup. You don't know your head from your arse. When you're in my position, you'll understand."

Harold pinched the bridge of his nose. "I've not been married a full week, not been home from the last trip to London more than two weeks. This could be delayed."

A slap to the desk answered the request. "We need this sorted in advance of the ship setting sail. What if we miss our window of opportunity? What if the deal goes through before our backing arrives? I can't take that chance. You leave on the morrow."

Head bowed, Harold tried not to weep. His father would ruin them before the year ended. His only hope was that he would be proven mistaken and the investment would turn the profit his father anticipated. But then what? The profit, no matter how large, would be reinvested in another scheme, another opium deal, another chartered ship, perhaps a fleet next time. None of it would be used to pay the debts, none applied to the estate. He wanted to believe in his father. He did. Experience taught him otherwise.

Shoulders rounded, Harold wordlessly swept up the papers before leaving the study in defeat, the day spoiled.

Hazel greeted him in the entrance hall, her lips frowning but her eyes expectant.

He shook his head. "I'm afraid we must postpone."

She nodded, feigning a half-smile. "I understand. We can go tomorrow."

"Two weeks at least. I'm leaving tomorrow for London."

"London?" she echoed. "Tomorrow?"

"It can't be helped. My apologies." He regretted the briskness of his tone, but there was little he could offer to assuage the rejection she must feel.

They stared at each other, each silent, each calculating their next words.

The idea was farfetched, but what if she traveled with him? At least then they would have more opportunity to become acquainted. He would not feel the trip wasted. She would not be left in an unfamiliar house with his parents. It did complicate matters, as he would need to travel by carriage if she accompanied him, which would slow the pace and delay his arrival by at least a day, perhaps two, if not more, depending on how well she traveled — assuming his parents did not require the use of the carriage, of course. There were other complications. Morals. Conscience. It was *her* dowry and *her* family's income he was required to sort, applying them to an opium shipment, no less. There was naught he could do about it, but it plagued his conscience nonetheless.

All considered, he wanted her to come. Would she?

"The trip is business, not pleasure," he explained, hoping she would understand the situation fully so as not to be disappointed. "No parties, shopping, socializing. Only solicitor meetings and the like."

That was not how to invite a bride to accompany him. Would she prefer a lie? Or something more akin to the truth but far more lascivious? He could not very well say, *this is an opportunity for me to seduce you*.

Hazel made to speak several times but stopped herself. She tugged at her bottom lip instead. At length, she said, "I've always wanted to go to London, but…" She breathed a laugh. "Solicitor meetings sound dreadfully dull. I have much to sort here. My luggage has yet to arrive. Being here to receive it is best. I couldn't possibly go without my possessions or more clothes. It's a business trip, not pleasure."

Harold frowned. Was she making excuses because she did not want to go with him or because she truly wanted her luggage? Did she not want to be alone with him? The past few days of progress waned. If he were Driffield, she would not have hesitated to express her interest in going.

He ground his teeth.

"If you'll excuse me," he said. "I need to notify my valet and ready for departure. I—I apologize." Harold bowed then turned to take the stairs two at a time.

Chapter 13

L ady Collingwood flicked her wrist. "Greenery. We need more greenery. We can secure more from Lady Winthorp's hothouse. I *must* have greenery for the party."

Hazel took notes at the escritoire in the parlor. Her mother-in-law had been planning a supper party for the past hour, all of which sounded tedious and expensive, not that Hazel knew anything about finances, and not that the family needed to worry about such matters, but she could not recall her father going to such lengths for a simple supper party. From what Hazel was coming to realize, Lady Collingwood planned supper parties nigh weekly, each ranging from elegant to extravagant regardless of the number of guests.

"Do you think a soiree would be more appealing?" Her ladyship looked to the window. "The weather can be so dreary this time of year. Music ought to cheer spirits." Rather than wait for Hazel to answer, Lady Collingwood continued, "Strike out the greenery. For a soiree, I want more lighting instead. Candles. Candelabras filled with candles. Chandeliers filled with candles. Mirrors angled to reflect the light. Doesn't that sound lovely?"

By the time the list was completed to satisfaction, the longcase clock read half past eleven. Nana would be expecting her at noon.

Hazel changed into a warm walking dress as quickly as her lady's maid's fingers could work then headed for the dower house. Only one day since Harold had left for London, but already Hazel's schedule was filled. Not for a second would she mourn not being asked to go to London. Rather than invite her, he had insisted it was a business trip. She could see it as a sign that he did not want her there with him, or she could assume he meant what he said—it was a business trip wherein he would spend all day, every day, sequestered in offices with peri-wigged men. The latter made her feel more confident about staying at Trelowen. Had she gone to London, she would have been bored silly.

Nana welcomed her with an embrace when Hazel entered the parlor. The dowager baroness had dressed with exquisite perfection for a casual call, her coiffure as immaculate as the dress. The contrast between this version and the version of Nana that had stumbled into the drawing room barefoot and in her nightdress was astonishing. Hardly the same woman.

"Sit." Nana's voice crinkled like tissue paper, the hint of a sensual soprano beneath the cracks. "Tea is on the way. I've sent Mildred on an errand; we won't have her dreary face spying on us."

Hazel suspected Miss Mildred Pine would extend her errand overlong. The companion had failed to impress thus far.

"You're dressed for royalty, Nana." Hazel admired the dress's embroidery. "Are we expecting company?"

The baroness preened. "I have something special in mind, but it's not company. Something to show you. If you promise to call on me every day at noon."

Not that Hazel had pressing engagements to compete with the offer, but she would not have declined even if she did. She very much liked Nana. "I'm honored to be invited."

"Good. But I shan't show you my secret yet. I shall tease you for half an hour at least. Ah, here's tea."

A footman carried in the tray, bowed to them both, then closed the door behind him. As the leaves steeped, Nana placed two biscuits each onto the saucers.

"Lady Collingwood and I have been planning a supper party," Hazel said. "Or maybe it's a soirée. I'm not certain she settled on one over the other."

Nana snorted a laugh. "My daughter-in-law is the least sensible person of my acquaintance. Pretty as a parasol and just as useless."

"Nana!"

"I can say these things because I'm the one who arranged their marriage. I couldn't resist her for Eugene. Those big blue eyes and simpering sighs. The belle of the county in her day. Still is. But I hate to think of her guiding you. You need a mentor. Allow me."

Hazel accepted the teacup with biscuit-adorned saucer, looking wide eyed to Nana who was as lucid as Hazel had ever seen her. "For whatever purpose?"

Nana tasted her tea, made a face, then added two lumps of sugar. "There's a great deal to learn about running a household, more so for an estate. Tell me, what has your mother taught you?"

"Nothing, I'm afraid. She died in childbed with my brother."

The baroness polished off both biscuits before adding two more to her saucer. "Then you have a hand in running the household in her stead?"

Hazel shook her head. "My father runs the household. I've never had a part in it."

Nana harrumphed. "It's these modern sensibilities. No one knows how to raise children anymore. Too lackadaisy. Lazy and ignorant children. From the cradle, they must be taught how to manage the household; men learn ledgers and accounts, tenants and farming, and politics, while the women learn leadership of the staff, hosting and entertaining, socializing with other families, and house upkeep." She took a bite of her third biscuit then waved it in the air. "There's a great deal more than that, but you understand my meaning. One cannot simply walk into a household and *not* know what to do. These are important matters! One cannot learn early enough one's roles and duties."

Hazel gulped as her grandmother-in-law finished another biscuit.

"God willing," the baroness continued, "it will be a long time in coming before you become baroness, but I'll not have you unprepared. Helena can't be trusted to guide you. Head of fluff." Two more biscuits down. Two more added to the saucer. "Have you met the staff?"

Nodding, Hazel gave her first biscuit a little nibble — *mmm, divine*. Nana added two more to Hazel's saucer.

"Good. Let's begin tomorrow. But first, we must establish the most important point. Eugene has an air of self-importance, always has, even as a child, but don't let that depress you. He can be managed. As his wife, you are in the perfect position to do so."

Mid nibble, Hazel stilled.

Nana continued, "The best way to handle him is just that—to handle him. Don't let him bully you with arrogance. Stand your ground."

"Do you mean Harold? Harold is arrogant and bullying?"

The baroness's teacup rattled in its saucer. She looked back at Hazel, startled. "Harold isn't arrogant or bullying. He's an angel. Why would you ask such a thing?"

Setting her tea aside, Hazel shook her head and smiled. It was a subtle lapse, nothing terrible. Nana had slipped into a memory of having this same conversation with Helena. A brief lapse, nothing of concern.

"Oh!" Nana leapt from her chair, nearly spilling her tea in the process. "The surprise!" Shoving yet another biscuit between her lips, she scuttled to an embroidery basket near the hearth, her dress swishing in accompaniment.

Rather than bring the basket, as Hazel expected, the baroness tossed out the thread and fabric, dug deep into the basket, then carried back with her a stack of paper. However helpful this mentoring sounded, reading lists of instructions was as unappealing as taking notes for her mother-in-law. She glanced around the room for a clock. Nothing. Excuses formed one after the other as to why she would need to return to the main house. Would the baroness require her to memorize the staff hierarchy, study the duties to accomplish between fixed hours of the day, analyze scenarios of what could and could not be said to guests? She grimaced at the stack when Nana returned to her seat.

With a gleeful sort of smugness, the baroness rifled through the pages then pulled one out to thrust into Hazel's lap.

Mouth agape at the paper before her, Hazel's expression betrayed her shock.

Nana giggled.

Oh my!

Hazel turned the paper one way then another. The image remained the same from every angle. Her cheeks flamed with embarrassment.

Oh my!

Sketched in red chalk, a woman reclined on a settee. Nude. The woman, not the settee. *Nude.* Nothing left to the imagination.

One leg stretched before her, one bent at the knee. One arm draped over the edge of the settee, one curved over her head.

Through Hazel's shock, Nana continued to giggle. "Do you like it?"

That was not a question Hazel was prepared to answer. Was it too late to wish for the hierarchy of staff? The sketch was painstakingly detailed.

"Do you see the resemblance?" Nana asked.

With much effort, Hazel lifted her gaze.

"It's me. You see now?"

Her eyes trailed, unwilling, back to the paper, the fire rekindling in her cheeks. Yes, she saw the resemblance now. Only just. The pucker of the lips. The shape of the eyes. The baroness could not be more than twenty in the sketch.

Nana shoved another paper into Hazel's hands, this one another nude, but rather than one sketch, there were many scattered across the paper, all at different angles, all a different pose. As Hazel turned the paper this way and that, she realized there were more on the back. Her grandmother-in-law rustled the papers. So many pages. *So many*. Did she plan to show Hazel all of them?

Grimacing an attempt at a smile, Hazel said, "They're, um, lovely."

"My Horace was an artist. I was his favorite subject. Let's keep this between us, shall we?"

As if Hazel planned to tout the news around town that the Dowager Lady Collingwood had a propensity for posing in bare flesh and that the newly minted Mrs. Hobbs had admired the result. No, that was not a topic Hazel ever wished to share with another living soul.

"This one," Nana said, pulling out a new sheet, "is a personal favorite."

While smaller sketches adorned the edges, the center of the paper focused on a woman in repose at the bank of the lake, as naked as the others but less scandalous since the woman's eyes were closed rather than staring unnervingly at the viewer with a look that shook Hazel to her heels. This sketch was bound to be a favorite. The chalk, black this time, spoke of a soul-deep admiration of artist for subject no viewer could fail to see.

For another hour complete, Hazel remained with Nana, the two poring over the drawings. By the tenth work, Hazel had grown accustomed to the sight, the shock having run its course. Seeing how proud Nana was to share them with her helped abate their scandalous nature, and truly, what was so scandalous about two people in love? What should have shocked Hazel more was the sly smiles and innuendos Nana made with each new drawing. That she said these things was shocking. That it was she saying them was more shocking. Once past this shock, as well, Hazel concluded she liked the Dowager Baroness Collingwood very much indeed.

Rather than take the path to the main house, she ventured to the lake, curious if she would recognize the sketch location.

The water was still, reflecting the grey sky above. As inviting as the bank, the promise of cold earth deterred her from sitting. Next time she would bring a blanket. Next time she could walk the perimeter.

Until her toes turned icy and her teeth chattered, she stared out to the lake, admiring the peacefulness. Twice now she had missed the opportunity for a boat ride. Something to look forward to rather than something to regret, she reminded herself. However lonely the coming weeks might be with only Lord and Lady Collingwood for company — the former ignoring her and the latter considering her a personal secretary rather than a daughter-in-law — she did not think she would be lonely. Alone, yes, but lonely, no. Now she had Nana. Should Nana be too busy for company despite her solicitation for daily visits, there was a house to make her own and staff to befriend. If all else failed, Hazel had herself for company, and no one had ever accused her of not liking her own company. Yes, it was for the best she did not go to London. She and Harold had all the time in the world to get to know one another.

When she turned towards the path to return to the house, she laughed to have spied at last the spot sketched in infamy.

The next day followed similarly. Lady Collingwood dictated to Hazel the invitations for the supper party. At noon, Nana regaled Hazel with stories, lessons, and more artwork — to Hazel's relief the deceased baron's sketches were not all scandalous. Two hours later, the lake reflected a leaden sky that promised bone-chilling rain, a threat Hazel ignored in her admiration of the landscape. She breathed in the wonder of this being *hers*.

Not all proceeded as it had the day before, for today brought an unexpected visitor.

Hazel emerged from the wilderness path and burrowed deeper into her winter cloak. Without the protection of the trees, she was at the mercy of the biting wind. Only days prior, it had been warm. Autumn played the trickster this year.

Some kilometers ahead, a figure and horse approached the stables, little more than a silhouette against the grey backdrop. Hazel squinted. A groom trotted to the figure, exchanged words, then escorted the horse to the stables, leaving the caller to head to the house. When said caller turned, he spotted Hazel and waved.

Although she could not yet make out the gentleman, her heart skipped a beat. Had Harold's plans changed?

"Mrs. Hobbs!" called out the man as he drew closer.

Hazel quickened her pace, all aflutter with anticipation and giddiness.

"Mrs. Hobbs, what a delight to spy you here, for you are the very person I've come to see." Dressed for riding, Lord Kissinger jogged the short stretch between them.

Disheartened that the viscount — cutting a fine figure in his buckskins and caped greatcoat — had not been Harold, but not disappointed by the caller's identity, Hazel smiled in greeting.

"Good afternoon, Lord Kissinger. You're in time for tea." She nodded towards the house.

"I had planned to invite you for a turn about the garden since time is not on my side today, but given the bluster of the weather, I'll accept." He fell in step with her. "Would a cup of chocolate be out of the question?"

"A request I can oblige with relish. To be honest, I've had enough tea today to last a week. Oh, and biscuits, as well. If I see another elderberry biscuit before this week ends, I may faint."

Lord Kissinger laughed. "It is a memorable day when you're forced to partake of endless tea and elderberry biscuits. In the event I find myself parched and near starvation, desperate for the sustenance which only tea and elderberry biscuits can provide, where should I look?"

"No further than the dower house, my lord."

"Ah, yes, Nana. It's been more than three years since I've had the pleasure of her company."

They entered by way of the terrace door, the most direct route to the drawing room. In short order, Hazel summoned for two cups of chocolate and saw to the seated comfort of her guest. Her first guest!

"The last time we spoke," she said, "I had only days prior traded my family name for Harold's. Do you find me much changed after a week of marriage?" She pulled back her shoulders and struck a pose.

Lord Kissinger assessed her in a dramatized perusal. "Indeed, you are much altered. From supper guest to hostess, confident and content. You *are* content, are you not?"

She hoped her composure did not slip or betray her hesitation. Content was an apt word, she supposed, although not a sentiment she would have immediately attributed to her feelings. Each day brought a new surprise. Each day she made herself a little more at home. Content might be an accurate assessment of her state of being, as would titillated, anxious, excited, or any other word that expressed conflicting emotions of anticipation. Would she be more or less content with Harold home? Both. Was it possible to be both more and less content simultaneously?

Her answer was less involved. "Yes, I'm content."

The drawing room door opened, then, to admit Mr. Quainoo with the tray.

Once the butler retreated and the door closed, Kissinger said, "Daunting is your task, Mrs. Hobbs, to make a home amongst strangers. I commend you the ease with which you've accepted the role of hostess, wife, and daughter. My friend is a lucky man to have a wife such as yourself."

Although he did not know anything about her outside of the scandal, Hazel nevertheless blushed and believed him earnest. He sounded earnest.

He added, "Trust me when I say he knows how lucky he is."

Tilting her head slightly, she quizzed him with raised eyebrows.

The viscount mirrored her expression. "You wouldn't have me gossip about my own friend, would you?" When she did not reply, he said with a conspiratorial smile that implied he had intended to do just that from the start, "He was taken with you at first sight."

Hazel gasped. "Poppycock!"

"'Tis true."

She hid her grin behind her cup of chocolate, hoping her trembling fingers did not give away how eager she was to hear more.

"He could speak of little else, I assure you. Intended to pay you court once he ascertained if his attentions would be welcomed. You've made him the happiest of men, Mrs. Hobbs."

Could it all be true? Had he intended to court her? Goodness. She was as flustered now as she had been when she hoped the caller was Harold.

Kissinger had more to say. "You'll find him to be the very best of men. All he needs is a nod of encouragement, and he will be the most devoted husband."

The viscount did not stay above half an hour. Before leaving, he invited her to call on his family and implored her to consider him her friend. Should she need ought, send word.

Her new friend may have absented the room, but his words had not. Hazel reflected on those words for some time, each passing second curving her lips into a broader smile. Harold had been taken with her at first sight!

"No, not at all scandalous. Liberating!" said the Dowager Lady Collingwood. "You're tempted. I can see it in your expression. How is it you've never tried it before?"

Hazel could not imagine how her expression revealed temptation when she more likely resembled a startled hare. "It's never crossed my mind. Not once."

"Fiddlesticks." Nana leaned forward. "You can tell me."

"Honestly! Never." Angling closer to Nana, she swept the room with a quick glance. Not that anyone had entered since bringing the tea tray, but she dared not take the chance of a rogue parlor maid lingering in a corner. In a whisper, she asked, "What does it *feel* like?"

Nana's eyes glinted with mischief; the same mischief Hazel swore she had seen in Harold's eyes on more than one occasion.

"It tickles in all the right places, if you catch my meaning."

Hazel gasped. "Nana!"

"You asked, child." She leaned back against the chair and laughed. "Pray, more tea and, I think, one more biscuit."

The dutiful pupil, Hazel tipped the pot to refill and added three biscuits to Nana's saucer, winking as she passed the cup.

"There is nothing more freeing than that first dive into the lake," Nana said before taste testing the tea then waving for more sugar. "The water glides over bare skin like sauce over goose. A little nude bathing does the spirit good. I challenge you to try it. Although you should wait until the weather is warmer. Would catch your death this time of year."

There was no denying it, Hazel thought during her walk home after the third day of visiting the dower house. Nana was improving. Every minute, every hour, and every day Hazel spent with her, the baroness was more lucid, less likely to confuse Hazel for Helena, less prone to drifting in and out of memory. Oh, she shared memories aplenty, but she always knew she was sharing a story of the past to someone in the present rather than reliving a lost moment. Given how well the baroness was doing, Hazel wondered if her lapses were due to loneliness rather than any grave malady. The poor dear must be dreadfully alone in the dower house with only the frowny-faced faradilly of a companion to keep her company.

It was with this promising realization that Hazel returned to the dower house on the fourth day.

The sky rumbled with ominous, charcoal clouds. No nude bathing today, she thought with a quiet laugh. A knock to the front door brought the butler who guided her to the parlor she now knew so well. Rather than find Nana waiting for her with the usual biscuit-laden tray, Hazel found Miss Pine embroidering by the hearth, back stiff and movements halting.

"Good afternoon, Miss Pine," Hazel said, glancing around the room for clues to Nana's whereabouts. Granted, it had only been a few days, but not once had the baroness missed their standing appointment. "Is Lady Collingwood not expecting me?"

The companion gave a sniff and shrug then turned back to her embroidery hoop.

Unsure if she should interrogate the girl, find the butler, leave, or wait, she chose the path of least resistance. Perching on the edge of her usual chair, she waited. And waited. And waited. So quiet was the room, she could hear the tug of Miss Pine's thread through the fabric.

Either fifteen minutes or fifteen seconds later—she could not be certain which—she turned sideways in her chair to eye Miss Pine. "Is Lady Collingwood joining us soon?" Hazel used the word *us* loosely since the baroness would boot out the companion the second she arrived.

Miss Pine shrugged again. Only after a lengthy pause and when Hazel suspected she would say no more, did the girl volunteer, "I spose so. She's out for her daily constitutional."

Thunder vibrated the windows. Dead leaves rustled by on a gust of wind.

"She's *outside*? For a *walk*? For how long has she been on this walk?" Not that Hazel was privy to Nana's daily schedule, but a walk prior to tea had never been mentioned.

She racked her memory for some hint that perhaps Nana was to meet her at the main house today.

There had been idle talk of spending time at the main house so Nana could show her a few things, features of the old house she found remarkable, tips on handling entertainments such as where guests should sit so as not to view the servant entrances, and so forth, but Hazel could not recall any mention of that happening today.

Miss Pine did not bother to look up from her frame when she said, "I'm not 'er keeper. She's a grown woman, ain't she? Gone walking is all."

Fidgeting, eyeing the windows as the sky darkened and the wind swayed tree branches, waiting, waiting, waiting, and finally heaving a harrumph, Hazel took her leave of Miss Pine to find the butler. The gentle soul that was Mr. Somners had the thoughtfulness to be easily found in the entrance hall, sharing a word with the footman who oft brought their tray.

"Pardon my intrusion," Hazel said when they halted conversation at the sight of her, "but I was wondering if you knew the whereabouts of Lady Collingwood. Was she not expecting me today?"

Mr. Somners's forehead wrinkled in surprise. "She's not with Miss Pine? She should have joined you by now. I had assumed her to be with her lady's maid — she prefers looking her best when you call — delayed only briefly."

The butler fidgeted with his waistcoat, as discomposed as Hazel felt.

The footman looked from Mr. Somners to Hazel and back again, his features pinched. "There's her morning walk. Did anyone see her return?"

Tension choked the air. Had it been anyone other than Nana. Had she not had prior lapses.

The hair on the back of Hazel's neck stood on end as thunder shuddered the front door and another gust whistled around the corners of the small manor. In short order, the butler dispatched two footmen to explore outside and one to check the main house, as well as one to inquire after the lady's maid. Hazel, torn between staying and searching, at last donned her cloak to brave the outdoors, against the butler's advice. Her destination the lake.

She could have sent a footman to the lake, but nothing nor no one would convince her to wait in the parlor with Miss Pine, not while distraught. Had it been anyone but Nana, the whole of the household would have assumed her enjoying a respite or taking advantage of solitude in another room. But it was not someone else. It was Nana.

And it was about to chuck down rain.

The wind tore through Hazel's cloak and dress, raising goose flesh on her arms and shivering her limbs. The weather had no right to turn this cold so fast. She crossed her arms over her chest to hold in warmth as she headed for the wilderness path.

As soon as the trees welcomed her into their fold, a chilling darkness descended. Bare branches waved; trunks creaked; the leaf-covered forest floor crackled in muffled protest. In the distance, a footman called Lady Collingwood's name, still in search for the baroness, his voice a mere whisper as the copse suppressed the sound. Veering at the fork in the path, Hazel quickened her pace to the lake.

Ahead, the still water peeked through the part in the trees.

A sound stopped her in her tracks.

A *pitapat*, like fairy feet running through the underbrush. A *tink*, like the clang of hammer against anvil.
A *potsun-potsun*, like a spoonful of sugar into tea.

The forest gave nothing away, but the lake ahead
muttered the sounds of rain, rain against dead leaves,
rain against the boathouse, rain against the lake water.
Hazel hoisted her petticoat and sprinted. Fat rain-
drops splayed her curls across her forehead when she
reached the edge of the path. Wiping a hand across
her eyes, she surveyed the bank and surrounding
clearing.

Her heart pounded in competition with the rain.
What if Nana had slipped? What if she had fallen?
What if...

There. At the site sketched in infamy. The
Dowager Lady Collingwood stood, bare fleshed,
staring absently at the lake. Careful not to slip on
grass moistening to mud, Hazel scrambled for her
grandmother-in-law.

She wrenched off her cloak. "Nana!"

The baroness jerked at the sound, turning to face
Hazel. Her brows knit in confusion as she took in her
surroundings.

"Where's Horace?" she asked.

Hazel wrapped the cloak around Nana's trembling body, the woman's skin icy and pale.

"Where's Horace?" she repeated.

Nowhere could Hazel spy the baroness's clothes.
The cloak would have to do. Rain pelted her cheeks
and blinded her between rapid blinks. She guided
Nana back to the path, the woman's shoulders rounding in compliance. The one happy thought Hazel
had—the silver-lining in the chalk-grey clouds—as

she wrapped an arm around Nana's waist to hold her steady was that at least her grandmother-in-law had not put up a fight to return to the house, for that was a moment's concern when the baroness's body tensed as Hazel tightened the cloak about her.

The baroness stumbled a time or two, her bare feet pink and muddy, but she held her own until one of the footmen caught up with them at the fork in the path. With a muttered apology and a hasty entreaty, he hooked a hold behind Nana's legs and shoulders and hoisted her into his arms as though she weighed no more than a babe.

Looking over the man's shoulders at Hazel, Nana said, "You always spoil my fun, Helena."

Chapter 14

Empty London streets greeted Harold that evening, his second evening in town. He had made excellent travel time, arriving on the third day, far better time than he had made on the prior trip, but then he did not have a wife waiting at home on the previous occasion. His valet and trunk beat him by an hour, much to his surprise and Abhijeet's conceit.

Supper at White's awaited him. Drowning his guilt in the best meal London had to offer was his plan. On the morrow, he would meet with the solicitor to sort out the accounts, distributions, and investment, so for now there was nothing to do except eat his guilt over leaving Hazel at Trelowen and knowing his father's trickery of the Trethow family. Hindsight showed him he should have insisted she join him, commanded she join him. At the very least, he could have *asked*. His implications of her coming along had seemed clear at the time, not so upon reflection.

The first night in London had him tossing and turning, despite his exhaustion from the trip, for he could not remove the vision of her sitting at home, dejected, ignored by his parents, regretting the marriage. So alone she must feel. So rejected.

His thoughts ran a darker course this evening. Would she take advantage of his absence to write to

Driffield? Try as he might to heed Patrick's advice to rid himself of thoughts of the Earl of Driffield, the ghost of the rake haunted the shadows of his mind, leering and jeering, free to carry out his wicked plans now that Hazel was safe under the guise of marriage. Adultery happened every day, after all. Marry for family, status, and wealth; love could be found elsewhere. Harold could not return to Trelowen fast enough, if for no other reason than to assure himself she was still there.

What he did not expect that evening was a run-in with the devil himself.

As though summoned by thought, the Earl of Driffield walked out of the card room as Harold reached the top of the hall stairs by the dining hall at White's. The two locked eyes.

Harold curled his fingers into fists. Driffield showed no signs of recognition.

With a curt nod, Harold entered the dining hall and made for his reserved table, hoping that would be the last he saw of the villain. Of all people! The odds were astounding. What the man could be doing in London, and so soon after the hunting party, Harold could only guess. Gambling, among other vices?

For the stretch of a glass of wine, he brooded. But oh ho, a happy thought intruded — if Driffield were in London, he could not be in Devonshire serenading Hazel. Happy thought indeed! His smugness lingered only long enough for his meal to arrive, for as soon as he skewered his meat for the first savory bite, Lord Driffield approached the table, pulled out the chair across from Harold, and sat without invitation.

Fork suspended, Harold stared. Blinked. Set down his cutlery.

"Have you heard," Driffield asked, "that White's is rumored to relocate next year?"

Harold frowned. "I've not."

"Now you have. A house on the east side is the rumor."

"Ah." He resumed his meal, taking a meaty bite and chewing slowly, his eyes trained on his opponent.

Could he call the man an opponent? Harold was the victor, was he not? If one called marriage victory, then he was the winner and Driffield the loser. But did the earl see it that way?

Driffield nodded to a waiter for a drink. "I assume you're here for the opium deal."

Harold stabbed another piece of meat.

"Lord Collingwood promised to move swiftly by sending you to arrange for the investment. I admit I had hoped our paths would cross. I have questions about the deal, specifically about the disbursement of profits when this succeeds."

"I'm afraid you'll have to communicate all questions to my father. I'm only the messenger." His appetite waned each time the man spoke. A small favor the topic was the investment and not Hazel.

"My questions are simple enough, even for you." Driffield gave a slow smile, a cunning smile.

With a dab of his napkin, Harold once more set aside his cutlery, his appetite lost. He leaned back, crossed his arms over his chest, and waited.

For twenty minutes while his supper turned cold, Harold fielded questions about the deal. Which ship?

Who was the captain? Where were the ports? How many others invested? On and on the man questioned, every movement that of a hunter assessing his prey, but Harold suspected it an act—the man was nervous about the deal, in need of money, perhaps in as much need as his own father. A risky gambler he was rumored to be, and Harold had just seen him coming from the card room. The man needed money. Fast. And in large quantities.

Driffield's motive clear, Harold relaxed. This was the last man he wanted to converse with, and he did not particularly care for the conversation topic, but it could have been worse.

Once the waiter cleared Harold's plate, Driffield rose to leave.

Smoothing his coat, he said, "Good talk, Mr. Hobbs." He turned away and took a step before swiveling back. "On second thought, I should take this opportunity to thank you for cleaning up the… inconvenience. It's men like you, Mr. Hobbs, we can count on to smooth…indiscretions."

As Driffield turned away again, Harold stood so quickly his chair rocked, nearly toppling. He took two steps to the earl, his hand touching the man's coat sleeve. Driffield looked down at Harold's hand, his eyes narrowing.

In a low rumble, Harold said, "If you bother my wife, you'll answer to me."

So tense was the air, Harold felt a bead of sweat form at the base of his spine.

The earl cocked his head to one side. "Your wife?"

Through gritted teeth, Harold said, "My wife." His hand remained on the coat sleeve.

"The busybody?" Driffield frowned. He stared over Harold's shoulder in thought, then with a brusque laugh looked back. "Yes, we can always count on men like you." Shaking his arm free of the grasp, he patted Harold's shoulder. "If there's one thing I can promise you, Mr. Hobbs, it's that I have less interest in your wife than I have in a broodmare for my carriage." With another laugh and shake of his head, Driffield strode out of the dining hall.

Abhijeet wiped a cloth over one of Harold's riding boots. "Curious."

"It is, isn't it? His expression when I mentioned my wife…it was as though he didn't know her. When he remembered, he called her a busybody. What do you make of it? A red herring? A forgettable flirt?"

Harold sat in the dressing room an hour after his encounter with the Earl of Driffield. His valet listened to the exchange with interest.

Abhijeet ran a final stroke over the newly polished boot before swapping it for the other. "I hesitate to say this. I don't wish either of us to misinterpret a situation about which we already know the facts, but rumor belowstairs has changed course."

Resting his forearms on his thighs and lacing his fingers, Harold prompted, "Tell me."

"I've not said anything since all is better off forgotten and rumor adds to more rumor."

Harold circled his hands as if he could reel the information out of his valet.

"It's the parlor maid, sir. She believes Mrs. Hobbs is innocent. Claims to have attended a Miss Plumb in the reception room adjacent to the parlor while the earl and Mrs. Hobbs née Trethow were compromised together. Answered the bellrope, Polly did. Says Miss Plumb was in a state of chaos and pleading to summon Lady Williamson. Polly did just that. Her ladyship escorted Miss Plumb to the guest wing, and that was that."

The tale hung in the air. Harold covered his face with his hands, trying to make sense of what Abhijeet revealed in light of Driffield's reactions.

Without moving his hands from his face, Harold asked, "Do you suppose Miss Plumb was serving as sentinel? To allow alone time between Driffield and…"

"If Polly is to be believed, it was the other way around. She didn't like to speak ill of an unmarried woman, but she insinuated that the condition of Miss Plumb's dishabille did not speak well of the situation."

"What the devil happened in that room, then?"

"I don't know, sir," Abhijeet admitted. "It's one reason I never shared what I heard. Complicates what doesn't need to be complicated. Two women in the parlor with one gentleman? Not something to be said to the husband of one of those women."

Harold slid his hands down his face as he peered up at his valet. "The devil."

Abhijeet bowed his head to concentrate on extracting a scuff from the boot.

"No. No, *she* was serving lookout," Harold muttered more to himself than to his companion.

A flash of memory. A memory that had haunted him just as Driffield had. Walking the wilderness path, he had come upon Hazel, seemingly alone in the forest. Then he had spotted Driffield in the distance. A lover's tryst. The whole scene unfolded in a far different way than he had first seen it, with Hazel serving sentry for her friend's tryst with Driffield, Miss Plumb hidden by the undergrowth, supine before Driffield.

The devil.

Why would Hazel not tell him the truth? Why allow herself to be ruined to save the guilty party? Ah, foolish questions. She would still have been ruined. Why not confess after marriage? Then, when had he ever given her a chance or a reason to trust him? Even after marriage, she protected her friend's honor.

All speculation. He would know nothing until he confronted her. But he knew he was right.

The blazing fire warmed the drawing room of the main house, a coze contrasting the frosty deluge outside.

Hazel stared aghast at her mother- and father-in-law. "She could have died!"

Helena flicked her wrist. "So dramatic. After a time, you'll become accustomed to her need for attention."

"Her need for—" Hazel bit back her anger-weighted tone. The last thing she needed was to insult her new family or appear ungrateful for all they had done for her and the Trethows. She took three deep breaths and said, "I'm concerned for her safety and wellbeing."

Lord Collingwood eyed the clock. "Yes, well, we've offered for her to move in, but she won't hear of it. Too independent, too stubborn."

Helena chortled. "You both forget. She already has a companion. We needn't worry. The companion keeps her content. If you're concerned, simply instruct the companion to keep a better eye on her. That makes perfect sense to me."

Toeing the line of insolence, Hazel replied, "The companion wasn't the least concerned about Nana's whereabouts. A good companion would have accompanied her."

"Independent and stubborn," Lord Collingwood muttered, leaning an elbow on the arm of the chair, ready to rise.

Lady Collingwood shook her head at Hazel as though pitying a puppy who had messed on the rug. "It's all so clear. Don't you see? The companion needs instruction. Remind her of her position and instruct her to follow Nana. She'll understand and obey."

Meeting adjourned, read Lord Collingwood's expression.

Why it should fall to Hazel to have a word with Miss Pine made little sense. She had been an official resident of Trelowen for eleven days, not exactly an authority who wielded control over the companion's position. The mere thought of confronting Miss Pine and ordering her about made Hazel's stomach churn. A sniff and shrug would be the response.

Hazel spent a sleepless night, struggling against the recurring vision of Nana rooted at the edge of the lake, despondent, waiting for her husband. The next morning was the first opportunity for Hazel to return to the dower house, the rain having abated in the wee hours. When she arrived, Mr. Somners escorted her to the first floor. The Dowager Baroness Collingwood's bedchamber took Hazel by surprise, although after the time spent together, she need not be shocked. While the furniture was sparse, the paintings were not. If wallpaper adorned the walls, Hazel had no way of knowing. Every inch of every wall was covered by gilded art, the subjects varying from the estate's lake to the baroness herself.

She did not know where to look first. That was until her gaze fell on the French Rococo bed in the center of the room. Propped on countless pillows, each as ornate as the bed frame, and enveloped by blankets sat Nana, looking one-part regal and one-part worryingly frail. As soon as the door closed, the baroness waved Hazel to sit. A chair had been positioned next to the bed, awaiting her arrival, alongside a table with a tray full of elderberry biscuits. Hazel could not resist a smile.

After kissing Nana's cheek, Hazel fluffed her skirts and sat, wasting no time to ready the tea as though it were a normal day and a normal visit, not the morning after chaos or in a bedchamber with a weary widow who bore sunken eyes framed by dark circles. The episode had taken its toll. What Hazel wanted to know but dared not ask was if this was the worst incident or merely one in many.

Words raspy, akin to claws against fabric, the baroness asked, "Are you shocked?"

"By what, Nana?"

"The tea tray. That I knew you were coming. You're far too early for our appointment." Before Hazel could answer, Nana winked. "I have spies everywhere. I knew you were on the way before you had left the house." Her chuckle dissolved into a wheezing cough.

"I see you're in good spirits today," Hazel said once Nana stopped coughing long enough to lay her head against a pillow, a satisfied smile curving her lips.

"You've fallen for my ruse. How else was I to get you into my bedchamber to show you the paintings?" She arced her arm at the walls. "They're all tokens of love from my husband. Our world memorialized by his hand."

What Hazel wanted to do was look at each painting, one at a time, no matter how long it took, but now was not the time, not with the pressing matter of Nana's safety.

"When you're feeling spry, you must tour each painting with me," Hazel said, working herself up for the task at hand. "For now, drink your tea, and tell me when the physician is coming."

"No physician. A walk in the cool air does the body good, balances the humors. A sedentary day with pleasant company is all I need. Now, are you going to put those biscuits on the plate, or shall I starve?"

By Nana's maneuvering, the conversation turned to pleasantries, paintings, and pillows. Hazel would not be distracted from her mission, although she wondered if it were too soon to broach the matter. No matter how much the baroness smiled or how many jests she shared, no matter how cheery her disposition between bouts of wheezing, Hazel was not fooled and would not be deterred. If rejected, she would try again tomorrow. And the next day. And the day after.

Her chance presented itself when Nana said, "A pity we could not proceed today as planned. I had hoped to show you the sneak-and-peek servant hall behind the first-floor saloon. I wager that's a feature Helena excluded when she showed you the house."

"About that…" Hazel folded her hands in her lap to still the tremble of anticipation. "I've been thinking. Since you have so much to teach me and show me, would it not be easier if you lived with us at the main house? Not to say you cannot retreat to the dower house whenever it pleases you, but it seems a shame for us to be so far apart when there is a perfectly lovely room down the hall from me waiting to be adorned by all these paintings. An ornamental ceiling, latticed casement windows with a splendid view. We would be doors apart rather than a forest apart. At least for the winter months?"

Nana rested her saucer atop a pillow, laid her head back, and closed her eyes. For so long was she silent that Hazel began to suspect she had fallen asleep. Her chest rose and fell in deep breaths.

"The yellow room or the green?"

"Either? I had thought the yellow cheeriest." Hazel laced her fingers, anxious and hopeful.

Another stretch of silence passed, filled only by the rasping inhale of those slumberous breaths. "Harold tried this, as well, I'll have you know."

"To convince you to choose the yellow over the green?"

Nana wheezed. "I'll tell you what I didn't tell him. I believe you'll understand. A woman should.

No one wants to live where they are not wanted. To be a nuisance. To be powerless in one's own home, scorned or ignored. A fate I wouldn't wish on anyone, least of all myself. And before you protest with what I would have expected from my grandson had I told him this — all that rubbish about how I really am wanted and not a nuisance — know that I would have believed him had he said it, for he would have meant it, but what good would it have done me had he left for India again? A young gentleman has no use for his grandmother, even if he means well."

A coughing fit interrupted her. Hazel refilled the teacup and held it out, but the baroness waved it away.

Rubbing her chest, Nana continued, "We have much to accomplish, you and I. Mentoring from inside this mausoleum is impractical and undesirable. Until you become so busy that I collect dust, I'll take the yellow room."

Hazel exhaled her worry. How easy this had been! She had expected an epic battle of dueling words.

Nana added, "My companion may have the green room."

"And about that…" Hazel took another breath, readying once more for battle.

"Don't say it. You can't abide her. She may be Friday-faced, but she doesn't fuss as would another companion. I can't stomach being fussed over. I won't have it."

"But, Nana, your safe — "

"I won't hear it. I'll not have a do-good following my every step. Miss Pine serves me well and reads a good tale. The green room, please." She paused, then clapped her hands and chortled. "The *green* room for Miss *Pine*. What a lark!"

The print on the newspaper blurred. Harold stared, unseeing, his mind kilometers away. For much of his morning meal, he had absently read the same line, each time his attention drifting away from the article and back to the encounter with Lord Driffield, followed closely by a recounting of Abhijeet's tale from the parlor maid. There was a great deal to analyze. Every memory of his wife was unpacked. Every look. Every word. He recalled each time he had watched her for signs of affection for the earl, even at their wedding breakfast, and each of those times he had seen only a blushing young lady with gaze fixed on her husband.

Through two cups of coffee he revisited their wedding night. How daft could he have been?

"If you're not going to read the paper I so painstakingly acquired for you, pass it my way," Abhijeet said from across the table.

Harold looked up, eyes unfocused, his mind lingering on other matters.

"Pass it." Abhijeet nodded to the paper and beckoned with his fingers.

Pushing it across the table, Harold walked to the sideboard to refill the coffee. Not that he needed a third cup, but it was so weak he might as well have been drinking flavored water.

The two men broke their fast together in the second-floor sitting room adjacent to the dressing room so that Harold could confer with his valet before the meeting with the solicitor. Harold needed to focus. Once he instructed the solicitor, his hands would be tied. His hands were already tied, truthfully, for he could not disobey his father, nor did he possess any legal power over the finances, but he was hopeful he could reconfigure the numbers with a touch of cunning. He just had to focus.

Abhijeet poked at the newspaper, *The West-India Monthly Packet of Intelligence*. "Nawab is raising trade taxes again."

"How trustworthy is news from the west about the goings on of the east? He raised trade taxes before we left. The information could be dated." Harold took his seat and buttered a piece of toast.

"Undoubtedly a new tax."

"Splendid." Harold groaned. "Do you think the captain will raise his demands again? I told Father I didn't trust the man." Dipping the toast into his now cold eggs, Harold tried to enjoy his sawdust-flavored breakfast. No offense to the cook. Nothing had flavor while his mind was so unpleasantly occupied.

"The captain has risks of his own," Abhijeet said. "The next article mentions traders' shifting allegiance by fair or foul means. Our intrepid captain risks a run in with the East India Company, as well as the authorities in China. With each new risk, the price rises. And now the tax to contend with."

"More credit than I afford him. What assurance do we have the investment is safe? None. It is one thing to trade in tea with reputable traders, quite another to trade in opium with a man motivated by greed. Cargo chartered by Englishmen with shallow pockets is too easily acquired by the Company with deeper pockets."

"Here. Read." Abhijeet pushed the paper back across the table.

Resuming where he had tried to read earlier, Harold focused his attention on the article. His valet understated the situation. Rumors were that the smaller trading ships "lost" at sea were not in fact lost but being made examples of as a threat for the larger trading ships to heed — join the Company or face the same fate. Countless captains became faithful by coercion, allowing charters only by the Company and forfeiting any capital earned from non-Company investors. It was the stuff of stories, no proof to any of it. But that was the funny aspect of stories. The more ridiculous, the more likely true.

Harold exhaled from his cheeks. There was nothing he could do. He might as well set fire to every penny in their account. As far as he could see, there were one hundred thousand reasons not to invest in opium trading and only one reason to do so. Luck was not a sound reason. Yet he had no authority to do anything other than act on his father's wishes.

Tossing the paper aside, he reached for the ledgers he was to give to the solicitor on behalf of his father. How many times had he and Abhijeet already combed the numbers?

One hundred thousand.

An awe-inspiring number.

That was not the number of times they had examined the ledger in search of a loophole that would allow Harold a way to reconfigure the amounts without legal or paternal repercussions. That was the cost of the charter.

Hazel's dowry, he saw, was twenty thousand. What had Hazel's dowry been before his father's extortion? Two thousand? Five thousand? Mr. Trethow had anticipated Hazel's marriage to Harold, a promise made between friends, nothing to do with wealth. The tragedy? Harold would have married her without a dowry. Guilt of his father's deeds weighed heavily on his shoulders.

The dowry did not include Mr. Trethow's investment capital, making the combination a shocking enough figure to have Harold questioning if his father had bankrupted Trethow. Even these two figures excluded the percentage of annual income Trethow contracted to go to the Trelowen estate coffers. Elbows on the table, Harold rested his forehead against his palms, staring at the ledger until it went out of focus.

Chapter 15

H azel ate another biscuit out of obligation. It would be unconscionable for Nana to be the only one noshing. At the rate her grandmother-in-law consumed the sweet delights, encouraging Hazel to join her each time, Hazel would need a new wardrobe before her luggage arrived. The number of biscuits had increased by leaps and bounds in the three days Nana had lived at the main house, no longer a treat reserved for afternoon visits but a near constant companion for the baroness. Biscuit eating had become a new way of life.

Hazel licked a crumb from the corner of her mouth, one-part *mmm*ing and one-part *ugh*ing. Was it possible to tire of a favorite treat?

"Why my son has dismissed so many servants, I can't understand," Nana said, complaining after a morning spent introducing Hazel to the staff for the second time in as many days. "When Horace ran the household, there was none of this stinginess. Take that as a lesson. One can never have too many servants."

Hazel nodded then redirected. "What did you think of the supper party?"

From Hazel's perspective, it had been divine, as had the company since Lord Kissinger made a point to sit beside her and engage her in conversation for the whole of the evening.

Nana wrinkled her nose. "Gauche. What was the intention of all the greenery? Of all the candles? I expected the dining room to burn down. One whiff of a breeze and the candles would have taken the ivies. Here's another lesson for you. There's elegance in simplicity."

The drawing room door opened, catching the attention of both Hazel and Nana.

Mr. Quainoo bowed. "The luggage carriage has arrived."

It took Hazel a moment of blank staring for his words to register. Her luggage! From Cornwall! Oh, at last, she would have her wardrobe and whatever possessions Papa had sent. Had he thought to send her journals? What about her jewelry? There was the desk set Cuthbert had given her for her sixteenth birthday — had Papa sent that?

As she rose from the chair in eagerness to intercept the trunks, Mr. Quainoo added, "A Miss Plumb arrived with the luggage. Shall I show her in?"

Hazel blinked. Agnes? "Yes, of course, bring her without delay."

She sat and stared wide-eyed at Nana whose expression mirrored hers.

"Who is Miss Plumb, dear, and why has she arrived with your luggage?"

"A friend," Hazel said without reminding her that she had met Agnes only two weeks ago. "Although I wasn't expecting her, certainly not with my trunks."

Perplexed but delighted, she stood again when the drawing room door opened. Agnes's presence was not the only surprising aspect. Her pale and haggard complexion shocked Hazel; had she not slept since leaving the hunting party? Agnes's eyes brightened when she saw Hazel.

Arms outstretched, Hazel greeted Agnes, embracing her before tugging her over to the baroness.

"This is Miss Plumb, if you'll recall?" Hazel looked from one to the other. "You remember Lady Collingwood?"

Agnes curtsied with a shy smile. Nana nodded but showed no signs of recognition. Hazel would not blame it on poor memory since Nana had only briefly met Agnes at the wedding breakfast, a morning in which the baroness had met a great many new faces for which she could not have cared a fig to meet.

The three sat together, Hazel offering tea which Agnes declined, Nana making polite conversation. Agnes was less than forthcoming. Time and again she caught Hazel's attention with beseeching looks, clearly hoping for a private word. As much as Hazel adored Nana, they could not very well speak candidly. No, that was not true. *She* could. Nana would not judge anything the two shared, but Agnes would not know that.

With a cheery smile, Hazel said, "You've traveled so far. I hope you'll stay the night. Mr. Quainoo can prepare a room."

"That's precisely what I had hoped, to be honest." Agnes stared at her hands.

"Splendid. I'll let him know, and to prepare an extra seat at supper." Turning to Nana she asked, "Would it be too much of a burden to ask you to tell Helena of our guest while I take Miss Plumb upstairs?"

In short order, Hazel and Agnes walked arm in arm up the staircase, neither speaking. The trouble was, they could not very well seek refuge in Agnes's guest room since the staff would be preparing it, nor could they speak in Hazel's room since the luggage would be carried there without delay. The parlor was in poor taste since that was the setting of tragedy. The most private room she could think of was the sitting room she shared with Harold.

Not until they were settled in the snug did Hazel prod.

"I'm all shock and amazement you're here!" She reached over to squeeze Agnes's hand. "Only two weeks, but it feels like a lifetime. I had hoped you would come, but I never expected it to be this soon. Why didn't you write to say you were coming? How in the world did you find your way onto the luggage carriage?"

Agnes cast her eyes down and chewed her bottom lip. Hazel could not recall when she had seen a shy or sheepish Agnes. All was not right with her friend. Was it Mr. Plumb? Was it Lord Driffield?

"Father found out about my governess and the gardener," Agnes said, her navel-gaze unwavering. "He dismissed them both without reference."

Hazel nodded, patting her friend's hand and wondering what the governess and gardener's affair had to do with anything.

"When she told me she was leaving, the two setting off for Hampshire where the gardener's cousin has promised him a new position, I begged her to take me along. It wasn't until we were at a posting inn to change horses that I realized the luggage carriage in the stable yard was from Teghyiy Hall, *your* luggage. Mr. Holderman, the gardener, had words with the coachman to arrange for me to travel to Devonshire with him instead."

"You traveled alone?"

"Yes. Well, no. My lady's maid accompanied me."

Hazel had more questions than answers but knew not where to start. "Your governess should never have let you travel alone, even with your maid. She's fortunate she's not here, or I'd have a firm word with her."

"Don't be angry. I was no longer her charge, and it was my idea so I wouldn't inconvenience them."

"Inconvenience them!" Hazel sputtered. "It was her obligation as a fellow human being to see you to safety." Fuming, Hazel muttered to herself, "I'm not sorry to see her go." Then with a look at her friend's ashen complexion, she said, "Oh, but who cares about the governess? Why did you leave so hastily? It was a foolish thing to do, and I don't mind telling you that because I care about you and your safety. Has Mr. Plumb's temper flared? I wish you would have sent word instead. I could have arranged for a visit, all proper. Now…" Her words trailed. Now…what?

"I'll not go back. Ever. If I can't stay here, I'll—I'll find somewhere else. I need only enough for the post, and I can go to Melissa."

Alarmed, Hazel clasped Agnes's hand in a vise-like grip. "Enough of this nonsense. You're safe here. What's happened?"

Agnes gave her hand a half-hearted tug then dissolved into tears. The tears turned to sobs. The sobs turned to hiccups. Hazel remained still, enveloping the cold, limp hand with her warm palms.

"I've missed my courses," Agnes stuttered between choked sobs.

Frowning, Hazel studied her friend's profile. What course? Then it hit like an oar to the head. *Her menses cycle*. But Agnes was not married…

In the length of a minute, Hazel struggled with tumultuous emotions. Shock at the news. Disappointment that her friend had never confided in her. Appalment that Agnes would do such a thing. Anger that Agnes had ruined herself, not just with love for the wrong man but ruination before marriage when she knew the risks. Pity for her friend's plight. Determination to find a way to help.

But first… "You can't be certain," Hazel reassured with a lighthearted laugh to brighten the melancholy. "It's only been two weeks since the hunting party. My courses are rarely punctual. You're only a little late." She patted the clammy hand.

Agnes shook her head, her face blotched with red and lined by tears. "I've missed three courses."

"Three?" She stared, confused again. "*Three*? As in you've not had a cycle for three months? As in…"

Agnes chewed her lip again.

"But you've said nothing until now!"

"I didn't think I would have to. He was supposed to propose at the party. We were supposed to be married without my ever having to return home. Once married, it wouldn't matter."

So much to digest. Hazel tried to wrap her mind around all of it, but struggled. This whole time, Agnes had known and kept the secret. It had not merely been about love. Good heavens.

Squaring her shoulders, Hazel asked, "Have you told him? Does he know? I'm sure if he knew, he would break his betrothal to Lady Whatshername, despite the scandal, and risk of a breach of promise suit. It was likely a betrothal arranged by his family."

"He knows," Agnes said in naught but a whisper.

When she did not volunteer more information, Hazel gave a curt nod and said, "We'll resolve this. I don't know how, but leave it to me. For now, you're safe at Trelowen."

Trelowen looked just as he had left it, only a might colder. It was far colder in Devonshire than in London, too cold for October. He buried his hands under his arms and shivered his way from the stables to the house, his first stop to be his dressing room, second stop his father's study to announce the accomplishment of the deal, third stop his wife. Sometime during the day, he should find his mother and call on Nana, but he had a mind for no one except Hazel. If he did not have to stop at the dressing room or his father's study, he would be all the happier, for Hazel had been his one and only thought for days on end, the rose-cheeked, bright-eyed woman who just might fancy him and only him.

He quickened his pace. Did the stables have to be so far?

He rushed past Mr. Quainoo with a nod, not quite hearing what the man said about the drawing room, and took the steps two at a time to his dressing room. He paused to listen at the connecting door to the shared sitting room but heard not a stir beyond. Hastening to the dressing room, he groaned to realize he had beat Abhijeet to the estate. His shave would have to wait. A hand to his morning stubble assured it light enough not to be seen only felt, a prickly scratch against his palm.

With a tug at the bellrope, he ordered a bath, then dug around for a change of clothes. The wait was interminable. To bide time, he jotted a note for his mother, a note to Nana, a note requesting to meet with his father, a note requesting Hazel's company in two hours, and finally a note to Patrick that he would pay a call in a day or two.

At last, the bath was ready.

Did he hum while he bathed? He might have done. Not a joyous occasion to know he had shipped off their money in a deal sure to ruin them; yet he hummed nonetheless. A smile tickled his lips a time or two. *Hazel.* Soon now. So soon he could taste the moment approaching. His first sight of her would be like nothing he had ever experienced. He would see her as she was, *his wife*, his *loyal* wife, the potential *love of his life*. He might have even given the water a bit of a splash in his eagerness to see her.

Half an hour later, he stood on the other side of his father's desk, breaking the much-anticipated news. Lord Collingwood celebrated with a glass of brandy and a drumroll to the desktop. *We're set, my boy. Mark my words!* was uttered a half dozen times. Harold reserved his opinions on the matter for his future discussions with Abhijeet and Patrick.

At last. Time with Hazel arrived.

He rubbed his hands together as he left the study and headed back to his bedchamber. His note had instructed to meet in their shared sitting room.

One hand on the door handle, the other fidgeting with his poorly knotted cravat — how he wished he could have arrived better dressed by his valet's expertise — he hesitated outside the sitting room door. The moment he had been waiting for. To behold the woman he could not wait to woo, a process he had started before leaving for London and a process he aimed to continue, this time without the shadow of fear or jealousy. He closed his eyes, listened to the increasing beat of his heart, took a deep breath, and opened the door.

Empty.

His smoldering gaze, prepared to charm her, flattened to a frown. A note on the table awaited his attention.

Come to the drawing room.

Not the romantic return he had envisioned. In truth, he doubted he would have had the courage to pull her into an embrace at first sight. That did not stop him from fantasizing about it or being disappointed that he would miss the opportunity of daring passion. The drawing room was no place for kissing.

Shoulders stooped, he made for the stairs.

Any preconceived notions that Hazel might be alone, lonely, and dejected were dashed the moment he stepped inside. Perhaps not the precise moment, for his first sight upon entering the room was Hazel, only Hazel, a brilliant smile lighting her heart-shaped face, almost as though she were as happy to see him as he to see her, as though she had been counting down the days to his return, as though she knew his thoughts and wanted to embrace him, a woman with a heart available for love. Ah, but then crept the realization that she was not alone. The smile was a polite welcome, nothing more. He had read too much in her expression. Had he not?

He surveyed the guests. To his surprise, Nana and Miss Plumb.

"Mr. Hobbs, welcome home," Hazel said, offering the empty chair next to her. "You remember Miss Plumb?"

He bowed over Miss Plumb's knuckles. "Come to keep my wife company?"

The young lady flushed and flashed Hazel a sidelong look.

Nana was more welcoming, accepting his kiss to her cheek with one of her own, followed by a sharp remark about his unshaven prickles. He took his seat, looking from one lady to the next. Tedious. He wanted Hazel alone.

The first to speak was Nana. "Well, young man, you've gotten your wish."

Taken aback, he looked to Hazel rather than his grandmother. How the deuce did his grandmother know?

Since he stared at Hazel, it was Hazel who explained, "Nana has moved in with us. For the present time. It's easier for her to help me become acquainted with the house if she's living here. Helping in tandem with Helena, of course."

Oh. Oh! So, not the wish he had in mind but *that* wish. The news came as quite the surprise given how adamant his grandmother had been about remaining independent. Rather than look to Nana, he maintained the study of his wife. Somehow, in the stretch of not quite two weeks, Hazel had accomplished the impossible. Who was this remarkable woman he had married?

"You should know, as well," Hazel continued, unperturbed by his stare, "Miss Plumb is staying with us. She only arrived three days ago, but already we've had a marvelous time, haven't we? She'll be staying for the foreseeable future. Her, er, departure date has not yet been decided. Isn't this lovely? Now there will be four of us should Lord Kissinger call, even numbers."

All he could do was award Miss Plumb a tight-lipped smile. That she had been Lord Driffield's paramour was the least of his concerns, but rather that he would be competing with her for his wife's attention while she stayed. Why the devil was she here? They were, technically, still in their honeymoon days, never mind that he had spent the past week and more in London. Granted, it had been his idea for her to invite either or both Miss Plumb and Lady Williamson as guests, though he had not meant this soon. Discourteous for him to be annoyed. Annoyed he was, all the same.

With a polite albeit hollow chuckle, Harold said, "It would appear the past week and change have been productively busy at Trelowen. Here I thought you might be so stricken with loneliness you'd miss me." Wincing, he bit his tongue as soon as he said the words.

Hazel's lips formed an O. Then she laughed. "There's that sense of humor of yours, Mr. Hobbs." She turned to Miss Plumb. "Have I mentioned what a jokester he is? Are you shocked?"

Miss Plumb did not meet Harold's eyes when he looked to her.

Nana said, "My grandson has a sharp wit. Takes after his grandfather. So much like his grandfather." Surprising everyone in the room, she patted Miss Plumb's hand and said, "Come with me, dear. I've something to show you. And—" Her voice dropped to a not-so-subtle whisper. "These two need time alone. I'm perceptive about these things, you know. Newlyweds always need time alone."

Harold cleared his throat. Hazel blushed and picked invisible lint from her dress.

Miss Plumb looked for all the world as though she would protest. In the end, Nana tugged her from the drawing room.

Wasting no time, Harold stood and turned to Hazel, ready to pull her into the embrace he had dreamt of for the entirety of the journey home. He took a step forward, their knees almost touching. She looked up at him and smiled. The smile was so bashful, so genuine, he stepped back again, awe-struck, taken, an awkward schoolboy.

"I, uh, see you're well," he said dumbly.

"Yes, quite well." Her soft laugh fluttered his stomach. "Was your trip successful?"

"Depends who you ask." Curse his awkwardness. "Yes, successful. Would you..." He searched for what to say. *Would you let me kiss you? Would you tell me the truth of what happened? Would you care to make a real marriage of this situation? Would you consent to fall in love with me?* More than a dozen possibilities popped into mind. He said, instead, "Would you join me upstairs?"

At her startled expression, he clarified, "In our sitting room. We could exchange tales of our past week and a half. That is, if you're not busy. If you've the time. We could wait—"

"No!" she interrupted, rising in haste. "I mean yes. I mean I have the time. Now. Yes. Let's go upstairs." That pretty blush again, the one that pounded his heart. "To the sitting room."

A low but warm fire crackled in the hearth, dispelling the cold seeping past the window edges.

Hazel was a blushing bride all over again. The first sight of Harold stepping into the drawing room sent her stomach to her feet and her heart to her throat. How was it possible for him to become more handsome each time she saw him, even more so after only a brief trip to London? For the length of a shared stare, she had forgotten they were not alone and wished him to rush across the room and embrace her, two newlyweds in love. Then the truth crept over her. They were not alone. They were not in love. She was, in his eyes, a fallen woman forced to marry.

Even now that they were alone, he was wooden. His lips frowned, his movements jerky and hesitant. He did not want to see her as much as she wanted to see him—a humbling realization.

Did this change her decision to tell him of Agnes's condition? No. She had made the decision after much fretting and at least one sleepless night, worried he would judge her more harshly than he must already, merely by association, and worried he might refuse to allow Agnes to stay as a guest. Neither of those

actions matched his character as far as she knew him.
He had, after all, married her under similar circumstances. Although she had not been in a delicate way,
Harold had been concerned enough to question her
on that point in advance of the marriage; yet he married her anyway, even consummating the marriage
to legitimize any potential child conceived from her
supposed dalliance.

His actions proved him a good man, a trustworthy
man. If anyone could help, he could.

Should she ask about London or get straight to
the point? Hazel feared she must get to the point or
she would lose courage. And how was she to pay
attention to his tales if Agnes shadowed her conscience? Best get that out in the open, then she could
hear all about his journey and how dreadfully dull
London was without her company.

Hazel looked up to find Harold standing by the
fireplace, arm propped on the mantel, studying her.

"About Agnes," she began.

"I already know," he interrupted. "In full disclosure, it is what I had hoped to discuss."

She gaped at him. Impossible! "How?"

"Lord Driffield cornered me in London."

"*He* told you?" Hazel could not be more shocked.

"Not in so many words, but I pieced it together.
I want to hear it from you, Hazel. Your own words.
The truth."

Nodding, she smoothed her hands over her dress
and clasped them in her lap. This would be easier
than she planned since he already knew, although his
opinion of her must be lower than ever, for he would
think both she and Agnes were involved with Lord

Driffield. How humiliating. At least he acted accepting of Agnes's condition. If he objected, he would not have wanted to talk about it.

"I want to do all I can to help her," Hazel said, voice firm, though her whitened knuckles belied her nervousness. "But whatever I do, I need to work quickly. Time is her enemy."

Harold propped his chin on his open palm, covering his mouth with his hand.

When he did not respond, she continued, "I've been thinking about matchmaking. I know you'll protest, but it's a viable course of action if I can move fast enough. Have you any available tenants? Friends? Relations? Anyone eager to fall in love with an amiable young lady who is talented at the pianoforte?"

His features darkened the more she talked, looking quite ferocious now.

Tapping a finger against his mouth, he shifted position and stretched his arm across the mantel. "I know it's been a long morning for me, and a cold morning at that, so I'm afraid I'm not following. What has matchmaking Miss Plumb to do with what happened?"

"I knew you wouldn't like the matchmaking idea. I've other possibilities, none as good or as plausible. Do you have a better plan?"

Harold stared at her for so long she thought he was trying to read her thoughts. "Start from the beginning? I'm sluggish. Miss Plumb arrives at Trelowen in your carriage…"

"Yes. In the luggage carriage, of all things. I only learned the truth of her situation after she arrived. I was as shocked by the news as you must have been to hear it from Lord Driffield, although I can't see what he would gain from confessing. When I learned she's three months and will start showing, well I could have swooned, for I never knew she had…oh, let's not discuss that further or I'll swoon now. I said to her — "

Harold's palm met the wood with a *thwack*. "Miss Plumb is increasing!"

All Hazel could do was look back at him.

He crossed the room in two strides and sat beside her, draping an arm over the back of the chaise. "As much as I'd like to hear about Miss Plumb's plight and your plans to save her, *again*, I'm far more interested in *you* and how the blame of the parlor scandal came to rest on your shoulders rather than hers when Lord Driffield was her paramour, not yours."

Hazel covered her mouth with both hands. He knew! *He knew.* Why tears chose this moment to prick her eyes, she could not say, but they blurred her vision and stung. Before she could say anything more, she wrested the handkerchief from her pocket to dab at eyes and nose.

"What did the earl tell you?" she asked, her voice cracking.

"Never mind him. I want to hear from you what happened. The truth."

Nodding, kerchief held to her nose — how dreadfully embarrassing to have a runny nose and waterpot eyes in front of the gentleman one hoped to seduce in the near future — she confessed all, recounting the event in question and backtracking to when Agnes's and Driffield's affair first began, sparing no detail, not even how infuriating it was that his charm had beguiled them all. The story ended at her father's announcement that she would marry Harold to save the family's reputation.

Clearing the air was a far greater relief than she could have expected. Now, he would not see her as a fallen woman, disloyal of heart, mind, and memory.

Throughout her confession, she stole glances, hoping to read his reactions. Whatever his thoughts, he hid them well. She thought she saw a flicker of anger when she spoke of Driffield's behavior in the parlor. She thought she glimpsed the hint of a smile when she admitted her failure as sentry was caused by spying on Harold on one occasion and bumping into him on another. But she could not be certain his expressions showed those reactions. What she saw in his features could be what she wanted to see.

When she finished her tale, he remained silent for some time, his gaze roaming her tear-streaked face.

"And so," he said, "you married me. A tragedy you had to sacrifice love to marry for convenience."

Her chin trembled anew.

His tone was not flippant, accusatory, or resentful. He did not spit the words. He did not enunciate with cynicism. The declaration lifted as though in question, as though gauging her immediate reaction to the sentiment. Her reaction, though not visible as far as she knew, was a wrench of the heart, a fear that *he* would see it that way, that he had been the one to sacrifice.

If true, nothing she said would make a difference.

Her voice wobbling, she said, "There's no one else I would have wanted to marry, with or without the scandal." She did not look up, but she heard the *hiss* of his breath.

The backs of his fingers found her cheek, caressing the wet skin from temple to jaw. Hazel shivered at the tender warmth of his touch.

When she met his gaze, she found him smiling, a dreamy sort of goofy smile that made her laugh. To her relief, rather than be insulted, he laughed with her. Neither spoke, only laughed, but Hazel believed this moment marked the beginning of something beautiful, something that felt astonishingly like the first stirring of love.

Chapter 16

Sunrays full of promise woke Harold the next morning. When the slats of light crossed his face, he did not cover his eyes with his forearm, rather he tossed the bedding aside and leapt to his feet, eager to greet the day. There was a striking young lady to be wooed.

If he had expected everyone else to be abed or to have Hazel to himself in the morning room, he was set for disappointment. The morning room was bustling with conversation when he arrived, everyone present, everyone breaking their fast. So much for thinking he had arisen early. Nana and Agnes were deep in conversation. Hazel and his mother were chattering. His father was cupping steaming tea while reading the newspaper. The domesticity and familial nature of the scene set him to smiling as he heaped bacon onto a plate and took a seat next to Hazel.

That striking young lady to be wooed turned a cheery smile his way—a clear admission, if Harold had ever seen one, that she knew she was going to be wooed.

"Good morning, Mr. Hobbs."

"And a good morning to you, Mrs. Hobbs."

Their gazes lingered just long enough for Nana to titter across the table. "Observe, Miss Plumb.

Newlyweds. I do believe you'll be helping me with my needlework today."

His mother poked at Lord Collingwood's arm, sending the tea sloshing. "Remember when you looked at me that way?"

Harold cast his mother and grandmother a smirk before turning back to Hazel. "Is it too early for a row on the lake? I believe we're overdue."

Her eyes brightened.

Before she could respond, Miss Plumb spoke up. "I've never rowed on a lake before. What a wonderful idea. We could take turns."

Harold's smile slipped as he looked to the guest.

Nana came to the rescue. "Don't forget about the needlework. I couldn't possibly finish without you. You wouldn't break my heart, would you? The lake will be there forever, but I won't."

A morbid thought, but Harold hid his smile by sampling the bacon, all too familiar with his grand-mother's dark humor and methods for getting exactly what she wanted.

Unable to deny a woman her dying wish, Miss Plumb bowed her head. "I would like nothing better than to help you, Lady Collingwood. You're too kind."

An hour later, Harold handed a bundled Hazel into the boat, a diligent footman holding it steady. The sun shone above, but the chill bit through his great-coat and layers. At least she was warm. Or appeared to be. Over a wool dress, she wore a second layer bodice — whatever women called that in fashion terms — and on top of that a hooded cloak, and even on top of that a fur-lined pelisse with matching muff.

Once settled, he nodded to the footman to push them off. The wind nipped at his cheeks.

Harold hunched into the coat, determined to make this outing undeniably romantic despite the weather's insistence to the contrary. Hazel looked about her, taking in the serenity. Every so often she would watch the oars dip into the still waters then steal a glance at Harold, each peek warming him against the cold.

When he had decided to pay her court after returning from India, he had hoped for a marriage of contentment. Luck might turn contentment into companionable love over the years, but he never expected a love match from the start. Arranged marriages between dissimilar people rarely equated to love, after all. Now, as he looked across the little boat to his wife, he realized how unjust that hope had been, denying them both the potential of something greater. Hazel deserved the deepest and most passionate love. With her, he coveted the same.

Giving the oars firm pulls, he propelled the boat across one side of the lake. Once they reached the deepest point, he tucked in the oars, the boat drifting to a standstill.

Hazel made a showing of breathing in the crisp air and sighing. "Divinity. It's far more romantic than I expected."

Waggling his eyebrows, he said, "Perfect. It's one of my methods for wooing you."

"*Wooing* me?" she questioned with a laugh. "How chivalrous of you. I've never been *wooed* before. What does this entail?"

He gestured around them with a stretch of his arms. "Behold. Stage one of wooing has commenced."

"Does this method have proven success?"

"I wouldn't know. I've been in India since I was seventeen so never had the opportunity to put my wooing strategies into action. But I've imagined a time or two that this might be a successful approach. Is it working?"

Hazel hid her smile in the fur collar of her pelisse. "It would spoil the challenge for me to say." She studied him from beneath long lashes. "You rowed at least one lady on the lake at the hunting party. Was it not successful then?"

Harold had to think for a moment to recall. With a sly smile he said, "Indeed I did row a lady or two across the lake. But I wasn't trying to woo anyone at the time."

"No? Not even Miss Evans?"

He laughed at the hint of jealousy in her voice. "Especially not Miss Evans. In fact, you'll be amused to know that not only did she nearly tip us over when it started to rain, but I spent the whole of the outing thinking of you."

She snapped her face forward, her eyes wide. "Of *me*?"

Nodding, he said, "Of *you*. I had planned to travel to Cornwall after my return from India. To pay you court."

"What a ridiculous tease you are. Is this stage two of wooing?"

"Not in the least, unless honest confession counts as a stage of courtship."

"Oh, good heavens." She waved her muff. "We're already married. You needn't court me."

"No? Then I've already won your heart? A record this must be. A single visit to the lake, and you're already madly in love with me."

Hazel buried her face in her muff and mumbled unintelligibly. Her shoulders shook with embarrassed laughter. It took her some time to recover from her fit of hilarity, or whatever it was her reaction showed, but when she sat up and schooled her features, she asked, "Why would you come to Cornwall to court me? Why not fall in love with some beautiful, flighty creature of your acquaintance? How silly of you to want to court a complete stranger."

"But you weren't a stranger. I grew up knowing we were intended for each other. For me, that was a greater intimacy than any acquaintance could afford. I never gave another woman a second glance. To you, I was faithful."

"Oh." Hazel stared at her muff.

They had drifted further across the lake, moving out of sightline from the boathouse and bank. He dropped the oars into the reflective surface to guide them back to sightline.

After he brought the oars to rest in the boat, she asked, "How would you have courted me in Cornwall?"

"Hmm. I'd not gotten that far in my plan to be honest. I don't suppose there are any lakes with rowboats near Teghyiy Hall?"

She shook her head. "You hadn't a plan because you were overconfident of your success. We were, as you said, intended. You would have stridden into the hall, full of expectations and arrogance."

"Quite the opposite, my dear. I would have feared you'd already promised your heart to a freckle-faced lad of your acquaintance with no thought to the stranger your father wanted you to marry. I would have arrived with a genuine and heartfelt suit, knowing I would be pitting myself against every face you knew, handsome or otherwise."

"Oh," she said again. "And if you had arrived to discover I was pockmarked with dragon breath?"

Harold chuckled. "I would have made an elaborate excuse for being in Cornwall then ridden back to Devonshire by first light of the following morning."

"Nonsense! You would have remained loyal even if I were ugly," she said.

"Then it's fortunate I've found you the most exquisite of beauties instead."

She had nothing to say to that, only to turn her head to take in the leafless trees. They shared silence, each shivering in the cold, the temperature all the colder for being out on the lake. He could not feel his lower half anymore.

"Do you row well?" she asked, breaking the silence.

"Out of practice, but before India, I rowed every morning."

"Then impress me."

Harold arched a single brow, his lips angling into a grin. He sliced the water with the oars and said, "Brace yourself."

With a powerful lean and pull, he lunged them across the lake, ripples waking the sleeping waters. His muscles burned from lack of practice, but he put his weight into it, rowing them well past the sightline and around the bend to the length of the lake that ran across much of the estate grounds. He went for speed and agility, aiming to send the wind whistling past their ears and to untidy her carefully rowed curls. Hazel squealed and grasped the bench. Her muff lay forgotten in her lap. When they reached the edge of Mr. Jones' land, he used both oars to spin them in the tightest circle his muscles could muster, one arm pulling, one arm pushing, his enjoyment at her reaction fueling his daring. As they whipped into one circle then two then a final third before turning back the way they had come, Hazel threw her head back and laughed, begging for more.

By the time they reached the deepest part of the lake and set to drift once more, Harold's teeth were chattering. He did not dare end the fun. Not until she was ready to return to the warmth of the house. If she so desired, he would stay here all day and freeze for her pleasure.

Tucking her hands into the muff, she said, "While we're confessing, I'll admit I've thought on more than one occasion we might have noticed each other had it not been for our parents' promise. That was my only objection to you, you see. My father's expectation of the match." She teased him with a smile before adding, "Well, that and my first impression of you."

"Pray tell what was so objectionable?" He scowled.

"You walked into the supper party looking…rustic. I was almost embarrassed for you."

Harold crossed his arms over his chest. "I see."

Unperturbed by his reaction, Hazel continued, "Your hair was unpowdered, sir! And that tan!" She tutted. "For all your posh demeanor, you looked like a gardener."

"Right. So, you'd prefer a foppish peacock."

Her smile deepened in wickedness. "That's what every proper young lady wants. But I've never admitted to being a proper young lady. In fact...I thought I might faint when I saw you on the wilderness walk that day after you'd mended the fence, or whatever it was you said you were doing. Not faint of fright, mind, but faint in the hopes you'd have to carry me back to the house."

Uncrossing his arms, he reached up to loosen his cravat. She watched him, her eyes widening as he unknotted the linen. Leaving it to hang about his neck, he slipped the top two buttons of his waistcoat through the holes and parted the stiff fabric to expose the hollow of his throat to the frosty air. He shivered at the kiss of cold but was undaunted. Hazel pursed her lips, saying nothing as she continued to watch.

Holding onto the bench, he leaned over the side of the boat and cupped an icy palmful of water. With a quick glance to ensure she was still focused on him, he dumped the water on his hair, followed by two more scoops until his hair was decidedly soaked. Hair powder streamed down his temples. He shuddered when the frigid droplets dribbled under his shirt collar and down his back. He combed his fingers through his curls and gave them a fierce shake.

Since he could not see himself, he could not truthfully say if he looked frightful or masculinely disheveled. Wishing for the latter, he asked, "Am I rustic enough now to entice you into a hot chocolate in the sitting room?"

She visibly swallowed, her eyes still wide as teacup saucers.

"In fear of ruining my potential success during stage one," he said when she showed no signs of responding, "I'm going to admit that with or without the enticement, I'm for the sitting room and hot chocolate because my teeth are chattering, and I can't feel my face. I do, however, hope you'll join me."

This time, the hearth fire in the sitting room roared with a fiery passion. Hazel wrapped the blanket around her, still trembling despite the warmth of the flames. That she had nearly frozen on the lake did not bother her one whit, for it had been the most fun she could remember having.

Harold shared the sentiment. He, too, was buried beneath the warmth of a blanket, contentedly smiling regardless of his wet hair. At least he had taken a moment to rinse out the remaining hair powder when they had returned to change clothes in their separate dressing rooms. For her part, her lady's maid could not work the laces and pins fast enough. Hazel had been giddy for more of his company, more of his flirts and compliments, all so unexpected from the reserved toff she had originally thought of him.

Though they shared the chaise longue, neither touched, each snug in their own coverlet. She wondered if they would warm faster by sharing a blanket. However exciting the thought, she dared not say such a thing to him. But she thought it. An ever-present desire to inch closer.

Tucking the blanket around her stockinged feet, slippers having been tossed to the floor the moment she found comfort, she asked, "Is this stage two of your wooing strategy?"

Russet strands curled as they dried, framing Harold's lean face. Although he so rarely wore powder, unlike the other gentlemen of her acquaintance, seeing him so undressed felt intimate somehow. Did other wives' husbands sport natural hair in private? Powdered or unpowdered, he was handsome. Not the kind of handsome she was accustomed to or ever thought to be attracted to, certainly not the kind of handsome found in fashionable circles. There was no denying, though, that he sent her pulse racing, more so with each conversation. As far as she could recall, no one had affected her thus, not even Lord Brooks. But she did not want to think of anyone else, only Harold.

Her husband drew the blanket more tightly about himself. "To which *this* are you referring as a potential stage two? The secluded setting? The decadent chocolate? The shared settee? Our shivering state?"

"Any of those. All of those. Methods not immediately evident could be at play, as well, all deviously contrived to win your suit."

His grin was positively diabolical. "I can't give away all of my secrets. You'll only know if I've employed stage two after you've succumbed to the charm of said stage."

She giggled and hoped she did not sound too vapid for doing so. The half-lidded look he gave her told her he did not find her remotely vapid. His flattery and flirting had all the appearance of being genuine. Harold liked her. He had thought of her while rowing another woman on the lake!

Tugging at her bottom lip with her teeth, she asked, "Will you promise to answer me honestly if I ask you a question?"

A quizzical quirk of his head. A blink. A nod. "Ask me anything."

"If you hadn't discovered the truth…you know, about the…parlor…would you have ever been able to look past it, or even if it had been true, would you have ever forgiven me enough to, um, woo me?"

"Hazel, understand this," he said, sitting up straighter. "I looked past it the moment I said *I will*. I wanted to win your affection even when I believed the scandal was true. A challenge, yes. Impossible, perhaps. Outside my purview, no. My concern was not the scandal but if you had any room in your heart for someone other than him."

"Oh." She said the word she had already repeated uncountable times today. The blanket seemed over-warm of a sudden. She slipped her feet out from under it.

"I can't deny that knowing the truth is a weight lifted. I don't have to compete with the memory of some great, lost love. I have only to compete with your ideal of a perfect husband, whatever that might be. Have I answered your question? Was that all you wanted to know?"

Hazel nodded. "Lord Kissinger was right about you."

He leaned towards her, propping his elbow on his thigh. "I beg your pardon."

"He called on me when you were in London. Said you were the very best of men."

"Did he now? The sly dog." Harold chuckled. "Is that all he said?"

Grinning, Hazel looked at him sidelong. "He might have said more. But what's said between friends stays between friends, so you shan't wheedle anything more out of me."

Harold clucked his tongue. "I see how it is. Betrayed by my dearest friend the moment I turn my back."

Brave, Hazel drew her legs onto the chaise, tucked her feet under the blanket, then dared to inch one of her feet across the cushion to the edge of Harold's blanket. She watched him watch her foot slide beneath the fabric. The corner of his lips twitched, eyes trained on the outline of the foot. A flex of her toes and she found his thigh. She wiggled her toes against him, then pulled her foot back to the safety of her blanket.

In dramatized slowness, Harold's gaze followed the path her foot had taken before meeting her stare. "I believe you're flirting with me, Mrs. Hobbs."

"Who says I don't have my own stages of wooing?" She drew her bottom lip between her teeth again and fluttered her eyelashes.

"Then in the name of fairness, you must allow me a question in return."

"Go on then."

"If I were to fetch a bit of paper, would you permit me to sketch you as you are now? Between the firelight flickering on your features and the sunlight haloing your hair, you're angelic. I want to capture it."

Hazel's heartbeat quickened. "You're an artist?"

"I dabble. May I? It won't take a moment to grab my things."

She nodded, at a loss for words. Which was more surprising, that he was an artist or that he wanted to draw her, she could not say. Both perhaps. He folded his blanket and slipped into his bedchamber for only a moment before returning with paper, wooden tablet, and graphite in hand. When he sat down, he was startlingly close, his leg brushing against her tucked foot.

"No need to move, Hazel. You're perfect as you are." Holding the tablet in his lap, his free hand arced across the paper with a furious flurry of movements.

"Did your grandfather teach you?" she asked, craning her neck to see the paper as he worked.

He tilted it just out of sight, never moving his focus from her face. "Self-taught. No one in my family knows. There, you know a secret about me."

"But your grandfather was an artist. Why didn't he teach you?"

The graphite strokes stopped midway across the page. "My grandfather was a gamester, not an artist. His addiction to gambling nearly ruined him. To the great fortune of my father, he won the largest amount of his life days before his death. I suspect it's why my father —" He stopped midsentence, a crease forming between his eyebrows. "Why would you think my grandfather was an artist?"

"Because he was," she insisted. "Has Nana never shown you his work? He was prolific. Her entire bedchamber is covered with his art."

Harold sat back and studied her. Hazel hoped she had not disclosed a secret Nana had entrusted her with. It had not seemed like a secret.

"She's never spoken a word about it to me," he said.

The bone and graphite drawing instrument rested between his index and middle finger as he reached for his hot chocolate. Staring into the cup, he swirled it one way then another. Hazel peered over his hand at the sketch, taking advantage of his distraction.

Harold snapped the tablet sideways with a "Ha!" before setting down his cup and resuming his sketch. "I'll ask her about it this evening," he said. "Curious she never told me about it. I wasn't close to my grandfather. He wasn't close to anyone that I know of; he was a man who kept to himself when not out gaming."

"Oh, but theirs was a love match!"

His hand stilled again. "Was it? I didn't realize. But then, he was in his sixties by the time I was born. Had no patience for children, only his vices. I know nothing of his youth."

"She's never spoken of his later years. The way she speaks of him, you'd think he was still alive, both of them young and deeply in love. It's all delightfully romantic."

He smiled. "She must confide in you for that reason."

Angling for a peek again, Hazel asked, "Do you have other sketches? May I see them? What do you sketch?"

"Yes, yes, and mostly landscapes. I sneaked a portrait or two in India from subjects none the wiser, mostly street vendors and urchins. You're my first permitted subject."

Graphite between his fingers again, he reached a hand to her, hesitated at her cheek, then tucked a strand of hair behind her ear. His fingers lingered there. Then with a slow sweep of his fingertips, he traced the heartbeat thumping along her neck. The pads of his fingers, in their tender caress, trailed a path of fire, Hazel's skin aflame where they touched, the warmth spreading through her body, igniting an inferno in her abdomen.

When his fingertips reached the top of the blanket, just above her collarbone, she laughed softly. "This must be stage two."

He did not respond right away, and she wondered if he had heard her. But then his eyes met hers, his lids hooded, the brown of his irises so dark they were nearly black. His thumb traced her lips, slightly parting them.

"May I kiss you?"

Her heart pounding and her hands trembling, she nodded and closed her eyes in anticipation.

Rather than press his lips to hers, as she expected, he brushed them, a featherlight touch of his to hers. Tender and gentle, a tease of skin to skin. He exhaled shakily, his breath tickling her cheek, scented of cocoa. Only after tempting, coaxing, courting, did he press more firmly, but even then, his kiss was soft and pliant, not demanding, rather kneading. She parted her lips, bracing for the invasion. Instead, he teased his tongue along the seam of her lips, flicking the tip of hers with a taunt. Her stomach fluttered. Her breath shuddered. Her toes curled.

Her eyes were still closed, her lips still puckered when she realized he had long since backed away.

How had she missed the end of the kiss? She shivered from the heat coursing through her.

Harold was looking back at her when she opened her eyes. The sketch was held up for her to see. Although she stared at the paper, she could not make immediate sense of the blends and shades, still dazed from the life-altering kiss, the kiss she had always wanted, the kiss as she had dreamt kisses should be.

"Well?" he prodded.

She focused on the drawing, forcing herself to make sense of the lines.

Goodness! Captured on paper, but a moment's work, was her perfect likeness, only not as she saw herself but how he must see her, unblemished by imperfections, the shading creating an aura, her likeness radiating happiness. It was breathtaking. More so than the chalk sketches she had seen before. Hazel pressed a hand to her chest.

"It's captivating," she said. "I'm breathless, in awe."

"This is how I see you. I can't capture the inner qualities with graphite alone, your loyalty, your kindness, your cleverness, but it is, as best I can create in a handful of minutes, how I see you."

She admired the art, her thoughts not on the shades but on Harold — his kiss, his compliments, his everything. Thinking more to the continued success of his courtship, she mouthed with a barely audible whisper, "Well done."

Chapter 17

Patrick arrived on horseback the next day, eager to hear the tidings from London and also desirous of an escape from his parents who had invited to tea a young lady readily available for matrimony. Since he arrived not long after Harold, Hazel, and Miss Plumb sat down for their own tea in the drawing room, there was not an opportunity for Harold to speak privately to Patrick. A candid talk would have to wait. With the London trip on Harold's mind and the discovery of the scandal's truth, he was champing at the bit to confide in Patrick.

If he had any doubts about sharing Miss Plumb's misfortune, her behavior at the viscount's arrival sealed his decision. Miss Plumb fluttered her eyelashes at Patrick after the initial greeting.

At such blatant flirtation, Harold raised his brows to Hazel. Hazel gave a little shrug and passed him his tea. Obviously, Hazel had not shared with her friend the preferences of the viscount. If Miss Plumb thought to ingratiate herself to the man or entrap him as a way to save herself, she would have a rude awakening, for not only would Patrick see through her ploy, he would laugh her out of the room.

Thus far, Miss Plumb had failed to make a favorable impression on Harold. On more than one occasion in the past two days, she had attempted to monopolize Hazel's time and invite herself into an invitation he had extended only to his wife. He knew she was a guest. He knew she was alone. He knew she did not mean to intrude. Those factors did not excuse her. If she were a traditional guest, she would be entertained by her hosts morning, noon, and night. As it was, she was not a traditional guest, but a destitute woman invited to stay in their home until further notice. If she were to live here, she could entertain herself. At the very least, she could be conscientious of their needs.

That did not seem unreasonable, did it? He was polite to her, but that was all. From his perspective, the girl owed more gratitude to Hazel than she could pay in a lifetime, yet he did not see evidence of her appreciativeness, only a dependency on Hazel's goodwill. He hoped this perspective did not make him insensitive. His heart went out to her, truly. Foolish though she may have been, a young woman had little defense against a man like Lord Driffield and his ilk. Under different circumstances, it could have as easily been Hazel, not in rumor but in fact. That did not convince him to forgive Miss Plumb for trying to steal the attention of his wife. And now she was trying to ply Patrick with flirty glances. Devious.

Some minutes into the conversation, Hazel set down her teacup. "Is it too cold for the wilderness walk? I think a stroll along the lake sounds invigorating."

It was too cold, Harold thought, but a walk would provide him the opportunity to separate Hazel from Miss Plumb. On second thought, perhaps he ought to rescue his friend. A glance to Hazel's pink lips settled the matter. Patrick could hold his own.

Within a quarter of an hour, bundled for the biting wind, the troupe traipsed outside for the wilderness walk. The wind kept its promise. It nipped at exposed skin, sending shivers down Harold's spine. The temperature, however, had warmed noticeably since yesterday, the determined sun high above. Cups of chocolate might not be necessary today.

As Harold stepped towards Hazel to offer his arm, Miss Plumb intercepted, tucking her hand under Hazel's elbow to lock arms. He grumbled to himself but let her have this victory. Just this one.

Patrick smirked and offered his arm to Harold.

"Cheeky." Harold clasped his hands behind his back and walked alongside his friend.

While it presented an opportunity to talk, it did not offer the privacy he would need to talk about the more sensitive topics he had in mind. Not that he could concentrate. With Hazel and Miss Plumb walking ahead of him, he had the fine view of Hazel's shapely derriere. Granted, he could not actually see the shape of it or her figure past the winter cloak, but there was a noticeable jiggle where he thought her derriere ought to be. He leered, feeling like a prized jackanape. Next to Miss Plumb, Hazel's figure showed to advantage, even with the figureless cloak blocking her assets. Miss Plumb was tall and slender, all boney angles. Perhaps some men found that attractive. Hazel, however, was of petite height with delectable curves. This was not the first time he had admired her physique, but now he did so with renewed appreciation, the appreciation of a husband.

More to the point, the appreciation of a man wooing a young lady he hoped to seduce mind, body, and heart.

A handkerchief waved in front of him, blocking his view.

"For your drool," Patrick said.

Harold cringed. "That obvious?"

"That obvious."

Taking the proffered kerchief, Harold dabbed at his chin and wiped at his waistcoat before returning the linen.

"Now who's cheeky?" Patrick tucked it back into his waistcoat pocket. "I called on your ladylove while you were in London, you'll be envious to know."

"So I've heard. A little birdy told me you sang my praises. Whatever you said made an impression."

"How could it not? I told her you saved kittens from burning barns in your spare time." Patrick winked. "I spoke only truths, my good man. From the way she keeps looking over her shoulder at you, the impression was more than favorable. She's smitten."

Coy would have been Harold's choice of descriptor, but he would take smitten. He would also take beautiful. The wind had pinkened her cheeks most becomingly.

Slowing his pace just enough for the ladies to be out of hearing range, Harold said *sotto voce*, "I'll call on you in a day or two. Much to discuss."

Patrick cocked his head. "Intrigue. Suspense. In regards to?"

"London, investments, a certain earl."

"Developments, I see. Speaking of a certain earl, a certain guest's presence is curious. I'm all agog. Give me a hint or I'll perish of anticipation."

Harold slowed their pace a tad more since the ladies had slowed theirs, obviously hoping the gentlemen would catch up.

Not wanting to appear too obvious about holding back his friend for a private conversation, he said brusquely, "The earl prefers plums to hazelnuts," then enlivened his steps to reach his wife and guest who had all but come to a complete stop.

Although Patrick's forehead wrinkled in surprise, he did not respond. The ladies turned to face them at the fork in the path. Miss Plumb relinquished Hazel's arm only when Patrick offered her his arm in its place. The man must be a saint. Harold did not give him a chance to change his mind. He linked arms with Hazel and drew her close to his side.

Beaming at him, Hazel said, "I've decided to host a supper party next week, with the help of Helena and Nana, of course."

Harold replied, "To what do we owe this honor?"

"Not to what," she said, "rather to whom. It'll be my first endeavor to matchmake Agnes with an eligible bachelor."

Miss Plumb turned red, and not from the wind chill. "Hazel!"

Hazel tittered. "I think a widower might do. Someone who is charmed by accomplished and stunningly beautiful ladies." Looking to Patrick she said, "Harold won't approve of me matchmaking, but once he sees how very good I am at it, he'll have to admit I'm right. I aim to impress him, you know."

Patrick laughed. "What makes you think Miss Plumb with all her stunning beauty and accomplishments needs your help finding a husband?"

"But it's not about finding a husband, Lord Kissinger. It's about finding the right match. Anyone can find a spouse, but not everyone can find their perfect love match. If you were to entrust me, I could do a bit of matchmaking for you, as well."

This time it was Harold's turn to exclaim, "Hazel!"

Patrick merely laughed more jovially. "You offer a fine character reference for your services, but I don't believe you could invite anyone who would entice me, and certainly not tempt me to leave bachelorhood behind."

With a twinkle in her eyes, she said, "That, my lord, is a challenge I accept with relish."

Harold was practically growling as they turned towards the lake, but he was too amused by his wife to scold her. Instead, he tightened his hold on her arm to draw her flush against his side and guided her in the direction of the boathouse, still some distance away. As he had done with Patrick, he slowed their gait in hopes Miss Plumb and her escort would gain distance.

Hazel squeezed his arm. "Are you trying to get me alone, Mr. Harold Hobbs?"

He grinned but said nothing.

"This must be the start of stage three of wooing," she said. "How many stages are there?"

"However many it takes for you to be so enamored with me that you lose count."

They drew ever closer to his destination, a two-story, stone structure built by his grandfather. The bottom floor housed the boats and opened onto the lake. The floor above was empty but had a Juliet balcony to take in the views. At one time, the space might have served as lodging for a groundskeeper or domestic boatswain, or perhaps additional equipment.

Once Patrick and Miss Plumb walked past the boathouse, Harold asked, "Would you care to see where the boats are stored?"

Hazel stared askance. "Hmm. That doesn't sound as appealing as a row on the lake or hot chocolate. Is there a reason you think I might enjoy seeing boats in storage?"

"There is."

She slowed, eyeing him suspiciously. "And what might be that reason? You'll have to do far more than this to induce me into a cold, wet building."

Harold leaned down to whisper in her ear. "I'm hoping to kiss you again."

Hazel snapped around to face him, nearly bumping noses with him. She made to speak, laughed instead, then side skipped, giving his arm a tug. He took that as a promising sign he was going to do more than hope.

Heedless of Patrick and Miss Plumb, Hazel screeched, "Catch me if you can!" and raced for the boathouse.

All Harold's attempts at discretion failed as the duo ahead turned to watch Hazel skipping and laughing with Harold having no other course of action than to chase her, grinning like a boy on twelfth night. She reached the double doors first, unlatched them, and wrenched open one squeaky side before disappearing into the darkness beyond.

Had he thought to do so, Harold would have stopped to offer a brief apology to the members of their party, but his mind was focused on a singular beauty, her pink lips, and her jiggly derriere. In the stretch of a few feet, he had lost all semblance of a mature adult. His one thought, if it could be said that he had a thought outside of an alluring woman named Hazel, was that this had turned from being an attempt to make a potentially unpleasant union into a workable marriage to blossoming into a romance, a passionate and undeniable attraction between two people.

In short, he was confident Hazel liked him.

Following suit, Harold darted past the wooden door into the semi-darkness of the boathouse. He stopped just inside when he did not find her waiting for him. A vaulted opening at the opposite end invited light through the slats of the closed waterway doors, but the only light on his side of the room spilled in from the open entrance. His eyes tried to adjust. He listened for the rustle of her petticoat. Silence. The only sounds the echo of water lapping against the wind and the gentle howl of funneled air.

Just when he was about to call her name, a hand reached out from the alcove behind him and pulled him into the blackness.

Caught off guard, he pivoted and stumbled, landing with one hand braced against the cold wall, his body pinning Hazel to the stone. She gasped then giggled. Saucy bird! This had been intentional. Perhaps not exactly how she envisioned, but most decidedly intentional.

In the shadowed recesses of the alcove, he could make out her outline. Capturing her cheek in his palm, he combed his fingers into her scalp, disheveling her tightly curled rows. As he angled to find her lips, she shocked him to the tips of his powdered hair by standing on tiptoes, clasping his arms, and kissing him first. Their lips met, hers moist and parted. Any plans he had for a stolen kiss with puckered lips were lost to the bold invitation of his wife.

Harold slipped his tongue past the parted seam to tease and tantalize hers. He flicked, licked, and kneaded until they both moaned, her fingers digging into his upper arms and pulling him closer against her. Winter layers be dashed, he nestled himself firmly between her legs. She arched her back in greeting, rubbing against his erection.

He groaned then leaned back, kissing her cheeks, her eyelids, her forehead, back to her mouth, then her cheek again. A turning point in their relationship? Undeniably.

"I do believe," she said, breathless, "you promised me a kiss."

After a throaty laugh, he asked, "Then what do you call what we just shared?"

"No, no, no, that was *me* kissing *you*. It doesn't count. You still owe me a kiss."

With the steady pulse of fire flowing through his veins, he dared not tempt another, not here, not with their guests waiting outside.

"I'm afraid, Hazel love, it'll remain a kiss owed." He caressed her cheek with the backs of his fingers, enchanted by her. "Come, I need to pin your curls. Step out into the light so I don't make more of a mess."

His fingers trembled as he pinned the curls back into their tidy rows. How was he expected to carry on through the day after such intimacy? His body, his mind, his heart, they all thrummed with awareness.

Hazel appeared similarly affected. Her cheeks and neck were flushed, her lips red and ever so slightly swollen, her eyes half-lidded with heavy lashes.

They stayed in the boathouse for several long minutes, embracing the cool air, taking in deep, slow breaths. Neither spoke. He wanted to ask if he could come to her tonight, but he had not the courage. Not yet. They had shared only two kisses. They had spoken truths only two days prior. He would wait until she invited him.

When they finally stepped out of the boathouse, it was to find they were alone. Neither Miss Plumb nor Patrick were anywhere in sight. How much trouble could a woman in the family way and a gentleman who preferred the sterner sex get into if left unchaperoned? With a shrug, he and Hazel headed back to the house.

Agnes turned her head this way and that, angling for a better look at her lady's maid's styling. "Don't you think he's handsome? I'm inclined to say he's the handsomest man of my acquaintance."

With a slow drawl, Hazel said, "Yeeees, he's handsome." She eyed her friend warily. "I don't, however, think that's an avenue you ought to consider."

Agnes waved a dismissive hand. "He already told me he's not the marrying kind, prefers the tall, dark, and handsome, he said, but I can still find *him* handsome, can't I? One needn't bed a man to find him handsome."

"Agnes!" Hazel shrieked, appalled by such talk.

The two sat in Agnes's dressing room, the latter still preparing for the rout Hazel was hosting that evening. Dressing had turned into a multi-hour affair. The dress Hazel had given Agnes had needed substantial adjustments to fit Agnes's figure, the lady's maid letting down the bottom hem and arms for length, taking in the waist, expanding the bust, and so much more. The dress was nearly unrecognizable. It would all be worth it to see Agnes safely wedded.

The rout had been prepared over the past several days with the help of both Helena and Nana, especially in selecting the guest list. Card tables and refreshments were the highlight of the evening, intended to provide opportunity for conversation that a supper party would not allow. Neither woman knew of Agnes's circumstances, but both were excited about matchmaking plans. Since Hazel could not very well host a rout with *only* men for guests, unmarried men at that, an equal ratio of ladies had been invited, including a few married couples, but Helena had selected with care the ladies to be invited — no one who would offer Agnes any great competition. Helena won favor with Hazel during one particular planning discussion by suggesting a few gentlemen who might turn Lord Kissinger's head.

"A pity he's not the marrying kind," Agnes continued. "I'm already taken with him."

Hazel shook her head. "Clearly he was warning you away."

"No, it wasn't like that. We spoke candidly, as friends, picking up where we left off from the hunting party. I even told him about my situation."

"Agnes, no!"

"I know I shouldn't have said anything, but it seemed natural. It's as though we were separated at birth, he and I, destined to become the very best of friends. We disclosed secrets we never thought to share. I'm sure Mr. Hobbs will disapprove. *He* doesn't like me, even if Lord Kissinger does."

Hazel could not disagree on that point. While Harold had not spoken to her about Agnes, she could tell he was annoyed by her.

Instead of disagreeing, Hazel said, "You'll both warm to each other after a time. It's inevitable that my best friend and my husband should get along."

Much to the consternation of the lady's maid, Agnes turned to face Hazel. "I know you've forgiven me, but I shall never forgive myself for putting you in this position. Is it horrible? Is he horrible? He couldn't be more of a stuffed tart if he tried, always so serious, a right bore. He's nothing at all like the man I envisioned you marrying."

"You're quite wrong about him." Hazel blushed and looked down at her hands. "He makes me laugh. And he's kind, and romantic, and ruggedly good looking, and…" Her words trailed off as she tried to capture what her heart felt about a man she knew so little about. "He's the kind of man I believe I could love."

"But could he ever love you?"

Hazel worried her lips. "I believe so."

There was so much more she could say, regale in every look, every smile, every touch, every joke, the boat ride, the afternoon spent in the sitting room, the boathouse kiss, the drawing room conversation after supper, the walk in the garden the next morning, the whispered compliments after church, so many moments. Sharing them felt like a violation of their intimacy. Those moments, all of them, were between Harold and her. There was no doubt in her mind she was falling in love with him and would continue to fall deeper, just as she was convinced he felt the same. At the very least, he *liked* her a great deal. He had a way of looking at her as though she were the only woman in the room, more so, the only woman he had ever truly seen. How does one explain that? Or share that without losing the magic in the explanation?

She kept it simple. "We suit, Agnes. We really do."

Agnes turned back to the mirror. "That's a relief. I'll never forgive myself for depriving you of a love match, but at least it's not bad."

Hazel did not respond, though she felt quite the opposite to her friend's assessment. Theirs *was* a love match. Or it soon would be. She smiled to herself at the memory of his whispered compliment this morning, that she was breathtaking in blue.

"Do you think," Agnes asked, "there's still a chance I could find love? Is it all over for me? Have I ruined my life?"

Hazel looked up, startled at the crack in Agnes's voice. In the mirror's reflection, Hazel could see Agnes's eyes watering.

"There's always a chance. I'm positive we'll find a good match, not just a husband."

"How am I supposed to find love in this condition? Who could love a woman carrying another man's child?"

Hazel reached over to take her friend's hand. "Someone who loves *you* will understand. It's not over."

Agnes sniffled but nodded. "I thought he was my true love. I want you to know that. I never thought to trap him. I never thought to be…one of those women. I—" Her voice broke. "I *knew* we were in love. I never would have done it otherwise. You know that, don't you?"

"Of course, I do! We were all fooled. Even Melissa believed his heart true."

"I won't trap someone to save myself. Know that I will be forthright should someone want to marry me. I'll not have them finding out after the wedding. They must know before and must understand that I'm not a—I'm not a whore."

"Oh, Agnes." Hazel stood up and wrapped her arms around her friend's shoulders, the maid standing back, looking teary eyed herself. "We'll find you the right man, and he'll fall so deeply in love with you that nothing else will matter."

Hazel observed the scene with satisfaction. A grin tugged at the corners of her lips as she surveyed the crowd, her gaze falling on Agnes at a card table with three gentlemen, all laughing. Yes, this was perfect! Her first hosted party, and it was a success.

Lord Collingwood sat at another card table, and from the looks on the faces of his peers, was winning. Helena enthralled a few ladies with conversation. Nana, who Hazel had insisted attend, stayed by the fire, talking mostly to Harold and Lord Kissinger, but from time to time she chatted with guests. Her companion hovered behind her, as frowny-faced as always but at least attentive. Although there were any number of gentlemen who might interest Lord Kissinger, he did not appear interested, instead speaking to a few ladies or couples on the rare occasion he was not with Harold or Nana.

Well, pooh. She had hoped to make two matches.

The rout was boisterous, intentionally so. Rather than a refreshment room, footmen circled with trays at timed intervals. Entertainment stations were set up around the room to keep guests engaged in one activity or another, be it cards, games, charades, pantomimes, or uninhibited gossip. Never did the voices dim nor people bore. Even the knot garden drew the attention of those willing to brave the cold.

All in all, Hazel was pleased with the turn out.

The only concern was Agnes. While Hazel did her best to ensure Agnes was the center of attention, expressly by circulating her around the room to sing her praises to all and sundry and press a commonality Hazel had "coincidentally" discovered between Agnes and whatever guest they spoke with at the time, no clear contender stepped forward. Some flirted. Then, who would not? Agnes was remarkably pretty. But no one extended the conversation beyond the initial flirt. It was most vexing. The current card players showed the most interest thus far. Hazel decided to leave Agnes at the table a while longer in hopes some progress would be made.

In another sweep of the room to determine which group she should visit next, her eyes fell to Harold. At present, he stood alone, watching her.

Hazel's cheeks warmed. No matter how many of the gentlemen she compared Harold to, there was no comparison. He stood poised, every inch an aristocrat, yet he emanated masculinity. He was a head taller than everyone. His physique filled his silk attire to admirable perfection with his broad shoulders, tapered waist, muscled legs, and the evident lack of padding his counterparts wore. Harold was not a large man, never to be mistaken for a laborer, but he was unmistakably fit.

The tip of Hazel's tongue wet her lips. His breeches hugged his thighs in sinful ways.

Every evening since the boathouse kiss, she had lain in bed, wondering if he would come to her. He had not. She appreciated his respect for her but was disappointed each time she doused the candle. He must be awaiting invitation.

Her gaze flicked from his face to his chest, then to his breeches, and back to his face, and yes, well, maybe back to the breeches a few more times. How did a wife invite her husband to bed? Was there a code? Maybe a look that conveyed the desired visit? Or was it more direct? No, surely not direct. That would be too improper, scandalous even. She could not *tell* him. There must be a phrase, something implicit that husbands understood as a euphemistic invitation. Or…

Oh, she had a delicious thought! But no, that would be even more scandalous than a direct invitation. But it would be understood… She would think more on that later.

What she wanted from him, exactly, she could not say. She had not particularly enjoyed their wedding night, no matter how much she tried to convince her-self. There had to be more to it. His kiss promised more. The drop of her stomach, the flutter in her abdo-men, the heat that coursed through her. *There had to be more to it.* If she had to judge by the penetrating look in his eyes now, she would swear on there being more.

Did he look at her as an artist might a subject? For a giddy moment, she wondered what it would be like to be his model, to pose for him as Nana had posed for Horace. To pose *nude.*

Her hand found her lips as she tried to smother a laugh and hide a smile. Wicked thoughts!

From across the room, Harold winked at her.

She could not very well talk with other guests now, not when the direction of her thoughts was painted on her cheeks, not when he stared so boldly at her, his eyes smoldering, igniting an inferno within her. Tugging at her bottom lip with her teeth, she blushed her way around the perimeter of the room to sidle up next to Harold.

With a hostess-friendly smile, she asked, "Enjoy-ing the party?"

Harold leaned down and said in a deep rumble, "I'm enjoying the view more."

Hazel laughed. "Yes, there is a good deal of lovely silk embroidery to admire." She winked so he would know she was fully aware he had not meant the dresses or coats.

"I was curious how long it would take you to find your way to me. I've been waiting with bated breath."

"Flattery, Mr. Hobbs, will get you everywhere." She slipped a hand into the crook of his arm; never mind they were standing still, and she was steady on her feet. "What do you see when you look out at the crowd?"

"Do you mean who would be a good match for Agnes, or do you mean what do *I* see?"

"Hmm. Both?"

Harold nodded once, then studied the guests. "The first is easy, the second more complex. I don't see a good match, sadly. Yes, my mother chose eligible bachelors, but most are popinjays. They're more concerned with themselves than they would be with a wife. Unlikely they would pursue her. Equally as unlikely would be her happiness in the match."

Hazel pouted but said nothing. She had thought as much. That did not stop her from being hopeful.

"I'll consider the situation. There are alternatives to marrying. With ingenuity, I'll think of possibilities. You don't carry the weight of this on your shoulders alone, darling."

Surprised, she looked up at his profile with its strong nose and angular jaw. The word *darling* struck her more than the offer to help, but combined, they made her heart skip beats.

He continued, "As to the second, what I see is not just a brilliantly hosted party — yes, that was a compliment, my dear — but a compilation of shades, hues, angles, perspectives, and lines."

Hazel tilted her head.

"I see everything as a potential sketch, how it would feel to put graphite to paper, where I would focus attention, how I would frame the subjects. For instance, observe Miss Snow talking to Mr. Sunderland. The contrast of light and shadow make them a fascinating subject. Notice how the light plays on

Miss Snow's features, yet Mr. Sunderland is darkened by shadow. The light enhances the lines of
Miss Snow's face. Now, before you take offense that
I mean to say she's wrinkled, let me explain that lines
express personality and emotion. A slight change in
line shape and placement could reveal the subject
laughs a great deal or frowns more. In Miss Snow's
case, she's happy. See how the lines form a crescent
to either side of her mouth?"

He glanced down to Hazel who was looking to
him more than to Miss Snow. From anyone else, she
might be jealous he was looking at another woman's
mouth, but from Harold, it was logical and artistic.

"The lines, if sketched just so, convey to the
observer a happy woman, not just in the moment
but the person herself," he continued to explain. "The
hues and undertones would be fantastic to paint,
especially given the warm colors of her dress in contrast to the cool colors of his attire, but I sketch more
than I paint. I would pay special attention to the negative space between them. Do you see how little space
there is in comparison to the people around them? I
could do a great deal with that space. The space itself
doesn't simply show where an object is not, rather
it shows a relationship between all that's around it.
It tells me that Mr. Sunderland is in preparation of
courting Miss Snow."

As fascinated as Hazel was by how he saw two
people talking, that bit of insight caught her attention. She looked from Mr. Sunderland to Miss Snow.
Sure enough, those crescent lines around her mouth
deepened each time Mr. Sunderland spoke. The light
on Miss Snow's face changed in intensity each time

she leaned closer to Mr. Sunderland to respond. Curiously, the shadows over Mr. Sunderland's face were not menacing or obstructive, rather intimate. To see the world through Harold's eyes! Goodness—what did *she* look like? Her free hand touched her face in search of lines and shadows.

The hand holding his arm shook as he chuckled. "You're all light and warmth," he said. "At present, I'd add a miniscule line between your brows to indicate curiosity, but there would be no escape from the two lines at the corners of your eyes, a woman who laughs often. Oh, and lest we forget, the angles would be slightly tilted from horizontal since you're leaning towards me."

"Well, then, Mr. Clever, what would you convey in your sketch if we were the subjects?"

He angled closer and moaned a *hmm* into her ear. "I would blend the shadowed space between us to show us as a pair, as two halves of a whole. The space between a darker blend, the space around a lighter blend. With the right angling, shading, and blending, the observer would know our relationship without us needing to pose, say with your hand over your heart looking up at me as I gaze adoringly back. There's power in what you do with the spaces *around* the subject, you see."

His words blended. All Hazel heard was their being two halves of a whole. How she heard words over the pounding of her heart was anyone's guess. This near stranger who liked her called them two halves of a whole. Despite the chill that crept in from outside, she desperately wanted a fan to cool the flush.

"Would you sketch or paint us?" she asked, her tongue dry, heavy, and altogether too large to speak.

"Sketch." After he said the word, he shifted his weight to lean farther in, his lips so close to her ear, his breath tickled her skin. "Although… I would love to apply a light brush stroke to your canvas."

Hazel gasped aloud, so loudly nearby heads turned.

She covered her reaction with a lively laugh, swatted at his arm, and said louder than necessary, "Mr. Hobbs, you do tell delicious tales." Looking to the faces of those around them, she smiled and gave a little shrug.

Heads swiveled away, disinterested.

With a boldness she did not feel, she batted her eyelashes at Harold and said before walking away, "Be careful what you wish for. You might just get it."

Chapter 18

The party guests gone, the candles doused, the family asleep, Hazel lay awake, the blanket pulled to her chin, her eyes trained on the coffered canopy as the reflections of the flames diminished with the dying fire. She waited. She wondered. She hoped.

Had she any forethought, she would have slipped a discreet note into his hand. *Sitting room. Paint me.* Or something bolder. Whispering such a request would have been better, as her words would have carried her true meaning. Realistically, her voice would have hitched from nervousness. At least he would have understood her meaning. Although being sketched or painted was infinitely appealing, strokes on canvas were not the kind she craved. Not yet.

Of all people to think of, she thought of her friend Melissa. Brave, passionate Melissa. Could Hazel be as bold?

Be brave, Hazel, she said to herself. *Be brave.*

She sat up to spy the table clock above the mantel. The clock face blurred. She squinted. The clock face blurred between narrowed lids. *Hmph.*

It must be close to midnight. Probably later. Probably much later. Hazel leaned back with a flop, tugging the blanket back to her chin.

Tomorrow was as good of a day as today. She could slip him a note tomorrow with a reference to paintings and canvases and brushes. Yes, tomorrow. Resuming her study of the retreating flame reflections and the texture of the woodgrain in light versus shadow, she wondered what Harold would make of it. The canopy hues, not the note. Oh, of course she meant the note.

Tossing back the blanket, she rose, donned the night wrap, then coaxed a brush through her hair. *Be brave*. It was not like he would reject her. What did she have to fear?

Drawing back her shoulders, she marched past the clock reading a quarter after two and opened her bedchamber door to the sitting room. The fire, unused that evening, greeted her with dying embers and a crackle. In a few tip-toed steps, confidence waning with each curl of toe to rug, she reached Harold's bedchamber door. Hand trembling, courage cold, she touched the handle with a fingertip. She stroked the metal.

In the chill of the room, she shivered. Her toes tingled. Her weight shifted. She pressed an ear to the door. Silence. He must be asleep. How selfish to wake him. How startled he would be!

With another *hmph*, she padded back across the sitting room, but then stopped at her open bedchamber door. If not now, when? Would she make this trek every night for the rest of their lives? Would she ever hand him a note of invitation? Once more, she padded back across the sitting room, stopping at his door. Hand to handle. Her fingers wrapped around the metal. She took slow, deep breaths.

Behind her, the fire crackled again. A log shifted.

She pressed the thumb latch and pushed open the door, stepping inside before she lost her nerve. Hazel blinked. The fire roared warm and inviting, brightening the room. It took her a moment to orient herself. To find the bed. The four-poster with carved columns stood against the far wall. Empty.

Oh.

The bedcovers had been turned down but were undisturbed.

"Hazel?" questioned a deep voice from near the fireplace.

She choked a strangled cry. On a couch in front of the fire, legs stretched out before him and ankles crossed, Harold sat with wood tablet on his lap, graphite in his hand. He wore a blue embroidered banyan. His legs were warmed by wool stockings. A night cap perched over his russet curls, those delectable curls unrolled and unpowdered, shaping a halo that framed his face.

Oh!

Her hand still gripping the door handle, she asked conversationally, as though they were not addressing each other in nightwear or standing in the same bedchamber in the wee hours of the morning, "What are you sketching?"

One corner of his mouth twitched a smile. "Us." He held up the paper for her to see, but she could not make it out. "I couldn't stop seeing us standing in the drawing room as I had described. I knew I'd never sleep until I sketched it." His gaze swept over her. "You're shivering. Come by the fire." He set the sketch aside on a low table and sat up, patting the couch for her to join him.

Shutting the door behind her, she obeyed. The fire did not warm her, though. She shivered more furiously, her muscles tensing, her fingers curling about her night wrap. Why had she not grabbed stockings? Her bare feet were numb. She chafed them against each other to stimulate warmth.

He scooted closer and wrapped a warm arm around her shoulders. At the contact, she relaxed, the shivering abating, though her feet remained numb.

In a husky voice, he asked, "Did you want to talk or…"

Hazel stared at her hands, willing herself to be brave. She had come this far already. Heart pounding and stomach fluttering, she turned her head to meet his eyes. His face was so close. Kissably close. She had never noticed how long his eyelashes were.

"I want you to take me to bed." To ensure he understood, she added, "Your bed."

Brown eyes lowered to admire her lips before Harold dipped his head to kiss her, a chaste kiss, but his lips were tender and slightly parted, sensual and teasing. Hazel's frozen toes curled.

Wordless, he stood, offered his hand, and pulled her up, pressing his lips to hers once more in that gentle, sensual way. In unhurried steps, his hand still holding hers, he escorted her to his bed. She could scarcely breathe. He pulled back the blanket. Only then did he release her hand, enabling him to unbutton his banyan, one slow button at a time, his eyes unwavering from hers. She watched. Her body throbbed. He slipped the banyan from his shoulders and let it fall to the floor. Removing his nightcap, then his stockings, also tossed to the floor, he then reached behind his neck to tug at his nightshirt, pulling it up and over his head in a smooth movement.

Not wanting to shock him yet unable to resist, she touched her fingertips to the reddish-brown curls dusting his chest. He sucked in a breath but said nothing, allowing her to explore. She swept her fingertips over his chest, raking the curls through her fingers. Though her eyes darted lower, she dared not stare or touch below his navel. What would he think of her or her behavior? She tugged her bottom lip between her teeth.

Harold did not allow her to lose confidence. With both hands clasping her hips, he lifted her night wrap up and over her head. When he reached to do the same with her nightdress, his hands stilled, fabric grasped in his fists, then he pulled her against him with a sudden roughness that made her gasp. He nestled his long, hard body against hers and captured her mouth for a hungry kiss, a needy kiss, a kiss that pushed boundaries. His tongue probed. Though he held her body tight to his, he relaxed his kiss, flicking the tip of his tongue to hers in invitation, prompting her to take control. She took it.

Wrapping her arms around his neck, she circled her tongue around his, kneading it, licking it, dueling for dominance. Instinctively, she wriggled her hips against him. Harold stepped away, but only to remove her nightdress.

As soon as the garment hit the floor, Hazel shrank back with self-consciousness.

Before she could cover herself with her hands, Harold palmed her face with both hands and said, "My beautiful, beautiful wife. My beautiful Hazel."

Whatever Hazel had been thinking dimmed. She melted against him. In one fluid movement, he scooped an arm behind her legs and lifted her as though she were weightless, then laid her on the bed before climbing onto the feathered mattress beside her. He pulled the bedcovers over them before his hand found her waist and his lips found her mouth.

The contrast between the two swirled her senses. His kiss was urgent, demanding, more provocative than before, yet his hand flowed against her skin with such gentle persuasion, such slow and methodical precision, her mind rippled with need.

And then she understood. He was holding to his promise. He was applying his brush stroke to her canvas.

She stilled, then said against his lips, "Paint me."

He leaned back only enough to see her face, his eyes a devilishly dark brown, his lids hooded, his lips reddened. While he studied her, his fingers trailed over her hip, shading a crosshatch pattern across her skin, one part with fingertips, one part with a gentle tickle of well-manicured nails. She made a sound mixed between a giggle, a gasp, and a moan. Dragging his fingers, he smoothed his palm over her hip and across her abdomen. The focal point her navel, he circled, then drew up and down her torso asymmetrical geometrics, his touch one moment light, fluttering, and silky, the next feathering against her skin, and then with a subtle move of the wrist pressured and coarse, hot and fast.

The sensations blended, muted then vibrant, shadowed then dramatic. She squeezed her eyes closed and pushed her head against the pillow, focusing on the contradictions, her skin aflame and sensitive to his touch. Just as his fingers brushed below her navel, his mouth covered her breast. She wrenched her eyes wide. He looked up to meet her gaze, her nipple between his lips, and flicked the bud until the skin puckered, embossed. *Oh my!* She had no words, no thoughts for the sensation, for the action. Arching her back, she reached a hand to his shoulder and dragged her fingers against his skin as he had done to her.

Harold shifted to move from her breast to her lips. His kiss distracted her only long enough for his hand to trace the triangle of her mons before slipping a finger between her lower lips and inside her core. She gasped in surprise.

He rubbed his nose against hers, then shifted his weight slightly away from her. Propping himself on an elbow, he smiled, a slow and sleepy smile.

She suspected he was about to say something, maybe ask a question, maybe make a joke, but she did not give him the opportunity. Tucking her hand behind his neck, she pulled him back to her for a kiss intended both to seduce and distract as she hooked an ankle over his hip and tugged. He needed no further persuasion. Angling himself over her, he brought his legs between hers and nudged her thighs apart.

As the weight of his chest pressed against hers and he positioned himself, Hazel braced for discomfort. She tensed and waited for the startling pain she recalled from their wedding night.

Instead, she felt his lips feather over her cheeks and down her neck. He shifted just so, then thrust not into her but against her, rubbing himself over her lower lips with a determined, wet friction. The motion caused a dizzying wave of euphoria. Her hips lifted to meet his next teasing thrust. Color filled her vision behind squeezed eyelids, vibrant, dynamic, a palette of shades, her world a distortion of gradient hues, tones, and textures. She met him thrust for thrust, rubbing her body against his, mumbling against his lips nonsense sounds, giving herself to the most glorious pleasure she had never known possible. Her limbs quivered. Her heart raced. Her senses layered. She dug her fingers into his back as a color wheel dazzled her in exquisite ecstasy.

In that moment, Harold repositioned and thrust inside of her. There was no pain. There was no discomfort. There was only bliss. She cried out. His depth deepened; his rhythm quickened. She rocked against him, layer after layer of saturated color overlapping. Elongated strokes. Short strokes. His rhythm turned erratic. Then he, too, cried out, burying the sound against her neck as his thrusts continued to bring her pleasure until they both tremored into a breathless, sweaty embrace.

His weight still atop her, he chuckled. She laughed, her lips pressed to his shoulder. What they laughed about, neither could say, but they both laughed. Even after he rolled off her, pulling her against him so she could rest her chin on his chest, they still laughed.

Hazel looked up at him, her husband, and admired the dishevelment of his hair, sweat drenching an inch into his hairline, frizzing his curls into wild disarray. His face was flushed. How could she ever have thought him a staid gentleman? This was no serious-minded bore. This was a man of passion. She wondered if it was too soon to ask for a second round.

Two days later, Harold sat in the private parlor of Ship's Anchor Inn, savoring a bite of fish. The cook's specialties were veal and West Country tart, both already on the table alongside a plethora of other culinary delights.

Patrick took a swig of ale then said, "Mr. Jones expressed the most interest. That is to say, the most *genuine* interest rather than obsequious interest."

"I'll call on him again next week and bring Hazel with me. She'll like Mrs. Jones. If he's sincere, now's the time to make arrangements."

An apple orchard should be one of the last items on his list, for once planted, it would not bear fruit for another five years. There were more pressing estate needs and faster yielding possibilities. But Harold wanted to consider long-term, as well. Not to mention he thought Hazel would like it. There was potential with an apple orchard, fruit to eat, cook, store, juice, and even turn into jam and cider. If Mr. Jones would agree to devoting a portion of his letted land for the orchard, Harold would promise to hire an extra farmhand, someone versed in orchard cultivation.

"Not that it's my business…" Patrick began before taking delight in the veal. Waving his fork at Harold, he continued, "But I'll make it my business since I'm your wise counsel." He took another drink of ale then poked the air with his fork. "How the devil are you going to pay for it?"

Harold cringed. "Since London, I've been study-ing the accounts, working and reworking figures. If

I can lay out the plans and numbers, maybe Father will listen."

"And maybe fish will learn to walk."

"I know. I know. But I have no control over the accounts. The best I can do is craft a proposal that will help him see reason." Harold stabbed at the last piece of his fish, his good mood plummeting.

After spending an evening, a full day, and another evening sequestered in his bedchamber with Hazel, he thought nothing could dispirit his mood. Splashing him with cold water was talk of his father and account ledgers.

Patrick asked, "What about the money from Trethow's estate?"

"The extorted funds, you mean? I'd rather Father not touch it. I'd rather strike it from the settlement." Harold set aside his cutlery, his appetite going the way of his mood. "In the end, we may not have a choice. At least not until we get the estate earning a profit again."

"Harold, I say this as a friend. You need to handle your father. He's destroying not just his own life, but yours. It's time to take control. Handle him."

Anger pulsed through his veins. "Like you're handling yours?"

Patrick looked up, his expression first registering shock then in equal parts anger. "That's different, and you know it."

"Is it? I don't see you putting your foot down. I don't see you telling him to sod off. Young lady after young lady you allow them to invite for supper, yet you say nothing. Here's a deal for you. You handle your father, then I'll handle mine."

Patrick pushed his plate away and crossed his arms over his chest. He made to speak several times but swallowed the words, choosing instead to shake his head and glower at his plate.

As quickly as the anger rose, it diminished, leaving Harold chagrined and guilt-ridden. He should not have lashed out. Patrick had only said what needed to be said. The trouble was Harold had no footing to handle his father, and that was the most infuriating part, for he could do nothing but watch the man sink the ship. He had not, as his father often and so eloquently reminded him, even reached his majority. Harold was not the head of the household. He had only prospects, plans, and pleas, a soundless voice against his father's greed.

Harold cleared his throat. "I had no right. Forgive me."

His friend continued to shake his head. "No, you *are* right. It's time I spoke honestly with him."

After a minute of silence, each staring at the table, Harold chided, "Or you could marry one of the young ladies your mother has picked out."

Patrick chuckled hollowly. "Nothing says masterfully clever like appeasing the sire while simultaneously making the bride and bridegroom miserable. Think Miss Plumb would consider a lifetime of misery?"

Harold gave that the laugh it deserved. "If you deprived Hazel of the opportunity to play matchmaker, she may not soon forgive you."

Patrick winked, harsh words of earlier forgiven.

After the meal, Harold returned home for vis-à-vis tea with Nana. He had looked forward to this conversation all morning, but he dreaded the thought of endless biscuits after his meaty meal. When he joined her in the parlor, the tea tray did not disappoint those expectations. He sighed, resolving himself to the inevitable stomachache.

A kiss on the cheek. An accepted cup and saucer. A curious glance at the leather portmanteau.

Nana unbuckled the straps and flipped open the bag, extracting a stack of paper. "I want you to come to my bedchamber. The paintings adorn the walls. I had Mr. Somners and Mr. Quainoo arrange between them to move every single frame from the dower house to my new room. When I die, I want them all buried with me. It'll require a mausoleum, of course." She chortled at her morbid jest. "These are a few of the sketches."

Harold set aside the saucer to take the stack. Nana began rifling through more paper in the portmanteau, but he focused his attention on the sheets in his hand.

Page after page, front and back, corner to corner, were chalk sketches, the style similar enough to his own to startle him but individual enough not to be mistaken for his work. Most of the sketches were landscapes of the lake and estate grounds, a few of the house, but there were some portraits of people, mostly house and grounds staff. The majority remained unfinished. These represented an artist's eye, the interpretation of the artist's world. A great deal of experimentation could be seen, namely with shading techniques and perspective.

Harold studied each page, critiquing, admiring, in awe that these were the works of his grandfather.

He turned over a sketch of the boathouse to find a corner of the wilderness walk drawn on the backside of the page. "Why did you never tell me?"

Nana waved a hand. "You were only a boy. You left for India not a day over fifteen."

"I was days away from my eighteenth birthday."

"Too young. Art is serious craft, not to be unappreciated by youth fancying Grand Tours and girls."

Harold frowned. "I went to India on business at Father's command, not for a tour or recreation or…girls."

"And look how you've grown. I shouldn't have recognized you."

"You didn't." That was unfair. Her mistaking him for his father could not be entirely her fault.

"But you see," she said, "now you can appreciate your grandfather's craft with the eyes of maturity."

He stopped himself before mentioning he had appreciated art since his youth, since as far back as he could remember. Harold was here to learn about his grandfather and spend time with his grandmother, not argue. Truthfully, she would not have had any reason to know him appreciative.

A pity. From the moment his hand gripped a writing implement, he had been drawing in some form or another, even if he had never shared his passion with his family. Had he shared, would she have told him? He would have liked to, but his mother had been too absorbed with her own life to notice him, his father too busy losing the family fortune in schemes to care, and his grandmother too focused on entertaining her friends at the dower house to attend to a child. His nanny was attentive. His tutor was attentive. The short stent he spent at Eton produced an attentive friend or two before his father sent for him to return and resume with the tutor. And then India. His art had been his own, a passion he never thought a family member would share.

"Yes, Nana, I can better appreciate his work now. Thank you for sharing." He traded the stack for a new stack.

What he would not give to have known his grandfather, to have shared this with him. So much he could have learned. Would his grandfather have critiqued his sketches, taught him more? The little bit he knew of his grandfather was in such stark contrast to the man he felt etched into the pages. He ached to ask his grandmother more questions.

"Will you come to see the paintings?" she asked, her tone more needy than curious.

"I would be honored."

"I *had* planned to show you. I thought you'd return after a few months, but you were gone so long. I worried."

He covered her hand with his.

She could not have worried more about him than he worried about her. Having her living in the main house was a relief. Here, in the house, she would be safe. No one could deny she was doing better. Her episodes of forgetfulness and confusion were less frequent, though not gone altogether. From what he had ascertained, she kept busy. She also socialized more, especially now that Miss Plumb was in residence.

While he could happily express many reasons he was thankful for his grandmother and Miss Plumb's attentions to each other, he would never vocalize some of those reasons, namely his infinite appreciation that Miss Plumb had been so distracted the day before by his grandmother's need for company, she had not once come to knock on Hazel's bedchamber or burst through the door to see why Hazel remained in bed all day. Harold almost laughed aloud at what a chaotic moment that would have caused.

Ah, yes, but above all, he was thankful his grandmother was safe and content.

A scratching sound awakened Hazel. She blinked at the darkness. The sound was akin to arms arcing angel wings into sand, something she had not done in years. A muted lap of ocean wave. A gentle tap-tap of feet on hardpacked beach. Unsure if she was dreaming, Hazel blinked again. As her eyes adjusted to the black, a glow became visible, a teardrop shape outlined on the wallpaper. When the glow flickered, she realized it was candlelight. The fire had long since died to embers. Giving her legs a firm stretch, she rolled over.

His back against the headboard, Harold sat next to her in bed, his knees bent to prop up his drawing tablet. Sweeping across the page in swift motions, danced the graphite.

For all her stretching and turning, he had not noticed she was awake. She kept it that way for now. The moment offered an intimate glimpse of her husband enjoying a different kind of passion than they had shared for nearly a week. His attention riveted,

Hazel could unabashedly admire not only the bareness of his flesh, but the fixed focus of his brown eyes, always slightly wild when sketching. This was the rawness, the ruggedness she had found so attractive. Now, it was within her reach every evening, physically and emotionally.

Inching closer, she propped herself with her elbow and laid her head against his chest, the skin cool from exposure, the hair tickling her cheek. His heartbeat sounded *thump thump* in her ear.

Harold's hand stilled. "I hope I didn't wake you."

She nuzzled him. "Who's to say I wasn't planning to wake *you*?" Her tone had intended to be teasing and implicit, but the grogginess of her voice gave away the truth.

He kissed the top of her head. "What do you think?"

The unfinished sketch was of her. Surprised, she sat up, her shoulder leaning against his. In the sketch, she lounged on the chaise in the sitting room, her arm folded beneath her head.

"From this evening?" she asked.

"I had wanted to capture it then, but I didn't dare disturb the moment, not when I was so enjoying your tale of Miss Plumb's first visit to the ocean."

"Liar. You were bored silly." Hazel pulled her knees to her chest.

Harold chuckled, then began shading her hair in the sketch, the strands unbound and spilling over the arm of the chaise.

It did not take long for Hazel to realize he had slipped back into focus. An idle bit of shading, and soon he was lost in his craft. Did he relive the scene as he drew, focus on the single moment, or recreate a new scene to enliven the memory? She watched him work until he finished the shading. When he began adding background, she decided to be daring. For several evenings, she had wanted to say something but never knew the best moment or the right words. This was not something a lady should think about much less say. After the intimacy they had shared, he could not possibly judge her ill. Surely.

Breaking his concentration with a kiss to his shoulder, she adjusted the blanket. Harold's hand stilled again, and he watched her out of the corner of his eyes. Hazel slipped the bedcover over her bare shoulder, exposing not just her upper arm but a glimpse of a single breast's curvature. She rested her chin on the same shoulder and fluttered her eyelashes.

She challenged, "Sketch me like this?"

In a measured tilt, Harold angled his head to face her fully. He caressed her with a look.

"Or…like this?" She let the bedcover slip below both breasts.

However calm she appeared on the outside, she was tumultuous inside. Her heart pounded. Her stomach clenched. Her knees knocked. Feeling exposed would be to state the obvious, but it was more than that. So much more than that.

He wet his lips.

"Or…would this be better?" Motion deliberately paced to tease, Hazel coaxed the bedcovers over her knees to pool at her feet.

Without a word, Harold turned over the paper. His hand worked magic, scratching, rubbing, shading, blending. Hazel dared not move. She watched him, fascinated, nervous, relieved, aroused.

After what felt like a lifetime, she was embold-
ened. Hoping not to disturb his work but curious all
the same, she lowered her knees a tad, arched her
back away from the headboard, and tousled her hair.
She saw, as she did this, his hand stop, his attention
fixed on her movements. When she posed, just so,
he adjusted the positioning of his paper and began
sketching anew.

Three or four more poses later, each time his paper
adjusting so he could start a new sketch in an available corner or edge of the sheet, she angled to see
his work.

Harold's throaty laugh interrupted her curiosity.
He turned away from her to set his tablet and graphite on the table. She squeaked, thinking he meant to
hide it. Instead, he handed it to her, his hands free
to flex and pull the bedcovers up to his chest. Hazel
grappled the sheet with glee.

One look and her fingers crept to her mouth.

In the short span, he had covered the page with
half a dozen different sketches, each unfinished
but each dynamic and emotional. Although she
stared at herself holding a pose, she hardly knew
herself. Staring back with sultry intensity was a
bold and confident woman, a woman with charm
and beauty, nothing like the woman she saw every
day in the mirror. The woman in the mirror always
looked back with courageous resignation. She was
what she was, and she accepted that. The reflection knew what she wanted in life but doubted she
could achieve it, not a plump country bumpkin. But
this woman, the woman in the myriad sketches, *oh*,
she wanted to be this woman yet could not readily

admit that she already was, at least from Harold's perspective.

So enamored was she, she forgot to be embarrassed by her nudity immortalized.

A tickle at her knee distracted her. When she swatted at the sensation, the back of her hand clipped Harold's fingers.

She had not noticed him move. He sat facing her, propped on one hand, the other hand tracing her kneecap with a solitary fingertip. The bedcovers had been tossed aside. Her eyes widened to see him boldly sprawled, as aroused as she. Absently, she pushed the art aside and trailed a hand up and down his thigh.

Though he sucked in a breath, he made no notice of her attentions, instead continuing his exploration of her knee. For all her curves, she had bony knees. There was nothing remotely sexy about her knees. Yet that same fingertip circled with the barest contact, a tickle, a tease, a flicker to skin. The fingertip turned to four as they drummed light as a feather down and up her shin, then back to circling the knee. Then down the back of her calves and up again to the knee. Fingernails grazed the inside of her thigh, then back to her knee. Her skin became so sensitive that a single circle about that bony kneecap had her clenching and tensing.

Harold leaned his chest against her shin, his chest hair intensifying the sensations. When he pressed his lips to her knee, she thought she might die. Her body throbbed with need. Her apex pulsed with a fiery heat. He was in no hurry, the devilish man.

He pressed another kiss to her knee, just on the outside, then one on the inside, parting her legs as

he did so. With a look of malevolence in those dark
eyes, he traced the same circle around the knee's peak
with his tongue. She moaned and tried to straighten
her leg away from him. How could one knee be so
endlessly sensual? He held fast to her ankle, pressing his lips to the inside of her thigh, his fingertips
circling where his tongue had just been.

Then spreading her legs wide, he crawled between
them, but rather than entering her, as she expected,
as she desperately wanted, he leaned over her and
kissed her abdomen.

His lips touching her skin, his voice a murmured
tickle, he asked, "You remember the brush strokes
I used?"

Oh, she remembered. She moaned an affirmative.

"I'll use the same techniques tonight, but with a
different brush."

She looked down at him, confused. In a long
sweep, he licked her from hip to navel. Hazel's gasp
turned into a cry as she braced against the bedsheets.

True to his word, he painted her torso with a
mouth made of fire, passion, and sin. She wriggled;
she panted; she moaned; she begged for mercy. He
captured her skin between his lips, swirling and
suckling, covering every inch of her torso. When he
slipped lower, she was sure she would go mad.

He palmed her mound, parted her lower lips,
and circled her bud with the tip of his tongue before
enveloping her in the moist heat of his mouth. With a
jerk of her body, she climaxed into a burst of shades
and blends, feeling every inch the confident and
sexual woman in the drawings. He joined her, skin
to skin, and came into her. She drew in his length,

tightening around his girth. Looking up to him as he found his pleasure and brought her more, she palmed his cheek. Harold's eyelids fluttered open. Gazing down at her, he turned his head to kiss the inside of her wrist.

Was it too soon to fall in love with her husband?

Eugene Hobbs, Baron Collingwood, clinked cutlery against his wine glass to capture everyone's attention at supper the next evening. "I've arranged a supper party for the end of the week. Special guests have been invited. Partners of mine. As it is only supper, not all my partners will attend. A select few. My point is, I want to make a memorable impression. The best attire. The best food. The best entertainment." He stared at Miss Plumb. "Do you play? Sing? Something of value?"

She glanced at Hazel before replying, "I'm tolerably good with music, my lord."

Hazel's laugh tinkled with merriment. "She's modest. You'll not find a better pianoforte player in the West Country."

Patrick cleared his throat. "I've been told I can carry a tune — should the best pianoforte player in the West Country care to accompany."

Harold leaned back in his chair, surprised by Patrick's admission and willingness to be center stage for Father's guests. Admirable offer, though. Now, Miss Plumb would not be volunteered to entertain guests alone.

"Good," said Eugene before turning his attention to his wife. "Perfection in arrangements, nothing less." Without letting her respond, he cut to Nana. "And you will busy yourself upstairs. This is an important supper."

When Harold saw Hazel about to protest, he shook his head. His father would not take kindly to dissention.

Nana harrumphed but nodded. "I wouldn't have attended if you invited me. I don't like your *partners*. Greedy gamblers, the lot of them."

Harold's mother began to scold, but Eugene held up a staying hand. "Now, if the ladies would care to retire, I'm ready for my port. Lord Kissinger, how is the earl? I had hoped he would join us this evening."

At the dismissal, the ladies made for the drawing room, leaving Harold behind with his father and Patrick, the latter having been expressly invited by Eugene in hopes of luring the earl, a wealthy man Eugene had yet to snare in one of his schemes despite years of trying. The conversation over port and cigars centered around the Earl of Winthorp. Harold lost interest quickly. Knowing Patrick could hold his own, he stayed only as long as was polite, then bowed out to join the ladies in the drawing room.

Although he did not slip in unseen as he had hoped, the ladies were too deep in a giggled discussion of the supper party to pay him any mind. He took a seat far enough to observe without interrupting.

Observe was a misrepresentation. Stare. Ogle. Drool. Those would be more apt. He watched Hazel exclusively. Her animation. Her smile. Her laugh. Earlier that morning, he had taken her with him to call on tenants, especially Mr. and Mrs. Jones. The experience had been enlightening. Simultaneously, she was friendly, chatting unreservedly with the couple as though they had been neighbors for years, while also emulating the poise and respectability of an aristocrat.

Her behavior with the tenants should not have surprised him. She was, after all, a gentleman's daughter. He suspected, however, his grandmother had influenced this elegance and maturity, for he did not recall this side of Hazel at the hunting party. She had been friendly, yes, but more youthful than poised. His grandmother had to be the influencer. The Dowager Baroness Collingwood, despite age and infirmity, defined poise and respectability, an earl's daughter who had been groomed from childhood. How remarkable that Hazel took on these traits with ease, combining them with her natural amiability.

His admiration of her was not because of her behavior, but seeing her in different situations increased his admiration, nevertheless. She was, to him, already perfection. He could not take his eyes off her. He could not stop thinking about her. He was a man obsessed with his own wife. Even now, the way she held herself, the way the light shimmered off her hair, the way she laughed, *everything*. Perfection.

"What do you think?" Hazel asked, turning to him.

He sat up. All eyes were on him.

After a moment's consideration, he said, "Your perspective is best." He had no idea what they had been talking about, but he hoped that would cover his ignorance.

His mother asked rhetorically, "What is it women want in marriage? To have their opinion valued. Aren't you the lucky woman!" She patted Hazel's arm.

Hazel's expression to him before she returned to the conversation was sly enough to reveal she knew all too well he had not been listening.

The remainder of the evening went by in a blur. Conversation turned to card games, embroidery, and reading after the gentlemen joined the group.

Later that evening, Harold sat in the private sitting room, warmed by the fire, his banyan, and his wool stockings. He waited for Hazel to join him. In hand, he held a brief collection of papers. On and off for the past several days, he had worked on this, hoping to finish his plan before presenting it. She should not be disappointed.

Flipping through the papers, he reread the letters.

When the adjoining door to her bedchamber opened, he grinned. Hazel posed against the doorframe, one arm over her head and one foot raised behind her. As concealing as her night wrap and nightdress was, they hid nothing from his memory and certainly not when she posed so provocatively. He forgot the letters in his hand.

She giggled, pulled the door shut behind her, and sat next to him on the chaise, her foot tucked beneath her. "Are those new sketches, or are you ready with blank pages to fill?"

"Neither." Laughing at her crestfallen expression, he leaned in to kiss her neck. "I've saved those for later."

The papers passed from his hands to hers. She started to read the first letter, cocking her head to the side.

He draped an arm on the back of the chaise. "They're character references."

"I see that." She eyed him askance then turned back to the letters.

"I can hear your thoughts as though you spoke them aloud, my dear. You want to try matchmaking at the supper party. I'm not opposed. I do, however, want you to consider two complications. For one, my father's *partners* are exactly what Nana claimed. Greedy gamblers. I don't mean to paint my father in a bad light, but, well, you know who they are, for most of them attended the hunting party. They're people like, and pardon me for mentioning his name, Lord Driffield. They're not the kind who need to be matched with Miss Plumb."

Her nod was slow, measured. "And the second?"

"After ten soirees, fifteen supper parties, twenty routs, and however many other events you hope to host or use for matchmaking purposes, there remains a slim chance for a good match. Lest we forget, we're also on a deadline that doesn't allow time for ten soirees, fifteen supper parties, or twenty routs since Miss Plumb's condition will become visible soon, despite how well her lady's maid hides the evidence." He waved a hand at the letters, feeling a little smug about his genius. "I promised to help. This is my idea."

"Character references." Her tone was more incredulous than pleased.

"It's the best course of action. I've listed the few people I know who would consider, in light of an outstanding character reference, employing a woman with child. The work is nothing menial. If employed, she would have housing and a way to support herself and the child. I know it's not ideal, but it's the most realistic idea I've had. If you'll read the references, you'll see I've taken a few liberties."

He watched her read over each one, not that they changed much from one to the next. Her brows puckered. Her lips frowned. This was not the reaction he wanted. His smugness wavered.

Pointing at a line in one of the letters, she read aloud, "Mrs. Plumbtree."

When she did not say more, he ventured, "A liberty, I know, but I thought presenting her as a widow was best. I couldn't very well recommend an unmarried woman, nor would I advise her to use her maiden name since that would too easily tie back to her family. A different name? I can rewrite these, of course."

Dash it all. He could tell she hated his idea. It really was the best he had devised.

Rolling up the references, she asked, "But how would we call on her? A former employer and his wife would not visit a former employee as a friend."

Harold pinched his chin. He had not thought of that. While he had not exactly lost sleep over plotting alternative solutions for Miss Plumb, he had put a fair bit of planning into this. How had he glossed over something so obvious? Of course, Hazel would want to call on her friend.

"What about this…" He drummed his fingers on his chin. "I'll write to an old acquaintance of mine. Just the one. Same plan. But I'll ensure he doesn't ask questions and understands she's a friend."

The crease between her brows deepened. "That makes her sound like your former mistress."

He exhaled from his cheeks. "Let me think about the wording. I'll sort it."

She shook her head. "I don't know how she'll take to employment either."

Without a ready response that would pass for polite, he remained silent. Miss Plumb would be fortunate to find employment. No one aside from the few gentlemen he knew personally would take in a woman with a child, widow or not. Without employment, she had no way to support herself. Miss Plumb had no choice. It was lucky indeed she had Hazel or Miss Plumb would have found herself not only homeless, but without the means of employment. Not without references. This was a grand opportunity. The only opportunity.

For how long she would be allowed to stay at Trelowen depended on his father's charity, and Harold did not consider his father charitable, not without some return for his efforts. It was crowded enough for the man with Nana and her companion under foot. Although Eugene did not blink at adding more debt and making more promissory notes to host parties, he would consider Miss Plumb another mouth to feed that he could not afford. Illogical. One mouth compared to the many he would happily and daftly feed at a supper party, but there it was. Miss Plumb was on borrowed time.

Hazel said, "I like the widow idea."

"A relief there's something of value in the plan."

"Don't pout, Harold. It's a good plan. Just not for Agnes. At least not yet. I'm not dismissing this. I'd rather, if we can, exhaust other ideas before we consider this one. What if we set her up not as an employee but as a tenant? A widow letting a cottage. That's respectable. Not uncommon. We would still be able to call on her. If these people, these friends of yours, would take in a widow as an employee, they would be as likely, if not more so, to take her in as a tenant."

"An easy arrangement to make."

Hazel smiled at that declaration. "There. We have it, then."

Shaking his head, Harold asked, "But without employment, who is paying the letting fees? Food? Supplies? Baby's needs? She could live frugally, but she can't live on nothing."

"Oh." Hazel bowed her head. Less than a minute later, she was smiling again. "We could cover her costs."

He coughed.

"As you said, she would live frugally. We could certainly pay to set her up at least."

How he was supposed to respond to that, he did not know. Admit they were paupers? Admit that his father racked debts on entertaining he could never pay but had no coin on hand to let a cottage or even lend? Admit he had no access to funds of his own? Hazel may have a heart of gold, but Harold had no way to see her idea to fruition. He rubbed his forehead at the onset of a migraine.

Hazel huffed. "Well if you won't, I will. While I don't know the exact figure, I know my father paid handsomely to secure this marriage. I'll pay for her needs out of my dowry. That should be more than enough to help her."

His breathing shallowed.

She continued, "We've not yet spoken about an allowance. I formally request pin money. Take it from my dowry. Since I may use my pin money however

I wish, I'll use it to help her. Now, what amount do you suppose is fair, and when shall I receive my first installment?"

Good heavens. He covered his mouth with his hand.

What she asked for was conversely reasonable and impossible. Would she understand if he explained the fate of her dowry? He thought not. The realization that she would have no money of her own or even a widow's income — perish the thought — might come as a rude awakening.

Now that the moment presented itself, should he explain their situation? If he did, how much should he tell? That they were destitute? That they were waiting for a risky investment to pay off? That his father had coerced her father to the point of Trethow's possible ruin? Then there was the explanation of where he fit into that dismal painting. He had little part in any of it, yet he was not certain she would see it that way.

Moving his hand to cover his eyes, he tried to think of where to begin. He could not. He needed to think this through first.

Harold raked a hand through his hair. "Give me a few days. I'll sort it."

She gave a brisk nod and a satisfied smile, likely assuming he not only meant he would sort the allowance but also the living arrangements of her "widowed" friend. He had not the first idea how to sort any of it.

Victorious, she reached over to tug at his buttons. Her flirty smile helped him forget his turmoil. Almost.

Chapter 19

The family gathered in the drawing room, awaiting guests. Hazel had not yet mentioned to Agnes the possibility of an alternate plan, and she was pleased she had not, for Agnes was all too clearly hoping tonight would be a promising opportunity for a match. Although Agnes was naturally beautiful, she had taken pains this evening to look stunning. Whatever gentleman did not fall for her tonight was mad.

A quick look at Harold confirmed him mad. His eyes were trained on Hazel. Only Hazel. Her cheeks warmed at his open regard.

There was so much about him to love. Every day presented a new discovery, some new reason to fall for him, and oh, she was falling. If she were being truthful, she had already fallen for him; his honesty, his respect, his humor, his cleverness, his talent. The list was endless, and she knew; she had tried to list all his assets one evening while she waited for him. Even when he joined her in the sitting room, she was still adding new items to the list and had countless more to continue adding. How she had not recognized him at first sight as her life's match, she would never know, for he was undoubtedly just that. It was more than him, though. It was how he made her feel. How he made her feel about herself.

She had not spoken about him much to Agnes. The two had once shared everything with each other, but no longer. There was an inexplicable chasm between them that widened every day. Hazel hoped that would not last, for Agnes was her dearest friend and had been for as long as she could remember. Together, they were supposed to raise their children. Together, they were supposed to grow old. But she found herself not confiding in Agnes as she might have done before her marriage. And of course, there were all the secrets Agnes had kept from her regarding Lord Driffield. In time, all would be resolved. She hoped.

The brief mention she had made to Agnes about her growing affection for Harold had been met with a dismissive wave and an impertinent, and rather shocking statement that it was only the intimacy Hazel liked. Well, Hazel had not been about to discuss that aspect of the marriage, but she did soundly disagree. Yes, the intimacy was surprisingly wonderful. Their marriage was not traditional; their evenings together were not duty bound. Everything about their time together was freeing. But that was not why she had fallen for him. Had she never visited his bedchamber, she would feel the same way, for it was *Harold* she had fallen for, not…well, not *that*. Convincing Agnes seemed tedious and unnecessary. In time, with a love match of her own, perhaps Agnes would understand.

Ah, the first guest.

The knocker fell four times at the front door. Voices could be heard from the entrance hall as Mr. Quainoo greeted the guest.

Hazel sidled next to Harold as the family assembled, ready to begin the festivities.

The drawing room double doors opened, and the butler led Lord Kissinger into the room. While Lord and Lady Collingwood visibly relaxed since it was *just* Lord Kissinger, Hazel, Harold, and Agnes stepped forward with hearty welcomes. For at least another ten minutes, they talked together, Kissinger joking about the song choices he had considered for the post-supper entertainment.

At length, the knocker fell again. Voices in the entrance hall. Mr. Quainoo's appearance.

Agnes was the first to see the guests and exclaim, "Melissa!" With a bold break from decorum, Agnes dashed across the room to embrace Melissa and curtsy to Sir Chauncey.

Once Hazel's father- and mother-in-law said their greetings, and Lord Collingwood engaged Sir Chauncey in conversation, Melissa joined their little group, Agnes's arm hooked with hers.

Hazel kissed each cheek. "What a wonderful surprise!"

"I would have written," Melissa said, "but we didn't receive the invitation until yesterday."

While her friend and Sir Chauncey had been at the hunting party, Hazel had not realized Lord Collingwood and Sir Chauncey were partners. She wondered if it was the same investment her father had been so excited about. A pity her father could not be here, but from what she understood of the invitations, her father-in-law had only invited those who lived within a close enough proximity to return home after supper.

The knocker once more. This time, Mr. Quainoo escorted a gentleman and his wife who Hazel could not remember. Two more arrivals followed that. It was to be a small gathering, she knew. The evening seemed overly extravagant for so short of a guest list. What was the point of impressing guests who were already in business with him? Lord Collingwood did love to flaunt his wealth. Hazel was relieved that Harold never showed the same inclinations.

Melissa leaned in to ask for Hazel's hearing only, "Is that doe-eyed expression for appearances or…?"

Flushing, Hazel said, "I hadn't realized I was staring at him."

With a touch to the back of Hazel's wrist and a teasing smile, Melissa said, "I know that look. I never thought to see it directed at Mr. Hobbs. You must tell me everything."

Hazel promised with a nod as the knocker sounded yet again.

When Mr. Quainoo stepped into the room this time, a hush fell. The Earl of Driffield walked in, on his arm a blonde who looked down her nose at everyone in attendance.

Out of the corner of her eyes, Hazel could see Agnes stiffen.

Harold stepped away from Kissinger to come to Hazel's side, his hand to the small of her back. At the same time, Kissinger moved to Agnes's side. Good. Should Agnes swoon, he could catch her. Hazel took one step closer to Harold.

Harold fumed. Thankfully, Patrick had understood his nod and stepped to Miss Plumb's side. Harold could not offer support to both ladies, and his priority was Hazel. He imbued strength into the hand he touched to the small of his wife's back.

The effrontery of his father to invite Driffield both angered and disgusted Harold. While his father would not know the connection between Miss Plumb and Lord Driffield, he did know there was a connection between the man and Hazel, even if that connection was erroneous. That fact made this all the more heinous. Driffield may have invested, but that did not give him the right to step foot into this house again. This affirmed what Harold already knew: his father thought of no one beyond himself. To his father, Hazel was nothing more than a means to have acquired ready financing, forgotten the moment the settlement was signed and the vows exchanged.

She was Harold's *wife*, yet his father showed her no more respect than he would a servant.

As the son of the host, the heir to the barony, and a respectable gentleman, Harold schooled his features into a mask of polite reception, thankful that they had not stood on ceremony this evening by forming a receiving line. With any luck, Driffield would ignore this corner of the room. Harold could then approach to welcome him without causing discomfort to Hazel or Miss Plumb.

Conversation did not immediately resume. Harold's companions watched Driffield guide his guest around the room to introduce her. Harold wondered how annoyed his mother would be when denied the privilege of making the introductions.

As the earl moved closer, Lady Melissa Williamson broke the silence to say, "What lovely greenery! Does Lady Collingwood have a hot house?"

Patrick replied, "Lady Collingwood has an infatuation with my mother's hot house."

The two continued discussing the hot house with far more animation than was required, and soon Hazel and Miss Plumb joined in with equal enthusiasm. Harold remained ever watchful. Driffield laughed at whatever Mr. and Mrs. Pottington said, then led his guest to Lord Wilkerson. The young lady, Harold could not help but notice, must think herself above all in attendance, for she held her nose high, her mouth pouted, and her eyes narrowed. She might have been attractive if she had relaxed and smiled. Alas, she looked like a cat who licked soured cream.

Harold tensed. Driffield had turned their way.

The enthralling conversation about hot houses increased volume.

"Mr. Hobbs," Driffield said with a stiff nod. Addressing the lady at his side, he said, "This is our host's son Mr. Hobbs and his wife Mrs. Hobbs. You'll wish to know Lady Williamson, as you've already met her husband Sir Chauncey."

Out of the corner of his eye, he saw Patrick raise his eyebrows at being ignored. The color had drained from Miss Plumb's face, but she held her shoulders back and her head up.

"At her request," Driffield continued, "I've the honor of introducing Lady Felicia, daughter of the Duke of Milford, and my betrothed."

Harold might have guessed. If anyone in the group was surprised, no one displayed the sentiment.

A round of *well met, how lovely for you,* and *a pleasure* was exchanged before Driffield turned away with his betrothed on his arm. Just when Harold thought he was going to give the cut direct to the Earl of Winthorp's heir, the man stopped, pivoted, and partially turned to face Patrick, though he did not encourage Lady Felicia to do the same.

Lord Driffield inclined his head almost imperceptibly and said, "Lord Kissinger," before guiding his betrothed across the room.

Harold's eyes met Patrick's. The corners of his friend's eyes crinkled in amusement. Acknowledged but not introduced.

More pointedly, he had given Miss Plumb the cut direct. It was not a risky slight on his part, as his betrothed would simply think her of no consequence, a poor relation invited out of pity. But it was humiliating for Miss Plumb. Both Hazel and Lady Williamson offered Miss Plumb their support, though discreetly. Lady Williamson, for her part, laughed and smiled at an unspoken joke as she clasped Miss Plumb's hand.

Harold stepped over to Patrick and asked under his breath, "Any reason for the tension?"

"No idea," Patrick said, expression still bemused. "Best guess? He assumes I'm one of the investors, an unworthy partner given any money I would have offered as capital would be from my father's accounts. Less likely guess? I was standing next to Miss Plumb."

"Both perhaps. Easier to cut Miss Plumb if he also cuts the person standing next to her."

Patrick chuckled. "Actually, I was thinking along the lines of his being envious I was standing at her side while he escorted the marmalade tart."

Harold snorted a laugh.

Not long did they wait before moving into the dining room for supper. Patrick sat to one side of Miss Plumb, Harold at her other side. Any concern he might have had about having to carry a conversation with the pale but stoic Miss Plumb was relieved by Patrick asking her about this evening's musical selection. Ever the chivalrous viscount.

Harold was free to converse with Hazel, his confident, lively, and lovely wife. This evening she glowed with the beauty of a woman in her element, surrounded by guests to entertain. Hazel did not appear discomfited by the earl's presence aside from her concern for Miss Plumb. Any worry stirred by Lord Driffield's arrival was allayed. Gone were Harold's worries of old of stolen looks between Hazel and Driffield, but he had fretted she would be uncomfortable that guests would recall the scandal.

Hazel angled closer and invited Harold to do the same. She whispered, "I don't think there are any matchmaking prospects here."

"I suspect you're right. Although...Lord Wilkerson is unmarried."

Hazel harrumphed but cast him a sidelong smirk. "He has too many chins."

Harold nearly choked on his drink. He took a moment to recover then said, "And here I thought the gravest insult was that a man had no chin."

Beneath the table, she pinched his elbow.

His mother's voice rose above the din, her question quieting conversation. "Lord Driffield, when is the wedding?"

Rather than the earl answering, the hitherto silent Lady Felicia responded. "The morning of the Countess of Driffield's first ball of the Season. Her ladyship wishes her first ball to celebrate the nuptials between her son and me and the union of our two families."

"How lovely," Helena said. "At St. George's, I presume?"

"No other location will do," said Lady Felicia.

"Are we the first to know of the happy event? Oh, I should like to think my little party is this important!" Helena tittered.

Speaking again for her betrothed, Lady Felicia said, "Indeed not. We've been engaged these past two years, plans delayed only until my father could return from France where he's been restoring his chateau. We had not intended to announce the wedding until the first ball, but after discussion, we've decided we've waited long enough."

"Isn't that lovely?" Helena looked around the table at her other guests.

As more questions and answers volleyed, Harold eyed Miss Plumb. The poor girl had stopped eating, and try as she might to carry on a hushed conversation with Patrick, she looked peaky.

Mr. Pottington said, "Must be a hardship to have waited so long."

This time, Lord Driffield spoke rather than Lady Felicia. He aimed his words well, his tone clear, his voice robust. "Time is unimportant when a gentleman knows his perfect match. Lady Felicia is, always has been, and always will be the only woman of my heart."

Nothing to do with an absurdly large dowry. Harold scoffed to himself.

Supper conversation changed course until the ladies returned to the drawing room to allow the men to talk business, which was the sole intention of the party. As Hazel left, she looked over her shoulder at Harold and smiled. The smile, he felt, spoke not only to her affection for him but her reassurance that she would see to her friend. Harold would be shocked if Miss Plumb remained in the drawing room when the men joined for entertainment, conversation, and tea before the end of the party.

Lord Collingwood smiled through his best performance yet, his finest periwig perched over a powdered forehead. "You must agree, I brought you only the best of news, gentlemen."

The guests concurred. With the mood light, the investors pleased, and Collingwood the bearer of glad tidings, the investment talk over port and cigars was worth the travel efforts and evening spent at Trelowen.

"My man has done right by us. I knew when I received written confirmation that the ship had sailed, it would by now be entering its first port. A two-week stretch from departure to first port. Assurance is a grand thing, is it not?"

Hearty agreement. A toast. Idle chatter about when they might receive the next notice of progress.

Harold listened for clues of his father's true motive for hosting the supper, and with so select a band of partners, but he could not decipher the meaning. Everything his father said rang with truth. While it was unlikely they would hear word of the ship's progress once it hit the stretch to China, it was likely they could have received notice of the departure. Surprising but possible. Certainly encouraging. Letters could take anywhere from a month to a full year, so his father's contact in India had gone to lengths to ensure the letter would be received to assure the investors.

Not for a moment did Harold let down his guard, though. His father could be a superb actor. It was one of the prime elements that kept people lending him money, opening accounts, writing vowels. Despite the frayed curtains, threadbare rugs, peeling wallpaper, and other signs of a man on his way to financial ruin, no one would guess his father to be anything but one of the wealthiest men in the West Country. He missed his calling for the stage.

Yet why go through all this trouble if the missive had not been received? Harold propped an elbow on the table, analyzing everything his father said.

The fellow investors had questions. The baron had answers.

His low faith in the ship's captain wavered. Misplaced mistrust. As unsavory as the man and as risky as the gamble, Harold felt a swelling of hope in his chest—all his doubts, all his worries, all for naught if he had misjudged the situation. This investment *could* pay off. With the wealth of this windfall, Harold could persuade his father to use a portion for the estate. Mr. Trethow would reap the rewards, as well. Harold's thoughts shifted to the problem he promised Hazel he would sort—with the success of the investment, it would sort itself. All his worries lifted in a single evening.

He had been planning to confront his father. To say what, he had not decided, but it had been time to do the very handling Patrick had prompted, but now… This changed everything.

Harold was biting his knuckle, lost in thought, when Lord Driffield turned to Patrick to make a comment loud enough for all at the table to hear.

"Kissinger, I'm surprised to see you at a table of investors. Did your Papa loosen your purse strings?"

Patrick chuckled. "Hoping I'll tip some coins into your empty coffers? Alms for the poor?"

Driffield raised his glass with a throaty laugh.

Conversation at the table shifted to politics. The earl showed every sign of disinterest, picking invisible lint from his spotless silk. From time to time, his eyes darted to Patrick. When the conversation over the Lord Mayor of London became heated, Driffield leaned towards Patrick and Harold.

Voice low, the earl said, "I offer this advice because I like your spirit, Kissinger. Stay away from Miss P. She's a trollop out to trap a title." Eyeing Harold, Driffield added, "You'd do well, Mr. Hobbs, to see she's barred from the estate. I would hate to see your reputation tarnished by association. How easy it is for a woman like her to take advantage of a man such as yourself."

Harold could see Patrick's jaw tick with tension. This time, the viscount did not rise to the goading. Harold thanked him for his advice but said nothing more. The more he was exposed to Driffield, the more he hated the man, however strong the word to describe a sentiment for a near stranger.

It came as a relief when the baron rose from the table and suggested they join the ladies in the drawing room. Promises of musical entertainment awaited their pleasure.

To Harold's immediate shock, he found Miss Plumb still in the room, content in conversation with Hazel. Lady Felicia sat ever so slightly away from them, conversing with Helena. As soon as the gentlemen entered the drawing room, Helena announced that Lord Kissinger and Miss Plumb would grace the party with a song. While Miss Plumb smiled prettily for the audience as she made her way to the pianoforte, Harold noticed her hands shook as she held them over the keys.

Hazel took her seat next to Harold, her leg a hair's breadth from touching his. Resting an elbow on the arm of his chair, he caressed her hand with his pinky then hooked their pinkies together. The song began.

Patrick truly did have a magnificent voice. There must be Welsh in his bloodline, Harold had used to tease him. For all Miss Plumb's nerves, she played an exquisite accompaniment, offering the crowd an undeniable glimpse of her natural talent.

A voice, discordant with the music, said something unintelligible then laughed. Harold frowned. The voice came again, louder this time, but not loud enough to dominate the entertainment, only interfere with the acoustics. Turning his head, Harold spied Driffield talking with Lady Felicia, the two carrying on a conversation as though a performance were not underway.

For the entirety of the song, the two conversed. It was not uncommon for guests to continue conversation during an informal performance, but in this instance, no one else talked, and all had been

arranged for attention to focus on the musical entertainment, part of the charm of the evening. This was,
quite obviously, not intended as background music.
Lord Driffield's behavior was in poor taste. He dis-
respected not just Miss Plumb and Patrick but also
his hostess.

When the music concluded, applause congrat-
ulated the duo. Miss Plumb curtsied with more
confidence than when she had first sat at the keys.
Patrick bowed and held his hands to say a word
about the music. Only, it was not about the music
that he spoke, as Harold and everyone else in the
room expected. What he said caused more than a
few gasps. Even Harold sat straighter in his chair and
leaned forward, Hazel grasping the arm of his chair
to brace herself.

"If I could have your attention for a moment
longer," Patrick said. "I have an announcement to
make. In honor of our hostess, we've chosen this party
to be the first place for our news."

Patrick held a hand for Miss Plumb to stand beside
him. When she clasped his hand, she did not let go.

Hands held between them, Patrick said, "You may
all wish us happy, for Miss Plumb has accepted my
proposal to become my wife."

Harold's shock was reflected in Hazel's expression.
The two stared at each other, wide eyed, lips parted.
Applause and congratulations greeted the couple,
Helena in particular clapping with vigor, undoubtedly

more excited about the announcement occurring at her party than about the engagement itself.

All Harold could surmise was Patrick took chivalry too far. In a noble act to protect her from the harsh words of Lord Driffield, the viscount had acted spontaneously, Miss Plumb too disoriented by the party events to decline his act of kindness. With strategic planning, they could arrange for an amicable break in a few days. From Hazel's bearing, Harold assumed she was coming to the same conclusion.

The guests milled around the newly made couple, offering their well wishes. All except Lord Driffield and Lady Felicia. The two remained at the back of the room, deep in a riotous conversation of laughter and smiles, seemingly unaware that the announcement had even taken place.

Harold rose with Hazel and waited for their turn to offer felicitations. There was nothing more to be said until he could get Patrick alone for a heart to heart. By all appearances, the pair was overjoyed. The guests had already forgotten or excused the cut from earlier—how important was a cut from one earl when the young lady was about to marry a future earl?

Oh dear. A complication. Harold wondered if Patrick realized it yet.

Breaking the engagement would be difficult once the Earl and Countess of Winthorp heard the news, and by the morning, they would have most certainly heard it, if not from Helena than from their lady's maid or valet. There could be no doubt that the footman in the drawing room would carry the news downstairs in a matter of minutes. From there, word would travel from staff member to staff member and straight into the Winthorp's estate, possibly before the evening ended. If the footman did not spread the news, the guests would, intentionally or not, as they talked casually to their own lady's maid or valet or even to each other in the hearing of staff. No matter how one looked at it, Patrick's parents would know before he could break it off. The work of a moment turned into a life sentence.

As the crowd dissipated, Harold dressed in his best smile. He reached for Patrick's hand and shook it, Hazel hugging Miss Plumb.

"The surprise of the evening," Harold said. "Could have knocked me over with a feather."

"I hope you'll forgive me for not telling you. I couldn't resist the element of surprise."

He was about to respond when the two least likely people made their way across the room. With a glance, Harold saw Hazel and Miss Plumb had not spotted the interlopers. At least the other guests had moved away. No one cared that Lord Driffield and his betrothed approached to wish the new couple well. No one except Harold and Patrick, and soon Hazel and Miss Plumb. As if to prove Harold wrong, Lady Williamson touched her husband's arm to say something then headed in their direction to offer Miss Plumb further support if needed.

Lady Felicia, none the wiser of the true tension of the moment, offered stiff congratulations to Miss Plumb, her tone proudly conveying her disapproval for the heir of an earldom to marry so far below him. Lord Driffield said nothing until Lady Felicia turned her attention to Lady Williamson. Once she was distracted, he stepped forward, taking Patrick's hand for a shake.

"I see my advice was unnecessary, Lord Kissinger. I wonder, though, if you've fallen into her trap or set one of your own." He waggled his eyebrows and said, "A ready-made heir is perfect for someone like you. Am I right?" The earl laughed heartily, his hand still gripping Patrick's.

The viscount's expression darkened. Loudly enough to be heard, he said, "Thank you for your felicitations. I'll share them with my betrothed."

Before Patrick could extract his hand, Driffield tugged him closer to clap a hand on his shoulder.

Although Harold was standing close enough to hear, Driffield whispered for Patrick's ears only, "No need to thank me yet, not until you need a spare for that heir."

He winked as he released his grip on Patrick and collected Lady Felicia to move to another group for conversation. Neither Harold nor Patrick spoke for some time. Thankfully, Hazel and Lady Williamson continued to occupy Miss Plumb, none of them privy to Lord Driffield's words.

At length, Patrick asked, "Can I trust you to be my second?"

Harold faced his friend, taken aback. "You needn't ask, but are you certain?"

Patrick answered with a brisk nod, then said, "Wait until after the wedding ceremony to issue my challenge."

"You mean to go through with it, then?"

"If you mean a duel, undoubtedly. For the honor of our ladies, I will meet him on the field. If you mean

the marriage, I already have the license. Forgive me
for not telling you. It was between Agnes and me
and not something we wanted to share until made
public. Tomorrow morning is the wedding, a private
ceremony in town. We've been planning this for two
weeks, and not entirely for the reasons you must suspect. Platonic love is potent. If the duel doesn't go as
planned, at least she'll have my name and my family's protection."

Harold was speechless. This whole time, they had
been planning a union. Had Patrick been planning to
challenge Driffield the whole time, as well? Harold
did not ask.

Instead, he inquired, "What of your parents?"

Patrick's smile was sardonic. "They'll be at the
ceremony. I've already told them she's with child. It
wasn't something I could hide, not when she'll soon
show, not when the baby will arrive nearly four
months early. The irony? They think it's mine."

"Their reaction?"

Patrick laughed. "Ecstatic. I've never seen my
mother happier. It's just as well because from the
moment Agnes and I made the decision, I accepted
the baby as mine. Girl or boy, the babe is mine. Con-
gratulate me, Harold. I'm going to be a father."

Chapter 20

T he vestry was crowded with only three people: Hazel, Agnes, and Agnes's lady's maid. Rather than Agnes and Lord Kissinger marrying at the church in town, Hazel had insisted they marry at the chapel on the estate, the same chapel in which she and Harold had exchanged their vows. The curate had not been fazed by the change in location, but then, who would be when it was a viscount and heir to an earldom who was bridegroom?

Where Agnes could not be persuaded was the wedding date. Hazel wanted to arrange for a wedding breakfast, but Agnes would not be moved. The ceremony was a mere formality, she had insisted. They could always plan a larger celebration later. It was fortunate Hazel had even been able to invite herself. As far as she could surmise, Agnes had intended the only guests to be the two witnesses, Lord and Lady Winthorp.

Hazel watched as the lady's maid tidied Agnes's hair, fussing despite the simplicity of the style. The chasm between Hazel and Agnes widened. So many secrets. And now a surprise marriage. She wanted to feel happy about this monumental moment, but instead, all she felt was the heartache of losing her friend.

"You'll be moving after the wedding?" Hazel asked, her voice wavering.

In contrast, Agnes's voice was firm and confident. "Yes. I'll be taking up residence at the Winthorp estate."

"Nana will miss you." Hazel could not meet Agnes's eyes. "As will I."

She tried to tell herself to be happy. This was not a betrayal of friendship, rather Agnes finding a way to save herself.

Agnes fluffed her petticoat. "Patrick has already written to Father to ensure my possessions are sent. I'll finally have my dresses, not that they'll fit for long."

"What did Mr. Plumb say? Did he respond?"

"Oh, yes. He and Patrick have been in correspondence. As much as I didn't want Father to know my whereabouts, I couldn't marry without his permission. We would have eloped had he said no, but Patrick was determined to try. He convinced Father of the match with more ease than I expected. I honestly thought we would have to elope." She laughed, lighthearted and cheery.

How could Agnes be so merry? This day was the sacrifice of happiness and love, the trapping of a gentleman who did not wish to wed and could never make Agnes content or be contented by her in return. Yet she smiled and looked for all the world like a bride on her wedding day, appropriate given that was exactly what she was.

Agnes must have seen Hazel's reticence. "Won't you be happy for me?"

Hazel met her friend's gaze at last. "Of course, I'm happy for you."

"No, you're not. I don't know why you insisted to be here. You don't want to be here."

"But I do!" Hazel avowed. "I would never miss your wedding day."

Agnes sighed and took Hazel's hands in hers. "You're angry. Perhaps because I didn't tell you. Perhaps because I'm marrying Patrick. Perhaps because you think you're losing me since I'm moving. Hazel, I'm marrying Patrick because I love him, and because he loves me. Before you protest, let me be clear. Although he and I have known each other only a short time, we have connected in ways I never thought possible for two people to connect. It began at the hunting party. We spoke at the dining table every evening. I was not romantically interested in him, but I felt an inexplicable connection even then. When I speak, he hears me. He is selfless and loving. I intend to make him the happiest of wives."

"But he —"

"No protests. We've fallen in love. As hard as it is to believe, we're a love match. Today, I'm marrying my best friend. Something I've learned since meeting him is that there are different kinds of love. I was a fool with Nathan and thought love was sexual and physical, but Patrick has taught me without meaning to that not all love is sexual or physical. Be happy for me. Today, I'm not marrying a man with whom I intend to share my bed, but with whom I intend to share my heart."

Agnes's face blurred as Hazel's eyes teared. Nodding, she squeezed her friend's hands.

"And neither of us can deny that he is terribly handsome." Agnes winked. "You're going to ask next," she continued more seriously, "why I didn't tell you. A simple answer. I didn't want you trying to talk me out of it. You would have thought of a dozen reasons why we shouldn't marry, and then you would have tried to come to my rescue. Again."

"Well," Hazel said, choking on her words, "at least you won't live far."

Agnes wrapped her arms around Hazel and hugged her tightly. "We could take tea every day if we wanted to. But please, no more elderberry biscuits."

They both laughed, Hazel's laugh sounding more like a sob. While her heart still ached, she saw the chasm bridged to a renewed friendship. She had not lost her friend after all.

Hazel wiped her eyes and freshened her complexion of any blotchiness or tear streaks before slipping into the transept to meet Harold for the ceremony. She laced her fingers with his and stood on her tiptoes to kiss his cheek. Was he remembering the last time they were here? The twinkle in his eyes hinted that he might be sharing the same memory.

Spending an afternoon writing one's last will and testament was not Harold's idea of a good time. As Patrick's second, it was a necessity. After issuing the challenge, the two men met with the March family solicitor, a gentleman who had been the family solicitor since before Lord Winthorp inherited his title, and a gentleman who lived nearby, unlike the Hobbs's family solicitor who resided in London.

A humbling experience.

Sitting in the solicitor's parlor.

Harold and Patrick writing their wills.

For Harold's part, he wrote a letter to Hazel, instructing the solicitor to hand deliver it personally to Mrs. Hobbs in the event of his death, not to a family member on her behalf but directly into her hands and only her hands. In the letter, he detailed the family's financial situation, explained the fate of her dowry, and instructed her on how to obtain her widow's income. The letter was not without personal sentiment.

The morning after, a foggy and drizzly Tuesday, Harold and Patrick waited in an open field before dawn, the solicitor, Patrick's valet, and the family physician standing nearby.

The duel was an unexpected turn of events. Harold doubted this was Lord Driffield's first duel. With the man's reputation, it was inevitable that someone would challenge him or had called him out already, be it father, brother, or husband. But it was Patrick's first duel. Harold certainly had never been involved in one, although he had witnessed one in his youth. Never in his wildest dreams would he have thought Patrick the sort to challenge a gentleman, even a gentleman who deserved it.

The sound of an approaching carriage caught their attention. Flamboyant. Lord Driffield arrived in his coach and four, coat of arms emblazoned on the side. Flamboyant *and* indiscreet. With the earl was his second, Viscount Brooks. Two outriders accompanied. From their attire, Harold assumed them to be valet and physician.

Once all were assembled on the field, Viscount Brooks and Harold approached each other. The fact that Patrick had once fancied Brooks was not lost on Harold, although he had never inquired if Brooks fancied him in return. The two meeting on the dueling field was somehow paradoxical from Harold's perspective. At least Brooks was only the second.

Extending his hand, Harold shook Brooks's before asking, "Does Lord Driffield wish to forego the duel by apologizing of all wrongdoing to both Lord and Lady Kissinger?"

"From Lord Driffield's point of view, no wrongdoing has occurred." Brooks's tone inflected an arrogant boredom that had no place on a battlefield.

Harold nodded, then loud enough for all to hear said, "Make ready. Disarmament satisfies honor. Let there be no bloodshed."

Harold returned to Patrick's side, his heart thumping wildly.

The weapon of choice was the rapier. Patrick had admitted his disappointment. He had hoped for pistols. Driffield had a keen advantage over his opponent, for while Patrick had experience fencing with the rapier, it was not extensive. Enough, he hoped, to block and disarm.

Readying his sword, Patrick took several deep breaths before heading out to meet the earl.

Like Patrick, Harold had minimal skill with rapier fencing. Should they both walk off the field today, he vowed to strengthen that skill. A great sport, really, since he could wield a sword indoors during the winter months, something he could not say about rowing. How different was it from painting? The sword was an extension of the arm, just as the paint brush, the flicks of the wrist narrating the canvas. God willing, he would not have to find out today the accuracy of the comparison. Tugging his greatcoat tighter, he huddled against the cold and wet drizzle.

The two gentlemen faced each other, bowed, and positioned for battle. In a heartbeat, the rapiers thrusted.

Unlike sabre bouts, the movements were more subtle and nuanced. The best way Harold could describe the scene was painting *impasto*. The thrusts of the rapier were bold but also smooth and delicate, each designed to guide the focal point, to control the opponent's next move. It was a style he had never used when painting, his hand and eye preferring the dramatic relationship between light and dark, *chiaroscuro*. There was no contrast in the duel, no light or dark, no blending or shading. There was only a harmonious texture of thrust and retract, the sword drawing the directional line, giving the illusion of distance and proximity, power and retreat.

Harold blinked.

Neither man's torso moved, only the feet, only the wrists.

Driffield thrusted. Patrick counterattacked.

Driffield parry-riposted. Patrick feinted to disengage.

Their eyes remained locked. They circled, struck, circled again.

Did Agnes March née Plumb, Lady Kissinger, appreciate this man who was at this very moment risking his life for her honor? This was not a duel to death. This was not a duel to first blood. This was only a duel to disarm. But duels always came with risk since not all gentlemen were honorable or apt to follow etiquette.

A step and stab. Another step and stab.

Harold blinked.

Driffield stepped and stabbed. Blood pooled on Patrick's white sleeve.

Harold blinked.

What the devil just happened? The movement had been so swift, he had not seen when or how the rapier point made contact, but there on Patrick's dueling shoulder, vibrant crimson bled through the linen. Harold cursed. He should have known Driffield could not be trusted.

The drizzle of rain turned from moist fog to a more determined patter, soon soaking Patrick's shirtsleeves, his shoulder a mottled pallet of rust to burnt umber.

Patrick disengaged to strike.

Driffield dropped his point, sidestepped the thrust, grabbed Patrick's guard, and punched the bridge of Patrick's nose with the quillon of his own rapier.

The valet beside Harold hissed.

Patrick recovered, moving into a counterdisengage, his rapier held steady though his nose ran with blood. Harold could see his friend blinking rapidly against the rain.

Patrick gave his head a shake.

His feet stumbled, sluggish and heavy.

He feinted and thrusted.

Retreated.

Shook his head.

Wavered, unsteady.

Blinked rapidly.

Harold's concern mounted. If he was not mistaken, Patrick was either about to swoon or be skewered by Driffield, perhaps both. He dared not think of the consequences of either.

A violent shake of his head, Patrick shuffled his feet, deceiving Driffield with a feint, then thrusted.

Driffield parried and riposted, his blade stabbing the air inches from Patrick's head.

The viscount bent low, feinted to his right then thrust high above Driffield's dueling shoulder.

Blood sprayed into the rain.

Driffield dropped his rapier, clasping a hand over his ear.

Harold closed his eyes — disarmament meant the end of the duel. He tilted his head back to feel the rain against his face, the drops now large and heavy and cold as icicles. Had Patrick swooned, Harold would have had to finish the battle on his behalf. Had Patrick moved right rather than left, he could have died. The cold splashing against Harold's face was a reminder of life.

A groan shook his relief.

He looked up in time to see Patrick swaying on his feet, rapier still gripped in hand, the shirtsleeve a troubling shade of red from shoulder to wrist, not to mention the blood now draining down his face and dripping onto his waistcoat. In quick strides, both Harold and Patrick's valet reached the viscount in time to catch him as he slumped towards the ground.

The rain pummeled the windows outside the solicitor's parlor. What started as a light drizzle on a dreary morning had turned into a deluge of water and ice. A week from November, yet the weather already threatened frost and snow. Harold and the solicitor sat in silence for a long stretch of time, neither seeing the point in filling the void with noise and empty words. On the couch in front of the fireplace lay motionless Patrick.

The physician's words of comfort brought little solace when Patrick remained unresponsive even after smelling salts. For an hour Patrick had lain unconscious. The physician had left once the wounds were bandaged and the blood was cleaned.

Only when the viscount gave the faintest of moans did Harold sit up in his chair. He watched his friend's eyelids flutter open. Patrick tried to raise a hand to his face then cried out when his shoulder protested.

"Welcome back," Harold said.

"Go to the devil." Patrick groaned but tried to sit up. "Tell me he looks worse than I feel."

"Indeed. I can't say for certain, but I think you took off the man's ear."

"Damn. I had been aiming for his eye." Patrick chuckled.

"Good news," Harold said, "You'll keep your pretty face once the nose heals. Before you're overcome with joy, I bear even better tidings. You won't have Driffield's death on your conscience, for one. You've helped bring justice to however many other young ladies Driffield has wronged. And last but not least, he won't be so attractive to future young ladies from this point forward."

"My life's work is complete. Now, I could kill for one of Nana's elderberry biscuits."

Harold soaked in a hot bath while Abhijeet whinged behind the screen in the dressing room about the soaked mess of the day's clothing. He responded with grunts and *mmm hmm*s, not hearing much of what his valet said. His thoughts were on life.

While he had not come close to death, being only a second on a wet dueling field and observing his friend nearly slaughtered, the whole of the event put life into perspective. By walking onto the field, he had agreed to place his own life on the line should his friend be incapacitated during the duel. That alone was humbling. Watching Driffield grab Patrick's guard for the punch was even more so, for with a simple turn of his wrist, the earl could have pierced Patrick's liver rather than break his nose. Not that Harold would ever thank Driffield for anything, he *was* thankful the man had chosen the latter. The day could have ended much worse. Even the shoulder wound could have killed Patrick. He had lost enough blood that the physician had expressed concern.

Satisfaction had been met. Driffield received his comeuppance. But the cost had been too high.

Come dishonor or ruin, Harold would rather have life. He knew many did not feel the same, and some levels of dishonor and ruin could be akin to losing life, or the quality thereof, but he far valued life.

His first task after the bath would be to request a meeting with his father. He needed to speak to Hazel about the family's situation, but before he could do that, he wanted to better understand the status of the ship. The letter had sounded promising, assuring investors the ship had sailed in good standing. Since his father had not read the letter aloud at the supper party, Harold wanted to read it himself and discuss the plans for the profits. That was not to say he did not still have reservations about the investment, but the hope that the letter brought was too great not to be discussed.

How wonderful to be able to explain the situation to Hazel with the qualification that all would soon be set to rights. Especially regarding her father. The whole of that deal brought Harold shame. He was ashamed of his father's greed, ashamed of his father's treatment of a man who was supposed to be his friend, and ashamed this was the situation into which she had married. Most of all, he was ashamed he was powerless to do anything about it.

The trouble was he did not want to upset her or make her uncomfortable around her father-in-law, much less have her upset at her own father for going to these lengths—not to save her reputation but to ensure he was able to invest. Both fathers had been greedy. How to explain it all to her without destroying her rose-tinted view escaped him, but if he had a way to right the situation with untold profits, the explanation seemed easier, or at least more hopeful.

With luck, his father would be available in the morning.

Leaning his head against the back of the copper tub, Harold sank lower into the water until it lapped at his chin. *Ah.* To be financially stable. To bedeck Hazel in jewels — emeralds, he thought, to match her eyes. To travel the continent with her. To see the estate restored. To —

"Out! Out *now!*" shrieked a voice from behind the screen.

Harold sat up so quickly, water sloshed over the edges.

Sounds of a struggle could be heard, scrambling, stuttered protests from his valet, a *thwack thwack*, followed by the closing of a door. The screen blocking his view was shoved aside. Standing where the screen had been, hands on panniers and wearing an expression seething with anger, was his wife.

"Foul man!"

Harold stared up at her, alarmed and exposed.

"How dare you participate in a duel! You could have died! You thoughtless, selfish man." Her voice cracked, anger oscillating to teary upset then back to anger.

"Ah. Word travels fast," Harold said.

"What did you think would happen when Lord Kissinger returned home with a broken nose and arm in a sling? Did you think Agnes wouldn't notice? Did you think she wouldn't send word to me?"

"Not faster than I could tell you myself. I've not been home longer than an hour." He did not mention that he had no intention of telling her about the duel. Now he was tempted to break Patrick's nose anew for telling Lady Kissinger.

"Even in the rain, messages travel quickly. Did you think to hide your brush with death?"

"Poor messenger," Harold muttered. "There was no brush with death. I was only his second, not directly involved.

"That makes no difference. You could have been required to fight as a second. You could have *died*! Lord Kissinger could have *died*! How did he end up stabbed and with a broken nose, hmm? Those are not idle injuries."

"Could have been worse." Harold winced as soon as he said the words.

"You're an odious man. A horrible, thoughtless, odious man. What did the two of you hope to prove? Nothing is worth your life. *Oh*!" Hazel hid her face in her hands and sniffled. "Had you no thought of the wife you'd leave behind? If I had known you were this odious, I never would have fallen in lo—" She clamped a hand over her mouth, her red-rimmed eyes widening.

Too late.

Harold's lips curved into a slow, broad smile. "What was that?"

She shook her head, both hands now clapped over her mouth.

Harold cupped a wet hand behind his ear. "You've what? You've fallen in…*love*? With *me*?"

"Don't be silly. I could never love someone careless enough to engage in a duel." Crossing her arms over her chest, she raised her chin and sniffed.

Harold's smile only broadened. "Well, well, well. My wife *loves* me, does she?"

"Not for a second." She harrumphed.

He hooked a dripping elbow over the side of the tub. "You *love* me. You think I'm devilishly handsome, don't you? An irresistible piece of man flesh." He leaned over the edge of the tub as the corners of her mouth twitched into a near laugh. "You pine over me when I'm not in the room, all because of my superior intellect, my cunning, my talent, my—"

"Oh, would you stop!" Hazel could no longer resist her laughter. She swatted at his arm as he gave her dress a playful tug.

"You *looooove* me. Say it. Admit it. Over head and ears in love."

When she wiped a tear of laughter from her cheek, Harold grabbed a fistful of her dress and drew her to him. She gave a little gasp as he lunged to grasp her at the waist and pull her down into the tub with him. The gasp turned to a shriek. Water splashed over the edges. She flailed briefly then sank onto his lap with a laugh. With a bit of persuasion, he wrapped her arms around his neck so he could kiss her.

Falling into her green eyes, he said, "I hope you're planning to tell our fifteen children we're a love match."

"Fifteen! Oh heavens. Not so many, I hope. Wouldn't one do? If I ensured it was an heir?"

Harold rubbed her nose with his. "What if I want a daughter? A little Hazel to spoil."

"Hmm. I suppose we should have two, then. A girl first, then a boy. I grew up in a house of boys, you know. I wouldn't know what to do with a daughter."

"Fourteen daughters and one son?" He jested.

"We'll not have any if I remain clothed." She smiled coyly.

Not one to miss an opportunity or daft enough to remind her why she had sought him out in his dressing room, he obeyed like a good husband and undressed his wife.

Chapter 21

L uck was on Harold's side. The next morning, his father was available to meet in the study.

Harold had a skip in his step all morning. For the first time in years, he saw real hope for the future, not a bleak stretch of financial ruin that would one day see the family destroyed, not a loveless arranged marriage, not another several years spent in foreign countries doing his father's bidding. He saw before him financial stability, a restored and profitable estate, a renewed relationship with his father, and a loving and ever-happy marriage with his soul's mate.

In anticipation of the meeting with his father, he invited Hazel for an interlude at the boathouse. She promised to meet him in the entrance hall in half an hour. A crew would now be prepping the top floor of the boathouse for romance. Cleaned and decorated with candles, pillows, blankets, a table and two chairs with tea and treats, and an easel and art supplies. As cold as it would be, he hoped to create a haven with a stunning view, something special for the two of them, where he could try his hand at the first oil painting of her since he had heretofore only sketched his wife.

Somewhere in their romantic escape, he would announce the good news of the investment since he would have the details of the letter by then. Premature to consider it a success when the ship would only be at its first or second port at this point, but Harold embraced the potential after so much doubt. He also would explain to Hazel the poor choices of his father. If she were to learn part, she needed to know all.

Harold's vision was for them to laugh about the disaster that brought them together. It was not a laughing matter, and had he thought about laughing at it a week ago, he would have considered himself mad, but now that financial freedom was at their fingertips, the whole of the situation that brought them together seemed worth a laugh. The greed of gentlemen had led to an unexpected love match. Well, it still was not entirely a laughing matter, but he was positive she would find humor. He hoped.

When he stepped into his father's study, he was smiling.

His father sat behind the desk, a brandy in his hand, cravat loosened, his periwig propped on the *porte perruque* behind him, leaving his head bare with wisps of grey in disarray over a balding scalp. Harold thought it an occasion to celebrate, as well. Although not a fan of brandy, he poured himself a sampling to toast with his father. Only after taking his seat on the opposite side of the desk did it dawn that the baron did not return his smile or acknowledge him. The multitude of wet rings on the desk surface hinted to a long morning of sloppy indulgence, not the reception Harold had anticipated. His smile slipped.

Without looking up, Eugene passed the creased letter across the desk. Wet splotches adorned the paper. Harold exchanged his glass for the letter.

He scanned the contents once, twice, then said, "I'm afraid I don't understand."

The baron tipped his glass between his lips before answering. "Not much to misunderstand."

Harold reread the letter again, more slowly this time, trying to make sense of it. The contents contradicted the letter his father had received last week. Which letter was to be believed?

Setting the missive on the desk, Harold asked, "When did this arrive? It can't be true if the ship set sail weeks ago. Where's the first letter?"

Eugene's eyes traced a path from the letter to his son. "That *is* the letter."

Harold shook his head. "But what of the letter you spoke about at the supper party?"

"Have you never lied?" Eugene scoffed, tipping the cup to his lips again. "*That* is the letter I received. I told them what they needed to hear."

The information took a moment to digest. Even then, Harold continued to shake his head. "You never received a letter saying the ship set sail." A knot tightened in his stomach. He thought he was going to be sick.

The baron pushed his empty glass across the desk as though willing it to refill itself. "Astute observation."

Ignoring his father's sarcasm, Harold said, "This letter says the ship remains docked, both captain and crew unaccounted for. But what of the cargo?"

"Deviled if I know." He reached for Harold's glass, sipped, then rested the rim to his chin.

Why Harold wished to deny this beggared belief. All along he knew the captain was crooked. All along he knew this deal would fail. Yet wrapping his mind around his father's performance of the previous week, that he had fallen for it along with the investors, and the dashed hopes he had entertained for days now was a heavy burden for both mind and heart.

What was he now to tell Hazel? The truth in all its grim reality.

"The investment capital?" Harold questioned.

"I know as much as you. The letter in front of you is all I have. Martins promises to do all he can to find the captain. From there, we could recoup our losses, force him to sail, or..." Eugene circled his hand in the air in search of other possibilities but finally let it fall to the desk.

Harold rose from his chair.

He walked to the hearth, rested his arm across the mantel, and stared into the fire. Flames licked at the logs. Red and orange teeth gnashed at the lumber, blues swallowing the kindling.

He flexed and relaxed his fingers, curling them into his palm until the half-moon nails dug into flesh. More irrationality — what was there to be angry about when he had known this would happen? What *this* was, he could not yet say, for nothing was definitive, not until they received more information. At this point, the direction seemed clear enough, but there were still possibilities. Until the baron's man of business — Martins — sent a letter declaring the fate of the captain, crew, cargo, and capital, all was not lost.

This did change the conversation he needed to have with his father. Rather than make plans for the profit, they needed to make plans for the loss of...well, everything. There were debts to be paid, an estate on the way to ruin, an in-law on the way to poverty, staff wages to be paid with more than empty promises, and… Harold closed his eyes. It was all too much.

"We need to talk about this. We need to plan." Harold spoke to the flames. He could not face his father. "Had I known… I'm taking Hazel to the boathouse. When I return, we'll devote the remainder of the day to making a plan. Before you brush me off or remind me of my youth, know that I'm familiar enough now with the accounts to quote your sins. No more, Father."

"Know the accounts." Eugene snorted. "Your priorities are clear enough, boy. Too busy dipping the wick to know the sacrifices I make, the lengths I go to dress you and your mother in finery. While you're off playing the happy husband, remember all I do to ensure our comforts, far more than you've ever done, only a leech to the coffers. Better yet, while you enjoy the pleasures of your wife, remember who arranged the marriage."

Harold's jaw clenched too tightly for him to speak. He ground his teeth, enraged. Although he remained silent, he pivoted to face the devil himself.

Eugene bellowed, "Wake up, boy, and admit I was right. Trethow's estate will keep us afloat and ensure our legacy. Pure genius. The fee tail I convinced him to make on Teghyiy Hall will award us the estate itself, as long as you plow the field to produce an heir. With the estate in our hands, we'll have a new source of income, lucrative income. Until then, we'll milk his annual profits. There's only one kind of friend in this world, and that's the kind daft enough to disinherit his line to save a lightskirt, all for our benefit. There's nothing more to plan, you see? All has already been arranged by the Collingwood cunning."

The cold-bloodedness astounded Harold. His father showed no remorse, no empathy, not even a shred of guilt. Logic was missing from the equation, as well. The annual percentage they were set to receive would do little to right their situation, not if their estate continued to produce nothing of its own, and certainly not at the rate of his father's expenditures and mounting debt. Percentage of Trethow's income or not, they were being buried alive by debts. The fee tail was not something to consider, either, for it could be decades before the estate changed hands, if it ever did, and the one estate could not support two separate estates. Harold wondered if his father had gone mad.

What was he to say? He wanted to defend his wife, defend her family, defend himself. He wanted to show his father reason, work the basic numbers for him to see his plan was as worthless as the investment. Frankly, he wanted to plant his fist against his father's cheek. But he was not a man of violence. The angrier he became, the more he sank into himself.

When he spoke, his voice was soft, his tone controlled, no indication of the anger funneling into his clenched fists. "Your perspective is clear. Use Hazel as a pawn. Coerce your childhood friend out of his family's fortune. Ruin everyone through an investment gone wrong. The Collingwood cunning failed you, though, for you could have simply taken their money and kept it rather than invest it, for what difference would they know? Then we'd be rich as Croesus." His words were embittered, filled with venom, yet to his ears they sounded flat, hollow.

The baron's eyes flickered in response. "By Jove, that's brilliant. Why didn't you say that before? Why didn't I think of that?" He leaned forward, stretching his arms across the desk, his expression lined with greed.

Harold palmed his face and rubbed his temples. If he did not leave this room in the next minute, he would do or say something he would regret. His best option was to retreat and regroup. Patrick had been right. Harold needed to handle his father. Not the easiest task. His father was a peer of the realm, while he was an heir still in his youth. Facts aside, he needed to handle his father.

Time to think.

Time to speak with the solicitor. As much as he dreaded another trip to London, it must be made. He could not stand by any longer and watch his father destroy them all. What choices did he have? The solicitor would know.

Time to think.

Harold slid his hand down his face. The table clock awarded him reprieve. Hazel would be waiting in the entrance hall by now. The romantic interlude he had planned for them had lost its appeal, but he needed her optimism more than anything. She would know what to do. Together, they could devise a plan. Together, they would go to London.

Yes, get out; get to Hazel.

Rather than take his leave of his father, he simply walked out of the study. He doubted his father noticed or cared, for the man was mumbling to himself about new investment ruses.

When Harold stepped into the anteroom adjacent to the study, he received the second shock of the day.

Hazel stood in the middle of the room, staring up at him. His mouth formed the words of a greeting, but his voice failed when he registered her expression.

Her cheeks were tear-streaked, her eyes red-rimmed, her chin trembling. She did not speak. She studied him for a silent century before bowing her head and leaving him alone in the anteroom.

Hazel leaned against her bedchamber door, vision blurred with tears.

Betrayed.

Utterly betrayed.

All this time she had thought the family her saviors, her father's friends who stepped in to protect her and her family from ruin, even sacrificing their only son and heir to save her reputation. The truth hit her boldly in the face. She had been used as a tool. Her father had been used as a tool. Her brother had been disinherited somehow. The marriage had been contrived from the greed of her father's money.

The worst betrayal of all was Harold's involvement. The marriage had been a sham. She did not want to doubt he loved her, but if he did, it had occurred by accident, and how convenient that he should get dowry *and* love. Did the love matter in light of the circumstances?

No.

A convenience for him. An inconvenience for her. A cause for deeper betrayal.

Knock knock.

Behind her, knuckles rapped smartly at the door. She jumped away as though burned, one hand clasped to her stomach, the other covering her mouth.

"Hazel?" Harold questioned from the other side of the door.

Panicked, she reached to the handle and flipped the lock, barring him from entry. The decisive click was met with silence.

Hazel waited.

More silence.

She closed her eyes, hoping he had left. As soon as she could collect her thoughts, she would request that her lady's maid pack the necessary items. She wanted to go *home*. Her father needed to know what they had done. She needed to know what her father had done. What fee tail? What percentage of income? *Oh, Papa.* How cruelly they had taken advantage of a man desperate to save his beloved daughter. Was it too late to repair the damage?

"Hazel? Let us talk. Please," came her husband's voice again.

Choking on a sob, she ignored him. Vile man! A trickster just like his father. He had conspired and plotted with his father to steal her father's money. Did they strategize with Lord Driffield, too, to force her into the compromise? She had not overheard enough of the conversation to understand much, but she had heard enough to know they had used her and her family abominably and to know Harold had some part in it or at least knowledge of it. From the way it sounded, he could have been the mastermind.

So much deception!

"Hazel, love, please let me explain. I understand you're distraught. Let's talk about this. If you need time, I'll understand. I'll be in our sitting room when you're ready, even if that means staying there all night."

This time, she heard the pad of footsteps down the hall. The faint *click-click* of a door opening and closing. Then another *click* of a door. He had walked around and into their sitting room.

Biting the knuckle of her forefinger, she stared at the sitting room door, then to her dressing room door, then back to the sitting room door. With a whimper, she went to the dressing room and rang for her lady's maid.

Fifteen, twenty, as much as thirty minutes passed. Hazel changed out of her warm walking dress, instructed her maid to pack enough for the journey, and cried anew — curiously, more about the loss of her boathouse romance than the situation. Before packing, the maid brought Hazel a cup of hot chocolate. By the time Hazel checked the table clock above the mantel, it had not been fifteen, twenty, or even thirty minutes, rather over an hour.

The truth was, unless she planned to steal the carriage, bribe the coachman, or some other silliness like whisking away on a horse in the dead of night, she needed Harold if she hoped to return home. She abhorred the thought of talking to him — villainous blackguard!

Tears dried, shoulders back, chin high, she marched to the sitting room door.

Hand to handle, she questioned if she could write him a note instead. Resigned, she opened the door and stepped inside.

True to his word, Harold remained in the sitting room, waiting. He was doubled over on the chaise longue, his head buried in his hands. At the sound of the door, he looked up with a jerk of his head.

Hazel covered her heart with her hand. It thumped and bumped at the sight of him. *How could he?* For that matter, how could her traitorous heart thump happily after a single look from those brown eyes and that unruly russet hair, the latter untidy from having fingers dragged through the locks for over an hour. His expression broke her heart. He looked for all the world like a wounded stag.

But *he* was not wounded. *She* was. She would do well to remember that it had been he who wielded the bow and arrow that struck her.

To safeguard her from her disloyal heart, she left open the door to her bedchamber. Nodding to him with a brisk and unfriendly acknowledgment, Hazel sat at the far end of the chaise and arranged her dress so it would not brush against his leg.

She said, looking into the fireplace rather than at him, "I'm going home to my father. Please arrange for the carriage to take me. Tomorrow morning at the latest."

If he showed surprise or bitterness or any reaction at all, she did not know. Her gaze remained on the fireplace.

Harold's voice, when he finally spoke, was quiet and soft. "I'll escort you there myself."

"No!" she protested, looking over at him in dismay before she remembered she was avoiding all eye contact. That same wounded expression met her glance. She hastened her gaze back to the fireplace, her heart giving a predictable *thump*. "No. I need away from you, your family, here, everything."

The chaise dipped as he shifted his weight. "I'll not have you travel alone. I'll send a message to Patrick."

"Not with his injury. I'll…I'll…I'll take Nana with me."

Yes, that sounded reasonable. Of all the dastardly deeds the family had committed against Hazel, Nana would have had no part in any of it. If anything, she wanted to protect Nana, as well. Who would look after her without Hazel here?

The sound and peripheral glimpse of him rubbing his hands against his buckskin breeches wrecked her senses. She squeezed her eyes closed and tried to will herself to hate him. *He had used her!* Any desire to be consoled by him or held by those strong hands was gulped down. *He had tricked her!*

Harold said, "I'll speak with Nana this afternoon about the trip, but I don't want my wife or my grand-mother traveling alone. Two defenseless women on the open road? And what if she has one of her moments? I'll arrange for outriders, but I want a chaperone, a male chaperone." After a moment's silence he asked, "What about Sir Chauncey?"

"They couldn't possibly receive the message in time for tomorrow morning. But yes, if Sir Chauncey and Melissa could join, then that would be ideal."

"If you'll agree to wait a few days, I can arrange it."

She thought for a moment. A few days was too long. To stay under this roof? To stay with these people? These tricksters? She could hide in her room, have her meals brought to her. It would be worth the wait.

She nodded.

Harold said, "I'll have everything taken care of for you and send a notice to your father of your impending arrival."

She could hear him swallow.

He continued, "I don't know what you overheard, but I hope for the opportunity to explain everything."

"My father can explain it all to me."

A stretch of silence, then, "Yes, it would be good to talk with him. But please, can we talk through it before you leave?"

Pursing her lips, she granted a curt nod. She did not want to hear more lies, but it was the ransom she had to pay to return to her bedchamber.

Harold exhaled loudly. She could see him from the corner of her eyes run a hand through his curls.

"My father has made poor choices, a great many poor choices. He's driven debts higher than he can pay, using the estate's income to invest in ventures rather than putting the money back into the estate. Nothing was *this* bad when I left for India. He had a series of successful deals, profits he used to invest in riskier ventures. I went to India to see to the riskiest one to date. It yielded substantial profits. I returned home to find the estate in disrepair, the coffers empty, and the debts unmanageably high. He was set on using the profits for a bigger gamble, an investment I advised him against. It was that investment for which he needed money. I knew nothing of his deal with your father, however, until I was told we would marry. Believe me when I say I had no part in the settlement other than to be the bridegroom."

She interrupted him. "But you knew about it. You went along with it. You allowed my father to sell his soul to save me. Even after marriage, you've never said a word about it to me."

"I went along with it to save you, not because of the settlement. Finding the words to tell you you've married a family of paupers with a head of household determined to ruin us isn't so easy, Hazel, although I refuse to make excuses. I should have said something sooner. I should have. I suppose I worried you would see me as having played a part in the marriage settlement. What I should have realized is not telling you branded me guilty despite innocence. There is nothing I can do about the settlement now, but if I can set it right with your father, I will."

Hazel did not know exactly what her father signed into the settlement nor did she ask. She would ask her father and no one else. As for the rest of what he was telling her, she did not know what to believe or even what shocked her the most. The family was known for their wealth. All of the parties! All of the expenses! Their reputation was renowned. There had been signs of disrepair, so many signs, but she had ignored them since they contradicted what she and everyone else had known about the family. But what of Harold's innocence? She had heard how coldly and callously he had spoken with his father about other ways to cheat people from their money. Had he been facetious? That was not Harold's style. Then, what did she know of her husband? Everything she knew about him was called into question.

"My father is not well," Harold continued. "He's consumed not just by greed but by the fear of poverty. I don't believe he meant you or your family harm when he took advantage of the situation. He was guided not by malice but by fear and greed. I offer no excuses for his behavior other than to say I don't think he was in his right mind when he convinced your father of the settlement."

She offered no reply. There was nothing to say.

Her hands became infinitely interesting as she answered him with her silence. How curious were hands? They lay folded in her lap, a sign of calm in the storm, a calmness she did not feel but portrayed outwardly. Her wedding band caught the firelight with a glint.

"Do you think," spoke the gentle voice from the stranger next to her, "you could forgive me for knowing and not telling you? Not today or tomorrow, but eventually?"

"I don't know." Her chin trembled, fresh tears pooling. "You cannot imagine what it's like to feel so betrayed. I thought your family saved me because they were good people. I trusted you because I thought you loved me. Everything has been a lie."

"Not everything. I do love you. Does that not make a difference? Allow for a hint of forgiveness and understanding?"

Hazel covered her mouth and nose with her hand to stifle the sobs that began to rack her body.

When she felt his hand against her back, she leapt off the chaise. "I need to go home," she said between gasps of breath. "I need to get away from here. I want Papa."

Before she risked another look at Harold and lost her resolve, she barreled out of the sitting room and back into her bedchamber, shutting the door behind her.

Chapter 22

Four days. She had only been gone four days. Harold would swear it had been a year.

No one in the house knew the real reason why she left. By some inner strength, Hazel had worn a smile on her departure day, insisting to everyone that she was merely visiting her papa and brother, a casual visit, nothing to raise alarm. Even Sir Chauncey and Lady Williamson thought it a brief coastal trip, either at the behest of her father or from homesickness. It took the Williamsons only three days to arrive to Trelowen after he sent them the request to accompany her. They insisted on taking her and the Dowager Baroness Collingwood in their own carriage, the couple excited for an excuse to go on holiday. Neither asked why Harold was not going.

What his parents and the staff thought about Harold's reaction to her departure, he could not say, for he had not left his bedchamber in four days. Nay, before that. Except for arranging the travel and seeing her off, he had not left his bedchamber since their talk in the sitting room, one week ago.

He was uncertain if he would ever leave his bedchamber again.

It seemed reasonable to wait until his father declared bankruptcy and invited the collectors to ransack the house for whatever assets they thought would cover the debts. Even then, why leave his chamber? They could not very well take his bed.

Harold stared at the back of his eyelids, an arm draped over his face to block out light and sound. If only it could block out thoughts.

She had not *left* him, surely. She would return. Their relationship would never be the same, but she would return. Would she not?

Betwixt bouts of grief, he oscillated from anger and guilt. If he had spoken with her sooner, it would not have ended as it did. If *he* had been the one to tell her the details of the marriage settlement and the family's financial situation, it might have exonerated him. But then, he was not the guilty party. Like her, he had been a pawn in his father's greed. He hated his father for putting him in this position, and he railed at her for not trusting him enough to believe his innocence. Did their love mean nothing? How could one love another person but not trust them? The very nature of love meant trust. Did this mean she did not love him after all?

Dark thoughts had absorbed the past week's nights and days. He was drained. Physically and emotionally, he was drained. He had no more energy to be angry, guilty, or grieved.

Letting his arm flop to his side, he stared up at the canopy of his bed. Devil take it. When had he last bathed? The stubble on his cheek did him no favors.

If he were going to win her back, he could not do it from bed. He *would* win her back. Or at least try. That was the only way of it. If he did not do something, she would either never return or she would return with a steel trap around her heart, forever distrusting him and villainizing him. If she thought the worst of him, *how* would he win her back?

Somehow, he had to right their situation. He had to regain her trust. An impossibility from this vantage point.

If he found a way to right his father's mistakes, would that prove him trustworthy? If he found a way to reverse the percentage of her father's income, would that prove him trustworthy? If he groveled at her feet and cried like a babe, would that prove him trustworthy?

Whether Hazel could trust him again remained to be seen, but he had only one choice — to act.

What took him a week to accept was that he was not blameless. All this time he had enabled his father. His hands were tied financially, yes, but he had allowed everything to happen with his passivity. Aside from a few mumbled objections, he had never fought his father, never stood his ground or refused to do the baron's bidding. He had enabled him by obeying the man's every whim. His father's wishes had always come first, even at his own personal sacrifice. Obey thy father. To thy father be true. What about himself? What about what was right? Blind obedience could not possibly be what was true or right. If he accepted this blame, the blame of passivity, then he could right the situation by acting in the best interest of his family.

It was not until Sunday that Harold requested to meet with his father. He needed a few days to recover from wallowing. Circles had haunted his eyes. The stench of four days had taken nearly as long to wash. He had notably not wanted to confront his father without a clear plan. This was no idle confrontation but the moment to end all moments, at least for Harold.

He arrived at his father's study with a hardened heart and a bead of perspiration at the base of his spine. One did not confront his own father lightly.

The study door closed behind him, a quiet but firm *thud*.

He wrinkled his nose. The room stank of liquor and unwashed body. So pungent, Harold had to swallow down the bile. His own filth of four days could not have compared to this.

Slumped over the desk, glass of brandy gripped in a hand, was his father. The periwig had not moved from its stand. If Harold was not mistaken, it was the same waistcoat and coat his father had been wearing during their last meeting that now adorned the back of one of the chairs in front of the hearth. The man's white linen shirt was stained with sweat and drink. The baron lifted his head long enough to see Harold had entered the study, then he laid it back on the desk, his forehead resting against the wood.

Harold had never seen his father in this state. For a moment, he questioned if he should confront him now. No, stay on course. Now more than ever his father needed to hear what he had to say.

"Father," he began, keeping his voice strong and controlled, "I will no longer standby and watch you destroy this family. Your greed has already ruined others and now my marriage. I'll stand for it no longer. Either allow me to help set the estate to rights or I'm leaving."

Eugene's head did not lift, but his shoulders shook with laughter. "As I said. Nothing but a leech. Want me to pay for your living elsewhere, boy? Think again."

"Actually, I'm going to Cornwall to save my marriage. But once I leave, I will not return. I'll arrange for a quaint and manageable cottage for Hazel and myself. I have twenty thousand pounds for our survival."

That lifted his father's head. The man's eyes were bloodshot and watery, his skin puffy with red blotches. He swayed trying to maintain an upright position, even while seated.

"What's this? Where the devil did you get twenty thousand pounds?"

"My wife's dowry. You may have instructed to use it for the investment, but the dowry was part of the marriage settlement, *my* marriage settlement. While I didn't have access to anything else you put towards the investment, I did have legal right to the dowry. Hazel and I will use it to make a new life for ourselves. Away from you."

"The devil, you say." Eugene coughed, spittle dribbling down his chin.

"You are a fraudster and a crook, Father. You were not this man when I left for India. I don't know who this man is, but you're not the father I once admired. You've always taken risks, gambled more than you should, but you were never cruel."

The baron's fist pounded the desk. "I'm trying to save us from ruin! Don't you see that?"

"No, you're a gamester just like your father. And it'll destroy you just as it destroyed him."

"Don't you dare compare me to my father," Eugene sputtered.

"Do you not see it? You've surpassed his greed. Once the investors hear they've lost their money in this deal, word will get around. Creditors will learn of the loss. They'll know you can't pay the debts. You won't be able to keep them at bay. And if you try a new scheme to steal investor money, you will be hanged for fraud."

"I'm a baron, boy. I can't be hanged."

"Is that a risk you're willing to take?"

Eugene rubbed his neck with swollen fingers but did not respond.

Harold took a deep breath for renewed confidence. "I've seen the accounts, Father. I know them by heart. I can get us out of this predicament if you'll trust me. Allow me to help. You've ignored my advice for too long, and look where it's led. Either entrust my help or I'm leaving and not coming back."

The baron finished the remaining liquid in his glass then made to rise for a refill. His legs faltered, and he crumpled back into the chair with an expression of anger and frustration.

Cursing, his father said, "Then leave. Useless boy. Don't you know your obligation is to *me*? Your obligation is to be my heir, not follow the call of your tallywacker."

"No, my obligation as heir is to stop you from harming yourself and others. Listen to me, or I'm leaving."

"Then begone. I can always sire a new heir."

Hazel had always imagined she was a Londoner at heart. The wind and sand of the coast, despite the many good memories made with her brother and Agnes, could not boast the sheer fun promised by a bustling city. Soirees, balls, teas, suppers. What more could a girl want? Granted, she had never been to London, but she had dreamt about it many times, anything to escape the humdrum life by the sea.

Thus, it surprised her to spend every day after her arrival to Teghyiy Hall homesick for Trelowen. Helena's supper parties. Calls on tenants and neighbors. Visits by those same tenants and neighbors. Agnes. Lord Kissinger. The drafty boathouse. Her list carried on. Not the bustling city, but home.

She refused to admit it was Harold she missed. Dishonorable cad.

That he had fallen in love with her made it all the more odious. A simple plan to gain her father's money had worked out rather well for him. Dratted fiend.

To keep her mind off him — impossible task when his brown eyes haunted both her waking and sleeping thoughts — she spent copious amounts of time whinging with her brother, touring Nana about the area, and playing hostess to Melissa and Sir Chauncey. The talk with her father had been procrastinated. The whole drive home, she wanted to urge the carriage to go faster so she could tell Papa how the villains had tricked and ruined them. Once home, she could not bring herself to say the words. He would be devastated. Lord Collingwood was his childhood friend, a trusted companion. Papa had even entrusted his beloved daughter to the family. This betrayal was unforgivable in her estimation.

So contented was Papa by her visit, she could not tell him.

Until today.

Mr. Cuthbert Phineas Trethow summoned Hazel to the parlor. He opened conversation with questions about life at Trelowen, sharing with her a few anecdotes about spending summers there as a young boy. Lord Collingwood's great-grandfather, Godfrey Hobbs the fifth Baron Collingwood and builder of Trelowen, was Cornish born and raised and kept his ties to his parish. Those ties remained to this day in one form or another. Mr. Trethow's father had been close friends with Lord Collingwood's father, and thus their boys, being of similar age, grew close, as well.

Had Hazel discovered the yew tree he used to climb? He asked. Had she found the secret path through the woods leading to the folly?

Questions of his youth abounded. Hazel enjoyed the stories but had little in the way of answers. One question, however, caught her quite by surprise.

Following a question about her meeting a neighbor he remembered from his youth, he asked, in the same conversational tone, "I don't suppose you've heard any mention of the investment? No trouble if not. Only thought to ask in case something might have been said."

This was the opening for which she had waited. Now was the perfect opportunity to tell him the family had been duped. Opportunity or not, this was no easy task.

"About that…" she said, committing herself to the admission.

There was more to her hesitation than not wanting to hurt him. This meant harkening back to the scandal, something she had hoped he would have put out of his mind, something that humiliated her even now despite her innocence. Swallowing her pride was the only way, for if she did not speak now, she may not find the courage again.

"I have something to tell you, Papa. Something you won't like. It pains me to tell you."

She waited, a tiny hope in her heart that he would instruct her not to speak if it pained her to do so. The reprieve did not come. He waited expectantly.

"I have reason to believe…that is, I overheard Lord Collingwood referencing the marriage settlement. He…you see…he took advantage of the situation and tricked you. He's not the friend you thought he was. We were both fooled and used for profits." She took several deep breaths.

Rather than appear shocked or troubled, her father leaned away in confusion. He scratched his chin and said, "Did he mention the investment by chance?"

"Don't you understand? He's stolen from us! Whatever is in the marriage settlement, he wanted so badly that he pretended to help us. He was a first-rate rogue, playing the hero when he just wanted the money."

"So…no mention of a ship? Did India or China come into the conversation?"

Hazel huffed. "You're not listening."

Cuthbert waved a hand and leaned an elbow on the arm of his chair. "Yes, yes, it was a good settlement, but what of the ship?"

"I don't know," she said, exasperated. "All I heard him say was that the investment had gone wrong so what a saving grace he had the Teghyiy income to depend on and the fee tail. *What* was in the settlement, Papa?"

Pensive, he stared unseeing, then mumbled, "Gone wrong, you say?"

"Yes. Was that the deal you talked about on our drive to Devonshire? Oh, Papa, what did you put in the settlement? Has he truly ruined us?"

Cuthbert rubbed his cheek absently, paying her no mind. She thought he had not heard her. He stared. He harrumphed. He stared.

"Papa?"

The truth of what Lord Collingwood had done must have taken a toll. Her papa leaned back against the chair and closed his eyes. She knew this would not be an easy task and had not wanted to hurt him, but the hurt was inevitable. No one wanted to be betrayed by those they trusted.

"Is there no way of reversing the settlement? Taking him to task somehow?"

Cuthbert rolled his head her direction. "Settlement? What settlement?"

Hazel blinked. "The marriage settlement. Everything he stole from us."

He rubbed his eyes and pinched the bridge of his nose. "That investment was to be the making of us. I did what I needed to do to be part of the deal."

"No, he tricked you. This is his doing. Whatever you lost in this deal is his fault."

He waved a hand then covered his eyes, his words muttered, almost flippant. "Nonsense. If anything, I tricked him." He muttered again, unintelligibly, then leaned forward in his chair with frustrated animation. "You've no idea how badly I wanted this deal. It was to be the making of us!"

Eyes wide, she stared at her father, trying to sort out what he was saying, what he was implying.

"I can only hope you misheard," he continued. "Investment gone wrong could mean anything. I'll write to him tonight, get the truth of it. This deal is everything! The wealth, Hazel, the wealth! The settlement was nothing. A fee tail for your first boy to inherit the estate if Cuthbert Walter doesn't have a boy, which of course he will, so more the fool Collingwood, plus a trifle portion of the annual income, all to convince him to marry you to his son. He couldn't refuse my capital if you were married to his son. A clever plan. All the money we could have. All the money. A deal to end all deals."

"My marriage was *your* trickery?"

"Genius, yes? You know how badly I wanted that marriage. With a sweep of my signature, I secured both the marriage and the investment."

"But you've given away everything! What of my brother's inheritance? What of the money you put towards my dowry?"

His answers were muttered again. Her father could not be bothered with her. She saw that now.

The fifteen additional minutes she stayed in the parlor, wheedling answers from him, proved disheartening. She heard enough to understand the contents of the settlement and what the loss of the investment would mean to their finances and to her brother's future—something she normally would have urged Harold into helping secure out of their vast wealth and the kindness of her husband's heart, but that was hardly possible now, not when they were paupers. She heard enough to understand her father's role, or what her father thought his role had been.

Betrayed anew. Betrayed by her own father. In her naivety she had thought the two families worked together to save her from ruin because they cared. In the end, it was only about the greed of two men, each thinking to outdo the other to invest in some ridiculous financial venture. The two had used their children to achieve their goals.

After hearing the tale from her father, as much as she could ascertain anyway, she now realized only one person had stepped in to help her.

Harold.

He could have refused the marriage. He could have eloped with Miss Evans. Instead he sacrificed his future to save her reputation. While she did not condone his keeping this from her, she understood why he had, for much the same reason she had been reluctant to tell her father of the betrayal. How does a man tell his wife, especially a woman he loves, that she was used for greed by her father-in-law and her own father?

That evening, she missed supper with complaints of a migraine. In truth, she wallowed in guilt. She had left Harold without listening to him, without trusting him. What sort of wife was she? How could she claim to love him without trusting him? Without so much as the benefit of doubt, she had accused him of scheming and trickery. Her conscience weighed heavy with the shame of it all.

Hazel and Nana sat together in the parlor on a blustery Wednesday of the next week. Embroidery was their focus, something Hazel found tedious, but she endured the torture as an excuse to enjoy Nana's company. The two had the house to themselves. Nana's companion had walked to the village for shopping. Melissa and Sir Chauncey were paying a call to friends in the area. Papa was out doing whatever it was Papas did. Cuthbert Walter was riding with friends.

Time and again Hazel made to tell Nana about the whole ordeal but each time she stopped herself. While she wanted to talk about it and wanted Nana's wisdom, she hesitated to say anything negative about Lord Collingwood. The man was not just Hazel's father-in-law, but more importantly Nana's son. It would not be the thing to speak ill of him, least of all to his mother. And so, she maintained her silence. There was no one with whom she could commiserate. Melissa would listen and offer sage advice, but Hazel hesitated there, as well — one did not air the dirty laundry of one's family or marriage even to close friends, and not all of the problem was her secret to share.

The only person she could or wanted to discuss this with was Harold. What a kick in the shin.

"Missing that strapping lad who calls himself my grandson?" asked Nana with a teasing wink.

Hazel blushed. She *had* been missing him. Her own fault. If she had been sensible, she could at this moment be in their private sitting room, cuddled against him beneath a shared blanket, or better yet, freezing her toes off in the boathouse for that romantic rendezvous Harold had promised. The mere thought of his recommending they keep warm with body heat had her cheeks burning.

"Yes, Nana. I am missing him," she admitted.

"Then you'll be delighted to know he's heading this way after his trip to London."

Hazel dropped her needle. "I beg your pardon."

"It's all in his missive." Nana continued to embroider, oblivious to how the announcement affected Hazel.

"What missive?"

"That missive." Nana nodded to the mantel but did not look up.

Tossing aside her worsted work, Hazel rushed to the mantel. There, poised nobly atop the seashell carvings, was a refolded letter, the wax seal broken and the creases not quite in line with the new folds. On the front of the letter her name and post read in smart, looping letters.

"This is addressed to me," Hazel said, stating the obvious.

Nana shrugged a single shoulder, her lips twitching from a suppressed giggle. "It could have been for me."

"Is your name Hazel Hobbs?" She laughed despite her attempt at a scolding tone.

"It's these aged eyes. Can't see clearly anymore. I could have sworn it said from Horace, which meant it was for me."

Nana's giggles increased as she continued successfully with her needlework. Aged eyes, Hazel's left foot.

"You found the contents interesting, did you?" Hazel asked, eager to read the letter but not wanting to appear overly so.

"Not particularly. There was not a single naughty word to be read."

"Nana!"

The single shoulder shrugged again.

Her fingers trembling, Hazel unfolded the letter.

Hazel,

I am coming to Cornwall in approximately two weeks' time. I have business to conduct in London that I hope will right matters and secure your trust. I understand if this is impossible. Give me the chance to prove my business acumen in a way that ensures your present and future happiness. You are all that matters. Your humble servant

Harold

Good heavens.

He was coming here!

He had a plan to right matters. But how? Had he been standing before her, she could have told him he need not bother for she realized her error in judgement and should be the one securing his trust instead.

What in the name of star-crossed lovers was he going to do in London?

He was coming here!

Nana's voice broke her rapture. "You see? Wholly disappointing. I expected a vivid description of how he hoped to pleasure you within the first ten minutes of your reunion."

"Nana!" Hazel screeched once again.

"If I were you, I would look forward to whatever London surprise my grandson has planned. You deserve a treat."

After the way she had treated Harold? Hazel thought not.

Nana gave her a pointed look. "Don't think I can't see that pained expression."

On the tip of her tongue was the urge to remind Nana of her aged eyesight.

Continuing, the baroness said, "You deserve a treat. When was the last time you did something for yourself or made a choice about what you want in life? Not recently, I'd wager. And I know how to make a winning wager. Ask Horace. To thine own self be true, I say."

Letter in hand, Hazel rejoined Nana but ignored her embroidery canvas. She reread the letter instead. He truly loved her. A matter-of-fact letter to some, but to her it was boldly scrawled between the lines.

"Don't ignore me," Nana interrupted. "Tell me I'm right—I so love to be right. You're a woman ruled by the desire to help others, always putting their needs before your own. This lovely trip was for my sake, I'm sure."

Hazel began to object but Nana held up a staying hand.

"I know all about you, Hazel Hobbs. Miss Plumb, or whoever she is now, has told me all your secrets. You protected her from scandal and took her into your home, both times taking the brunt. You've hosted parties to help both her and her husband find love. You've seen to my comforts and amusements, no insignificant effort there. Do I need to list more? I can. I will. Make a decision for yourself for once. What does Hazel want? I think Hazel wants a treat. Let my grandson spoil you." Leaning closer to Hazel, never mind that they were alone in the parlor, she said, "I know he's talented like my Horace. Has he sketched you yet?"

Between talk of being selfless and being sketched, Hazel was relieved by the question. A personal question, but far easier to address than the motivation behind her choices in life.

Was she so selfless? Not from her perspective. This trip was proof enough. If she were so selfless, she would have put Harold's needs first. Then again, coming here had not been for her so much as for her father. When *had* she last made a life decision that involved her own needs? What did she even want from life? If she could make any choice for herself, what would she choose?

Well, right now she would choose to talk with Nana about art. There was little else that would bring a smile to her lips outside of Harold himself.

The hustle and bustle in the Trelowen courtyard could not be ignored. Hired coaches queued as servants loaded an endless collection of trunks. For Harold's trip to India, he had not packed half as much. Then, he had no plans to return this time. Below stairs was atwitter with gossip. Helena flitted about the house, distraught. The baron sequestered himself in his study. Harold remained the levelheaded and calm fixture in the eye of the storm. His plan was to send the coaches to Cornwall in advance of his travels while he saw to the dealings in London.

Everything listed in the marriage settlement was his to do with as he wished, including the income percentage from Teghyiy Hall. He fully intended to take advantage of his legal right to the settlement contents, with Hazel's consultation, of course. If his father thought to access that income or anything else to do with the settlement, he would have quite the surprise in store, or at least that was what Harold hoped to ensure after conferring with the solicitor.

Beyond his stone expression raged a maelstrom of emotion. Defying his father did not come easily. Guilt plagued his every waking thought. This was his *father*. A son should obey his father. With each hesitation, he thought of Hazel. A man must protect his family. Redefining family was difficult, for rather than thinking of his parents as family since they were beyond his reach, he had to focus on Hazel as his family.

She was all that mattered.

Not since Hazel's departure had he shared a meal with his parents. First, he had been absent. Now, his father was absent. Bless his mother for her heretofore cheery disposition. Not until the hired coaches arrived did her panic begin. She was inconsolable. He had tried. His mother might be flighty, but she was still his mother, and he loved her dearly.

The longcase clock read over an hour until Harold needed to depart. One task remained. To say goodbye to his father.

For what must have been half an hour, Harold stood in the anteroom staring at the study door, his legs numb and heavy from lack of movement. Packing and arranging the departure had not been difficult. After all, he had delegated those tasks. Facing his father for the last time was not something he could delegate. His imagination ran wild with farewell scenarios—a quick and heartless goodbye where neither made eye contact, a tearful goodbye wherein Harold lost his courage, a shouting match, a pleading for forgiveness on the part of his father.

Nothing prepared a son for a moment like this.

Drawing on the inner strength encouraged by thoughts of Hazel, he entered the study.

If he had thought the stench of unwashed body had been pungent before, it was nothing to now. Harold covered his nose and mouth with his hand. The room smelled of sick, sweat, spirits, and death. Alarming. His eyes swept the room.

Empty decanters littered the floor and tables. Parchment, scrolls, and books were scattered about the study in equal measure. An overturned chair suffered a broken leg. Most disturbing was his father. Eugene Hobbs lay curled on his side on top of his desk, cradling a dueling pistol. Harold's heart thudded wildly, erratically.

His body shook. His eyes watered. His face contorted. *Good God, no.*

The baron groaned, whimpered, then fluttered his eyelids open.

Harold closed his own eyes. It took him long minutes to compose himself. By the time he opened his eyes again, his father was propped on an elbow and staring at Harold.

Eugene spoke first, his words slurred. "Didn't expect to see you again."

The baron sat up, swaying as he dropped his legs over the side of the desk. His fingertips brushed the pistol. As if startled by its appearance, he stared at it before harrumphing and turning his attention back to Harold.

In an instant that sent a cold chill down Harold's spine, he questioned if this had been staged. His father's last-ditch effort to gain control. The man knew about the dowry. By now he would have realized Harold controlled the Teghyiy income, as well. Would he playact this dire of circumstances?

In another sweep of the room, Harold noticed in the far corner near the basin stand a curious spillage on the rug. He suspected it was bile. Closing his eyes again, he squeezed back tears. This scene could not be staged. He resolved to remain on his guard, nevertheless.

Eugene barked his words. "Well? Say your goodbye so you can leave me in peace."

Harold shook his head. "You're not well."

"Don't tell me what I am and am not. This is my house, and you're no longer a resident."

Walking to the hearth, eerily cold and devoid of fire, Harold turned one of the chairs to face the desk. He had to move a spilled glass before taking a seat.

"You're not well," Harold repeated.

"What do you care?"

"You know I do."

Eugene snorted then coughed until he hacked on phlegm. "If you did, you wouldn't leave. A son has an obligation to his father."

"You know why I'm leaving."

"Not going to stay to watch the creditors pick at my bones."

Harold was unsure if that was a question or statement, so he remained silent. Resting his elbows on his thighs, he laced his fingers and stared at the strewn paper beneath his feet.

Neither man spoke. Harold was torn. Should he walk out now? Should he find a way to console or help his father? Should he ring for someone to light the fire and clean up the mess? Should he send for a physician? He knew not what to do.

"Martins found him," Eugene said.

Harold looked up. His father bandied his hand about the floor as though trying to point to the letter, one of the myriad papers in disarray.

"Took the letter overlong to arrive. He found him the day after sending the first letter."

That the letter arrived within a month rather than a year was good timing as far as Harold was concerned, but clearly the news was not good. He surmised Martins found the good captain either dead or halfway to the West Indies with both cargo and money.

"Bastard's under the protection of the Company. Official EIC ship captain now."

Harold unlaced his fingers to stare at his open palms then laced them again.

"There was no cargo, Martins wrote. Never was. All a ruse. Not a lick of opium to his name. Money's gone. Word's out. Letter came from Trethow asking questions. They'll all know soon."

Consolatory words failed him. He had known it was coming. He had known it while still in India investigating the deal. Hearing the truth of it nevertheless dealt a blow to Harold's gut. His father was bankrupt. The only money they had remaining was the assets in the marriage settlement.

"I'm ruined," said the baron, choking on the words.

Harold's eyes flicked to the pistol within his father's reach.

"Worse, I've lost my son." Eugene choked again, this time on a sob. He covered his face with shaking hands and cried as Harold had never seen his father cry before. "My son." The man began to wail noisily, then blubbered. "Don't leave me."

Lost for words, Harold's jaw unhinged. He was ill-equipped for this predicament. Telling lie from truth was not easy. Hearing platitudes from a man incapable of affection, especially under duress, made telling lie from truth all the more challenging. His heart leapt to embrace his father and give him anything he wanted, but his head stayed the reaction.

Voice steadier than his nerves, Harold said, "You know the cost of me staying."

"Anything. I'll do anything." The words were muffled behind his hands.

"You have one and only one chance to make this right. If you're serious, I'll give you an hour to clean yourself, then you'll accompany me to London. One utterance or hint of balking, and you'll see the back of me. Understood?"

He hated that his words sounded cold, but he could not waver, not now.

"Ring for Shephard. He'll ready me. One hour, son. One hour."

It would take the baron far longer than one hour to clean himself from his drunken stupor and what smelled like two weeks' worth of stench, but Harold nodded. Would his father stay true to his word? Would he allow Harold to make this right? Hope once again swelled in his breast.

Chapter 23

Harold's heart was in his throat, as was his stomach. Really, his throat was a crowded place today, causing a parched tightness that had him swallowing every minute on the minute. He turned his horse down the lane towards Teghyiy Hall and passed beneath the gatehouse's stone arch. As eager as he was to reach the hall, he had spent the evening and early morning at the parish inn to guarantee he arrived clean of body and attire and scented of rosewater rather than road.

Abhijeet remained at the inn until further notice. Harold could not be certain of the reception at the hall. Although the caravan of hired coaches had been ready to head to Cornwall while he set forth to London, he had delayed their departure in light of the events with his father. Everything now depended on Hazel. Would she bar the door? Could she trust him again?

He touched a hand to the nape of his neck to ensure the hairbow felt straight. Not a hair out of place for his arrival. Since he had not seen Hazel in nearly a month, he wanted to be pristine for her first sighting of him.

But wait… Had she not confessed on countless occasions how much she favored him rugged and unkempt? Dash it. He reached back again and tousled

his hair, skewing the bow and tugging a few strands
to wisp about his face. The cravat received the same
treatment. A tug here. A tug there. Yes, that ought
to do it. Presentable for Mr. Trethow and family but
suitably disheveled for Hazel's pleasure. She could be
so angry at him that she would not give his appearance a second glance, but he hoped she might be so
taken with him that she forgot her anger. At least long
enough for him to make peace.

The hall came into view, a stately five-bay block
with two perpendicular wings. While the courtyard
was quiet, a stable hand waited for him, ready to take
his horse. A liveried man Harold assumed was the
butler waited on the portico. They had received his
notice of arrival, then, and were expecting him. His
eyes darted to each window for signs of Hazel. No
wafting curtains. Disappointing.

As soon as he dismounted, he was shown inside
and directed into a drawing room. The formality
brought foreboding. Would she not receive him
then? Well, at the very least he could ask to see Nana.
Surely Nana would not think him a thieving rogue,
too. *Oh dear*.

The drawing room door opened and closed
behind him before he had a chance to sit. He turned
to face his executioner.

A flurry of gold and white satin bull-rushed him.
It was a dazzling display of fabric and flesh as Hazel —
at least he hoped it was Hazel, for he could not be
certain given how fast it all happened — leapt into
the air to twine her arms about his neck and her legs
about his waist. Before he could speak, she set her
mouth to his. With wild abandon, she kissed him.

The stray hair strands must have had a more potent effect than he anticipated. He tightened his hold on her, a tad challenging given the width of the panniers, and explored the haven of her lips. He was a man starved of his wife's affection.

When she released her hold and stood on her own feet, she said, "You took ever so long. I had my apology speech memorized last week, but I've already forgotten it."

Quizzing her with knitted brow, he said, "I've been laboring under the impression that it was I who owed you the apology."

"Yes, well, I know when I'm in the wrong. After talking with my father, I realized you had no part in the plan other than to agree to the marriage, a decision I firmly believe you made because you were helpless to guard against my stunning beauty and charming wit."

"Ah, you've found me out." He returned to her lips, lingering but a moment. "With all forgiven, I suppose I needn't prove my business prowess anymore."

"If you don't tell me why you went to London, I'll retract my apology." Her scold was playful, punctuated with a moue.

She led him hand in hand to the chairs by the hearth, a warm fire blazing to heat his frozen limbs from the ride.

"I'm afraid," he said once they were comfortably seated, their fingers laced together, "this is a serious conversation. One that requires decisions on your part."

"Oh." She tensed. "That sounds ominous."

"No, promising, rather. Let me think how to begin. I, too, had a speech, one to convince you I'm not a black-hearted villain, but if we can skip that…" He paused in case she wanted to interject. She did not. "I can begin at the catalyst of the London trip, which, in full disclosure, took a far different direction than I planned."

Harold caressed the backs of her fingers with his free hand, wishing they were in their shared sitting room.

"After you left, I told my father I was leaving in pursuit of you and would not return. Ever. My plan was first to go to London and see that my father had no access to anything within the marriage settlement. Then I would come to you. I intended to propose we let a cottage on the coast."

Hazel thought for a minute, then said, "I thought we were poverty-stricken. How would we let a cottage?" More to herself than to him, she said, "You left your father…left your home…for *me*."

"Ah, allow me to clarify. I learned in my previous trip to London, the one I took after we married in order to secure the investment for my father, that the contents of the settlement are mine, not my father's. He intended to use the dowry as part of the investment, but I was able to keep it since I had financial right to it. All else in the settlement is ours, as well, including the percentage of your father's earnings. My point is letting the cottage *was* the direction I intended to propose. You must decide if it remains the direction. There's been a change of plans to offer alternatives. I entrust all choices to you, Hazel."

She gaped before asking, "What changed?"

"My father had a, shall we say, episode of hysteria."

Hazel gasped.

"He accompanied me to London—"

"You did not have him committed!" She wrenched her hand from his and covered her heart.

"Rest assured, I did not. He is not incapacitated and maintains all his faculties. He was…distraught. I will say that even if he had been incapacitated, I would have sought a different avenue. Declaring him as such would have involved the Crown. One does not commit a peer of the realm without repercussion."

"If he isn't well, why did he go to London with you?"

Harold retrieved her hand, lacing their fingers once more. "We explored our options with the family solicitor. Namely, how to stop him from making poor decisions and keep the creditors at bay. The solution we chose was to name me as asset trustee and beneficiary."

"That means…what exactly?"

"I control all his assets. *All* assets. From money to furniture. A trustee need only be eighteen rather than one and twenty, enabling us to make this happen now rather than waiting for my twenty-first birthday in March. In the trust agreement, we ensured he, the settlor, has no direct access outside of what I grant. You've been named my successor, as both trustee and beneficiary, should aught happen to me."

"Me?"

"You. Would you be bored silly if I show you the agreement and accounts later?"

"Never!" Hazel squeezed his hand. "I don't think I have a head for numbers, but I want to learn. If you'll teach me."

He smiled, beyond pleased that she had not objected to being involved in the financials.

"My father," he continued, "has entrusted me with everything. I am the decision maker now in what happens with the estate and where the money is spent. But I hope we can make the decisions together, you and I."

Her eyes sparkled. While he may not have needed to prove his trustworthiness, he hoped he had done so anyway.

"We have decisions to make now," he said, "if it's not too soon. Our only monetary asset is your dowry, but we do have the annual percentage of your father's estate profits promised to us. One option, should you not wish to return to Trelowen or see my father, is to use the dowry to let a cottage. Perhaps here on the coast near your family? I can then use this first year's percentage of profits to rehire the steward so that while we're living elsewhere, I'm still restoring the estate. With the steward, we can prioritize. The home farm needs to generate income, for starters. The tenant homes need repairs. New homes need to be prepared to attract more tenant families and farmers. New farming equipment is needed. The list is lengthy, I'm sorry to say."

Rather than her eyes glazing over as he expected, she listened, absorbing his words and considering their meaning.

"Another option is to return to Trelowen and live in the dower house. We'd be on the estate but away from my father. We could apply the dowry to the estate, and I could redirect Mr. Trethow's income back to him."

Hazel interrupted. "I realize you have a plethora of thoughtful possibilities to present, but I needn't hear more. I *do* have a say in what we decide?"

"Of course. That's the point, my love."

"Splendid. Then this is what I want to do. We return home. We use the dowry to hire the steward and purchase whatever we need to make the estate prosperous. We keep the entire percentage of my father's income from now until forever."

Harold leaned back, eyes wide. "Bold decisions. Are you certain you—"

"I should think I know my own mind, Mr. Hobbs." She flashed him a saucy smile. "It's *my* dowry, and I'm entrusting it to you to make wise choices for *our* home."

"You won't be uncomfortable seeing my father again?"

"As uncomfortable as seeing my own," she said. "He's no more guilty than my father. If I've already forgiven my own, I can certainly forgive my father-in-law. Hypocritical if not, don't you think?"

He did not think his father deserved her forgiveness and hoped hers appreciated its worth. He chose to remain silent on both matters.

"To my mind," she continued, "the only sin our fathers are guilty of is desperately wanting us to marry—and this is the narrative to which I will refer for the remainder of our days, so no talk of greedy and deceitful gentlemen. So determined for us to marry, my father gifted us with that lovely annual treat. I realize the damage of the lost investment, but he doesn't have debts and has a lucrative estate. He made this decision to settle our marriage. Besides, we need it more than he does. As for the entailment, we can worry about that later."

To say he was surprised would be an understatement.

"What of Lord Collingwood's debts?" she asked.

Harold cleared his throat and shifted in his seat. "As trustee, I am now liable for all debts my father incurred."

"Oh."

"Was that suitably dramatic?" he asked with a sly grin. "Now for the good news."

"Go on then. You have me on tenterhooks. I'm imagining creditors with battering rams. I'll have you know that debtor's chains would not match the bows on my dress."

"No battering rams or chains, love." Harold lifted her hand and kissed her wrist. "The trust safeguards my father's possessions, so creditors cannot take them in lieu of payment. The solicitor provided options for us to consider. For instance, if I name the creditors as partial beneficiaries to the trust, they will excuse a significant portion of the debts accrued. Another option is to request debt forgiveness. Since the assets are now in a trust, the creditors are likely to consider forgiveness. If four-fifths agree, then all are legally obligated to forgive."

"But wouldn't those options insinuate bankruptcy, the very thing we want to avoid people knowing? If word spread, it would ruin the family's reputation. And I'll say now that I don't like the idea of them being beneficiaries, even partially so."

Harold chuckled. His wife had more of a head for business than he would have ever given her credit for, a characteristic he found exceedingly attractive. He kissed her wrist again, closing his eyes to inhale the floral scent on her skin. If it were not conceited, he liked to think she applied it for him.

"What would you have us do?"

"Well," she said smartly, "for all anyone knows, we're one of the wealthiest families in the West Country. Let's keep it that way. We call on each of your father's creditors to introduce — wait, no, they wouldn't be overly fond of a woman talking business, so let's make it *you* who calls on them, but you must tell me everything or I shall relegate you to the dower house without so much as a kiss. Now, where was I? Oh, yes, you call on each creditor to introduce yourself as the trustee. Assure them you want to keep the tabs and credit lines open. How else will we continue to host your mother's parties? Give them a little something from the dowry as a good faith payment. We can use my father's annual marriage gift to pay a little on each debt. Go on and kiss my cheek for being so clever."

He obeyed, smiling broadly when he leaned back. "Then that's what we'll do, my clever wife, but know that I'll be having a word with my mother. No more extravagances. It's one thing to maintain a reputation and quite another to spend money we need to recoup. I'll not allow the debts to increase while we're trying to decrease them."

"This steward you want to hire. He's trustworthy?"

Harold nodded. "The best. Taught me all I know about keeping accounts. Had my father listened to him from the beginning, we wouldn't be in this situation. He'll know what to do that will have the most impact on generating estate income."

"And Lord Collingwood is well?"

"Well enough."

Harold tugged Hazel to him so he could kiss her soundly. He had far more pleasant ideas for their time together than talking about his father.

The reunion he both anticipated and dreaded had gone better than he could have dreamed. While he aimed to entrust important decisions to her, she in turn had entrusted him with the contents of the marriage settlement. By doing so, she had given him the greatest of gifts: her trust.

A voice broke their embrace.

"It's about time you pleasured my granddaughter."

Leaping apart, they turned to face the door.

In unison, Harold and Hazel cried, "Nana!"

When Hazel stepped over the threshold of Trelowen, she knew she was home. Never again would she think of her childhood abode as home. *This* was home. She breathed in the scents of timber and contentment.

This arrival mirrored her first when she had attended the hunting party with her father, but this time, it was by her choice. After a lifetime of having decisions made for her, she had made the choices of what to do with the finances and where to live. Choosing Trelowen was an inexplicable moment of triumph. With a new sense of confidence, she ran a hand over the banister of the main staircase. *Home.*

Harold approached her from behind and rested a hand to her back. "Upstairs," he whispered.

Hazel tugged at her bottom lip with her teeth, blushing with anticipation.

The front door swung open to Lord and Lady Collingwood escorting Nana. She was chattering non-stop about her grand adventure to the cliffs.

Hazel's breath caught at the sight of Lord Collingwood. The baron did not look well, but she supposed he could have looked worse. Bags underlined his eyes. Fatigue lined his face. His shoulders rounded forward when he walked.

Any expectation of apologies would forever be unfulfilled, she realized. He did not know she had overheard him, neither would he have cared if he did know. What apologies could he offer her anyway? His failing had been greed, little else. She only hoped he knew what a godsend was his son.

When she looked up at Harold, he nodded his head in the direction of the stairs and waggled his eyebrows. Hazel glanced at the family. They were enthralled by their own conversation.

One foot on the first step. Then another. She glanced back. No one paid them any mind. Hazel lifted the edge of her dress and scurried up the staircase, Harold following on her heels. She burst into her bedchamber, then spun around to receive Harold as he rushed in behind her, closing the door with his foot. He scooped her into his arms and showered her face with flirty kisses.

Before they made it to the edge of her bed, she said, "Tell me you love me."

"I love you," he said, nuzzling her cheek.

"Good. Because I love you. And…I have a request."

He moaned his response as he kissed her neck.

"Could you paint me first?"

Harold's lips halted their exploration of her ear-lobe. "If your intention is to torture me to madness, you enchanting minx, you'll succeed." His laugh tick-led her skin.

Hazel tugged at his cravat. "Actually, I rather thought it would be the other way around."

Leaning away to better see her, dawning lit his eyes. "You're not referring to paintbrushes and a canvas, are you?"

She shook her head and giggled.

With a throaty growl, he said, "Then prepare to be *painted*, my darling."

Epilogue

October 1760

Hazel stood in their apple orchard, arm in arm with Agnes. Together, they watched their husbands pander to the whims of their sons. Agnes's son Forrester, now five years old, straddled his father's shoulders while Patrick hoisted him to reach the tallest apple dangling just out of reach. Hazel's son Walter, four going on twenty it seemed some days, ran circles around Harold, trying to scoop up the fallen apples before his father could.

Circling another tree, picking their own fare, were Helena, Eugene, and Nana. Helena was clamoring about a cider party she wanted to host, while Nana regaled them all with a tale of when Horace had hosted a cider party — utter nonsense Eugene exclaimed, for there was not an apple orchard when his father was alive. The baron, who doted on his grandson as he had never doted on his own son, had lost a good deal of his robust girth over the years, now a quieter and more subdued man, affected in ways none of them could understand by his poor decisions, or so it seemed to Hazel.

Harold grabbed Walter on one of the boy's rounds and tossed him into the air. Hazel shrieked as Harold caught him, their son laughing at the fun.

"Excuse me, Agnes, but I must see to my husband."

She marched over to Harold, hands on hips. Even as she made her way to him, he lobbed Walter into the air again. She quickened her pace.

"You put him down this instant." She scolded Harold.

Addressing Walter rather than her, Harold said, "Your mother is envious that I'm not tossing her into the air. Think I should?"

Walter found that endlessly amusing.

Hazel narrowed her eyes at her husband. "I'll not have any of us disheveled for our guests. They're due to arrive within the hour."

"And here I thought you were worried for his safety," Harold ribbed.

"Nonsense. I trust you. But you'll have him sweaty before his grandpapa and uncle arrive. I want him looking his best."

"You don't fool me," he said, tapping the side of his nose. "You're hoping your brother's paternal instinct will kick in so that he'll be motivated to find love at last. One look at cherubic Walter and who wouldn't want a son of his own?"

"Don't be ridiculous." Hazel's cheeks warmed to be so transparent. "Although now that you mention it, Cuthbert does need a nudge in that direction. Do you suppose we should host that cider party while they're visiting?"

Harold ruffled Walter's curls before the boy stumbled his way past fallen apples to tug Forrester into a game of chase. "If you want Cuthbert to find love, allow him to conduct his own search."

"We didn't conduct our own search, yet we're a love match." Hazel poked his arm.

Harold's returning grin tied her stomach in knots. So distracted by her love's wicked smile, she did not realize what he was about until it was too late. Before the entire family and their guests, he grabbed her waist in a firm grip and tossed her into the air, sending her screeching upwards by a few feet then rescued by his strong arms.

He pulled her against him and, before his lips met hers, said, "Yes, we are."

A Note from the Author

Dear Reader,

Thank you for purchasing and reading this book. Supporting indie writers who brave self-publishing is important and appreciated. I hope you'll continue reading my novels, as I have many more titles to come.

I humbly request you review this book on Amazon with an honest opinion. Reviewing elsewhere is additionally much appreciated.

One way to support writers you've enjoyed reading, indie or otherwise, is to share their work with friends, family, book clubs, etc. Lend books, share books, exchange books, recommend books, and gift books. If you especially enjoyed a writer's book, lend it to someone to read in case they might find a new favorite author in the book you've shared.

Connect with me online at www.paullettgolden.com, www.facebook.com/paullettgolden, www.twitter.com/paullettgolden, and www.instagram.com/paullettgolden, as well as Amazon's Author Central, Goodreads, BookBub, and LibraryThing.

All the best,
Paullett Golden

If you enjoyed *The Heir and The Enchantress*, stay tuned for Cuthbert's story:

The Gentleman and The Enchantress

About the Author

Celebrated for her complex characters, realistic con-
flicts, and sensual love scenes, Paullett Golden has
put a spin on historical romance. Her novels, set pri-
marily in Georgian and Regency England with some
dabbling in Ireland, Scotland, and France, challenge
the norm by involving characters who are loved for
their flaws, imperfections, and idiosyncrasies. Her
stories show love overcoming adversity. Whatever
our self-doubts, *love will out.*

Connect online
paullettgolden.com
facebook.com/paullettgolden
twitter.com/paullettgolden
instagram.com/paullettgolden

Printed in Great Britain
by Amazon

58561922R00225